BLUFF CITY PAWN

BLUFF CITY PAWN

A Novel

Stephen Schottenfeld

B L O O M S B U R Y

NEW YORK • LONDON • NEW DELHI • SYDNEY

Published by Bloomsbury USA, New York

Bloomsbury is a trademark of Bloomsbury Publishing Plc

All papers used by Bloomsbury USA are natural, recyclable products made from wood grown in well-managed forests. The manufacturing processes conform to the environmental regulations of the country of origin.

LIBRARY OF CONGRESS CATALOGING-IN-PUBLICATION DATA

Schottenfeld, Stephen.
Bluff City pawn : a novel / Stephen Schottenfeld.
pages cm
ISBN 978-1-62040-635-9 (hardback)
1. Pawnbroking—Tennessee—Memphis—Fiction. 2. Contingent valuation—Fiction.
3. Brothers—Fiction. 4. Family secrets—Fiction. I. Title.
PS3619.C4548B55 2014
813'.6—dc23
2013041930

First U.S. Edition 2014

1 3 5 7 9 10 8 6 4 2

Typeset by Hewer Text UK Ltd, Edinburgh
Printed and bound in the U.S.A. by Thomson-Shore Inc., Dexter, Michigan

Bloomsbury books may be purchased for business or promotional use. For information on bulk purchases please contact Macmillan Corporate and Premium Sales Department at specialmarkets@macmillan.com.

For my mother and father
and for Susan

There once many a man
mood-glad, goldbright, of gleams garnished,
flushed with wine-pride, flashing war-gear,
gazed on wrought gemstones, on gold, on silver,
on wealth held and hoarded, on light-filled amber,
on this bright burg of broad dominion.

—ANONYMOUS, "THE RUIN, " EIGHTH CENTURY
(TRANSLATION BY MICHAEL ALEXANDER)

The true meaning of money yet remains to be popularly
explained and comprehended.

—THEODORE DREISER, *SISTER CARRIE*

One

OPENING THE STORE TAKES thirty minutes, but today, the Monday after daylight savings, he leaves twice that just to get in front of what might go wrong. Someone at the door saying it's nine and Huddy correcting eight and the guy saying we're both here. Daylight savings, a busted day, a day that won't get done. Time doubled over and Huddy's head blurred between what it was and what it moved to, a new hour that doesn't yet fit.

He unlocks the steel shutters and folds them back. Two men walking loosely down Lamar—both far enough away that Huddy won't worry about them running up. He unlocks the door and locks it behind him, turns off the alarm and locks it, too, because he doesn't want the customers' hands on the panel. Hits the lights and looks around for damage or items out of place, anyone hiding. He stares up at the ceiling, not that he's expecting a cut hole, but you never know. Then he walks back to the loan counter, unrolls the paper, and turns on the computer.

The pawnshop bust has moved off the front page, and Huddy checks to see if it's buried elsewhere. It's gone. Fast Pawn over on Winchester, only open a year, which means to Huddy they were criminal from day one. It's been over a year since a pawnshop got busted, that one on Park, where the guy got in so deep and stupid he was giving orders: You think you can get me computers, stereos, jewelry? And then before that the shop near the tool plant, where the owner had the employees from the plant stealing from the factory, and you'd walk in there and see shelves and shelves of brand-new industrial tools. These stories happening just often enough to make people think every pawnshop has a truck parked out back, doing these midnight deals. And sure, some of what's here is hot, you can't stop all of it, especially if no one's gonna write down serial numbers, but he's more often a buffer against crime, if anyone would ask him. The customer needs fast cash and they get a collateralized loan instead of robbing someone. The shops, Huddy would tell them, are *stopping* the crime.

He opens the gun room, sliding up the fencing, and puts out the pistols locked in the gun safe. Then he changes out the video, gets the oldest tape from the cabinet and rewinds it and sets it in. A newer technology would make things easier, but he's waiting for his brother Joe to pay for the hard drive, the same way he's waiting for Joe to fix the broken curb, so the customers don't keep tripping into the store. Or stripe the lot, so they know where to park. Huddy glances outside. At closing it'll be darker and the lot won't be lit up, even when he already complained to Joe. The lights are under city contract, so it won't really be his brother's fault, but Huddy still blames him. Joe far off in the suburbs, with a different mayor. "I don't want to live around all them Democrats," he'd said, which Huddy knows means blacks.

He gets the drawer set up. He checks the default list, checks the tickets, prices the merchandise up, goes to the back and starts pulling the inventory. A gun, a fishtank, two saws. He'll give Mister Terry a few extra days on the gun, because Mister Terry is always good on his loan, surprised he's defaulted, but the other items he'll put out on the floor. The fishtank: He can already hear the customers coming in, saying, "Hey, man, you're taking fishtanks? I'll get you a bigger one." Give him a month, he could turn the place into an aquarium. It'd be the same way if he bought an accordion, a bowling ball, frozen steaks. Whatever he buys, the street always wants to bring him more. "Steaks, man, I can get you beautiful cuts. All packed up, ready to go."

He cleans the tank, wipes and tests the saws. Deanie, his employee, who helps with the cleaning and ticketing, isn't here yet, and he wonders if she's confused the time, until he realizes she'd be earlier, not later, so it's him doing the confusing, and the forgetting—since he now remembers her saying something about the doctor. This nerve damage they can't figure out what from. Maybe it was even surgery, the conversation returning, so Huddy's alone today.

He goes to the back door to make sure there's nothing strange. Then he opens the valuables safe behind the loan counter. Keeps the handle down, so it looks locked. Puts the jewelry out. The bank opens at 8:30, but he won't go, not because of Deanie but because he went last Monday, so this week it'll be Wednesday or Friday. Instead, he'll Windex the showcases. He finishes and eyes the clock. Flicks on the signs, unlocks the door. No rain, so he wheels the two mowers and the bike from the entrance to outside, chains 'em up. The merchandise outside means you're open more than the Open sign does. He comes back in and decides to call home before his phone starts ringing. "Hey," he says when Christie answers.

"Hold on. Cody, no no no . . ."

Huddy waits. "If Harlan calls, give him my number. I already gave it . . ." Huddy's younger brother, Harlan, phoning last night to say he was leaving Florida, gonna try Memphis again. "Memphis?" Huddy had said. "You hate it here."

"No, I hate it *here*. New bunch of apples, new bunch of worms."

Huddy sorry for that but also happy to have him back. And Harlan always makes being around Joe bearable, feels less poor up against him.

"He give a time?" Christie asks.

"Wouldn't matter."

"Well, that's helpful. He going straight to you or here?"

"Guess that depends on the time." Someone at the door now. "I'll check in later," he says. "How are you today?" Huddy asks, always saying hello to see what's given back. A direct hello, or eye contact. Even a nod, a mumble. *"I'm shopping." "Just looking."* He'll take anything. The first customer is a loan, a guy pawning a Cold Steel knife, the next is Miss Daws paying the interest. Miss Daws could've bought the ring ten times over, all the years she's bringing in her twenty. Then it's Mister Isom picking up his tackle box. Huddy's gonna have to be careful with pickups today. Each one will be: Do I trust this person to leave on the floor while I go back to storage? And who else is here and in the lot? And what about the late-afternoon rush? Huddy might need to ask customers to wait outside.

A young mother with her two-year-old, making her way forward, until the kid bumps his head against the hard knob of the mitre saw, and he starts to cry, rubbing his head. "No, that didn't hurt," his mother says. "Shake it off. Come on, you're a tough kid." She yanks at him, but he drops to the floor, bawling, just when the father comes in carrying an infant. "I told him to stay close," she says, "and he goes and whacks something."

"Tyler, come over here," the father yells. And now the infant is crying, too. The father steps forward and scoops the son up, both arms full with crying, and he looks at Huddy and then at her and says, "Just get done with your business and come on." And he bangs outside.

Quiet again, but the woman is weakened by the time she reaches the counter, the item she's pawning turning cheap and bad in her hand. Her wrist, actually, the watch coming off. "I'm wanting to know what I could get for this," she says softly and Huddy holds it.

"Accutron," he says. "The first electronic watch. But it's a difficult watch to repair. Getting to be like a dinosaur. Sorry," and he hands it back, but she doesn't take it.

"I was hoping to get something for it."

"Yeah," he says. "This was really something back in the sixties. Kind of an innovation. But now, it's just a dinosaur," he says again, and he repeats the gesture, and this time she takes it.

She gives this dashed squinch. "I might could find something from home."

And Huddy watches her spread her hand out on the counter, look at her fingers, at the missing rings and stones.

"When you figure he's gonna start honking at me?" She looks around the store, like suddenly she's a buyer. "You know what I really need? I need about a week where everything's free. Either that or a lucky penny."

Huddy nods. And by the time the horn starts, she's already at the door. No one there to replace her, and Huddy sees a picture of the four of them, huddled in an empty house, wind going through open windows, the sound of the U-Haul driving the furniture away.

The car door slams. He wonders what bind they're in, what job got lost. Or maybe it's dope, drinking, gambling, people falling into everything. If they could keep out of these things in life, they wouldn't need him.

★　★　★

"Thought I'd check your pistols," a gun buyer says, and Huddy switches to the gun counter. Huddy's never seen him before, but he knows the type: hat, vest, pocket pants, fifties, white, wearing a beard. "Show me that Government .45," the man says, and Huddy unlocks the case, grabs the mat and sets it on the glass, grabs the gun and opens the chamber, closes it and transfers the gun to the mat, the handle facing the man, the nose away from both of them. He shuts the gun case and half-steps away.

The man lifts the gun, flips it over and back. "Looks real clean. Not shot much."

"I don't see any ring pounded on the back of the chamber," Huddy says.

"Yeah, that's right. Doesn't have a lot of wear. I like to shoot Governments. I like the man-stoppers. You know? Uncle Sam started doing these Governments in 1912."

Off a year, Huddy thinks. Gun buyers love to talk and he just lets them go.

The man glances at the ticket price dangling on the string. Flicks it with his finger. "I'm a big gun buyer. Buy lots of guns. You call me anytime you get a good one."

Huddy only listening with his eyes now, the man setting the gun back down on the mat.

"Might buy this tomorrow. I'll be in about the same time."

"There might be somebody from yesterday saying the same thing." The man smiles and leaves, and Huddy returns the gun to the case. He knows the pawnshop flies, like this guy Del waltzing in now who shows up twice a week, only buying if you've made a mistake. Because that was Huddy, before he worked here. He'd come for tools, but more than that, he liked the action, the treasure hunt. What's in today, what's behind door number three? And he liked the contest, your skills against theirs. "I gotta have a hundred and a half for this." And the owner Mister Jenks one day said, "You make a good presentation. You need a job?" And Huddy did.

He worked as an assistant for three years. The old man was amazing. Remembered every loan and could price the merchandise instantly. Books about guns, guitars, pool cues, everything on a shelf behind him, but never reaching there. And hardly ever testing the jewelry. Once in a while rubbing a ring against the touchstone, but mostly just knowing it with his eyes and hand, seeing the tone being off, feeling the weight, knowing the trademarks, how it's stamped, manufactured. Mister Jenks knew it all. *Sorry, miss, it's not gold.* He knew a person before they had two feet in the store. A quick glance—he knew every gesture and expression, every sob story and hustle, every thought and feeling moving beneath their skin.

But still, the guy wouldn't maximize. He didn't like the twenty-year-olds acting wild. Except, Huddy thought, what about a twenty-year-old bringing a fine diamond ring? Mister Jenks, as he got older, taking less risk, even shying away from electronics. He didn't understand the video games, the PlayStations. Customers coming in nonstop, "You got CDs, you got DVDs? You got Game Boys?"

"You're crazy, Mister Jenks, not taking in this stuff."

"I don't like the product. I don't like the customer. Why bother with videotapes? They're not even copies. They're copy-copies. I don't need the dollar sale."

Huddy thought he could do better. It would take time to learn jewelry, but in other merchandise he was solid. Like when that guy tried selling a fake guitar, just slapped a Fender sticker on it, and Huddy could tell from the weight, and the bumps on the frets, and he said, "It's a real nice, *light* guitar," and handed it back. Liked watching the guy's face fear up.

When the chance came, when the old man wanted out, Huddy couldn't buy his way in, but Joe's second marriage was ending—time to hide the assets—and Huddy said, "Set me up here," and Joe even bought the building. Silent owner plus landlord. Two more things for Joe to have, on top of the construction business, the foundation company, the gravel pit. Now a side cash business and a rent check. Huddy standing in the store one last time with Mister Jenks. Any final advice? And Huddy thinking he'd hear something tired, "If you don't know, loan low," but Mister Jenks just smiled, like he'd slipped Huddy a silver-plated store when Huddy thought he'd paid for sterling. But Huddy threw a counterfeit grin right back: Get going, this place is mine.

Huddy increased the size of the yellow-pages ad. He had a billboard built. Joe even paid for it. Bluff City Pawn. Same name, but now you see it. Gave the building a bath, fresh coat of paint. Put new showcases in, new velvet displays—Huddy unlocking one of the cases now for Del, who's looking for watches. "Man, I love watches," Del says, "never can have too much time. Let me see that wind-up."

Huddy slides the door, reaches in. Del examines the watch and names his price and Huddy won't bother negotiating, because Del knows the markup rate almost as much as Huddy does. Wouldn't be surprised if he'd cracked the pricing code at Cash America. Del thinks he won, but Huddy won, too. Buy low, the selling takes care of itself.

Del hands him the money and starts talking about pipe cutting and threading. "Having a devil trying to find it." Huddy nods, doesn't need to tell Del to check back, since he sees a guy like this too much. "You gonna miss this?" Del says, twirling the watch on his finger.

"I think the universe is full of stuff, and you gotta just jump in and grab it."

"I'll tell my wife you said that." Del closes his fist, and Huddy hears the metal click.

The mail lady, Miss Theresa, comes through the door and Huddy's glad to be done with Del—turning from pawnshop fly to pawnshop parasite.

"Next time," Del says, "just tell me what's mismarked, so I can go right to it."

He tips his hat, but Huddy's eyes are off him with the phone ringing. "Bluff City," Huddy says, and listens. "We have one laptop," he says, and hears thank you.

Miss Theresa hands him the mail, and then steps over to the jewelry, leans on the glass. "I need something to go out." She'll do layaway and she's good about payments, but sometimes when she stretches it, he feels like she's treating the mail like money—"For you, Mister Huddy"—when of course it's only bills. "Ooh, that one," she says, and Huddy follows her finger.

"That's a nice dinner ring," he says.

"Ah," she says, and then pushes away from the counter. "I'ma look at it more tomorrow. Don't you let anyone touch it. Heard about the robbery next door."

"What robbery?"

"The liquor store. Saturday."

Huddy checks his watch—Mister Barnes opened at ten. "Anyone get hurt?"

She shakes her head. "Just robbed."

And when she leaves, Huddy locks up and steps outside to peek in. Mister Barnes is reading the paper, and Huddy enters, doesn't see blood or bandages. "What happened Saturday?"

"What happened? Turn my back to get the liquor off the shelf, turn back there's a gun in my face." Mister Barnes saying the last part into the paper.

"What'd they look like?" Huddy figures it'd be good to know if they've been in his store, or what to look for if they do.

"Look like. They looked like three young thugs. Thug clothes, thug everything. You tell your brother Joe he's losing a tenant."

"Oh, come on, you don't mean that."

"Sure do. I must be crazy thinking I could run this place without bulletproof glass. Right now, we should be talking, there should be bulletproof glass between us, and if you want to say something there's a little airhole to do it, and you put your money through the slot—like a bank—and I put my liquor through the chute. That's how King's Liquor down the street doing it. They got *all* the liquor behind the glass, and if a customer wants to be robbing, he's gonna have to rob himself." His nostrils flare like all his liquor got skunked. "Whatever. It's too late for changes. I'm out."

"You're gonna let them run you?"

"Listen. I go down to the station, they give me the pictures, see if I recognize anyone. I recognize *everyone*. I'm flipping through the pictures, they all my customers. Half the people that come into my store. Now I've been held up three times and I chased 'em out twice, but all them photos, forget it. Time is up."

"You give the police a description?"

Mister Barnes shrugs. "Sure," he says. "A description."

Huddy microwaves his lunch, and while he carries the plate to the counter, he has a thought: He'll be alone. Not in the store today but around him *all* days. The grocer, Mister Sanders, on his left closed out six months ago, and now it's Mister Barnes, on his right. And this should give him leverage with Joe, who owns all three bays—you'd think he'd protect his last tenant and his middle brother—but it'll only make him increase the rent. He did that when Mister Sanders left, and Huddy knew the talk of taxes was a lie to cover the difference.

Plus Huddy wanted to leave, too. Not the business, but the location. Because he saw how for the past year his shop was dying. When he started, the pickup rate on the loans was sixty percent—and he used to listen to Mister Jenks talk about the good old days when the rate was as high as eighty, when running a pawnshop was just turning a key in the morning and letting the interest pile up. But now the rate's nearing thirty, two thirds of the customers forfeiting their loans. And the average loan keeps dropping, too. Instead of seventy-dollar loans, Huddy's averaging forty, so the interest is smaller. Last month, Huddy started driving, scouting locations, looking at traffic flows—although he hadn't told Joe about his plan, about bankrolling him one more time. But then Huddy scored a big hit here. A guy came in with a corroded ring, saying, "I know the stone's not real, but the gold's real and I'll take what you can scrap it for." And Huddy took his word on the diamond, because he was eyeing another customer snaking around the tool shelves looking for blind spots. Plus the diamond was rough, no sparkle, looking like a lump of coal. Huddy gave the man a hundred for the gold, and it wasn't until the end of the day that he put the diamond in the cooker and got surprised. Weighed it. Over a carat. One hundred dollars making twenty-five hundred. Huddy knew the ring was a blip. But it made staying easier. Might as well wait through Christmas, and then Valentine's for jewelry.

Now, with Mister Barnes leaving, Huddy's waited too long. It's gonna be harder to leave, and harder to stay.

A hollow boom outside—Huddy jumps, the shop rattles—then screeching metal. The two sounds, explosion and collision, confuse, and Huddy waits for more noises to point it somewhere, screams or curses, horns or sirens, and when he hears nothing he rushes out to see what accident or mess. He looks to his left past the grocery that's gone, and instead of chaos and flames there's a semi in the driveway, hydraulics raised, the offloaded Dumpster behind it.

Three Mexican laborers sitting on a truck bed, a contractor at the storefront. About time, Huddy thinks. The building's been abandoned for over a year, so at least it's activity. Maybe they're putting in something helpful, like an auto-parts store, which always works perfect with a pawnshop, brings in the working man. Or maybe some neutral business, insurance, whatever, neither help nor hurt. But don't let it be public assistance—or some nightmare like a methadone clinic, addicts hanging around pissing and crapping over everything. Once that scenario pops up, Huddy finds himself walking over there just to confirm what's *not* going in. He goes straight to the contractor, who's posting a permit on the wall, and then he sees another worker appear in the middle doorway, a set of plans tucked under his arm, looking like the superintendent, so he slides over. "What you putting in here?" Huddy asks.

The man untucks the plans, squeezes his hands over them. "XGC Services."

"What's that?"

The man squints. "Blood bank."

Huddy's face smacked with the news. "Blood bank?" he says, just sick to repeat it. This building, long and low, same size as his own, but now it's a tower, grown colossal.

"Manny!" the man shouts, decisive. "Wreck out the front room!" He jerks his thumb behind him and Huddy watches the lead guy turn and translate instructions to the other two, who climb back to the toolbox. "Who you?" the man says, chin up-twitched, eyes fixed and narrowed.

"I run a shop next door."

The man glances to his right, eyes passing around, then back at Huddy, annoyed to have searched. "Well, I guess you're getting a neighbor."

Huddy's lips pinch together. He scans the building's three doorways, the work crew going in to start the demo. "Where's it going?"

"Everywhere," Huddy hears back. "It's the whole place." And when he looks over, the man's eyes are wide.

"We already got a blood bank downtown."

The man shrugs. "Got another one now."

Huddy thinks, Blood bank. A bunch of people with nothing. They'll hang around and harass—need a drink of water, need the bathroom, need the phone. "When's it going in?"

"Three months," the man says casually, but to Huddy it comes out like a warning. "Gut it out, frame it. Could be six."

Huddy winces, like he's a donor getting his arm pricked without payment.

He hears the sledgehammer knocking down a partition wall.

The man's teeth flash as he watches Huddy leave. "Guess you ain't giving any blood."

Half of his meal uneaten, but Huddy can't touch it. It'll take less than a week after the bank's opened before it's wall to wall in there. And then they'll be here. On a rainy day, a crowd's gonna be all up under his canopy. Two hookers stroll by, one in red spandex, bright and tight; the other in jeans, whale-tail underwear peeking out the back. A car honks, hips sway and turn, but the driver doesn't stop, was only teasing.

He calls home again.

"Huddy, what you doing? It's naptime." Christie whispering mad. But the clock says earlier. "I thought I was calling before that."

"I put him down an hour ago. The time change."

He shakes his head, forgot. "Why didn't you turn the ringer off?"

"I left it on, in case Harlan called. Was he in Florida last night or did he call you from the road?"

"They're putting a blood bank in the next building."

"Damn, he's getting up. He's always *up*."

Customer comes in. "I gotta go," Huddy says.

The man dragging his way over to the counter. He holds out a necklace that's all kinked and damaged.

Huddy gets the scale, weighs it. Six pennyweights. "I can give you forty bucks."

"Forty?"

"This has no value as a necklace. I can only sell its weight. It's not a necklace anymore."

"Come on now." The man flings out a hand and glares. Points at the necklace like it was fine jewelry until Huddy smashed it and cheated with the scale. "That's more than forty."

"Not from this side of the counter," Huddy says and he pushes the scrap back. "Thanks for stopping in." The man's anger spreads to confusion, then grief. "Maybe you got something else you can bring me," Huddy says, and the man nods, slips inside himself, "Yeah, okay, might."

Huddy wants to shut the door and unplug the phone and think about his worries—Barnes plus blood bank—figure out how to tell them both to Joe. He calls Joe, gets the voice mail, hangs up, tries the office, gets the secretary: "Do you want his voice mail?"

"Just tell him . . . not to forget about my lights." But that's not enough of his worry anymore. *Tell him I'm tired of him getting his rent but me not getting my living.* Joe with his monthly rent and his weekly cash. And his shopping sprees, cherry-picking the best jewelry from the showcases, only paying cost so Huddy can't make a profit. Just saying, "Book it," then stepping to the back to tape his name on sale items that haven't cleared thirty days.

Huddy frowns at the bulky analog TVs on the shelf. He's in no man's land with televisions; the flats ain't coming in yet, and he's stuck with those.

Then a lever-action collector comes in, mentioning the L.C. Smith double-barrel he's just seen at Liberty Pawn, over on Summer, a gun he knows Huddy would want for himself. "Your eyeballs gonna jump when you see it. Man named Keller—he's got it locked away 'cause he ain't letting the yahoos play with it. It's so clean and smooth, you gonna think it's a reproduction." Huddy decides to close up and chase down a special gun.

Two

LIBERTY IS OLD AND tired, but the building is freestanding, the neighbors far off, and the driveway is big. When Huddy parks, he sees good bars on the windows. Inside, the lighting is poor, but a quick peek tells him the guy is killing him on merchandise. Like a fine catalogue of secondhand everything. Better saws, DeWalt drills, the tools mostly Black & Decker, Rockwell, Milwaukee, and not all used up. Huddy scans the guitar wall, picking out the Americans. One Martin, two Gibsons. And the handful of customers—busy for early afternoon—are nice working people. At the jewelry counter, a well-dressed black couple is picking out a ring, the woman in a sleeveless blouse, designer pants and sandals, hoop earrings and a purse on her shoulder; the man in a short-sleeved button-up. The white customer at the tools is wearing a tie! Huddy thinking, A guy comes in my shop with that, it's the taxman come to audit. Huddy walks behind the couple and glimpses the filled trays. Bigger stones. A two-carat, a couple larger than a carat. One Rolex with the watches.

"Can I help you with anything?" Huddy hears from the loan counter. Must be Mister Keller, since the employee at the guns is Huddy's age. Combover hair and a smile like a piano. Huddy points at the guns and Keller nods and goes back to his customer. Forty bucks on the counter. No merchandise, so the cash must be interest on a two-hundred-dollar loan. Huddy looks past Keller, at the solid double-door safe.

The L.C. Smith isn't on the racks, but there are others to admire: two Weatherbys, a Browning Citori over-and-under. The rest are Remingtons and Mossbergs and Marlins. Even a couple Sears. But three high-end shotguns, plus the hidden L.C. Smith, when Huddy is lucky to have one in six months. And the handguns are just as good. Not just the regulars like Taurus and Ruger, and a notch up with Smith & Wesson, but a Colt Python in its original box, and a Kimber. Huddy feels like he's browsing the Guns & Ammo store down the street. Doesn't even see the cheapies, Hi-Point and Jennings and Bryco, Huddy's bread-and-butter.

A customer grips a Ruger. "My brother, he been enjoying the Bearcat he got from you last month." The employee and the buyer walk over to the loan counter, and Huddy thinks, This place is hooked in with *families*. Got brothers bringing each other here.

"How about I help you now?" Mister Keller says, same wide smile at the gun counter.

"Bill Mowry comes into my shop talking about an L.C. Smith, because he knows I like doubles." Huddy hands him his FFL and watches Keller read it.

"Bluff City Pawn. That's where Nat Jenks was."

Huddy nods. "I've been running it six years."

"How's Lamar?"

"Terrible. But if I could see that L.C. Smith, I'd be happier."

Mister Keller steps over to the gun safe and pulls out the shotgun, and Huddy leans in, ready to grade. Case colors swirl the receiver, the bluing on the barrel is barely faded. When Keller breaks it open, Huddy hears the automatic ejectors click. Add five hundred.

The gun right there in front of him and Huddy's hand upon it. He shines his LED light on the chamber. No rust or dings or pitting. He closes the barrel gently, turns the gun over and back. The stock is triple-A fancy wood, French walnut.

Keller's eyes move up the frame. "Hand-engraved. No machine doing that. Guy with a little bitty tool going tick tick tick." His finger notch up and down.

Huddy wiggles the gun, no play in the metal. He scans the wood-to-metal fit, everything flush and continuous, nothing proud. "You mind if I take the barrels off?"

"Not if you're serious about the gun."

Huddy scans the steel for blemishes, studies every line and crease and edge, every number and proofmark. A Premier Skeet Grade. The gun needs to come home with him and he'll sell three, maybe four, from his collection to make it happen. "Little defect under the hand guard," he says, and Mister Keller's eyes twitch up, "Okay." Huddy reassembles the barrels, hands the gun back. "How's a pawnshop get a gun like this?"

"I got forty years in this shop. This is the only one I've ever seen come in."

Huddy nods at the racks. "You got other stuff, too. You got some primo guns."

"Some plain-Jane, too," Mister Keller shrugs. "A little bit of everything."

Huddy glances down at the case. "Python NIB. Wish I was selling this everything."

The front door dings open. A customer with tattoos, long hair, face grimed, looking like Huddy's clientele, but at the loan counter, he changes to here. "I come for my trailer," he says.

Huddy didn't see a trailer in the driveway, which means there must be a lot behind the building. Which means Keller is doing title loans. Huddy searches around for other secrets. Like maybe he's missed the platinum mine in the corner. "You say you been here forty?"

"My daddy did forty-four. And granddad did a stretch, when we were down on Beale."

Huddy imagines the green-visored father running the shop—maybe generations of Kellers going all the way back to year one, to the customer in a toga pawning his oil lamp.

"I'd like not to go as far as daddy," Keller says, "but my kids don't want to fool with it."

All the scouting that Huddy did—he never thought about moving his pawnshop into another pawnshop. "You thinking of retiring?"

"I ain't put a sign on the marquee yet, but my wife keeps telling me to climb up there."

"I wish I was off Lamar." Huddy scans the floor. Two new customers. A scummy, low-end guy at the tools, but also a father and son at the guitars. "I wish I was here."

"Yeah? Well. We should talk. I should listen. You want the book, the inventory, the building? If I talk too much, tell me to stop. We talking about the gun anymore?"

"Hell, yeah. But I don't see no sticker price."

"Price is up here," Mister Keller says, tapping his head. "I figure, we both know ballpark. We both know book." His hand opens in a giveaway. "I'll let you have it for five."

"Thanks," Huddy says before he can stop his voice, but he doesn't need to, 'cause eight would have been a steal.

"I'll take my five and you'll get your ten."

Huddy pays cash and wants Keller to think he can pay for the store, too. He drives east out of the driveway to survey the storage lot, and there are two, the front one a chain-link fence for trailers, and then another behind it, with wooden privacy fencing inside the chain. He hooks right at the side street, drives past the first lot and parks. From his car, Huddy peers through the gaps in the slats. A boat, a car. He sees a trenching machine. A stump grinder. A riding mower. Big tickets, quality loans. Keller is a pawnbroker, a repo man, and a high-dollar merchant, and Huddy wants to be all of them, instead of feeling like a small-time clerk. It takes half the drive home before the two deals—buying the gun and buying the shop—separate, the consolation being that Huddy is still holding his finest double. But he needs to figure how he can dig a couple hundred thousand out from his brother Joe.

The phone rings. Lost his pawn ticket, the caller says, and Huddy searches the computer, tells him the payment date.

He wants to hear from Joe, wants to see Harlan—Huddy's thoughts falling in a brotherly line, been awhile since that happened. Is Harlan showing today? He was first popping in on some buddy in Knoxville, just a quick hi.

Mister Ramirez comes up to the counter to purchase a caulk gun, a blaster, two scrapers; must've switched from carpets to painting. "You done with carpets?" Huddy says, and Mister Ramirez nods uneasily, so Huddy shows the price with fingers.

The phone rings again and Huddy answers.

"Sergeant Bell here, down at pawn detail."

"Hello, Sergeant Bell," Huddy says, taking a deep breath as he hears the damage, some jewelry coming up on the database. He copies down the tag numbers, and could Huddy have the stuff ready tomorrow morning for pickup?

"Sure thing," Huddy says, blood vessels about to pop.

The phone again—better not be pawn detail grabbing more merchandise. "Bluff City."

"Huddy, how many times you gonna call me about this nonproblem?"

"Joe, don't yell at me. It's not a—"

"Your lights will come on. I got a buyer here who's messing with the layout, wants to flip the design so the kitchen's where the living room is. She's moving things upside down and backwards."

"Listen, I wanna talk to you about more than lights."

"More than lights? You're calling me twenty times about lights and you want to talk about something else?"

"It's about the neighborhood."

"What about it?"

"It's picked clean. There ain't no money to squeeze from it. Guy came in yesterday asking if I bought *towels*. And it's bad. Bad dangerous."

"You're a pawnshop, Huddy. You're supposed to be in a bad area."

"Pawnshop should be *close* to bad. Right on the edge of bad. Just a little ahead of bad."

"Thanks for educating," Joe says. "You're fine, Huddy. Gold prices are through the roof."

"'Cept everyone and their brother's buying it." Huddy saying it soft, not to argue, fingers tapping air. "Furniture store down the street's got a sign in the window: We Buy Gold."

A black man in a hooded jacket.

"I'll call you back," Huddy says. He needs time to develop his pitch. He'll have to make Liberty Pawn sound like First Tennessee and make the blood bank sound like a contagion. "How you doing?" The man doesn't answer, so Huddy tries again. "How you doing today?"

"Fell through the floor," the guy mumbles. He smiles and shakes like he's being tickled. More muffled words, some sound thrown out, shifting. He's at the sockets bin, rolling his hand through them like he's combing seashells. Sockets spill over the sides, but the man doesn't react, as if the ocean were loud in his ears. Huddy looks at the nearby fishtank—this guy's making the whole shop feel underwater—then returns to the man. His hands are busy, but the rest of him is dead. The noise to Huddy is the sound of knuckles cracking. The sockets clicking together is the clock ticking wrong.

"Can I help you?" Huddy says.

There's no answer, every question needs to be doubled. "Hey."

"Couldn't find the right sizes," the man says, the sockets on three fingers like rings or brass knuckles.

Huddy eyes the bin and what's been spilled. "Dollar."

The man stares at Huddy through small eyes. His socketless hand curls up to his shirt and fidgets between his chest buttons, scratching or reaching inside for something, and Huddy watches and doesn't see black skin, but a white shirt, a second shirt, underneath with a front pocket where the money's at. A dollar comes out crumpled on the counter. The man nods, twirls his socket fingers, and Huddy watches him leave. It wasn't as if he expected the man to flash a weapon, but he wasn't looking for the money there either, the balled cash like a torn-out heart.

Huddy looks at his watch and decides to close early. But he

can't. Three white men walk in, scruffy, in hats, and Huddy recognizes the front man as a customer. The one in the back is wearing a coat. Heavy. The coat, not the man, who's stick-thin. The front man approaches the loan counter, the other two separate—the coat going over to the jewelry and leaning on the case, the third sliding over to the guns. Three pawn tickets on the counter, Huddy's problems multiplying. A shotgun, a necklace, a tool bucket. Huddy sighs. These tickets'll have him running around the store in ten different directions. He plugs the man's name into the computer. Tells him, "Five hundred." The man signs the tickets and Huddy takes the money. Always take the money. He does the jewelry loan first. Steps behind him to the safe—his back turned like Mister Barnes—gets the envelope and returns to the counter, the necklace spilling out with Huddy's fingers never touching it.

Now the gun. Takes the man's fingerprint on the pad, gives him the federal form while Huddy does the call-in. Everything's clean. No back child support owed, no domestic violence. Huddy logs out the loan, but now he's stuck. He won't give the man the gun until he goes to the back for the toolbox, and he can't go for the toolbox with all three of them here. "Gentlemen, I'm gonna have to ask you to step outside."

They all straighten and regard each other, the guy in the coat zipping and unzipping.

Huddy turns to the lender. "Just take me a minute to get your stuff. We're done here."

He nods, and the two follow him out, with Huddy trailing behind them, locking the door.

He fetches the tool bucket, all the way to the back of the storeroom, where there's fifteen other buckets of miscellaneous tools, then up to the gun safe behind the stock-room petition wall, where all the shotguns look alike so Huddy's checking fifty to find the one. And when he gets the gun and carries both back to the floor, he looks to the door and outside in the dimness there's four men huddled. What's forming, being planned? Huddy feeling like the redcoats are coming. Until the fourth one is Harlan. Tan skin. Looking even younger than when he left. Harlan sees him and waves. Harlan, three years gone in Florida, the last without a phone call answered. And Huddy knew Harlan wasn't bringing back what he borrowed, but right now that doesn't make him any less happy, Huddy almost running with the gun and the toolbox—when has he ever gone to this door like this?—he'll finish the exchange out there since there's no reason to bring the three inside. Carrying the pawns like he's bearing gifts, like some family gathering, greeting everyone, come in, come in. Even these party crashers can join the fun. The gang's all here.

"Look who's arrived," Huddy says, and he'd clap his brother but he's holding stuff.

"Am I late or early?" Harlan says, and Huddy doesn't know. The hour is early, but the day feels delayed, arrested. He surveys his brother. Harlan's got more hair, the same big smile, but the rest of him's less.

"Both." Huddy steps out and hands the shotgun to the loaner and gives the bucket to the guy not wearing the coat. The breeze feels good. Only a small bit of one but enough to cool Huddy's face, which is as hot and red as Harlan's is tan.

"We were trying to figure out what those balls mean," Harlan says. "This sign here." And he points to the window.

"That's your pawnshop symbol," Huddy says. "Three brass balls. Every shop's got that."

"See, I was trying to tell these folks it meant you got 'em by the balls."

Huddy smiles. And the others do, just less so.

"Hey man, can I see the gun?" Harlan asks, and before the owner can say no Harlan adds, "You got a premium gun there," and his hand is out, his eyes signaling he's not some stranger off the street. The owner offers it slowly, puzzled, like Harlan's the old friend he can't yet recognize.

Harlan steps aside, points the gun at the street. Puts his cheek against the stock, looks down the barrel. Then he wheels at Huddy. "Your money or your life," he says, in an old-movie stickup voice, and Huddy doesn't laugh, his back bumping the door, but Harlan does, then lowers the gun, returns it. "Yeah, this gun fits me. This gun is premium."

"What you think?" the pawner says to Huddy. "You think my gun's premium?"

Huddy steps forward, doesn't want to feel jammed. "I think it's a good, strong loan. You can bring it back anytime."

The three men troop off to their truck. If I was on Summer, Huddy thinks, I could loan on the vehicle, too. He shakes his head, not about title loans, but all the day's complaints and curves. He unchains the merchandise. "Grab this mower," he says. "I got no help today."

"Why not?"

Huddy shrugs. "Because my best employee is the computer."

They move the mowers inside and Huddy goes back for the bike, then back in to close out. He transmits all the sales downtown. Puts the pistols and jewelry in safes, puts the loans up.

"Fishtank, huh?"

Huddy looks up from the counter but Harlan's already off it, over to the jewelry.

"You stop in Knoxville?" Huddy says.

"No. Not really."

He checks the coffeepot, the back door. Pumps the hand sanitizer onto his hands. The phone rings. Damn, Deanie. Maybe Christie, or Joe again, so he answers. But it's just a man wanting to sell a pressure washer. "It's new," the man says.

Of course it is. "Bring it in tomorrow, we'll see what you got," Huddy says.

New, Huddy thinks. Tomorrow it'll be ten years old.

Harlan singing, "Golden rings, golden ring, with one tiny little stone. Waiting there, waiting there . . ." He looks at Huddy. "You gonna harmonize with me or what?"

Huddy croons his face, eyes closed, lips puckered.

"Man, where's the music? It's too quiet. Stereos on the shelf, stacks of CDs. This should be a party place." Harlan goes to the stationary bike, climbs on and starts pedaling.

"Come off of there," Huddy says. He turns off the signs, the lights, sets the alarm. Steps outside with Harlan and closes the metal shutters. Harlan's truck is double-parked, although who can see the lines out here? Huddy stares up at the darkness. "You see, these lights are supposed to be on. Joe's supposed to be taking care of that." He hears Harlan laugh about responsibility. "Near an hour ago they should be lit."

Trucks rumble down Lamar, shaking the air. "You got yourself in a no-neighborhood."

Huddy surveys the ruins. A sign down the street says, BEST PRICES IN MEMPHIS, but the store's gone. He knows the decline by heart. The office buildings going derelict. The projects torn down. Churches closing, too. The train container yard closed and the warehouses moved to Mississippi. Now Mister Barnes leaving.

"Surprised the sidewalks don't roll up." He scans the rooftops where thieves keep ripping up the A/C units, going for the copper.

"Everybody split but you."

I'm working on that, Huddy thinks. He looks next door at the construction, thinks of the needles sticking skin and the livid blood running all day, through veins and up tubes and into Huddy's mouth, thick and heavy, a coppery taste. "You know what's going there? Blood bank."

"That's good, right? It'll bring a crowd."

"The worst kind. Night of the living dead. They gonna hang out in my shop because it's warm and they think they belong here."

"You know what I think? I think the city ain't never recovered from King."

"I ain't talking about King. I'm talking about *me*."

"You ever think what this city'd be if King got killed somewhere else?"

And Huddy knows Harlan's saying it wrong—how some assassination should've been farther—and now a panhandler is creeping close. This lurker, working his way over, with a hurt dip to his legs, like every step's gonna make him take a knee. "Here comes the birdman."

Harlan shrugs. "That guy's just a methhead. He looks sprung."

"Huh?"

"Sprung. Where you done so much, you ain't coming back."

"Good to know."

The man reaches them. Eyes wasted and hungry, face mauled with sores. Huddy waits for the dirty hand, this guy looking like he's standing, hustling, and sleeping all at the same time. "Look here now, I've got a wife and—"

"No, you don't," Harlan says, and Huddy watches his brother

stare him down, daring. "Here's a buck," he says and reaches into his pocket, thrusts it forward.

The man examines Harlan and the dollar, the bill folded up so it looks like only a piece of something real, some trick money that couldn't open and be whole. The meth mouth—rotten, jagged teeth, the crocodile smile flashed at Huddy, and Huddy'd like to fend him with the gun, but his eyes are enough, pushing the man to go. And he does, away, but hardly making space with his injured steps, swerving like he's following a trail of switch-backs and it'll take him all the way to the next night to get distance.

"See, I usually say no to that," Huddy says.

"The city ain't got no loose money. Rich folks have it all tied up to themselves."

"So now you've come back to Memphis to give some away. You're in the right place."

Harlan smiles. "It was *your* money he wanted. I was just trying to distract him."

"Me? Don't got none. Pawnbroker with cash in his pocket ain't gonna live long. I already got enough of a bull's-eye coming out of there." Huddy checks around for more bum traffic while Harlan looks back at the store.

"I thought you might've changed the name to Huddy's. Unless it's supposed to say Joe's."

"Ain't Joe's," Huddy says, glaring. "You don't put names on it. You give it something neutral like Capitol, Empire. Liberty."

"Well, you can call it Harlan's." He makes a sign with his hand, then stops smiling. "You tell Joe I left Florida, coming back?"

"Nope."

"Yeah, I bet he'd say, 'That Harlan can cut and run with the best of them.'" Huddy watches his brother's mouth clamp shut, his body held still to kill the insult.

"Why you back?"

"Well," Harlan says and closes his eyes, tilts his head like he's draining water. "I guess I stayed too long to where my tail got torn off. Might see Joe, go watch him eat. Same house?"

Huddy nods. "It's bigger."

"Yeah, I gotta get me one of them houses that grow."

"I was thinking you'd come over to mine tonight. See my family." But Huddy needs a face-to-face with Joe now, not at week's end, when Joe gets his payment. "Let's go out there. Joe's." Not waiting to get robbed by Barnes's men, not waiting for no blood bank. I ain't a dead carcass on the side of the road for somebody to tear a piece out of. Ain't just twitching road-kill. Sorry, Barnes, I'm leaving first. He reaches for the phone, but he'll call Christie from the car. Tell her about Harlan, say sorry for interrupting Cody's sleep. Forget dinner, but he'll aim for bedtime.

He eyes the street. Any danger or demand coming off it is smaller with Harlan here, just a nagging threat or test, only spare-change, peg-legged shakedowns. Here's a quarter, go get your bang of coke. Just needy scavengers and addicts with diseased mouths and dead legs.

"If these lights don't go on, I'ma cut down Joe's chandeliers."

"Maybe you're supposed to clap 'em on." Which Harlan does, loud.

"Hey, quiet there."

"What, you scared? This is your place of business. Nobody's coming anyway."

"Oh, yeah? They'll come. And it ain't gonna be the church bus."

"What you got for me? You got that ho line down the road. Lamar and Getwell."

"Oh, they up here, too. Twenty dollars'll get you a big ol' lip lock. Too bad y—"

The lights come on, pieces of darkness burning away, the bulbs buzzing like voices, as if Huddy's walked into a room where everyone's saying surprise.

Three

JOE HAS A WATER garden. He already had the pool, a kidney-shaped, in-ground beauty with fieldstone edging, but now the yard's gone, replaced with pebble paths and paving stones and cantilevered decking and clusters of blooming flowers spearing the air with green. It's some alternate universe, Huddy thinks, surveying the scenery from the patio, or like some twister had lifted the botanical garden in the city and flung it all the way out here.

"Ain't it heaven?" Lorie says, with her hands spread wide to this new paradise, and Huddy wonders if he's supposed to applaud plant life. "Joe saw a picture in one of my magazines, and then he went out and got all these books on how-to and drew up the design and everything."

"When'd this happen?" Huddy says, his throat knotting.

"Summer."

All these months Joe coming into the shop and never saying what got switched and assembled. Not after he looked for TVs—or before when he took a two-carat solitaire, which Lorie's wearing now, or the ladies' Rolex, also there. Or the bracelet, the earrings. Huddy looks her over, picking out Joe's visits. Been married two years, enough time that she can't wear all of it at once—unless she's a pawnshop mannequin. Truth is, Huddy likes Lorie more than the other wives, but Lorie likes the jewelry more, so he should like her less. At least Huddy's lucky with Christie; about the worst he gets is her buying all these trinkets from flea markets and thrift stores and Huddy's always knocking them over in the hallway. Plus she gets the mall itch too much, but Huddy'll explain he's worked too long in a pawnshop to pay retail.

But this yard project, this refuge. A refuge from what? He's already in the suburbs, now he's somewhere else twice. Already gone to White America and now on a private island inside it.

"He's setting under the pergola." She points to the far-left corner, but the corner's blocked by ferns and shrubbery and shade trees, Joe tucked snug behind the foliage. "Joe!"

"Yeah?" they hear back.

"You got your brothers here."

"That Harlan, too?"

"Guess he can see *us*," Harlan says, and he brings fingers to his mouth and whistles.

"What you doing here?" Joe shouts.

"Came to smoke your cigars," Harlan calls and Joe replies, but Huddy can't hear the words, until he realizes it's not just the acreage but a sound drowning it. The pool, only it's too loud for the filter. A water noise, Huddy's sure of that, past the pool, bigger than a trickle, some rush of water going over rocks.

"What's the water I'm hearing?" he says.

"That's the stream waterfall," Lorie says. "It feeds into the pond."

"Pond?" Huddy pulls at the sides of his mouth, rubs knuckles against his teeth. Every day my heart's in my throat and Joe's coming home to tropics. But he can't say Joe's rubbing it in his face when he's never mentioned what got scrapped and added.

Huddy sees him emerge from the corner like he's tunneling

out, a hidden figure half-lit by the hanging lights, made partial by the mesh of ferns. Joe clears the shade trees but then he's screened again, big rocks blocking him and the high hedges and tall flowers a curtain of colors that he keeps coming through and slipping behind. They keep seeing more of him then less, here but not here, branches beetling down to take his face, then a clearing to see him whole until the spaces fill in again and the hedges get his legs so it looks like he's floating or cut in two; then he's broken up and flickering and gone, then the path straightens and unfills to show him once more whole. Harlan's the one who's been away, far off in Florida, but watching Joe weave through his backcountry, it's like he's returning, too, from the Far East of Germantown, the other side of the world—and Huddy's the only one who's been stuck. The path swerves again so it looks like Joe's walking toward them but away, passing through plants and flowers like some shifting disguise.

"Can I get you anything?" Lorie says, and Huddy feels like he should be ordering mint julep. She's dressed all in white, and he keeps expecting she'll offer a silver platter with tiny foods and napkins.

"He still drinking Buffalo Trace?" Harlan says.

"Working on a bottle out there, I'm sure." She turns to Huddy and he nods. "I'll get you glasses," she says. She twirls with a hostess flip and flourish, and Huddy hears the jewelry on her neck jangling while Harlan sniffs her perfume and eyes her ass and thighs. "Wife number three," Harlan says, and they wait for the door to slide. "'Member what daddy used to tell us: Didn't have to marry 'em all." Huddy smiles, then his eyes sweep the grounds. Firefly sculptures and a metal cowboy riding a propeller plane. He stares at the spinning parts. Past the pool, the path is bordered with rows of footlights that look like spaceships and Huddy's waiting for the little green men. When he shakes his head, it feels like a planet orbiting his body. "Life on Mars," he says.

"Ain't that."

He looks back at the spectral lights. "Well, it's some kind of afterlife out here."

"Ain't that either."

"Well, what *is* it then, Harlan? 'Cause it looks kind of *unusual* to me."

"It's a war movie, man," he says. Huddy watches Harlan sniff loud. "The generals setting under their tent, drinking their tea, while the battle's going to hell."

He looks at Harlan. Pictures white tablecloths and sprinkled sugar stirring into liquid. But then, he thinks: *I'm* the foot soldier, Harlan, dodging cannon fire. You're just the deserter.

Joe climbs the bridge like some carrying wave, held aloft, then dips down as if descending from air, out of the half-shadows and into the glow coming off the water, in full view, nearing them now, poolside between the webbed chairs and the water's edge and close enough for Huddy to see Joe's face, eyes beaming, lit with the surprise—and relief, maybe—of Harlan's return. "Harlan, Harlan ..." The second time louder, some bit of exhilaration slipping out.

"The man with the big watch," Harlan says, low and weak.

Huddy stares at Joe's hand extending, clamping down on his brother's shoulder.

"You come back a tycoon or a whipped dog?" Joe says. Harlan smiles, always a loose and easy smile, but this time small, tight. Joe's hand still hanging there and Huddy feels his own shoulder shake it off. "I'm sure you're real happy about being back."

Harlan's jaw tilts up. "Oh, I cried the whole way."

Joe glances sideways at Huddy. "He give you his story yet?" But he doesn't wait. "Last I heard, you were talking about running dozers and backhoes."

Huddy remembers the time Joe had stopped in, telling about a phone call he got from Harlan. They had him doing steep grades, Harlan had bragged, and Joe laughed, but then his lips pinched together, some memory sting of Harlan's struggles and mistakes— missed days, quitting or getting fired, starting and losing and striking out somewhere else—Joe knowing that Harlan's good fortune wouldn't stick.

"Yeah, was," Harlan says. He scratches at his neck.

"What happened after?" It's just a small question, but Harlan's silent and Joe's face sinks and Huddy feels the air collapse. "Well," Harlan says, swinging his legs. "Then I got to selling left-handed widgets." He pokes the ground like there's something dead beneath his feet but he's testing to see if it isn't. The sliding door cuts him loose, Lorie carrying glasses, walking briskly, her jewelry tinkling until Huddy realizes it's the ice. "Lorie," Harlan says, throwing his head back, "how'd this second-class brother of mine land someone like you?"

"Must have been my hair," Joe says.

"Oh, you're not losing it," Harlan says, "you just pulled out all the gray."

Joe laughs, rakes his balding hair, and Huddy surveys the deep yard, the light on the pool gleaming. The pool, the pond, the waterfall—Huddy wonders what else is out there, maybe creeks and brooks and lakes and a piece of the Mississippi and a sandy beach and way past some ocean with tides and currents pulling to the horizon, as far as Joe pulled himself up from the bottom, his trucks and haulers all over the city, making the city, and now he's made this. Wrought-iron fencing far off at the property line, but Huddy can't see it, feels like he's looking out at miles and miles to a mirage that never ends but stretches and spreads and goes everywhere.

"Why don't you show us this obstacle course?" Huddy says. "Make sure I don't fall in."

"You coming?" Joe says to Lorie, but his attention is full on Harlan, his eyes squinting like they're hitting the sun, trying to see what's inside, what's there and gone, Harlan eyeing the ground, patting his hair like a cap tipped down on his face.

"I might listen from here," she says and her fingers flutter. "Y'all be nice to each other." She doesn't look bothered by Huddy or worried by Harlan; she doesn't mind this one-time visit. Huddy feels like she's smiling at Joe's brothers—distant Huddy and nonexistent Harlan—as if they were some silly old rhyme.

"Oh, we just gonna kiss his rings," Harlan says. "You go first, Joe. You always been the line leader. I'll go behind so I can pick your pocket. Hold my hand so I can swipe your watch."

Joe leads and they follow, single-file with Harlan next and Huddy tagging. They pass the chairs and the pool and enter the narrow path and Huddy feels his feet crunch and skid on the pea gravel. Petals scattered about, plants tangled and dense crowding him, brushing his pants and skin as he passes, the pool's chlorine smell overtaken by the flowers sweet and fragrant. "That's an optic fiber plant," Joe says. "That's a butterfly bush, Japanese myrtle." Huddy doesn't know if he's naming three separate things or correcting himself on one, his hand thrown out in all directions, speaking some foreign language exotic to Huddy but not to Joe, just ticking things off indifferently as if he hadn't planted but discarded them. "Big tree is crape myrtle. That one's wax," Joe says, at some clump of foliage, and Harlan says, "Yeah, knew that," dumping the ice from his glass.

The water is louder now. They cross the bridge and Huddy stares at the side channel flowing underneath, curving and opening wide to the terraced pond with the stream waterfall pouring down upon smooth rocks. Light shining on the pond's surface and Huddy stares inside the water at the vivid fish, watches them circle and slip. Two dozen fish, tails waving and wriggling, orange and red like streaks of underwater fire, all in his brother's yard like they've been here forever, some low, sunken craterworld beneath the grass that Joe merely had to dig down and discover. All these happy fish with their flapping fins and little mouths open, set free from the cleared earth above.

"What's the fish?" Harlan says.

"Goldfish," Joe says. "Different varieties. Comets, couple of shubunkin, fantail. Fantail's the calico. Those bright gold ones is koi."

Huddy looks at Joe the new fish professor.

"They making babies?" Harlan says.

"Two sets already. Had to give some away."

"You give any to Huddy?"

"What the hell do I want with them?" Huddy says. He stares down at their gaping mouths, at their eyes never closing.

"You got that fishtank in your shop," Harlan says. "Plop 'em in there, sell the tank."

"I gave 'em to someone with a pond," Joe says, shrugging at Huddy, and Huddy wonders when ponds became such a common thing. Maybe a customer will pawn a pond and default and Huddy'll dig a pit and set the stones in his own yard.

"Well, *I'll* take some," Harlan says. "Put 'em in my pocket. Goldfish? I'da done bluegill. Or stocked it with bream."

"We ain't eating 'em, Harlan. Raccoons the ones eating. And the birds. That's why I built the deep zone three feet at the bottom. Got the strawberry pot so the fish got holes to hide."

So how is Huddy supposed to not feel burned when Joe's built a sanctuary, with fake herons as decoys, protecting his goldfish like they're endangered species. This hole in the ground, designed and terraced, and then the holes in the strawberry pot and maybe inside an escape hatch reaching all the way through to the ocean floor. At his feet are decorative rocks, large varieties of quartz, flecked and glittering. He hears Joe calling out more foreign names, pickerel weed and horsetail and umbrella grass; hears him name the water lilies. Next to some agate halves is a chunk of amethyst and then a nugget small and sparkly. Water lilies and oxygenators, Joe says, they competing for the algae. Huddy reaches down for the nugget.

"Ha," Joe says, watching Huddy inspect. "Figures you'd find my gold."

"Lemme see that," Harlan says and grabs it from his brother, grips it tight.

"You're rich now, Harlan," Joe says, and Harlan looks at Huddy, considering.

"Fool's gold," Huddy says. "Iron pyrite." It feels good to be the namer of things.

Harlan stares at his open hand. "Fake, huh?" Licks his lips, slow, like an old taste he can't recall. "Didn't think you'd go for phony." Harlan shakes the rock like dice, flings it in the pond and the water plunks, the fish darting as the rock sinks. "Hope your guppies don't choke on it." His thumb slides across his palm, feeling for any fakeness that might've flaked off. "You got any real liquor?"

They follow the stone path to the gazebo. Two stone benches with a slate slab between them, Joe taking one bench, Huddy and Harlan sharing the other. "Confederate jasmine," Joe says, pointing above and around, but Huddy eyes the lights twining the posts.

"There it is," Harlan says, snatching the bottle from the table and pouring big.

"I didn't even know you did this," Huddy says. He meant admiration, not rivalry, but his voice came out high and childish. He worries what else will sound wrong from his mouth.

"Yeah, Joe," Harlan says, "this is a real nice cemetery you built."

Joe laughs, coughs, like his laughter's been blocked up for years by living rich. He raises his glass and Huddy pours and reaches his glass high to clink against the other two. "So, Harlan," Joe says, thumping his thumb on the table, "what's next?"

Harlan's arm does a slot-machine pull. He laughs, takes his first drink. "Find a clock and punch it." He shakes his head, tongue pushing hard against his teeth. "Do anything."

"He just got here," Huddy says.

"Come work for me," Joe shrugs, some business deal ending, briefcase clicking shut.

"Might," Harlan says, and Huddy watches him throw his drink back. Harlan eyes Huddy, leans at him, but Huddy knows he's feeling like he's going the other way, ditching out, which is ridiculous since what Harlan needs is what only Joe can give, and what Huddy needs is for Joe to stop looking at Huddy like he's staring at a wall. "Thanks," Harlan says, his face flushed with shame. He slaps his thighs to stand, but doesn't. Shakes his legs like an engine running.

Joe's shirt is crisp as a hundred-dollar bill. His face is beat-down and tired from the long day, but the shirt, even untucked, looks pressed and perfect. Huddy drinks and swallows. "You could be his goldfish enforcer," he says to Harlan, teeth bared. "I'll get you a snake gun." And he feels cold for saying it, because he knows Harlan's come home tapped-out and small. Or worse, with bad debts to wrong people. Huddy looks at Joe's fingers, thinks of him pinching his fish food, the fish crowding and frenzied, snapping at their meal and each other, the water alive with their hunger. He eyes the shirt again, tips his glass, feels his body lifting into the chest pocket, arcing and about to drop in but Harlan's already nestled there, a handkerchief pulled over him like a nighttime blanket, so Huddy can't squeeze beside.

"Where you staying?" Huddy asks.

Harlan slides his hand along the arm of the bench, dances his fingers at the edge. "Saw this sign out on Stage Road: Win one year's free rent. Thought I'd stop in and go see about that."

Huddy watches Joe frown. "Stage Road?" Huddy says. "What you doing up there?"

"You, too?" Harlan says, neck twisting. But then he lightens, swings his neck back slow. "KayKay."

"KayKay . . . You two still close?"

"Look like you lost a few," Joe says, eyes narrowed like Harlan's starved out a new face.

"Ha," Harlan says, "I was about to tell you the opposite. You lookin' full-grown, that's for sure. I feel sorry for that belt." Harlan lights a cigarette, eyes pinpoints against the smoke.

Joe eases back, pats his belly. "Doctors want me eating a handful of pills."

"For what?" Huddy asks.

"For stuff I don't have yet. Make sure my blood moves." He rubs his stomach, some soft ulcer rub. "What you think—this brother of ours, he on the run? Hiding out from the world?"

Huddy watches Harlan's glass tilt at his throat. He wants to talk about himself, not Harlan, not now—Harlan siphoning off Joe's attention. Sitting beside Harlan makes Huddy feel identical, and Joe's not helping with his eyes shifting back and forth like he can't tell one brother from another. Joe getting it double, two needy brothers both at the margins, one without money and one without the means to free himself somewhere better. He'll quick-fix Harlan and be done. That's how Huddy'd do if he were staring at two kinds of favors.

"You the only one hid away," Harlan says. "You a hermit crab now? Maybe you hiding from her—your next wife-to-be-ex."

Huddy laughs, but he only wants to hear about his own relief. How am I supposed to talk out here, to tell what is happening to me, with the air so sweet and unreal, with all these blooming flowers and tree colors. He feels the water rolling over him, rounding him off, rubbing and wearing his complaints down, leaving him relaxed but weak. Water running everywhere and Huddy's mouth drying up. He sips, feels warm and better, but his tongue is still thick with all that he wants to say, so he fires another sip to burn words down. Joe is pointing out the helicopter plants and tiger grass, and Huddy refills his glass and realizes he's not just thirsty but hungry, since he forgot to grab dinner to hurry here. Another sip and more heat in his stomach and Joe's talking about water cannon, elephant ear, some frond or other, but there's too much to look at so Huddy'd like to chew the plants to not only clear some space but curb his hunger, and the trees need to be trimmed back too and Huddy'd like to do that also with his teeth. He'd like Joe to sit and watch while Huddy ate the entire garden, chewed it right to the ground, his mouth a plow filled with shreds of greenery, and then he'd go diving for the fish, and after he could have this talk and Joe would have to listen because Huddy's voice would sound so strange with all of Joe's plants stuffed in his mouth, fish scales jutting from his teeth like tiny pins.

"Listen, Joe . . ." But Huddy's not even sure which problem he's bringing up, he can't say Summer yet, he hasn't ordered his thoughts or maybe the drinking's scrambling them. He runs his hand across his lips. "I got a situation." His voice doesn't seem right, the only sound that fits here is water. He likes his job. He just wants a small do-over, a tiny nother chance.

"I heard about it. Barnes called me." Huddy watches Joe shake his head. Three feet away but it feels like what's between them is ten shut windows. "Great, another vacancy."

"Barnes called you?"

"An hour ago."

"Well I'm leaving before Barnes."

Joe's hand up to halt him.

"We gotta move the shop, Joe."

"I ain't touching your rent, okay?" His hand pushing out now. Huddy takes another sip, the glass sliding to his mouth.

"Tell him about the blood bank," Harlan says.

"Two rehearse this?" Joe snaps. He frowns, thought he was having a brotherly moment, some shared family history, but Huddy and Harlan have turned twins, two halves with the same face and one voice, side by side with secret talks and plans, and Joe on the other bench, outnumbered and apart. He tilts one way to Harlan, then scowls at Huddy, but Huddy glares straight back. How can you think we sharing something when you're living like this? Memories gonna get real blurry, the past going blank. There's no stories when we're all small, no older, other time—no us when there's this maze of trails where I need a map to find you.

"We got a blood bank setting up next door to the shop," Huddy says.

"So what? A few more lowlifes in your shop. Run 'em off."

Huddy sips through clenched teeth, his face seething. Blood bank, he thinks, but it slips in his head to bloodbath. "If we move—"

"Move? Leave me with an empty building? Before I've made my money back?"

"That money was *gone*, Joe. Remember? It was *quiet* money."

"You want me to fork it out again? *And* own a vacant building on Lamar? I'll have to board the building up for a year before I get tenants filling it."

"That's why I'm leaving!" Huddy stands up to go, but he's staring out at footpaths going every which way with a thousand hidden corners.

Joe sighs, lays his arms out. How does he get to be the exhausted one, the one with problems? Huddy hears the water pouring down on the pond, a current pushing his plans away, Joe sitting on his bench like a boat with the water moving him safely out to sea.

"Hey, man," Harlan says, "that white fish, with the itty-bitty tail, I'm calling him Stubby."

"Harlan!" Huddy says, hate flooding his face, shaking his head at Joe. "I got it all scoped out. Liberty Pawn, on Summer Avenue—"

"Summer Avenue?" Joe laughing, relieved.

"What's wrong with Summer?"

Joe trades grins with Harlan. Huddy can see how Harlan's giving him a lift—Joe gets to turn Huddy down and have fun doing it. "You must be the only person who drives down Summer and says, 'Count me in.' Summer and Lamar, they're both ghetto streets."

"Summer is doing business with the whole city," Huddy says. "Don't matter ghetto."

"Joe," Harlan says, "what Huddy's trying to say is congratulations on all your money, and let's just divvy it up three ways and we're all happy."

"I ain't saying that."

"Well, I believe in sharing. *Family.*" Harlan grabs the bottle and pulls directly, exhaling with a long, pleasurable sigh. "Family money. So how about sliding me twenty cents?"

"Will you shut up?" Huddy says.

"You gonna lose your customers," Joe says, still smiling over Harlan's act. "Nobody from Lamar coming over to Summer. Your customers can't even find Summer."

"I'll get double back at the new place."

"Just go to the bank, man," Harlan says. "Why you need his dough?"

"Ha!" Joe says.

"Banks don't do pawnshops," Huddy says, but correcting Harlan doesn't bring Huddy closer to getting Joe. "This other place, it's got a drive-around. Contractors on a lunch break, they got their equipment hitched up, they can be fifty feet long and get in there. And the building's freestanding." Joe shuffling his hands, so what? "I don't want no one connected to me no more. Nobody's breaking in next door and coming over to me. Barnes gone, I'll have empty stores on both sides. With Liberty, the only people coming into my lot would be for me. And it's got a thousand more square feet inside. I can put more out on the floor, more in storage. It'll give me a chance to spread out."

"Spread out or spread *thin*? Why you want more space to guard? Sounds like too much, Huddy. Too many arms and legs and tentacles."

"Sounds like you an octopus," Harlan says.

Huddy looks up at the house, all the big rooms lit on the top floor. "Too many arms and legs and tentacles," Huddy mumbles, feeling like one of his customers who echo his appraisals, like the guy who came in last week trying to get cash on a camera that was nothing more than a glorified piece of plastic. "Sorry, buddy," Huddy said, "technology's just a little old on that," and the guy threw the line back, and Huddy kept quiet, just cut him down with silence, the echoed line cracking out in every direction, to bewilderment and humiliation and fear and rage and grief, and Huddy watched for a reaction, the man's fingers hooking into the camera case, but then he left, his emotions twisting together at the door, which he yanked, calling the parking lot a motherfucker. But now Huddy's exchanged positions, on the wrong side of the counter, playing the sad and mad repeater.

"I'm sorry," Joe says. And he is, Huddy can see and hear it, Joe's scratchy voice, his hand across his pained face. "I got my money tied up in Arkansas. This tract of land I've been throwing money into 'cause a geologist says I should. I've got a guy not paying me on a contract, hung me up for eighty thousand dollars worth of concrete. Says it's not his fault, nobody has money anymore. Sure, I'm getting bigger. But I'm shrinking, too." His fingers make a cage of his hands. "The numbers are all over the place. It's not as much *live* money as you think."

Huddy chews at his cheek, eats his flesh. "Are we brothers, Joe?" Huddy looking around at jackpot and Joe telling him he's crapped out and bust.

"Don't make me sound mean. If I could give you this—"

"'Cause right now I feel like a brother's brother's brother brother."

Joe shakes his head. "Man, you don't make me feel likable." He stands and snatches the empty bottle. "You both drinking *my booze*—but I'm just the bearer of bad tidings." They watch him tromp off, feet crunching gravel, climbing and descending the bridge till he's half-seen through branches and leaves, then gone.

"Go count your money," Huddy mutters.

"He thinks he's bringing God to the world," Harlan says.

Huddy doesn't like Harlan feeling what he's feeling. Joe with fishes in his yard, Huddy with roaches in his shop. No matter how much he sprays and bombs and sets the traps, they keep coming and breeding, laying their eggs in the low heat of the electronics.

"Two kinds of living," Harlan says. "Shit and sugar. I guess the flip side to this is me."

Harlan's sorry voice in Huddy's ears, Harlan dumping his pain in Huddy's lap. "Where's that stuff I staked you?" he says, his voice angrier than he means it.

Harlan's hands come up to explain, but then twist open, empty. "Thought you forgot."

"You thought a pawnbroker forgot a loan?"

Harlan's lips press together. "Things just got tight." He looks back at his hand like Huddy's borrowed hardware should be glued there but it somehow got unstuck. "And then this guy got me out on a string and pulled it."

Huddy waves the story away. "I already wrote it off as a loss."

"Just a nail gun and chop saw," Harlan mumbles.

"Hell it was. It was a compressor. And a generator, too."

"Weren't no generator."

"Oh, yeah? I remember loading that truck up good."

Harlan whirls his head like the missing machinery just slipped past on a raft, got carried down the canal of Joe's yard. "Maybe I could work it off."

"Sounds like you've already got a job. He gonna set you up with some heavy-duty mulework, that's what he can do for you. Man, why'd you even go down to Florida? Drywalling? Like you had to go all the way to Florida to hang drywall."

"I was framing houses, too. I was getting my stripes. And then I had this big job—"

"Save it. My whole fricking day is excuses and everything's gonna sound double-stupid out here. I can't believe he did this. I can't—"

"Why you always hearing the bad part of me?"

"Huh? I don't hear from you for a year and you come back talking about your tail getting tore off. Damn straight—I'm thinking you sleeping with a shotgun under your bed."

"I was down there three years and the only part you want to hear about is the bad."

"The bad is the punchline. The bad is why you're here. The good don't really count."

"I ain't saying I didn't get crazy. But I stopped it. And then I got swiped. I come back to this armpit, this stinking place, and the two of you talking shit. Shotgun under my bed? Man, I was sleeping with a fishing pole. I didn't get so much as a hangnail down there." He flicks his fingers out. "The Florida me? It's done. I buried him. You hear me?!" He pulls at his shirt like it's dripping sweat clinging, but Huddy could care less about Harlan wrestling clothes. Harlan jolts up like he got stung and Huddy watches him repeat the walkout.

"Guess that makes two," Huddy mumbles. He loops his finger out to where Harlan split. That's right, get moving, get lost. Just like their daddy. Not that Huddy would give that a moment's thought, he cut out that dark spot years ago, except that's where Joe's money started.

Joe was fifteen, Huddy thirteen, Harlan ten, and when their

daddy left, Joe saw them through hard times. He started mowing neighbors' lawns, and since he was too young to drive, he made a deal with an older neighbor whose family had a truck and a trailer, to drive him around the city on the weekends and nights, and Joe would do the bulk of the work and the neighbor could split the cash. He'd come home smelling of grass and gasoline, his face streaked with sweat and dirt, the heat coming off him. A fifteen-year-old man of the house. Thick wads of cash from his pants pocket, one leg, then the next, and they'd watch him reach for it, the money warm and unfolding on the table, everyone staring at it, their mama, too, the money from her new job at the grocery store not enough, but now, with this, it was. Huddy thankful but jealous, seeing her look at the money with relief, Huddy wanting to be older for it to be him, Joe not having to say a word, everything he needed to say or do was right there on the table. Joe's little notebook, the neat rows of names and addresses and figures. Huddy asking to look at the notebook, wanting to see the numbers; Harlan wanting to hold the cash. Most of the money went to the household, but whatever was saved Joe threw back in the business. Upgraded the equipment, got a commercial mower, edger, string trimmer. Turned sixteen and got his own truck and trailer, went solo and made more, even had some old men knocking on the door looking for work.

When the grass went dormant, Joe worked at a gas station. Which is how he hooked in with short-haul trucking and then eventually with a building contractor. But that was later. At first, Joe even did some scrapping. Took his truck out and filled the back with metals ditched at the curb, ladders and dishwashers and water heaters and electrical motors and stainless steel sinks and aluminum cans. Went to restaurants, commercial businesses, siding shops.

Brought salvage wire out into the backyard and built a fire, and while he cooked out the insulation to get to the copper, he'd go work on the mower, sharpening blades. Huddy asking to work alongside him, Harlan asking to have some cash, Joe not answering either, so Huddy asking for advice.

Keep your blades sharp, Joe would say. Try not to run over anything.

Harlan asking about where he can get money.

"Go catch chickens," Joe said.

"That's what daddy did, way back," Harlan said.

Joe not looking up, so Harlan saying, "Money's right there on the table, too. That's easier to catch. 'Member daddy said catching chickens was 'bout the nastiest thing you could do. He used to say how bad the chicken house smelled."

Joe added some name or number to his book. "You know what your problem is, Harlan. You think you're a kid. You think you're a person. You ain't neither. You a laborer. Go bust some concrete. Go be a scrapper."

"Like that nigger, the one me and Huddy seen? Had his bike filled up with junk. 'Member, Huddy? We saw him go by and he got so much junk he tipped over."

Joe shaking his head, looking at Huddy, then fixing back on Harlan. "You gonna be a nigger your whole life."

Huddy stands, feels his head fuzz but not spin, but he doesn't want more brothers' voices. He flips open his phone to reach Christie. When she answers, he asks, "Wrong time again?"

"What are you talking about?"

"From before. Forget it. After lunch."

"You still at Joe's?"

"Guess I am."

"What's that mean?"

"I'm here—but I ain't never been back here. His new backyard. Yeah, I'm at Joe's."

"Hold on."

Huddy waits, looks around, stares at a glazed porcelain ball atop a pedestal. He hears shouts and cries and Christie shushing. "Dealing with Cody?"

"Who else is screaming in my face?"

"I don't know what's going on over here"—he eyes metal birds and butterflies, all these flying creatures stuck in the ground—"so I figure I ask what's there."

"What's going on is a diaper. Why's it so quiet on your end? How are you with Harlan and there's no noise?"

"Break in the action. Surprised you can't hear the ocean. That surf?"

"Hold on. Git your leg—shh . . . Damn tabs. What you saying?"

"Just me and the horsetail."

"Huh?"

"Helicopters and cannons."

"Huddy, what you babbling about?"

"Some plants. I'm sightseeing. I'm calling you from a different time zone. Is it morning where you at? I better check the tank, make sure I got enough to get home."

"Oh, you sound like you filled up fine. Look: I already got a one-year-old I can't understand. Try not to drive home to the wrong house. Good luck with the porch steps."

"Ain't all that."

"Did that car seat come out of pawn yet?" And when he doesn't answer she says, "We need it now, Huddy. Cody's busting out of the seat. I gotta get him the next size."

"This guy's gonna default, I'm sure of it."

"You always say that. I'm buying the thing."

Okay, he thinks, and he says bye. He follows the path back, his hands slashing at plants brushing his face, and he imagines his arms as saws, the branches lopping down around him. Harlan squats at the edge of the pond, staring at the water. He glances down at his hand and Huddy sees the right sleeve rolled past the elbow, the shirt wet to the shoulder, and when he hears Harlan's hand tapping on the paving stones he knows what he's holding.

Harlan turns and grins. "I don't got no fishing license, so I guess I had to get this." The hand comes up fast, the nugget held between two fingers. "Ain't worth shit?"

Huddy steps closer, examines the cavities and crystals. "Worth something," he shrugs.

"What'd you call it?" Harlan says, the glistening rock moving to his face like a magnet.

"Fool's gold."

"The other thing."

"Pyrite."

"Yeah, pyrite," Harlan says. "Semiprecious pyrite."

Huddy laughs, shakes his head. "Get you a gem box. You a gem salesman right quick."

"Fool's gold, pure gold. Sounds the same to me." Harlan blows on the rock like pyrite's just a dusty coating keeping down the value.

Huddy studies the others. "I'd go with the quartz, if you're taking. That pyrite's probably a tenth of the agate."

"Yeah?" Harlan says.

"Bigger," Huddy shrugs. "If you want to get scientific. Probably a fraction of the other."

"Well I'm sticking with gold." Harlan buffs the pyrite on his shirt, then pockets it. "Unless you want it? For collateral. Or how 'bout you scoop the rest up and then you and me square." But he doesn't smile. Instead he yanks his head back like his hair got pulled, his face pinched in anguish.

"The stuff I was saying before . . ." Huddy says.

"You weren't saying nothing." His shoulders jerk. "I know what I am. Third down the line. I know where Joe is and I know where you are."

"It ain't like that."

"Ha, I guess that makes me your buffer from the bottom." Harlan flexes his hand and the fish flee. "See, it's dark, so they getting spooked 'cause they think I'm a predator." He skims his hand along the surface and Huddy watches the water ripple out. "He really got the works out here," Harlan says, shaking his head. "This is some dream, ain't it?"

A dream or a display. But sure, Harlan's right, Huddy won't argue.

"Were me," Harlan says, "I'd build it exactly like this and I wouldn't even need the house. I'd just stay out here and make this my water bed."

And Huddy feels it, too, this floating peace. Moon and stars and the air a part of Joe's arrangement. You build something like this, you'd feel like you can reach up to the sky and move constellations around like potted plants, flick stars with your fingers. His eyes open dizzy to the fish, slashes of red and orange brilliant in the water. It's the biggest success story he knows, and it's gotta be a consolation that it's a brother.

"Can't everybody win, I guess." Harlan scoops water, spreads his fingers and watches it pour through. "This ain't just a pond. It's a wishing well. 'Cept everything already came true."

Huddy imagines a shining penny pitched out from his thumb, his life tossed away and remade. "If you work for me, Harlan, I can't pay you as much."

"Sounds like you needing me more. Unless you pulling the plug." Harlan steps lightly over stones, climbs the small embankment edging the waterfall. He reaches into the running water and pulls a clump of algae from the wet rocks and flings the slick green muck over his shoulder into the bushes. Huddy thinks of Harlan's arm sinking down, his panning hand moving through the water, groping for the gold, his fingers crawling along the terraced steps, circling until the nugget's pinched in his fingers.

"Lemme tell you something," Huddy says. "Some people. Like Joe, he got his gravel he's digging out the ground. Others digging gold out the ground. I dig it out of people. Out the ground or people is the same thing. As long as folks coming into my store, I'm fine, 'cause I'm mining." But he's shaking his head the whole time he says it.

"Good deal," Harlan says. He steps back to the front of the pond. "Now where's that fish called Stubby? I'm naming 'em all right now. That calico, she's thinking she's special. We gonna call her Lady Jane. This fantail, he likes me, he's my follower. I'ma call him Shadow."

Huddy watches Harlan rub his bloodshot eyes. "You really fixing to stay with KayKay?"

"Might." He slides his head. "You never liked her."

"Kind of a dark mystery, that's all. Crack her open, never know what'll pop out."

Huddy remembers her car. The front end bashed in. From driving into her ex's truck—and the way Harlan explained it, the ex had driven into her car the week before, so she was just retaliating.

Huddy thought there was a restraining order, but he couldn't remember which side, or maybe that was just him thinking there ought to be one. The guy had asked to marry her, right after he went to jail, and Harlan thought that was a hoot, the ex doing everything backward and late. "If you want," Huddy says, "I got a spare room. Till you lovebirds connect."

Harlan nods. "That's brain coral there," he says, pointing. "And water hyacinth. Gotta be careful with that one, it's a choker." He looks around for something else to name or know. "Those dots on the rocks is tadpoles."

They hear the glass door slide open, see Joe come out.

"I'll give your place a spark, man," Harlan says fast. "That's what I bring to the table. And I got the truck. It's running good."

"Harlan, you can be all that. But you also gonna be my guard dog."

"Hell, I can do that. Easy. See, when I told you about losing my tail, I didn't mention: I'm a salamander. So it grows back fast."

Huddy pats Harlan's shoulder, cups the back of his neck. "I know you everything from a puppy dog to a rattlesnake."

A twitch of a smile fading. Harlan's face darkens. "Florida, man," shaking his head, "nothing happened down there." Saying it like it did and it didn't and both were the problem, and Huddy can't tell which he's hearing more, Harlan worried or Harlan bored.

They both turn to look at Joe approaching, a six-pack hooked in his fingers. "Guess we're switching gears," Harlan says. "You think . . ." he says, staring hard at the water, his face concentrating, "if you'd been firstborn, this would've been you?"

"Can't know. He always been a workhorse, gotta give him that. Ain't just about order."

"I think it would've been good for me, if I'd been oldest. If it was me taking care of things, putting bread on ... if he'd been behind us, instead of vice versa ... me taking the lead ..."

But Joe's close enough to stop Harlan. "What are we arguing about now?" He shuts his eyes, rubs his lids, blinks himself awake. "She said she heard the whole thing. Got ears like a squirrel."

"Guess this is one big doghouse," Harlan says.

Joe glances at the pond and Huddy wonders if he's seeing the missing gold, if he might frisk them or just smile at their petty crime. "So what's with the blood bank? You got a name for the contractor? It's probably too late to snuff out the permit." Joe glances at his watch but then turns back to his house, the windows huge with glass. "Stay long if you want," he shrugs, ripping one of the beers and passing the rest. Amazing how little they had as kids, their daddy swiping the valuables on his way out the door, and now Joe's got all this, and he looks like he's about to drop, breathing hard from all the long years of climbing and chasing.

"You ever drive with this guy?" Huddy says, not knowing why he's saying it, because the last time he's been driving with Joe's been years, but man, what a maniac driver. He throws a hearty arm around Joe, hears himself laugh. "The worst tailgater ever," Huddy says, laughing more, three rear-end collisions to Joe's credit, Huddy in the passenger seat and Joe right up on the guy's ass, the guy thinking he's playing some sick game. "The guy flipping him off in the mirror and he's not even seeing it, 'cause he's on the phone, yelling about work." Cell phone, Huddy thinks, so it couldn't have been too long ago.

Joe smiles, smudges his fingers across his eyes.

"You done some craziness out here," Harlan says, and Huddy laughs, his arm still around Joe, thinking about a playful push toward the water, let's all jump in.

"Sit down," Harlan says. "You falling over. We heard your creaking bones from the door. We gonna drink that beer and name your fishes. That big one, we gonna call him Lucky."

Driving home, Huddy waits for Harlan's headlights to flicker and signal that he's peeling off elsewhere, but the beam stays bright and steady in Huddy's mirror. His cell phone rings and Huddy pushes the button to tell Christie he's nearing home.

"Miss Deanie called," Christie says. He checks his watch. It feels like he hasn't seen her for weeks, even if she went missing today. "Said she tried you at work."

"How'd the surgery go?" Huddy says, unsure if she's had one.

"She says she can't work for you no more. She finally got disability and she's scared to mess with it. If she comes in, someone might see her and rat her out. She knew her thinking wasn't running deep. Maybe she'll work with you later, she says."

He laughs. It's funny if it were someone else's life and since he's laughing it must be. "It's fine," Huddy says. He looks in the mirror, sees Harlan, his car staying tight. He feels like changing lanes to see if Harlan'd switch, too, some kid's game. "Harlan coming home with me," he says, and he hears hesitation before she says okay.

"Did you tell me that before, Huddy? I might've listened for that."

"First time. He won't stay long." But he hears more worry. "Where'd you think he was staying?"

"I didn't. And then you said you were going to Joe's. So I thought *that*. Why else would you go to Joe's? And Lorie—she's real strong on hospitality. She didn't offer no invitation?"

"Nobody did."

"Them two—they do whatever they want, don't they?"

"Harlan wouldn't want to stay there."

"Why not? I'd stay there."

"Well, I'm bringing Harlan home."

"I know. You *just* told me. You might've said it more. In case I forgot."

"Just a few days. Maybe even tonight."

"About tonight—Cody's asleep and I'm already in bed. I was dropping off when your Deanie called. I'll be better company in the morning."

"We won't wake you up, when we come in."

"Uh-huh. Just in case, I might just post a sign on the door."

"I'll tell him you were asleep when I called you."

"Sounds perfect. A little white lie. Goodnight."

Huddy knows what's supposed to happen when he gets home. He's supposed to sit out back and stare at what's not there and get bummed. Sneer at his tiny square of grass and his one tree and his no-smell of pool or flowers. But he won't be like that. Because this place is tons better than where he lived before, before he became a pawnbroker. Doesn't have the dope track running behind his house. No cars in neighbors' yards. No neighbor with two feet of meadowweeds that the city's gotta threaten fines before the home-owner gets his ass up and mows it down. Only two of the houses on the block are rentals, and even those aren't too-bad eyesores. The folks all around are solid. One neighbor works in the schools, another's an electrician, the couple three houses down are potters, got a studio out back, and a few more on the block are steady retired. Huddy tells them all he works in collateralized loans, and if they asked he'd be more specific, but they don't. He's got a family, wife and kid, never thought he'd have either, turning forty empty and now look at him, having both, and Christie wants another one, and damn right let's have three. And now Harlan's here, too. It ain't much, but Huddy's keeping every bit. Just put in a new lawn set, next was gonna be the swings. He can't wait to get there, go inside and say, "Here it is, Harlan, this is me. This is home."

Four

HUDDY WAKES FROM A starlight dream to laughter he thinks is his own until he hears Christie's voice and then Harlan's coming into his small room like a taunt. The dream—he *knew* he'd been dreaming, saw that what he was picturing for himself, a yard deep and endless, was jumbled with what Joe had created, but knowing that it was a dream rewarded it back, like some trick he'd outsmarted. And then came Harlan's voice, a lookout sound far away, faint and cold like a water drip, but there was a hammock spread between trees so Huddy climbed up and rolled in and nodded off, but Harlan's voice neared and sharpened, passing over and undoing the dream, and Huddy wanted to stop the voice but his own mouth was soundless, and he wanted to move—the land was a promise in his mind that he could gather up and carry to safety, if only he could move—but his body was too heavy, sunk down in the netting, the mesh bowl now a hole dug deep, and then Christie's voice, like a hand, slipped beneath him and led him back inside, and he woke, feeling the hammock, no, bed under him. He lay flat on his back, wrapped in a sheet, the dream severed, staring at the ceiling, a water stain in the corner because the roof wasn't on right.

He kicks away the sheet, whips his hand out as if a curtain hung there, his anger more than the hangover squeezing his head, but by the time he reaches the doorway he feels also a mild relief that at least he isn't being toyed with anymore, that his life is clear and true and not clouded by darkness and dreams. He showers and dresses and walks back to the kitchen, the hallway floorboards sloped, the settling cracks faultlining the walls, and he feels again the contrast of his dream and his surroundings. But then he sees Harlan in yesterday's clothes and hears him making fun of Joe's floating world, his hand dancing out Joe's cultivated tastes, and Huddy's so cheered and grateful for the company at his table: Harlan's been too far gone these past years. Christie spoons food at Cody's mouth, but she's looking over her shoulder to see the joke get told, and Cody's eyes hold there, too, his mushmouth bright orange and open like last night's fish. "I asked her, 'Weren't you Miss Waitress Tennessee?'" Harlan says, "but she said she ain't never been no waitress." And Huddy realizes Harlan's talking about Lorie and busts out laughing. He touches Christie's shoulder, rubs it, his other hand cupping Cody's head.

"Welcome back from Shangri-la," Christie says.

"Wasn't like our daddy taught us to be big," Harlan says, "but Joe sure done figured."

Huddy opens a cupboard, the wood sticking, and takes down a plate. He stands by himself at the barred window and stares out at the patch of weeds and dirt.

"Your brother say he'd sleep in the shed if we needed the space."

Huddy hears Harlan's fingers drum against the table.

"You giving me this food and . . ." Harlan's voice dropping.

Huddy looks at the flimsy shed, pictures Harlan camped inside with a wet bedroll. "You ain't some stranger," he says, half-turning, seeing Harlan rub his stomach and eye his finished plate, embarrassed, the half-drunk glass of juice sucked down like he'd siphoned it.

"I ain't feeding like little man here." He taps the rim of the plate, pushes it away, then wipes his hand across a pant leg. "This all from the store?" he says, throwing a hand out at the front rooms.

Huddy returns to the window. "Most of it," he hears Christie answer. "I told him I'm threatening to break loose and go to Wolfchase. Get the whole shopping experience."

Huddy thinking about that first year when he took home everything, but then it just became stuff. Sits in his store and turns invisible. He turns to see Christie, her eyes narrowed, and he thinks maybe it's about money, and he says What? and she blinks, her eyes moving across his face, and he realizes her glance was directed inward.

"What what?" her eyes lowered but then shifting back on him, harder, for being misread.

"Thought something was wrong."

"She just checking you out," Harlan says. "Her older stud."

"I was thinking . . . I don't know what I was thinking. I ought call my sister, okay?"

"She cute?" Harlan asks.

"Yeah, give Jeannie a call," Huddy says, unsure why he's naming her, since there's no deep sisterly feeling, no closeness but no division either, just some childhood residue. He says all the siblings to himself, as if it's giving him some power—over Harlan, he realizes—Billy then Jeannie then Christie then Jim then Johnny. Her order. Huddy and Christie had joked that they were both middle children, only Christie, being one of five, had the smaller middle. "I'll let you know about the car seat," he says.

"Already bought it," she says.

"You did?"

"I told you I was getting up early." Her eyes cut to the wall phone. And Huddy feels the room stop, with his brother being here and with Christie wanting to communicate with her own, the spoon held out frozen until Cody yells for the withheld food. As soon as he swallows, he's finished and squirms to get out of his strapped-in seat. "Look at this mud slick," Christie says, the plastic spoon drooping from her fingers as if it weighed of lead.

"You got houses today?"

"Two," she says, wiping Cody's cheeks, his face grimacing in a pucker, and then the tray.

Huddy stabs three quick bites with his fork and chews and feels himself strengthen. Coffee he'll drink there. "You ready?"

"What else am I doing?" Harlan stands, hops. Grabs his shirt and shakes it. "Already wearing my action jacket," and Huddy watches him shove his arms out at the air.

Two rights and the economy bottoms. Overgrown grass and trash piles and houses slumped and decayed and boarded-up. A tidy home and a few more scattered about, but losing out to the overall war-zone surroundings.

"Tell you what," Harlan says. "When God give Memphis the enema, he putting the hose right here." Time-warped shacks, a poverty old and eternal. "This city don't know—rest of the world's gone futuristic." Harlan already feeling stuck. "All right, explain this business of yours."

So Huddy tells a story about Jenks. About a customer with a TV, and Jenks would give him twenty-five dollars, and when the man picked up the TV, he'd give Jenks back thirty. "Sometimes, the man'd bring his thirty in a month, sometimes a week, sometimes just a couple days. This man's carrying his TV in and out of the store for years, Jenks making five dollars, five dollars. So one day, the man comes in empty-handed, depressed, and Jenks asks him what's wrong. 'My TV broke,' the man said, 'and now I don't have nothing to loan on.' So Jenks walks over to the TV shelf and grabs a set and gives it free. 'Here,' he says, 'now you loan on this.'"

Harlan smiles, laughs hard and fast. Too harsh, maybe, so Huddy adds, "I take their money and I take their risk."

"I ain't criticizing. Sounds so good it should be illegal. Twenty-five makes thirty. What's that, twenty-five percent?"

"Twenty," Huddy nods, but Harlan grimaces for the math lesson and for starting from scratch, back to another square one. A floor boy, a gofer. Huddy won't let him near the cash drawer—not for now—and he won't let him clean and polish the jewelry, and he knows Harlan'll get restless, and Huddy's gonna have to throw him a bone, give him something to be proud about. During the year of Harlan's silence and unanswered calls, Huddy thought of traveling to Florida. But he couldn't decide if his brother had disappeared and when to start looking. Wait too long and he's beyond help, go too early and he's just lying in the sand laughing at your concern.

"She fifteen years younger?" Harlan asks, and the grin tells Huddy it's Christie.

He nods—even though the age gap is less than fifteen, but it's closer to right than Harlan's guess about the interest.

"Man, I don't get my brothers. Joe's got a third wife, and she's old as him. A third wife who looks like a first. And you've got a first one who looks like a third. You ought switch."

Gang signs spray-painted on the blood bank. Huddy shakes his head at the neighborhood welcome. He won't let Harlan see the alarm code, so he hops out and goes to the door like a phone's ringing and turns around and Harlan's exited but moving slow, as if he knows what Huddy needs to do, and Huddy punches in the code. He looks back at Harlan and Harlan nods, and Huddy feels more correct than bad for guarding himself.

He shows Harlan the back room, and when they come back to the front, Huddy turns on the computer and gives him the tickets to retrieve the loans coming out of pawn. When he finishes, Huddy has him sit on a stool and watch him on the computer until Harlan glances at the wall clock and pops up. "Time for this guard dog to get armed." He reaches for the counter gun.

"Nah, stays there." Huddy thinks and swivels, picks another pistol from another drawer.

"I'm wearing it, right?" He grabs the belt holster from under the counter and straps it on. "You remember when we were kids and I climbed that tree and you and Joe chopped it down?"

"You remembering that now?"

"Must be all these axes I'm seeing. Joe done the chopping—but I whupped *you*."

"Yeah, well, not as bad as daddy did."

"Never as bad as that. He'd send us down to the basement."

"Send us to the *furnace*," Huddy says. "'Get down behind the coal furnace and wait for me.'" Huddy laughing at the remembered line.

"Yeah, he'd make you *wait*." Harlan smiling. "You knew he was getting the strap and you just had to sit there and think about it, and you knew he'd never forget you."

Huddy nods at the shared bruises and eyes the gun now holstered at Harlan's side. "Try not to hit anything I don't tell you to."

"Customer," Harlan says.

"I see him." A new customer bringing in an old story.

"How you doing, buddy?" Harlan says. "See anything you can't live without?"

My baby needs diapers. My truck needs gas. Old lines but it's all new to Harlan. Fresh ears, and a fresh heart. Huddy can see how he identifies with the clientele, knows their end-of-the-line feelings, whereas Huddy has long moved to cynical, with everybody trying to get into his pocket. Sob stories, cover stories—you weed through a whole day of lies to pull out the truth.

"Mister Durwood, how are you?" Huddy asks and the man replies, "Man, it's terrible when your pawnbroker knows your name." The joke thrown to Harlan as if he's already the audience. What would his business have been like if he'd been running it with Harlan beside him, adding a jump to the place, instead of just Joe above? And then, an old customer comes in needing to sell a Winchester '73, and maybe Harlan can be his good-luck charm, too. "Did something stupid," the man says. "How about twenty-five hundred? Man, I feel sick doing this."

Huddy knows the gun is legit, the man's owned it thirty years. And it's going to Huddy's favorite gun buyer: Mister Yewell, not just an enthusiast but a gentleman he trusts enough to let him take a gun apart. No one answers at Yewell's so Huddy leaves a message: "Mister Yewell, it's Huddy Marr from Bluff City Pawn. I got something here for you. A Winchester '73 just came in, if you want to check it out, put your name on it." Huddy hasn't seen him much lately, and the last time his health looked poor, but Yewell just shrugged, "Still cleaning my guns every day."

"That hasn't happened in *months*," Huddy says, smiling at Harlan and his future sale, but it's only a half-hour celebration till pawn detail crashes the party.

"I know, I'm the grim reaper," Sergeant Bell says, accordion files tucked under an arm, badge flapping on his chest like some harmless conventioneer. "He couldn't spell burglary, but he could tell us every house he hit. Drove us all around, confessing. Mighty white of him."

Huddy trading the jewelry for a receipt. He wishes he could get Yewell here right now, but of course he's gonna have to wait a legal month before he can make the sale.

"He should do some time," Bell says, the chain dropping inside a file, "if we still have a court system." And then he slips out the door.

"Probably keep the chain himself," Harlan says, watching the car drive off. "What'd your man look like?"

Huddy shakes his head, throws a hand out. "He was wearing a nametag that said 'thief.'"

"He black?"

Huddy nods. And the one before that, too, and the one before that was white and the one before that was black with a white girl waiting in the car, and Huddy would list every complexion if it got any cash back. He gets burned more by the blacks, but burned worse by the whites.

Huddy sees Tom, his scrap-gold buyer, pulling up—Tom always waiting for the midmorning lull and wearing his smoke-screen outfit of customer clothes to disguise his briefcase cash. "Got business," Huddy says, and he grabs an envelope from the safe and flips the counter for Tom, and the two walk back to his office. He'll watch the floor and Harlan on the monitor.

Huddy hands him the envelope.

"Light, huh?" Tom says, waving it, and Huddy shrugs. "Least we're catching the market good." The years of built-up trust, Tom just reads the figures on the envelope, what's fourteen-karat and what's ten, and plugs the numbers into his iPhone. "You got four seventy-five here," he says, and tags the envelope with the number and Huddy's name.

Huddy nods. Tom unlatches the briefcase on his lap, the envelope goes in and out comes the cash. He counts and Huddy glances at the monitor, split-screen showing nothing in the store and outside just Tom's car with his armed guard sitting inside, but then another car pulling up.

"Bought a thousand off a guy last week," Tom says. "This sanitation feller. Those sewer rats catch more gold. They got filters to catch it. Shit Gold, he calls it. Banged-up and dirty, but I tell 'em it's as good as clean."

A white woman enters and Huddy watches her. "You got it, Harlan?"

"I sure do."

The woman walks straight back to the loan counter, no picking through aisles or merchandise, and then Harlan puts his hand on his heart and fake-staggers his legs, and Huddy knows it's KayKay even before Harlan flips the counter to go to her. "Well . . ." Huddy says.

"Yep, time to fade into the crowd," Tom says, but Huddy sits watching KayKay and Harlan, two figures hugging like they're taking cover beneath a tree. Huddy is in his own store, but he feels like he's looking in on Harlan's life—and how quickly it's rejoining itself, to Memphis and Huddy and now her. He lays back for a while, watching them on the monitor like they're moving inside his own brain, then walks out. "Look who's turned up," he says, although he's the one feeling like he's come from nowhere, and KayKay gives a small sleepy smile like she'd just seen him yesterday.

A touch more wear and tear to her face, a white T-shirt with the neck stretched loose. Her legs look good in the jeans but are probably bony without them. But she looks clean and showered, painted nails and the perfume worn for Harlan, Huddy thinks.

"Called her, told her I was here," Harlan says, and Huddy wonders when, or if, a phone call was even needed. They're the same animals, two of the same species picking up each other's tracks. "I guess I better get on the right side of the counter," Harlan says.

Huddy looks again at her open neckline, thinks of a drunk hand clutching as she scrambles for the door. "He tell you his parole officer says he shouldn't be around women?"

Harlan laughs. "She knows you a windjammer and not to trust a word outta your mouth."

"I might believe *half*." She leans in, looks over the counter at Harlan's legs. "Maybe I should check your ankles, make sure you're not wearing one of them bracelets."

Huddy smiles. "What you been up to, KayKay?"

She exhales long and bored. "Oh, I don't know. I don't remember my life too good." Her dark eyes sweep the store like she's looking out at a dusty country. "Mom's having a classic fall-apart, if you want to know everything." She shrugs, scans the gun racks, then looks at Huddy. "Boys with toys," she says and wags a finger. "What's he having you do here?"

"He's the post commander," Huddy says.

Harlan huffs. "More like sit in a chair and be a hemorrhoid."

KayKay looks around, but Huddy knows where she'll settle. "You should let him show the jewelry."

"Oh, yeah?" Huddy says. "Might help if he knew a diamond from a piece of gravel."

KayKay shrugs. "He'd be good at it, that's all. Sell all this stuff like it was real."

"It *is* real," Huddy says.

In the doorway, the same gun buyer from yesterday, the nonbuyer, although maybe Huddy's wrong today. Already got the Winchester—waiting for Yewell to call on that—so maybe this is his gun day. Huddy watches him approach. "You back for your gun?"

"Then Harlan won't have to lie about it," KayKay says.

The customer's lips pinch. "Thought I'd check some other pieces."

Huddy nods but he's not gonna waste his steps, just turns a useless hand at the gun room.

Harlan at the jewelry case across from KayKay, and Huddy watches them huddle over the jewelry like it's throwing firelight to keep them warm.

"You like this one?" Harlan points out a chunky ring.

"Maybe if I had green teeth and lived in Frayser in a trailer."

Huddy laughs, but Harlan doesn't. "Looks like she's gone upscale on you," Huddy says.

"More like be a wannabe," Harlan says, and he waits for her fingers to select elsewhere.

Huddy studying their hands and faces to see what feeling or secret is passing between them. He can't say what's beginning or needs mending because he doesn't know what ever ended or got broken. She points at a necklace, and Harlan unlocks the case and his hand dips down to lift the glinting object off the bar.

"That bracelet, too," KayKay says, tapping on the countertop—a sheet of glass that's sitting in a room that's hers—and Harlan's hand grabbing again but Huddy says, "Nuh-uh. One at a time. People gonna try to get ten rings spread out on the counter. One'll go missing, fast."

"Too bad you don't have any SIGs," the customer says. "I got a SIG 210 at home. Thing's got the mechanical precision of a watch. Don't know whether to wind it or load it."

Huddy nods.

"People, huh?" KayKay says. "You don't gotta be careful with me. I ain't *them*."

"Course not," Huddy says. "I was talking others. Gypsies—they like to do it that way."

"Well, I ain't wearing ten scarves."

"Just trying to teach Harlan here. Second thing: They want to see something, you put it in their *hand*. That way, they have to give it back to you. On the counter, it gets gone."

"You sure talk suspicious," she says.

"Thanks for educating," Harlan says. "You mind if I put this on her *neck*? Turn around."

KayKay turns and leans back and Harlan spins the necklace around her and pulls it up, his hands glancing her shirt, her shoulders, the sides of her upturning neck, his knuckles brushing her ears and pressing the top of her spine while he hooks the latch—Huddy almost laughing at all the contact and handiwork. KayKay circles around to Harlan and he tilts the makeup mirror, hits the necklace right, and Huddy laughs aloud now, but he's still impressed with the form. KayKay tucks her hair behind her ears and her fingers slide across to trace the jewelry on her skin.

"I got a gun in every room of the house," the man says, and he makes a gun of his hand. "By the back door, too. Got a gun on top of the fridge by the back door, and if someone tries getting in they gotta go through my fridge gun." His voice booms. "And my fridge gun's a Smith, so you know it'll go bang forever."

"Sure will," Huddy says, rolling his eyes.

"I told you Harlan knew how to show jewelry," KayKay says.

"You tell 'em the price," Harlan says to Huddy, "I tell 'em why they need to take it home."

"All these people breaking into sheds. You go into *my* shed, you getting carried out." He looks at Huddy for approval, but Huddy's not gonna cheer his dead shed-invader.

Harlan extends his middle finger to impale the man and shut his mouth. "Huddy, what's she gotta do to get a necklace like this?"

"Save up."

"Well how 'bout installment plans?"

"Ten percent down for layaway. I'll waive the processing fee." He smiles his soft heart.

"How 'bout you just waive the price?" KayKay teases.

"Maybe your mama . . ." Harlan says. His neck yanks and his teeth bite down. "All that you done. Maybe she got something she ain't needing, and she help you with this here thing."

Huddy watches Harlan glance at KayKay, his eyes drawing out some memory pang, some kick to the muddy curb that KayKay closes her lips and blinks about. "She sure been walking on me lately. Ever since daddy died. I guess I backed the wrong horse."

"My son, he's over in Iraq. Sharpshooter like his dad."

"Hey man," Harlan says, his face burning. "Lemme ask you. How come every military man I meet is a shooter? You know? How come nobody's the cook?"

"Huh?"

"I mean, somebody has to be the cook, but every military guy I meet's some special-ops, Green Beret, ex-marine sniper."

The man studies Harlan, trying to measure out the insult from the spit-out craziness, but Harlan keeps adding, "I wish I met one guy from the military who'd say, 'I was the *cook* and couldn't shoot for shit, but I made the best damn chili around. I was the best damn food server.'"

Huddy watches the man's eyes go down to the gun at Harlan's hip and take it in, Harlan's fingers not there but his body dug in and steady as a duelist.

"I mean, somebody has to be the cook!" Harlan's face wild and his voice country-loud. The man frowns at the gun, trades stares with Harlan. Then he locks eyes with Huddy.

"He just got his jaw unwired," Huddy says, but he's smiling 'cause Harlan's crazy-assed antics got the guy moving on.

"Sounds like," he hears the man say at the door.

"Why do all gun buyers have short dicks?" Harlan says.

The door stays closed, the man stopped behind. He tugs and twists his cap and talks to himself and then walks off to his truck.

"Don't gotta egg, Harlan. Even a jackleg like that. Never know the day he's bringing."

"That guy thinks he's doing you a favor 'cause he's *white* and he's coming in here."

The man revs and guns the truck, tires spinning mad and screaming out of the lot and onto Lamar, but peeling out is the same as slinking off if you don't return to bash the store. Huddy looks over at KayKay. Everybody's been eyeing everyone the past minute, but KayKay's drawn a hood around her, paying no mind save to the mirror bouncing back the necklace, her hand to her throat. Huddy wonders if the storm even registered. Maybe a hothead with a gun is just an ordinary thing. Or maybe she needed a shootout with bullets ricocheting and ripping the air, gunsmoke and the screams of the dying, before she pried her eyes. Huddy shakes his head. The lights of her world have darkened except for the rainbow flying off the necklace. He kind of admires the focus. "Yeah," she says, her fingers going down to circle the red pendant like a lockpicker working the knob. "My mother might have something to trade for this."

"Mister Yewell, Huddy Marr again. Calling 'cause I really think you gonna wanna get a jump on this Winchester." Huddy hangs up, checks his watch and frowns. He can feel the low vibration of the jackhammer from the next building. Nothing can mask it. Try to cover it with stereo music and it would still thump in the background.

"You can trust me with jewelry," Harlan says, nodding. "I know how to loosen the ladies. I know their material instinct. Build a rapport."

"Yeah, I seen that." Huddy remembering Harlan's running hands and rubdown. "What you gonna do with the men? You gonna pet them, too?"

Harlan smiles. "I tell the ladies it makes 'em look taller and thinner and younger."

And then they go home and wonder what happened. "You bunking with her tonight?"

Harlan shrugs. "You meet Christie here?"

"Why?" Huddy asks.

"I figure, you sure ain't meet her square-dancing."

"She came in once. Shopping." Which is true, or enough true for Harlan.

When the phone rings minutes later, Huddy hopes it's Yewell asking for the gun, but it might be KayKay calling for Harlan, and instead it's Joe. "He's here," Huddy says. "Working."

It's a long pause before Joe says, "Fine. Let him be *your* sidekick."

"Oh, was he working by your side?" Huddy sees Del pull up. Even for Del it's quick, no day between visits.

"That Joe?" Harlan says.

"You two coming over again?" Huddy hears Joe ask, and he replies, "How 'bout you coming to *me*?" Which isn't what he wants, Joe touring his mud hut like some ambassador slumming the village.

"I'm building a house that's three-quarters done and I ain't been paid."

"Looks like you gonna have to pick up the hammer yourself. I got twenty of 'em here."

"What's different about me?" Del says, arms spread, and Huddy presses dead the phone.

Huddy seeing the same parasite, the same pawn bullshitter, same flapping mouth. "Am I supposed to ask about your weight?"

"No, it's different than that." He turns sideways.

Huddy rolls his eyes. "You got a twenty-year-old girlfriend and she works at Hooters."

"No. *Outside*."

Huddy sees a new used car. "Car."

"Bought it online. Guess how much. And Huddy, you know I'm married so I wouldn't have no girlfriend from Hooters."

Huddy stone-faced wanting to be nameless and unknown to Del.

"You ain't gonna guess the price?" Del looks at Harlan. "How about you? You gonna guess? I bet I'll make a thousand, for what I paid. They sold it like it's a beater but it ain't that."

Del makes a beeline for the jewelry and Huddy hears a buzzing noise from his lips, this fly-wing sound Del always makes when he doesn't see what he wants. "You still hiding those Rolexes?" He switches to Harlan. "He tell you where he's hiding them?"

"Not yet," Harlan says. "But I'm thinking he buries them out back."

"Ha. Well, how 'bout you and me go dig 'em up? I bet we strike oil, too!"

A black man comes in, approaches with a VCR, which he sets down carefully. "I'm wanting to sell this."

"Sorry, my man, I get those all day every day."

"For real?" His face falls.

Del smirks at Huddy, and stops when the man looks behind at the electronics and then carries his VCR out like a sad hat in his hands. Huddy watches Del sneer, like he's sitting on a mule grinding his bootheels into the world beneath him.

"You wouldn't even take it for *free*. He must be thinking technology stopped."

Huddy shakes his head, not at Del's judgment but his disdain, the door not even closed.

"Dolls!" Del moving toward them, two Teresa dolls inside their packaging. "My niece . . ." Then he waves his hand like an eraser. "I got this idea to bounce off you." His palms press together and flatten. "Gold. How much you getting for your scrap? I got the gold fever."

"Already got someone, Del." Trying to make his voice sound dull and valueless.

"What's he giving you? Ninety percent?"

Huddy crosses his arms, turns himself into a rock that Del can't push uphill.

"Damn, you ain't telling me nothing today." He looks around like Huddy's buyer is hiding. "Who's your guy? I bet you gotta count your money six times with him. Me, you know I got a clean score. I've been buying your stuff for years. Bought watches, rings, guns—how many guns I bought? Drills. Saws. Bought something from there and there and there. Hell, I probably bought a *vowel* from you!" Pointing to claim every inch of the room, the shelves, the walls all a part of his belongings, his fingers smearing the air. "So now I'ma buy your gold."

"Del, you really wanna drive around with all that money? It's nerve-racking work." But Huddy's also thinking, Bullshit you got the cash for gold.

"You the one to talk," Del says. "You got buzzards circling this place. 'Sides, I don't scare easy. Your buyer's paying ninety, isn't he? Maybe I do a notch better. He can't be giving you ninety-*five*? It's between, right? Yeah, I bet you got bagfuls of wedding bands." Huddy feels like the whole city is listening, Del's mouth moving through streets and alleyways and doors, bodies rising out of bed and coming to crowd their faces at his windows. "Go from penny-weights to grams to ounces to pounds and we all make money. Come on, Huddy, give me a piece of it. Whatever you get, I'll bump it *point five*. Let's say for example—"

"I get it, Del."

"Good." He sniffs loud like there's a gold dust in the air. "I'll make it work for both of us. Don't be hording. Gold. It's just some low-hanging fruit and I wanna taste it."

Give him more than a taste, Huddy thinks. Pour a stash down Del's mouth, fill his cheeks with bent bracelets and the gold grill that he bought last month from a black kid, the kid pulling the grill right out from his teeth. Del's mouth plugged with the gold brick Huddy'd set there.

"You see the quotes on platinum prices? You think there'd be a way to scrape the platinum off the catalytic converter."

Huddy stares at the back of his head. "Huh?"

"From my car," Del says, and he twists back and his face wrenches angrily. "The converter's got platinum. How you get the platinum out but keep the converter running?"

"I really don't know, Del."

He wrings his hands like the platinum's there, a polish he can't peel off. "Forget it. We talk price next time. Gold. Now it's me." He nods to himself until it's true and then leaves.

Harlan shakes his head. "What the fuck was that?"

"Del Twiggs." Huddy shrugs.

"Twiggs—that's about right."

He looks at the car, sizes up the value inside it. "Next time I see him, he better have an ATM strapped to his back. And money coming out of his mouth."

A white male looking to sell a mower and an edger, and Huddy doesn't pin the guy for a thief, although maybe he's stealing it from himself, doesn't want to tell the wife about the gambling so now he's gonna tell her someone broke into the shed and stole their lawn equipment.

A gun buyer in a camo cap but glazed eyes so Huddy tells him he can't show him a gun. And when the man protests, Huddy says, "Maybe tomorrow we find a gun to put you in."

"*Dying Young*," a customer says, looking at the VCR tapes. "Man, that's me."

When he leaves, Harlan asks, "You think our daddy's alive?"

Huddy makes a face. "He ain't in *Memphis* if he is. Hope that's not why you back."

"Sometimes I think he's living in our old house."

"You do?"

Harlan shrugs. "He's probably dead. But whenever I tell myself he is, he pops up in my mind as living."

"You got heaters?" a customer asks, and the phone rings, and Huddy points and answers.

"Is this Mister Marr?" a woman's voice asks.

"Speaking."

"This is Miss Millie. Lee Yewell's wife."

"Oh. Oh, yes."

"I'm returning your messages. I'm afraid . . ." Huddy already feeling a loss coming. "My husband passed away last month."

"Oh . . . That's terrible." Huddy sorry for her loss, and his—but he knows he can always sell a good gun. "I saw him, two months ago."

He's lost his best customer and he looks over at his gun racks—and thinks, What's she gonna do with the guns? And it's as if she hears his mind when she says: "Lee left us some instructions. He said you'd be the person to call about the guns. But I've never called a pawnshop before. You understand."

"Of course."

Two black men come in and one tugs at his neck and asks Huddy if he's got any big crosses, and Huddy holds up his hand and the guy breaks out his roll and Huddy watches Harlan watch the man flash it.

Every time the concrete goes into the steel container next door, it sounds like a building coming down.

"Would you like me to come look at them?" Huddy says, and hears back, "I suppose you should do that."

Huddy remembers selling Yewell a Winchester '76, a Winchester '86. He wants to open his gun book right now to see how many went to him.

"That didn't sound good," Harlan says.

"Good?" Huddy says, hanging up, and he can't even imagine the size of the man's collection.

"Well, he's dead, ain't he?"

"Yeah, dead." And Huddy'll miss chatting about the seasons. *How did the birds treat you, Mister Yewell? Gearing up for the deers now?*

"Well," Harlan says, puzzled for having to say what's obvious. "Tough selling a gun to a dead man." And he looks at the men and they grin.

And Huddy grins, too. "It sure is." Yewell coming in for years, *What you get this week, Mister Huddy?* A lifetime's worth of collecting and Huddy about to get his hands on them. This has never happened before. Not even in his dreams. "This is it, Harlan, this is my home run."

Five

THE DOORBELL IS REGULAR but the house isn't. A colonial with
columns rising higher than the roofline of Huddy's one-story
bungalow and the grounds unfurling to the street stretching as long
as Huddy's block. The ride over, Huddy was thinking about all the
Winchester rifles and shotguns Yewell had bought from him. He
was sure to see slide-actions and bolt-actions, along with handguns
and drillings, but Yewell's area of interest was lever-action
Winchesters—Huddy's mouth watering over the full scale of the
collection and the first look he'd be getting at all the different calibers and models, but staring at Yewell's estate now, Huddy can't
help but measure the enormous distance of their lives. He knew
Yewell was rich, and yet he still misjudged him. Yewell talked about
engineering, doing something mechanical, but you'd have to
succeed with more than new money to live out on Dogwood.

Quick steps from behind the door and Huddy wipes his feet,
tucks his tool bag and pad of paper to his stomach. He expects to
see a servant but instead a man beyond Huddy's age appears in an
oxford and khakis. And loafers. Huddy doesn't have to look down
to know they're there, the same way he doesn't need to lift the cuffs
to know the socks aren't. And Huddy knew he was right to change
out of his work clothes before driving out here, ditching the

pawnshop jeans and T-shirt for slacks and a button-up, plus a sport coat for extra impression, did everything but get a haircut to make himself shiny and closer to their kind. "You must be Huddy," the man says, and Huddy recognizes the resemblance to a Yewell younger than the one Huddy knew even before the two exchange hands, and the man smiles like he's just been promoted and adds, "I'm Kipp—Lee Junior." Junior. A similar face but softer, a trace of the daddy's drawl but flatter, more suburban and rootless, and Huddy can't imagine him holding a gun. Maybe a tennis racket or a golf club, which could be part of why the family's selling the collection, so it's good if the son's upbringing turned him into a yuppie prince.

Huddy steps inside the large entryway that feels like a lobby and stares at the formal dining room to his left and straight ahead the ornate staircase going up. "Sorry for your loss," he says, his voice bouncing off the marble floor and lifting up to the high ceiling.

"Thank you," Kipp says, nodding, "we're in the hunt room."

Sure, Huddy thinks, sounds sensible, picturing antlers and head mounts, wet noses and bright eyes gazing down from walls, and he follows the son through a living room as wide as the house, the wedge of a grand piano as big as a king-size bed Huddy doesn't own, the furnishings not brand-new this and brand-new that but better, original items you'd go to a deluxe designer store to get replicas of. Even the wallpaper looks antique, faded and peeling like paper money shedding off the walls, and the stains and age don't look like damage or neglect but a more authentic kind of elegance. Imperfections that keep the value of the room by not fixing it, like an old gun you know not to polish and destroy.

"Here we are," Kipp says, leading him through double doors into a pine-paneled back room in which are mounted not animals but black-and-white pictures that Huddy can't scan because across the room is the widow, who rises from a leather chair to receive him. Cotton money, Huddy thinks. Or railroad money. Either way, old, and Huddy realizes Yewell's job may have bought his guns, but his marriage done brought him here.

Her white hair as silken as the red sweater it spreads upon, like strands woven together and worn as a single uniform. "Can I offer you some ice water or tea?" she says, her voice warm and proper, her hands folded before her, and then she moves toward him— except it's only her voice moving as she remains there, so he advances midroom until she offers her hand, and he reaches out and takes it and almost bends in a curtsy. He could come into this home a thousand times and still feel it was a restricted area he needed a ticket to enter. He repeats his condolences, tentatively, his eyes dropping down to the rug—not bearskin but Oriental— scuffed and worn on the hardwood floor.

"I knew Lee ten years," Huddy says, nodding to connect what he knew to this. Curtains printed with horse scenes. First-place ribbons. Horse figurines and a carriage clock. "He once showed me a picture of you. Out at your cabin." And his eyes skim the photos to search for a cabin or the face of Yewell, but instead he's met with shots of horses and carriages, equestrian events that Huddy's seen in the *Appeal* but never on walls in a room he's been in. He stares at the marble fireplace. Carved above the mantel is a coonskin-capped hunter with a rifle aimed at the doors that moments before Huddy passed through.

"The hunting lodge," Kipp says. "Mama calls it the lake house, and daddy called it the hunting lodge."

"We were very close, Mister Marr. May I call you Huddy?"

"Of course."

"Lee had time to come home every day for lunch," she says. "And that's both a good and a bad thing, since lunch is every day."

Huddy smiles. But what he wants to know is, Close enough for him to tell you the values of his guns? He slips a hand inside his sport-coat pocket and finds a bottle cap hidden in the lint.

The widow laughs childlike and then a memory stiffens her face; she sits charm-school straight on the edge of her leather chair and directs Huddy to a matching one across the table from her. The son positions himself in the middle of the couch—a guard dog, between Huddy and the widow's money, dressed in Weejun loafers—then maneuvers sideways to cross his legs, showing the sole of one shoe. Across from him is an empty couch, like a missing fourth piece of the game about to be played, and Huddy pictures Yewell stationed there to complete the square, but if Yewell were here, Huddy wouldn't be.

On the table are printouts—the gun collection, Huddy knows. But he can't see the number of pages because they're stacked so exactly, the corners aligned in a perfect rectangle inside the rectangle of the table, like stationery set in a box. Huddy steals a glance at the widow's hands, her long fingers and manicured nails. Her gold necklace holds a diamond, U-shaped pendant that Huddy realizes is a horseshoe. He imagines her arranging the pages before his arrival, like a centerpiece, her neck tilted in contemplation as she surveyed its placement, her index fingers like rulers, her eyes scanning the compass points of the table. The pages are facedown, topped by a pen that cuts diagonally across, its tip pointing at one of the corners, which has enough separation for Huddy to now see at least three sheets, and he counts and figures seventy or eighty guns, easy. The direction of the pen makes Huddy feel as if it were spun and landed there, as if it were now his turn to act. He wants to jump from his chair and flip the pages, but he knows it's their move, so he looks elsewhere on the table, at a brass ornament saying TALLY-HO, at tiny jockeys on matchbook covers, and then around the room at a plaque saying SPIRIT OF THE SPORT, and a painting of a horse in close-up profile, the one big eye open and staring back at Huddy so he looks away, out the barless windows onto the backyard, but it's too wide and long and multiplied to call it that. A brick terrace and then gardens and ivy beds wreathing the thick trees, and Huddy's eyes keep filling, a pillared guest house that was probably the servants' quarters until they left and it was renovated, and then across the yard another house, this time a barn that you'd take for a house, and between these houses a riding ring that to Huddy looks like a winner's circle, and then pastureland and a vast expanse of acreage sweeping back and outward as infinite as the sky. He imagines flying out of the barn and riding out into that deep beyond—just amazing that you could vanish inside your own land, your vision of your property blotted out not just by trees or buildings but distance, a rolling territory that extended and probably came out east of Nashville—and then Huddy comes out of the reverie by realizing he doesn't smell manure. "You keep horses?" he asks. He looks back at her, her hands composed on her lap, as if she were part of the picture of what he'd been seeing outside.

"Not for a time," she says, her voice soft and small. "When I was a child, we had Morgans. Beautiful black Morgans. And I bought a little Welsh jumper for my daughter, named Royal." And Huddy doesn't ask if that's a horse or daughter. "My other son took two for his farm, and my daughter has the jumper in the country, and two other Morgans are retired over at Wildwood." She gazes outside as if hearing some faraway hoofbeat music. "I thoroughly enjoyed our horses," she says, her voice scraped with grief, and then her face flinches. She swallows, shakes her head, frightened but annoyed—for being unable to think of what to say next, for not containing her grief, much less to a stranger. She turns and blinks hard to switch off her memories, to not see a horse or a husband or anything else gone, and Huddy watches her hands wring, and then run along the sides of her legs, perching on her knees. A smile breaks across her face, as if she'd only been carried off by delightful dreams, and her shoulders spring up and her chin rises.

"Mama still has a clock that whinnies," Kipp says, his eyes holding on her, his voice amiable but uncertain. "You stay here long enough you'll hear it."

I'll stay forever, Huddy thinks. Hang around for months and months swapping stories: She'd tell him about her horses galloping over the ground, and he wouldn't tell her about his brothers shooting a turtle with a pellet gun—or maybe he'd say they'd kept it as a pet. He'll just listen to her stories about happy games she played with the servants' kids, like having them chase her or braid her hair. Swinging on swings and tree limbs, and dunking them in a washtub in a pretend baptism. Talk plenty and bond until Huddy isn't a stranger but someone familiar enough to become her little friend, and then the gun list upturning and offered like leftover wealth and his life rescued.

He can't imagine spending your entire life in this much ease, your days and years not divided between those and these times but one unbroken line of what you always had. What would his life have been if he'd been born into this instead of something low and puny? But then, look at Joe: grew up and shoved his way to the top. At least it seemed the top until Huddy got here and saw the tippytop. The inside of this house feels bigger than all of Huddy's pinched childhood, her outdoor world bigger than all the ground he ever covered.

"You would have seen more of the garden a week ago," she says. "You are late for the azaleas, but at least you're getting more than the garden's bones."

And Huddy suspects he's been staring long but then sees he needn't worry, because she's fogged up in her own words and losses, her memories growing on her face. Her hands knot. She searches the room, as if she were trying to find a vase or jar to deposit the memories. And then she bows her head at her son as if to apologize for her manners, and his eyes narrow, his face tenses. Huddy can't blame her—losing and dying seem unimaginable here. Or maybe this is the good place you go to after you die. When his mama got sick, six years ago, and talked her heavenly thoughts, was her vision of eternity as good as this? If he died here, Huddy wouldn't want to go anywhere *but* here, put him right out in that golden yard. He looks outside—doesn't see death but growth, life and afterlife— and then his mind conjures Yewell ripping out of the ground like some uprooting flower, dirt tumbling off him like a landslide, Yewell reborn and the torn-out flowers dead.

"My brother Joe," Huddy says, nodding to kill the vision. "He lives here. Germantown. Over on Wickersham. He just put in a water garden."

"Oh, that's very nice," the widow says, thankful to switch subjects. "I gave some thought to arranging a water feature. Wickersham— that's Kimbrough Woods." And Huddy watches opinions form between them, mother and son marking streets and incomes, Huddy for once not bitter but thankful that Joe lives here and is similar, their lives harmonizing with Joe's but maybe not joining his.

"That's right," Huddy says, staring outside.

"Kimbrough Woods has a garden club. I don't believe it's federated. I don't know if he's a member, or his wife is."

"I'd have to ask her."

"I've been a member of Suburban Garden Club for most of my adult life. My mother was one of the founders and I just followed her in. I do love the garden club."

"And the herb club," Kipp says, eyes rolling in fake exasperation. "And the charity horse show. And the neighborhood task force." His voice pokes at Huddy and Huddy laughs, nods knowingly as if they shared the same experiences, the same superior mothers, the same uncommon ground.

"I belong to too many things," she says, her voice a cheery protest, shaking her head as if she can't understand the busyness of her life, all the joyful ways of making the time pass. "When it comes to volunteering, I've always been a worker bee. Kipp here, he volunteers at church. And he belongs to Rotary. Mostly, he networks."

Kipp shrugs and folds his hands. And pauses. "I suppose you didn't come all the way out here to hear about our activities."

"Or floral arrangements," she says, leaning forward, the pages centered between them and all eyes finally pointed there, the room contracting as everyone quiets, and Huddy's heart quickens and he knows it's time to shop. Okay, Yewell, let's see what you put together. Let's see what your list says.

She grabs the pen and the pages fan out and Huddy sees it's much more than three, the figures climbing in his head just as she sets the pen aside, lifts the pages and taps them neatly back to one. "Huddy, Lee kept these records." Her hand quivers a little, but Huddy knows it's only age. The biggest deal of his life and he's never had a seller less desperate to make it, which means the desperation is his—or the son's, too, his eyes like edged weapons and his face bobbing attentively. "The list says one hundred and eighty guns," she says. "One eighty-one, to be exact." Huddy nods simply but the number screams in his head. "But Kipp has counted them and come out with less."

"*Two* less," Kipp says, to insist he doesn't share his mother's disinterest, but Huddy can't concentrate on his words and needs because the numbers still fill the room like a noise he can't yet talk around, a noise that would make him crazy if he weren't so stunned and happy. His head shakes at the son, then at her. I'm here, he says, but he isn't, his mind leaping out of the room and running through their house and opening doors, the next room and the next and the next, until he enters the gun room and finds racks and racks of long guns, racks on the floor and racks on the walls—the guns standing and horizontal and surrounding him in all directions.

"Maybe you will find the other two when you go through the collection," she says. "Lee had his gun buddies come over and he'd share his guns, and he might have traded a few or maybe Kipp has miscounted."

Two less, twenty less. It doesn't matter. One hundred and seventy, eighty, whatever guns—a fat number you could cut into but never thin.

"I have made a copy of Lee's list for you. And you may borrow this fountain pen if you'd like. Lee said a thousand times it's not called a fountain pen anymore, but I can't just call it a pen."

Huddy taps his shirt pocket. "Got one here," he hears himself say. And the tap is a sensation that brings him back, a pulse returning through him. He pushes his fingers into his flesh, like he'd found a seam to hide his nerves.

"As you will see, Lee wrote down what he paid for them. We know that what they're worth and what one can get for them are two separate things."

"That's right," Huddy says, feeling alert now, "what they're worth and what they bring," his voice measured and correct. He thinks about Yewell's gun buddies and what they'd seen and would want, and Huddy wishing Yewell had been some closet collector, the loneliest collector in town, everything put behind glass and in safes and in drawers and under beds, but Huddy knows Yewell wasn't that. Not in this house, where everything is like artwork, enjoyed every day. He reaches for the list, and she smiles as if she were greeting him again, the pages between their outstretched hands. He draws them toward him, the pages colder than her hand and heavier than his own, but in his mind he is not a dealer but an accountant, about to peruse a balance sheet that doesn't contain money in its numbers. A counting game in which the zeroes don't count or *only* count. Huddy blinks to decide which. He switches to the guns, telling himself they *aren't*, just bits of old gray metal.

He stares at the page and what he notices first is not the guns but the system that organizes them. Yewell the mechanical engineer, always a bit of a mechanism himself, coming in quick during the slow hours, and Huddy figured he kept his list precise, too. Along the top are the categories: the make and the model and the serial number and the type and the condition and then the price, but Huddy's not ready to read for dollar signs. "He sure was organized," he says, and she smiles and the son just nods, unsure if money got made. Huddy looks at the photocopied black circles on the left-hand side, like three bull's-eyes.

R1, R2, R3—the rifle numbers running fast down the page but the sequence of model '73s staying still while Huddy's mind jumps by the thousands. He scans the column of serial numbers, sees one of the serializations is only four digits, and he feels his shoulders pump. The '73s stop and then it's a handful of '76s and even more

'86s, Huddy catching all the odd calibers, and then the collection goes on repeat again with '94s, carrying over onto the next page, Huddy reading every configuration—Timber Carbine, Timber Carbine Scout, Timber Carbine Scout Takedown—like he's reading straight out of the blue book. On page three, the guns become bolt-actions, the Model 70s spreading through all production periods and capacities and chamberings, like Yewell couldn't die until he bought up the entire history.

"He sure liked his Winchesters," Huddy says, almost blurting it, like some pressure pushing out of his mouth. "Some people, see," more words surging, "they're gun accumulators, but Lee was a gun *collector.*" Which is what Huddy suspected and hoped for, Yewell trading up his whole life. Huddy scans the conditions, sees nothing less than good, and he knew Yewell wouldn't fool with fair or poor, but he's still surprised to see how many are graded as very good and excellent and NIB, Huddy picturing all those pristine guns in boxes. He'll need to check the conditions, but Yewell's eyes were as sharp as the pocket magnifying glass he always carried.

The widow smiles, appreciating Huddy's opinion and expertise, as if he'd said her husband was a rarer specimen than one of his prized Winchesters, but Huddy knows the son is here to make sure Huddy adds more. He'd tell them this list is a wish list—if only the prices weren't here. But they aren't. Next to the prices are dates, and Huddy sucks the inside of his mouth when he sees that the prices aren't current values but purchase prices, the dates Yewell took them in, some as old as fifty years. Huddy always looking for an opening in the deal—staring at one as wide as a howitzer. And sure, they would see these dates, too, but they wouldn't know what an old Winchester price meant. Unless they brought in an appraiser, and Huddy's not that.

Fifty-year-old prices. Before the Civil War centennial, before the antique-gun craze got cracking, back when you could get a musket for forty dollars. Huddy nods to himself. I can tell you something educational, give you the whole history of the Yellow Boy, and we can talk about the pioneer days, but today I will not tell you how Winchesters have appreciated. I don't understand your life; why should I tell you what is mine? I am not my brother's keeper, Huddy thinks, especially here in Germantown.

Even on the recent purchases, the prices look good. Yewell paid smart money for good guns, and Huddy liked to joke about Yewell's bargaining, how he had to insult the piece before he bought it. "The bore is terrible, Huddy, you're gonna have to cut me another ten percent." Yewell telling how somebody refinished the wood, how the model was common, how the bluing wasn't what Huddy graded it. But Huddy knew Yewell bought not just for condition but for romance, too, so he could push right back. "That ain't rust, Yewell, that's blood-rust. Sure it's broken, but things break when they fall off horses on the frontier." A deal they both enjoyed playing, as if they each rode a trail a thousand miles out west to win. And now Yewell's bargaining is part of how Huddy can win again.

He turns the next page, sees an 1860 Henry .44 rimfire and his heart just about bursts. Stops his hand from coming to his mouth. His fingers pinch pages. And then below the Henry is a Yellow Boy, as if Huddy weren't just reading the list but Yewell were reading *him*, taking his thoughts and arranging them on the page, a staring contest in which Yewell could X-ray through him to make Huddy blink. And he does. Then he reads the two rifles again—to make sure they don't disappear. And they don't. They're here, and Huddy can't believe it. His tongue pushes against his teeth. His head's down but he's aware of other eyes in the room studying him now, seeing that he's hooked into something first-rate but not knowing what. The holy grail of rifles, is what Huddy would say, if he were talking. It makes perfect sense that if you had a Henry, you'd have a Yellow Boy, too—a pair going together just like this mansion and this guest house. The purchase date on the Henry is forty years old, the price two thousand, and Huddy could sell it for forty, easy, the rate of return so large he can't do the math. The Yellow Boy is even older, bought in '56 for a thousand, the profit margin higher.

Yewell, you should've put an asterisk next to these. Huddy almost shaking his head, fighting his face, at what Yewell didn't do. Sure he put a space between the Henry and the Yellow Boy, between the Yellow Boy and the rest of the cowboy guns, but the spaces almost look like typos when they should look like neon lights. Yewell, how the hell'd you get these two? Thought they only went to presidents and kings. *Aw, Huddy, I just picked them up from some collector calling it quits. Some collector older than me, back when I was younger than you.* Huddy'd like to keep talking to unburied Yewell, but now he needs to know if these are the two missing guns, and he feels himself rising from the seat as if his body were helium-filled and he pushes himself down. He turns the page to slip away from his ballooning thoughts, because the deal is oversize—even without them knowing about the Henry and the Yellow Boy they'll still expect a too-big number, still want a number from their world—and he skims shotguns now, the long row of Model 42s and 12s and 97s, the fine guns popping out and Huddy almost looking for hundred-dollar guns instead of thousands, and then the list switches to pistols, ten then fifteen single-action Colts tumbling down the page.

"Huddy," he hears her say, "Lee said that you would know what they are worth and you would be able to propose a correct figure."

Huddy nods at this estimation. "I'll need to check the conditions," he says, as if what he'd been looking at were only dull utility guns, worn and bumped around. "Can't offer a price off of a list. These are fine guns. But I'll have to see how fine they really are. Condition of a Winchester is extremely important."

"I went on the Internet and checked some prices," Kipp says, as if Huddy had just tried undercutting, and Huddy'd like to ask him if he even knew where or how to look, but the Internet sounds good; with Huddy holding the pages, the son needs to show he's holding information, too. Huddy nods as the son cups his hands. "He also instructed if you couldn't give a right price, we should auction them off."

"I don't want auction," she announces, her hand waving dismissively. "I don't want people knowing they all came from this house." And Huddy's pleased to hear the irritation in her voice. She looks toward the double doors as if she hears a crowd banging and demanding she open up. "People'll think we had some arsenal here."

"It's not an arsenal, mama. It's daddy's guns." The son shakes his head and frowns at her for showing how much she enjoys having the guns in her home, for signaling what she expects for their removal. He turns to Huddy and Huddy can feel his annoyance transferring over. "You're prepared to buy them all?" he asks.

"Yes . . ." Huddy says, but his voice trails off. "We can do it as a bulk purchase. Or we can . . ." his voice tiptoeing, "piece it out, in stages, which'll make you more money in the long run. There's different ways." Because Huddy's plan going in was to take twenty of the best pieces, sell 'em and come back for more. But now the plan is wrong. Even if he'd wanted to cherry-pick the Henry and the Yellow Boy and . . . there's too many other special guns to pick out a best twenty—he can see they won't let him, the transaction is too long and messy. And not just *their* mess, either. Huddy knows if he stretches things the collection will scatter to other dealers and relatives and a dozen other ways of moving or going over him. So he'll buy them all at once. Now. The son is demanding Huddy be big and Huddy wants to be big, too. Why would he tell them that it's impossible to do what they want to do? Why would he talk about only what his finances make possible? Why lose a chance to see the guns?

"Are you talking consignment?" the son asks, confused, even accusing. Maybe they are both wary of him now, the widow not from what Huddy said but because he's a pawnbroker, a man who deals with the sad part of life and only makes it sadder. A place where needed belongings must be sold away.

"No, not consignment," Huddy says firmly. "Consignment is a pain. I don't wanna keep track of someone else's guns. Got enough trouble keeping track of my own. Sounds like you wanna do one-money," and Huddy nods at the son, "and that's fine. We can do it bulk purchase." His voice sounds final. He isn't here to talk about his problems, to tell them he can't get close to what they expect to hear.

"Huddy, where in the city are you located?" she asks, and Huddy says near Memphis State, which is false but being out here makes it true. "Lamar," he adds, regretting it, because it sounds like murder. He should've said Chickasaw Gardens. Or the Pink Palace.

She nods, as if to forgive him. "When I was a girl, that's all we wanted to do. To go to the city. Downtown, all by ourselves on the bus. We'd shop in the morning at Goldsmith's. See a fashion show. Have lunch there. And then we'd go to the Fun Shop. They had those glasses that spilled when you drank from them. And the . . .

gum that snaps on your fingers." She laughs, all the old gags returning. And maybe, Huddy thinks, the fond memories of old prices.
Get a Popsicle for a nickel and look how happy you were. "You
don't have to go there anymore," she says. "Everything is out here."

All inside this house, Huddy thinks.

"Would you be selling any of Lee's guns to the coloreds?" she
asks, and Huddy looks at her, and the son looks away. "I'm not
prejudiced," she says before Huddy can answer. "It's just that with
the crime and all, I'd hate for one of Lee's guns to wind up
connected to trouble. You read in the paper, there's already so many
guns on the street."

"These are collector guns, Missus Yewell. They'd be priced above
all that."

"I care about the city," she says, shaking her head. "It is hard to
watch the disintegration of something you cherish. There's just no
respect for life. And that mayor has set us back twenty years. He's
far too confrontational. He has fostered bad relations."

"He's crazy," Huddy says, "that's for sure."

"He's a drug addict," Kipp says, "is what he is." And Huddy
watches his face turn hard and contemptuous and certain. "We know
that for a fact. This city will eat shit as long as he's running it."

A hand twitches up to stop her son's anger, pushes forward
against his words. She is uneasy, not by what he has said, but by why
he would need to express it here.

Huddy nods—Herenton is an enemy, a poison the city drinks
every day—and he watches her straighten in her chair as high as
she can go, and the son keeps going, too. He sniffs loud, revulsed, as
if inhaling the rank and steaming air. But Huddy can assure him
the rankness and excrement are far away, unless they brought back
horses. "The city is out of control," Kipp says, throwing up his

hands. "There's no common sense coming out of it. The blacks here in Germantown, they're well-educated and you talk to them and they're devastated to see how their people live. Different fathers and the mother is on and off crack."

Huddy returns to the list. At the end is miscellaneous, which Yewell has listed as "junk," a couple dozen guns with missing or broken parts lumped together, although even the junk is pretty good. If the city burnt to the ground, the flames wouldn't make more than a vague haze in the Germantown sky, a far-off sunset flare. But it would show clear and close on your television—maybe you'd see the fire trucks arriving too late to save Huddy's house— the sirens and cries like news from another nation. Black-gray smoke and houses shriveling and unroofing, and your frantic hand reaching for the remote.

And suddenly she is gone from him, climbed a tower or maybe just a horse, so that Huddy feels like she's moving over him with her next address: "You and Lee Junior can arrange a proper transaction. I will trust you both to do what is fair and right."

And Huddy's gone, too, ready to find the damn guns.

"You can access the room through the garage," she says, and then a bright smile spreads across her face. "It's been such a pleasure meeting you." The smile stretches and clenches, like she's just come from a horse show and a wedding and a christening—three gifts all on the same blessed day.

Six

THE GUN ROOM IS a lost space in the house unfound until you enter the garage and come around the truck and enough into the lane between the truck and a Lexus to see a wooden door centered in the back wall, a door mostly hidden behind wooden ammunition crates glued against it. Kipp swings the door open to reveal a second door—not just a door but an old safe door—and Huddy reads the logo, Second National Bank, and halts while Kipp turns the combination and spins the wheel, and then he follows Kipp again inside the inner room, a windowless slab all wired up, the air smelling of oil and wax and steel, zebra skin over concrete instead of Oriental rugs over hardwood. In his sightlines—guns. Hundreds of guns you'd be tripping over if they weren't racked up neatly. Standing racks extending the entire left wall, two layers of racks like Huddy's seeing double, never seen a private collection so big, not even through bad vision or if the guns got cloned, and Huddy so eager to walk down that line. It's as if walking through that safe door vaulted him ninety miles to Dixie Gun Works—been awhile since Huddy's driven the road to Union City, so maybe he's now in Dixie. What he knows is that the countryside he saw beyond the hunt room can't match what's walled up here, not the buildings or the open land, not rainbow flower patches or deep woods or stands of centuries-old trees rising hundreds of feet and spreading thick canopies into the air. All of that together could never be as pretty as what's standing bare along this white wall. Huddy smells the pipe smoke but feels it wasn't smoking or age that caused a heart attack but the size of this lineup. If I'da had all this, I would've died, too. Maybe them black-powder granules got into your lungs. He'd like to go over and inhale the charcoal odor, but he'll wait for the son's clearance. Kipp observes the military scenes behind glassed cabinets, so Huddy does, too. He searches the combat photos just like he searched for Yewell atop horses. He sees a battalion at an air base, soldiers loading up trucks and engaged in a firefight, the faces too battle-blurred and distant, but then there he is in another shot at the far left with three other uniformed soldiers to his right, arms draped, the words FOUR BUDDIES written at the bottom, signatures and nicknames scrawled across their bodies. Found you, Huddy thinks, and it figures he'd be in this war room and not the horse world Huddy sat in to get to here. And there Yewell is again, smiling, shirtless in a tin bathtub. And then leaning against the big tire of a howitzer, until Huddy realizes it isn't, just like the grinning helmeted head popping out of a tank isn't him either. Crouched soldiers with hands plugging their ears as a howitzer booms; soldiers under an archway in an unknown city until he sees the handwriting on the white border that says SEOUL. "Your daddy bring that back from Korea?" Huddy nods at the flag in the next case and the remembered conversation.

"Yes," Kipp says proudly and admires the veterans display, an Ike jacket and fatigues with Yewell's name stenciled over the pocket. "I miss him every day of the week," Kipp says and Huddy nods at the uniform and looks down. On the base shelf of the cabinet, there's a helmet liner, an ammo case and gear pouch, manuals and maps and an officer's handbook, a booklet entitled "Characteristics and Effects of Atomic Explosion." Huddy returns to the fatigues and pays tribute to Yewell's military service while also knowing the value of militaria, just like there's money in the sharpshooter photos he observes in the next display case, trick-shot artists like Annie Oakley in hipshot pose, Lucky McDaniel in quick-draw, Adolf Topperwein pointing a six-shooter at one of his bullet drawings. Huddy leans in to check for autographs, but he won't ask about memorabilia.

"You shoot much?" Huddy says, keeping Yewell, father-and-son stories, out.

"Couple a times. Spent more time shooting at cans, with friends. I went in a different direction sportswise. But we worked on cars together. You see that GT in the garage?" Huddy did, the classic car on the other side of the brand-new Lexus. "Well, not that one, but the one before it. And before that. An MG. We had us some fun with cars." The son wearing a far-off smile, some enjoyed yesterday, that unnerves Huddy. He watches the son study the room and the guns, leaning forward, and Huddy senses a dangerous thinking. Talking about *we* and *us*, and Huddy knows he's gotta be careful with sentiment and nostalgia and dreams—long-ago days of being fifteen with his daddy beside him and wanting the guns now because he isn't a son anymore, can't feel twelve or ten or younger, little about being a Yewell to want to get away from, nothing hard or hateful back in the memories, nothing to snub or let go of but only what to hold, the guns never touching Huddy's hands but passing down to the son.

Huddy needs to calmly disconnect the past, drive the son out of his childhood and into this room which is still theirs but at least Huddy's here, too, and then he can give them a payday that won't mend hearts but is useful elsewhere. Their memories will have to return from other rooms. Huddy turns from the displays and sees an L-shaped couch, a desk with a bookcase of specialty books. A floor lamp made from an old rifle; shell casings making an American eagle. "This looks like his inner sanctum." On the wall, a bullet board. Model cannons and submarine deck guns on the desk.

"He built this room himself," Kipp says, which is better for Huddy, hearing admiration in what got assembled, but not shared experience. A place where Yewell went solo and separate. "He says he wished he could've put saloon doors in the wall, but he knew he was stocking more than bourbon."

"Yeah," Huddy says. "He sure went stronger than swinging doors."

Huddy seeing all the good-looking wood and the bluing and the beautiful scopes. You got your guns out, just like I thought. *I always liked to see what I'm collecting.* Who needs a safe when the room's a safe?

"Guess I'll migrate over," Huddy says as he moves toward the racks, having to control his skips or else he'll start hopping like some rabbit going over a fence. Kipp walks to the desk and sets up in the chair—to track me, Huddy thinks, until he hears the computer switch on, so maybe it's just bargain-hunting. Or last-minute price checks. Or just planning the next trip of a lifetime. Whatever, Huddy thinks, putting his eyes and mind forward, drawing tight on the guns. He unzips his pouch and slips on cotton gloves. Time to test. Lever-actions grouped together just like the list. Huddy starts picking, lifts a '73 off the rack, holds it by the wood. Checks the chamber, eyes the finish. See what's operating, but he ain't going in the field with these, ain't even gonna dry-fire. Only break the bank, and not the guns, to get 'em. Pulls the lever down. Removes a bore light from his pouch and shines it down the receiver—no pits or dirt. Closes it up. Holds the hammer, lets it down gently, works the action the same gentle way. Clean and tight. He inspects every rifle on the first rack, studying the outside and going inside the barrel and finding no residue—going from the list back to the rack, checking models and calibers and serial numbers, making his own column of prices, one for cost and one for retail—and it doesn't take long to see the list making sense with the guns; made sense as soon as he checked the first handful and verified the correct grading. So Huddy switches to ballpark, not opening every rifle but scanning surfaces, just a cattleman looking at fence posts, eyeing gaps and fits and edges and lettering and admiring case colors without expressing it outside. Doesn't want to bring attention. Wants the numbers to slide in, have nothing seen except what he's adjusting in his mind: these aren't blue Winchesters but browned-out guns, and guns are tools, so Huddy's just walking down the aisle of a hardware store looking at hammers and screws and pins. There they are, the Henry and the Yellow Boy—the Yellow Boy with its brass receiver, the Henry without the wood on the fore end and with the loading mechanism on the front—in the middle of a rack in the middle of the row, like all the surrounding rifles are a guarding posse. He doesn't even lift them. Never put his hands on these two except in a catalogue, but he'll work the smooth actions later, and he can see enough of the condition and care without touching. Already thinking about a few phone calls that'll make half the money he hasn't raised yet back.

"Nice, huh?" the son says, and Huddy steps away and says, "Sure are. Your daddy sure cleaned his guns."

He'd rather talk about gun care, rust prevention instead of prices, put the son to sleep talking about bore brushes and brass cleaning rods, and then wake him up after the deal's been made. Or talk about what's not here, cracks and scratches and all other downgrades.

"You don't need to check them all?"

"Well, these old utility guns got used real hard, so I don't wanna tear 'em up." Huddy looks back at the Henry and Yellow Boy without meaning to, so he adds a shrug, like they're two relics from some period of American history nobody much thinks of anymore, except for a few families feuding across the battle line.

On the rack, Huddy sees a tag hanging off the trigger guard of an '86 saying FAKE. Must've left your glasses at home, Yewell. Huddy studies to see what got doctored. Reblued it and then took part of the finish off, making it newer then older again. The fake could be a warning except that Yewell's the one that caught it, too late for him but early enough for Huddy. All in all, he's never seen so many original parts on so many old guns. "Sold this to your daddy," Huddy says, and he turns to show the son a '94 he's been reunited with.

"My uncle Pete wants the double that dad went hunting with."

Huddy sees a piece of paper unfolded in the son's hand.

"Model 21," Kipp says, and Huddy's happy that the gun language didn't come from the son's mouth, but he wonders what other notes are hiding.

"Twenty-one in twenty-gauge," Huddy says. "Side-by-side." Already passed it two racks back, but now it's gone farther. The seated son, but he just walked across and around and seized a ten-thousand-dollar Super Grade and walked it out the room. What other relations and favors and voices are hidden inside those pockets? "I'll be sure to set it aside for you," Huddy says, and he's done chatting. The son probably thinking about hand-me-downs— about next saying, "I might want to pick out a few for myself," so

Huddy moves away, hard not to feel hurried, but it doesn't matter, he's already seen his pot of gold in the first rack, and the rest might be maybe-gold, but he's long past making a mistake. Does quick work with the shotguns, which are superclean; he checks the martial marks on the militaries. He wishes he could tell a joke that would make the son laugh for the entire inspection. Or just lock him away in the pistols cabinet.

Huddy changes position, moves to the handguns hanging on L-hooks inside cases. All the good names, Colt and Remington and Smith & Wesson; S&W break-top, Colt SAA .45 with 95-percent case colors. Huddy pulls the latch, swings the cylinder out, pops it back. Checks the timing. The revolvers labeled proof he's gonna keep that way, leave the cylinder unturned. Won't talk to the son, only to the dead man, tell him about his select wood, his extra finishes. Yewell, this is one beautiful single-action. Too bad about the broken grip. You had it almost right. *That's why I had to get this one, too.* Huddy finding the next one more perfect. He sees ivory grips on handguns worth as much as the guns. This pearl grip with a chip out the side, but who cares? Little nick in the front sight but only a bit of holster wear. Dings on the grips of the next couple, but the fittings are tight. Checks the clips on the pistols and they all make sense.

"Myself, I haven't decided yet," the son says, his words again in the way. He gazes into a bottled boat and Huddy can't tell if it's a gun or the whole deal he's unsure about. "My mother wouldn't say this, but we've had other collectors call. Our attorney has recommended we go with a national concern."

"Well, thing is," Huddy says, his face and voice neutralized but his blood pressure climbing higher than the number of guns in the room. "With these big gun brokers, here's what'll happen. They charge twenty percent, and by the time they get through taxes and fees and all the other Mickey Mouse . . . you'll get your *check*. What you get from me is gonna be *money*. And I pay on the spot. You sell 'em to me and you're done. End of sale."

The son returns to the boat and Huddy to the revolvers, but what else is there to see? What's inside and outside these pistols is clearer than the smoke signals coming from the chair. Time to pull the trigger. Buy them at his price, but make it sound like theirs. If he offers silly money, they'll go elsewhere, so the figure must be big. Six figures. Just the bottom of it. "Alright," Huddy says, and he steps into the middle of the room and waits to be joined, but the son stays seated. "I'm not even gonna ask about the memorabilia. That's precious stuff. Can't put a price on that. The racks, you can probably find another use for. For the guns, I can offer you a hundred thousand. And I can have it in two days." Huddy hoping the speed counts as money, too. What he can get quick is what he can get forever, when there are only a few places it can come from. His voice sounded right, like the tool pouch he's wearing doubles as a money belt, and the rest is near, too, just needs to go home and collect what's dropped behind couch cushions and stashed in cigar boxes or wadded up in dirty jeans.

"A hundred thousand," Kipp repeats in a voice so concealed and equal to Huddy's price it's as if he's said it first.

Huddy waits for him to nod, but he doesn't. And Huddy doesn't know what's been accepted or passed. He's stuck—only a single shot at the offer—and how can a payment so large and unspoken in all the years he's been a pawnbroker still be low? And how can the number ever be high enough when he's saying it to someone born into the millionaires' club?

Huddy's thinking about step two. He'll go back to the widow

and tell her the whole world will know about these guns. Not just dealers but every scumbag and gunrunner calling nonstop, every Bubba and Bubbette that ever wanted a gun. Disconnect the phone but you're still a widow at night hearing gun taps on your night-stand, these guns locked away but loaded like an armory clogged up with ammo and about to explode, as unavoidable as the exhale of your held breath.

A palm uncups from the son's chin. "Hundred thousand," he says again, but the voice isn't matched—the pitch lifting to mean an answer, and he nods to tell him which one.

And Huddy's just won the lottery. His life has never felt luckier. He only needs to start buying the ticket.

"Just me," Huddy says to Joe, who looks around for a second face, then squints to the street like Harlan's split into the night. "I know, getting to be a regular thing," Huddy adds and waits to be let inside. "Thought you might be out back again, talking to your plants?"

"Was," Joe says. He eyes the dress-up clothes. "You must be find-ing a church."

"Something like that. Just down the road: Our Lady of Perpetual Help."

He gives Huddy a tired, beaten face, but Huddy won't take it. "I'm having a long day."

"Yeah, good thing about being a pawnbroker is each day you getting paid."

Joe gestures him in and turns and leads and Huddy pursues close behind, passing the living room, where the TV is on, and Lorie stands there but Joe veers directions and Huddy shrugs a greeting, which she answers with a friendly smile that still finds fault with his visit and needs. He follows Joe and because of seeing Lorie feels not just uninvited but a little like a beggar straggling in as they enter the stainless kitchen, the smell of made food, but mostly what scrubbed and cleaned it after, filling Huddy's nostrils. His stomach grumbles from the snack in his truck. Tiered against the center island is a table and Joe sits with his back to the window, and Huddy sits at the other end to envy again the grand landscapes people build for themselves or get handed down, but it's too dark with only bug lights to see; there's enough shining inside, the silver appliances and polished hardwood, the glassware in the glassed cabinets arranged in clinking rows. "You still liking grilled cheese and potato chips?" Huddy eyes the stove, the massive range hood motorized and gleaming with enough power to suck the air out of the whole house, like if you walked by it and bumped a button it would suck you up dead. "When you was a kid, I remember how much you liked eating that."

"You come out here to talk about how I ate?"

"Just seeing how tastes change. Anyway, I was just over on Dogwood."

Joe rolls his eyes. "Where's Harlan?"

"He's hanging with KayKay." And Huddy watches Joe shake his head as if Huddy's responsible for not sheltering Harlan from nonsense and trouble.

"The greatest clown on earth."

"Now now. Not all of us do our lives just perfect. He worked good for me today."

"Day One ain't never been his problem. It's the next when he starts acting like a mullet. He's gonna be chained up one day, you know that?" He makes a face and looks away, over at a corner of the room like Harlan's collapsed there, looking pitiful, kicked against the wall.

But Huddy doesn't want to account for Harlan's lowly story, to feel sorry for it, much less have it be his.

"What you got there?" Joe says, nodding at the papers rolled up in Huddy's hand.

"Bringing you a four-leaf clover." He shows them like a bouquet. "You know the Yewells, live over on Dogwood?" And Huddy knows he's repeating the street name, but it feels good to tell a suburban story containing not just a happy ending but happy all the way through. Joe's used to Huddy telling some ragtag bit about the city's sinkhole and instead Huddy's got a Germantown story even better than this sunny spot on Wickersham, as if Wickersham were knocked back across the city line.

"You think I know everyone in Germantown?"

"I'm sure you know how they *live*. Fancy-fancy. Man, I thought I was seeing the topside of things here," and Huddy taps the table, "and then you realize there's a whole nother world you ain't been invited to. Anyway, this widow, I knew her husband, Lee, and she's a lady extraordinaire. I mean, a prima suprema lady lady. We talked about her garden club, and I told her about your water garden, and she's real impressed. Thought it was very tasteful. I wouldn't be surprised if the ladies from her club visited one day with a welcome basket. Or decorated your mailbox. Whatever it is they do that's classy and society-like. Anyway, me and her, we had a long conversation. I think she would've liked me better if I was a plant, but like I said—Hey Joe, you listening? Your neck get snapped?"

"Huh?"

"Maybe you can look at me when I'm telling you this. Unless you're needing neck support."

"I'll look at you when you tell me something needs looking."

"Fine, I'll bring it down to your level." And Huddy presents the pages, spreads them out on the table like blueprints to the biggest project Joe never built. "See, we didn't just talk about flowers. We had ourselves a nice little tea table, and then we talked about the hundreds of guns she was wanting to sell." He releases his hands and the edges of the pages curl up.

Joe grunts, his shoulders slumping. "This all about moving off Lamar so you can stiff me with rent? Thought we already had a talk on that." His eyes close.

"You could make more on this deal in a month than ten years of rent money."

"Why . . ." And his head shakes all about and his mouth puffs in anger. "Why you keep coming here asking for stuff? What you bringing tomorrow?" He looks down, still shaking in a fit, like the pages have been torn apart from a single sheet and made meaningless, and could never be patched together to make sense again. "Guns? You come here to show me guns?" He starts to say more but gives up, tilts back in his chair and stares overhead at the ceiling. His hand rubs at his neck.

"Not just guns. The prettiest, best, rarest collection I ever seen."

"Oh, yeah?" says Joe, the chair returning with a thud. "Which one of these is the gun that killed Jesse James?" He hunches over the list, his face fake and bright. "Which one of these guns is famous? I've always liked a good Western." Huddy glares but Joe won't stop talking. "Gimme something personal. How about Buffalo Bill Cody? You got something about him?"

"They *all* famous. Don't need no sheriff or outlaw to make it so. You looking at Winchesters. The gun that *won* the West. If you knew guns, you'd know that. You looking at history right there. You just need to use your mind to see. Surprised you can't see a fur trader with his mountain rifle pointed right between your eyes.

Cutting you down like he's cutting buffalo." His eyes meet Joe's and keep there until Joe breaks away.

"Okay, so this society lady wants to sell her husband's guns."

"She weren't just that. You should have seen this house. Old-time mansion. Columns. Guest house. And the land . . ."

"Yeah?"

"Miles of it. Can barely see the house from the street—and you *can't* see all the backyard from the house. They used to have horses. She grew up there, on this estate, and she had horses all her life. Man, I wish I was raised in that barn. I'd be so comfy and secure, I'd just lay down in my stall and sleep. Probably get a nameplate on the door. A fan over my head to keep me cool."

Joe leans into the list or maybe it's just the table, and Huddy watches him freeze and think. "How much?" Joe says, a hand hooding his eyes.

"How much I offer?" Huddy says, but the question feels wrong and he's already catching the deal changing. He looks at Joe, waits for the hand to come off his rising face and see what's been formed.

"How much *land*?"

Huddy keeps still but his mind shakes no. "Why you wanna know that?"

"What'd you say the name was, Eubell? Husband—husband was Lee? You say widow—she talking about selling it?"

"We didn't talk about the land," Huddy says, slow against Joe's stirred-up voice. "We were talking about guns. Joe, this is *my* deal. And the deal is *guns*."

"If it was just your deal you wouldn't need me to make it." And he pushes the pages back.

And Huddy knows he should take off, gather the pages and go away, but there's nowhere else. Not until he collects this money first. "This help us both. I need it more, but it's win-win. Damn, you think I like crawling over to ask your help. Last place. If I could pay this myself I would. I'm asking you, brother to brother—"And he watches Joe's lips clamp shut. "I know, you think I'm always pulling the brother bit when I want money." And when he hears himself say it, it's true—it's like losing the argument to both sides of the table, Joe and himself both calling him out—and he shakes his head bitterly at what he's lost to two people. He pulls at the pages, slips his fingers between them, watches them slide and come apart. Flips them down so he can stare at nothing instead of the numbers taunting him on the other side.

"We sharing blood, Huddy," Joe says, his voice soft but set. "It'll always be that." And Huddy watches a finger smooth across his lips, then his hands link together. He rests his chin on top. His face turns blank. "How about this?" Joe says, and his neck tilts left to right as if to weigh his claim and compensation. "You tell me about the guns. And then you tell me about the land."

"Why?"

"The land—it's how Germantown grows. It can't grow any other way. 'Cause Germantown's surrounded. You got these old-time horsey people, and when they die or sell off their ranchland, somebody like me develops it. Call it infill. Only way to develop is to parse out these estates. That retirement home I built. The husband died and the wife moved out. Gave the big house to the kids and sold the acreage. And the way I got that bid was knowing the son. That's the only way. Knowing the family. Just like you got with your gun collector here. Inside dibs. And there's never a For Sale sign with places like these. That kind of property is never on the market. Maybe your widow ain't selling today . . ." Huddy watching Joe's eyes shine, feeling his own excitement rise because of it. "But it'd be a good thing to know her before tomorrow come. 'Cause when it does, it'll pay for years of tomorrows. Now: tell me about the guns."

And Huddy's head bobs with the rush and wonder, the guns and the deal kick-starting, Joe walking away but then walking a bloodline back.

"Going up now, Joe," Lorie calls out from the other room and Joe answers he'll be up soon, and Huddy'd like to ask about her overhearing or tell him that of all his wives, she's his favorite, but he'll save those jokes for another day. He doesn't want to look at Joe's marriage or disturb what's in place before them on the table.

"I knew the guns would be good," he says. "But there ain't a single wall-hanger in the bunch. A couple you'd even donate to the Smithsonian—except they don't know they could go there. These two guns," Huddy rifling through the pages, "he didn't even mark these! But I can't get to them without getting the thing whole. Which is fine, 'cause we'll make money on everything. He's got lever-actions with no levers broken. He's got every modification, primo condition. I mean, there ain't more than a dozen guns used up. The rest are just beautiful. Some generic stuff, but not much and even the generics is solid. I mean, it'll all sell."

"How much you gonna offer?"

"Like I said, it's all desirable. This is an advanced Winchester collection," Huddy says, wishing he could talk profit and not the money to get it. "Some junk, but no doggy stuff."

"Huddy, what's the outlay?"

"One hundred thousand. Hundred thousand to make three-fifty. That's a quarter—"

"You're not asking me for that?!" Joe says, eyes wide. But it's a false outrage, Joe objecting to the number but also not refusing the smaller numbers beneath it. Huddy can feel Joe's pride in his being needed, his understanding that the deal is solid 'cause the purchase is nearby.

"I'm seeing what you're willing to give. And I've got my own guns to sell. And then I'm gonna go to my gold buyer, my diamond buyer to raise the rest. I'm emptying out my cases." He looks at Joe, watches him concentrate and listen, his interest drawn in. "Sell my diamonds to the diamond buyer. The gold buyer, I'm dumping all my gold. People can't pay the price of a necklace. With the market as high as it is, I'll make the money as scrap. Scrap everything."

Joe's silent, and then he says, "Going for broke."

"I *am* broke. Or almost. This is so I won't be."

"Still. It's a gamble."

"Damn straight. It took years to build up those cases." But then Huddy shrugs. "The jewelry's just filler, sitting there."

"You really can't get any help from the banks? A little?"

"Sure. I'll just tell them I got five nice guitars. But I don't want them to laugh at me. I ain't in stocks and bonds and real estate. And banks have a thing about collateral."

"What's *my* collateral? On this deal."

"Your collateral is me. I'd offer you the building, but it's already yours."

Joe runs his finger along and off the table edge. "What happens if I say no to all this?"

"Well, then it goes to bye-bye land. Unless I can phone all the doctors and lawyers I grew up with." And Huddy's about to keep talking, but he can feel Joe moving to a decision, getting close, almost, and he figures he'll just pause and push with silence.

"What if I gave you fifty?"

This small-big number a stun gun out of his brother's mouth, but Huddy shrugs for more. "Sixty'd make it easier." Huddy trying to weigh what he needs from Joe with the profit he needs to start his new life on Summer. "Hey, it's your fault for being rich."

Joe laughs. "Sure, I'm rich. But it would help if someone paid me to do something more than fix a door or window. That's all *anyone's* doing. Everybody else in a bind puts *me* in a bind."

"But you got your money diversified. Nobody wants a door or window, you just get it somewhere else, right?"

"Multiple streams of income," Joe says, as if he were confiding life's secret. "'Cept they're all drying up. Six months ago, people were calling for everything. This one fella, lives on a dead-end street with the street named after him. He pays me to turn his garage into a bar, and then pays me again to build him a garage next to the bar. People were spending like they could never spend all they had ... What I'm saying, Huddy, is right now I don't have room for bad ideas."

"Only bad idea is not making this deal. It's the one foolish thing. You saying your business is coming to a roaring, screeching halt— this the perfect time. The surest thing. The only guarantee I can't give is timeline. It'll take six months to disperse a collection like this—I'm estimating—but most of them gonna move real fast. Heck, I could sell the whole collection online to Cherry's, get you your money back in thirty days. But if we do it right, piece it out, wait awhile longer, I'll get you double, triple of what I could get faster. And I'll pay you before I pay me." And he waits for Joe to nod. "Joe, we hit this right—"

"What about *wrong?*"

"How you mean?"

"You tell me," Joe says, his eyes popping. "You the gun expert. And there's always ways to hit wrong."

Huddy shrugs. "It ain't selling candy. It's involved. You don't just get a table and set 'em out on the sidewalk."

Joe waves his hand, bats away Huddy's corner lemonade stand. "What happens if some of the guns are stolen?"

"Say a few are. Two hundred guns. Some gun stolen in '72 and Yewell never knew it and we log it in and find it's bad, so we turn it over to the feds and that's it. They take it, we lose the gun."

"They don't take the rest?"

"We *sell* the rest. We just take our lumps. We let ATF know and they just take what's stolen. Look, I never been crossways with the feds and I ain't about to start. We just get the guns, log 'em in, run the serial numbers, and if there's problems, we give whatever up and that's it. Feds ain't gonna freeze the collection over a bad handful. Some bad ain't gonna make the collection radioactive, if that's what you're worrying over."

"I'm worrying over everything." And he leans in and stabs at the list. "You're talking about a hundred thousand this and a quarter-million profit and you're only giving me one way it can go wrong?"

Huddy nods, thinks about Joe's question, and the number of answers he can come up with. "Okay. Look here: I'm telling you about stolen guns. Well, you gotta worry about fakers, too. Put-together guns with mixed serial numbers. But you ain't gotta worry, because this guy was meticulous. Every collector makes mistakes—but he's got his mistakes *labeled*. Look," and Huddy searches the list and finds a page where a gun's marked FAKE. "I see this, and when I matched it with the gun, he got a tag hanging on the trigger guard saying, 'Uh oh.' "

"He wrote that?"

"I'm saying," Huddy's hand steadied against Joe's concern, "he knew when he stepped in it. Only happened to him a handful of times, and he didn't try to hide it. Joe, this guy's got everything labeled but a missing screw. He knew his guns. And I know 'em, too."

"You know your guns."

"I know how to spot a fake."

"You always saying you a jack of all trades at your shop. Maybe it'd be better if you rolled up all that knowledge and put it all here."

"Don't need to. Guns was the thing I knew before I started."

"So you're telling me you've covered everything that is or isn't supposed to happen. I don't jump off a cliff and figure my way down. Handful are stolen. Handful are oops, he missed that."

The cell phone rings, Huddy's, and he looks at the number and sees it's home. "I won't answer. Chri—"

"Best not," Joe interrupts, and Huddy nods, but he likes it better when it's himself saying what he'll take and ignore.

He stops it ringing and says, "Where were we?"

"We were going off a *cliff*. With a bunch of stolen guns. With errors. What else?"

"Nothing." Huddy's hands open empty, but Joe's mind is empty, too, all additional suspicions and complications and outcomes unnamed and unknown, so Huddy goes ahead. "That mean you in? I need to know before I call my buyers. You ain't just gonna get up to the line and stop?"

Joe examines the list, squints to peer in at what's wrong underneath but Huddy knows what's poking through is what's right. "Lemme think on this."

"Sure. Take ten minutes." Joe squinches a face. "It ain't me. We gotta be ready to go. People lining up to get at these guns. The son's gonna make trouble. Find a way to get between me and the deal. He's talking to his mama right now putting a ton of crap in her head about auction and keeping some guns for himself and he's got a wedding ring and you know he's got kids, and he's thinking about what Little Junior should have from granddad . . . and don't forget about Uncle Bubba and . . . and what we promised to Cousin In-law."

"Alright, calm down."

"I can't! Collectors gonna swoop down. His gun buddies—I'm surprised they didn't bring a checkbook to the funeral. Please. Carry the body out the front door and the guns out the back. Everybody's gonna get a piece, and if I'm calling the widow in a week it'll be a lawyer answering the phone. I can't sit on this, Joe. Yewell didn't just buy from me. I'm bringing the cash in two days or the guns start evaporating."

Joe's eyes circle the list, not following lines or moving up and down columns, unsure of the order and how it's divided and where to count, and Huddy's about to instruct, tell him how '64 is the magic date of Winchesters and everything here is pre-, but he pulls back from adding words and information when Joe taps his forehead and shakes his head and says, "I don't like not knowing what I'm looking at." He drops his hand down on the page.

"So go over there and look at 'em. See what's actual. That'll help you get it. You gonna get gun-happy. You be seeing the Golden Age of Guns. 'Course you gotta pay in first. Pay to play."

Joe nods slowly, his hand patting the list.

"That a yes?"

"You saying there's nothing stupid here? Nothing else we're getting hung by?"

But Huddy knows he doesn't have to answer because Joe's voice is calmer than the words and he's only staring inward.

Joe turns to the wall, studies it, his eyes squeezing small, and Huddy waits for him to return the short distance. "I'm saying yes."

Huddy brushes his hand across the table and his fingers stick; some small mess or spill getting missed. The feeling surprises him, he almost laughs at what he felt, but he's got bigger desires than pointing out an unclean table inside his brother's house. "You ain't just going over there to see about the land?"

"Fifty thousand dollars, you damn right I'm seeing about the land. But that doesn't mean I'm bluffing you. I'm gonna look over the land. Have a little chat with this Southern-belle land baron. And then I'm gonna check out the guns."

"But you paying in first. You ain't just teasing me with the brink of something, just so you can set yourself up long-term."

"Setting us both up long-term."

Huddy nods. "Well, if you're talking *us*—you can help me carry the guns out. 'Cause I'm gonna need more than my own hands. And you wouldn't trust me with all your guns, right?" Huddy laughs and Joe rolls his eyes but then looks square.

"You got the security to hold 'em?"

"My system locks up tight. 'Course, with your work crews not working, you can always build me something extra in the back room. If you're worrying. Build us a room within a room."

Joe smiles. "I might just have to do that. Maybe you need some security from yourself. Being as how you have a thing for pretty guns."

"You mean, the way you like to cream my merchandise? If it floats to the top, I can always count on you creaming it." And Joe rolls his eyes for Huddy bringing up some old unfairness to spoil this even moment. "Another time, sure. I'd want to squirrel some away. Guns like these, they'd gimme a woodie at midnight. Except I got bigger plans. I'm buying my freedom, brother."

"From me?"

"From me, too. And if you're speaking of trust, you and me ain't telling no one. This is a closed conversation. That includes wives." Which Huddy would've said anyway, but especially after Joe silenced Huddy's call. "No talk. Not until the guns are in the store, logged in, 'cause guns have a nasty habit of walking back out."

"Nothing's walking out." And his arms stretch, not to shake Huddy's hand but Huddy doesn't need a hand brought to his own to know he's made a bond with his brother. The deal is binding, the money's getting transferred and his life's becoming fixed.

Seven

HARLAN'S TRUCK IS IN the street. Parked in front of Huddy's house. Which isn't surprising, some instinct of Harlan's to be present when you don't need him nearby, to go into hiding when you want him at hand. It's like Huddy got followed from work, which was why he bought a home not only big and nice enough and in a quiet neighborhood away from the highway and traffic, but far enough away from the shop so no one ever tailed him back—except Harlan mistimed the arrival by getting here first. Still, after spending the hours in the big spaces of Germantown, Huddy feels where he works and lives are too close and the same.

He stares at the truck, the hood pocked from hail. The damage can't be seen under streetlight, but Huddy saw the dented metal earlier. He turns to his house. Behind the blinds, Harlan's head sits like a stone atop the armchair and Huddy studies it through the bars and glass. Then he climbs the porch steps and hears through the cracked window a cry that's only TV; the amplified voice makes him want to tune out real ones, especially Harlan's. He'll be happy to see him—tomorrow. He wishes the doorbell could swing a trap beneath the chair and send Harlan belowground for the night, and when daybreak came and Huddy rose and ate breakfast, he could later dig him out and pull him up to light.

"Look who looks expensive," Harlan says, his feet up on Huddy's chair in the room Huddy comes home to. "Whoever pawned that coat must've paid serious chicken."

Harlan's talk already feeling on and on. "Thought you'd be out with KayKay."

"I had to get back to my other job," Harlan says, and Huddy waits for the next joke. "I'm a test pilot for La-Z-Boy recliners." And Huddy still smiles at the rehearsed punchline, a line that wouldn't be pointless on a different night, and he imagines hearing it then and laughs. Harlan lays back satisfied, but to Huddy it looks like he's seated in a backseat, in a car that got pulled over. Or maybe he's up against a wall. "Thing is, with KayKay, we've always been fast sweethearts. She's not much into foreplay, dancing, songs. Ain't much into romantic requests." How little Huddy wants to hear about Harlan and KayKay's rutting session, until Harlan says, "'Sides, I wanted to hear about your bonanza," which is worse. "You find your fortune? Tell it, man. Don't be modest."

"It's late, Harlan." Huddy motions to the back room to start to leave.

"They sacked out. Little man must've took a tranquilizer, from the way he's snoozing."

Huddy crosses the room and hears from behind, "What was the family suicide gun? That granddad blew his head off with." He turns back not to Harlan but the TV to see what's reminding, if there's some crime show or corpse triggering memories, but it's a commercial, a skinny kid with a mohawk like a rat ate up the sides of his head, and the music's blaring from his ears and his parents stand stunned, unhappy until they next sit under sunshine on a beach and hear only birds and ocean—so maybe the killing was before.

"Why you talking about dead family?"

"'Cause of the dead man you seen. Seeing about. A dead man with guns. Which got me thinking about how our granddad made himself dead with a gun."

Huddy shakes his head at Harlan then at the TV, which is back to a program that isn't crimes but sports but Huddy still won't watch.

"Just saying how he ended it," Harlan says. "And it was cancer. Illness. Bad health. Ain't saying he gone crazy. Wait, it was our *great*-granddad, weren't it? It was our daddy talking about *his* granddad. See, it don't matter. He's even older than what I thought. Even more ancestral."

"How 'bout talking about his *life?*"

"That's the only thing I know. Nothing else got passed down, except for what he done to his brains. How he left. If I told you a story about his life, I'd just be making it up. But tell about the deal. You buying selling trading? Buying to sell? Trading to buy? You gonna need some big-dog funds, ain't you?"

"Which part you want me to answer?" Huddy feels likes he's losing something more precious than sleep. Maybe he'll doze through whatever Harlan says next.

"The last part. Well, you know where to go. You got one brother who's puking money. Just borrow his checkbook. That'll pay for you. Forging his signature'd be easy. His name's small."

And Huddy remains standing halfway in and out of the room, he won't sit close on a couch beside his brother but stay behind the divider he built with the other, the promise of money probably glowing on his face. As much as Harlan talks, he's alert to the business stored in Huddy's mind. "All sorts of ways to raise money," Huddy says. He wishes there was a door in the room to shut.

"Sure is. Lots of ways to scramble up cash. You ever think he got the wrong name? Huddy and Harlan—goes together. But Joe?

Daddy, after he named us, he should've gone back and switched it. To Hank. Harlan and Huddy and Hank. Or Huey? Harlan and Huddy and Huey. Howie?"

Huddy shakes his head, Harlan like some kid who can't tie the end of a string.

"Then we'd all sound the same. And equal. If I ever saw daddy again, that'd be the first thing I'd tell his face. His face—my face. Same, ain't it? I got his, don't I? More than two of you. I'm his lookalike, might say."

But Huddy can't tell which answer Harlan wants. But, yes: Put Harlan in bib overalls and he's the spitting image. Those overalls—real good for lifting daddy's drunk ass off the floor. When Huddy shakes his head of the memory, Harlan takes that for an answer.

"Fine. Anyway, what I'd say to him was he named the first one wrong. That he made Joe think he was different. Not that I'd want his name. Boring. But daddy, he made him a half-brother to us. You and me, we's full. I think his first name came from somewhere else. Good thing our daddy's name wasn't a J—or I'da thought you and me was adopted."

Huddy stares at Harlan's mouth, at his loud words and thoughts not stopping, listening to Harlan is like hearing two people talking together who can't understand who the other is, but then he remembers, suddenly, being little, his name fitting with Harlan and thinking, "Joe, what are you?" Harlan's problem is he's an adult with too much of his schoolboy self in his head. Too much of what should be gone isn't.

"You know, I'm still thinking of that tree I fell down with."

"Why?" Huddy says, and he shakes his head, but it's a memory of Joe and Huddy planning and playing together, and he smiles. "That was Joe's idea. He done the chopping. Said so yourself." The tree on the ground and Harlan, too, beside the stump.

"Yeah, but you were the one that got me to climb. Watched you go up first, and nothing happened so I figured nothing happen to me. Didn't know you two were scheming."

Huddy sees Harlan up in the tree, his climbing feet, his arms pulling up on the next limb, and Joe waiting for his footing to get high enough before grabbing the hidden ax to cut him down.

Harlan turns off the TV, which turns him serious, his eyes not moving. He collapses the footrest, leans forward on the edge of the chair. And Huddy waits to hear him say, Me, too. Let *me* be necessary. He feels stingy for thinking this, for neglecting Harlan if he asks about income, but it's not Huddy's fault for keeping his own life to himself, for judging Harlan an intruder. "Truth is, Huddy. Me and KayKay, I told her I was working for you tomorrow early, and I wasn't 'bout to mess with that. Heck, I even cleaned your kitchen. I'm being straight here." He blinks and looks around the room. "I wish you had a lie-detector machine. One of those ever come into your shop?"

Huddy grins. Sure, Harlan. A lie-detector machine, a pair of mink goggles. Flyswatter made of . . . Huddy can't complete the thought. Snakeskin. Snakeskin flyswatter. He waves his hand at items he's making up.

"I wish I could talk to you with one of those strapped to my skin, so you'd know how much you could trust me."

"I trust you, Harlan."

"I'd trust myself more, if I was wearing one all the time. Name: Harlan Marr. Place of residence: my brother's house." And he smiles but then the smile gets swamped, and Huddy watches what empties and fills in, Harlan's pain and contempt for how his life made him answer where he was. His body anchored in the chair; he shakes his shoulders free. "Name of brother: Huddy. Other one is Hank." And

Harlan laughs a little as the machine catches him, his finger rising and falling to signal his first lie.

Huddy steps quietly to the crib, his eyes seeing nothing. But then they adjust to darkness, and when he reaches the railing his son is visible, asleep on his side, lying in pajamas without a sheet or blanket covering. A squeak comes out of his nose. Huddy watches him breathe through his tiny new teeth, his gentle chest lifting and falling and lifting, the cartoon pajamas snug to his belly, and beneath his body more cartoons on the sheet. His son lightly snores and Huddy hears himself hum along with the noise.

Christie stirs awake in another dark room Huddy enters. She rubs her eye, squints for the night hour on the clock. Her face bunches at his lateness. The TV is on—the beam flickers and flashes—but without sound.

"Was just watching Cody sleep," Huddy says.

"He's getting good at it." She props up in bed. "Where you been?" she says groggily.

"Germantown."

"Joe's?"

"And elsewhere. A house I always thought I needed a passport to walk through."

"And that's why you're smiling so much?"

"Well, I'm having a good day."

"But you're not gonna tell me about it."

Huddy zips his mouth and then talks. "If I tell you why I'm happy, you'd just say, 'You're gonna spend what?'" And Huddy can't help it, he's already messing up, saying too much, but after a day like this, and the hopeful ones to come, he'd like a small applause. He'll shake a finger at himself in the morning. "Let's just say, I found a bird's nest on the ground."

"A bird's nest on the ground. Maybe you can tell me something that's not in code."

"Chirp chirp." He pulls off his shoes, feels like juggling them but instead flings them at the closet. He's gonna wear an all-night smile, a loud one, because making Joe agree to stay silent made Huddy want to talk. "Some news, but I can't say what."

"Thanks. You're really painting a picture."

He laughs. His mind fools with him, imagines his pillows stuffed with cash. "What time Harlan get here today?"

She shrugs. "Dinner. Sitting in that chair since then."

And Huddy thinks of Harlan pleased after his La-Z-Boy line hit the mark. But then he remembers the device cuffed to his arm, his answers graphing up and down in measurements of true and false and true enough. "He cleaned the kitchen," Huddy says.

"Yeah," Christie shrugs, "sort of."

"How you mean?"

"I don't know, Huddy, I guess he did."

"He says he did, is all."

"Well, okay. I don't keep track of his chores. Stacked the plates in the sink. Stopped there. Whatever, I ain't grading. He had us laughing. You know how he is."

Sure, like telling how granddad finished himself. Funny, morbid stuff. Huddy drops onto the bed, stares at the ceiling.

"He asked if you owned a motorcycle," she says.

"Why?" he says, rolling to face her.

"He says he couldn't understand all these people who own houses but no motorcycles. Thought people had their needs all backwards." Her eyes pinch. "You know, it ain't much fun if you aren't gonna share the good days. 'Cause you never tell the bad."

"You wanna hear the bad?" Huddy stares at the TV. He can hear the low voice from the other set, like some sound being thrown. "Why's the sound off?"

"I fell asleep to it that way."

He looks at the sheets and blanket bunched at the foot of the bed, like she'd got up to leave but fell asleep suddenly while rising. The pillows aren't flat on the mattress but tilted up against the wall. He stares at her angled shoulders, at her neck almost upright. "You sleeping funny tonight."

"It was Harlan—what he said."

"The motorcycle?"

"About how we met. He was asking."

Huddy shakes his head, Harlan pulling at the strand of a personal story, pulls and pulls until it loosens and out it comes. Harlan in his shop, and now in his own rooms. Huddy glances back at the TV, expecting to see a picture of Harlan inside, but it's just a car chase, cars moving and going, engines gunned. The first car makes the tight turn, but the second one charges the corner overfast and skids, fishtails. "You tell him?"

"Sort of knew already. But you skipped the rest. Part before."

"None of his business."

"Maybe you just didn't want to tell him what I been."

"It was before I knew you. That was something you'd settled out of. Said so yourself, your wild teenage years."

"Before you knew me—but it was still me." She looks at him, long, her eyes lowered but her face staying turned, as if she wanted Huddy to not only see her now but also then, to recognize behind this face to what she looked like and took prior.

"You know what I mean. Just some bad bit." Huddy remembering her first appearance, twenty-four, coming in to look for a ring she'd pawned to Mister Jenks six years earlier. She figured it was gone, but she had to see, because the ring was special: an elephant ring, with ruby eyes and a diamond headdress. Huddy checked but there was no paper trail. Maybe Jenks had held it for a bit, or shopped it to some specialty buyer who liked oddball things, but more likely he just chopped it up, plucked the bigger stones, if there were any—Huddy suspected they were just tiny diamonds clustered together to give the illusion of more diamond—and sent the gold to the melt. Huddy said sorry, wished it was here, but she didn't go. She turned over her shoulder to the display cases and squinted, as if the elephant ring were there but she couldn't quite pick it out. And then she told him the reason the ring got here—although Huddy mostly knew, can't imagine this ring as a teenage gift, so he'd assumed it was one swiping account or another. He realized he was hearing some twisted-up nostalgia, not some sunny tale about what she used to have or be but instead an upsetting, darker story, told by this changed person who beforehand had acted worse and crooked and stolen a ring from her grandma. She'd straightened herself out, had her own housecleaning business, but she was still feeling bad about her past trouble. Huddy had never had this return situation, someone looking for a ring, much less an elephant ring, and hoping to amend a wrong. He felt like they shared a disbelief: He couldn't believe she'd tried retrieving a long-lost ring and she couldn't believe she'd ever needed being here before. She wore no wedding ring, and when she mentioned later, over the phone, that she lived nearby, he was surprised, since her life had traveled to a different part, that she wasn't from farther.

"I pawned it," she says, "because I thought I'd be able to get it back. But I couldn't."

"Probably better that way."

"That I couldn't?"

"Better that you pawned it, instead of wanting to sell. Look, we don't have to talk about this."

"Because it made me less suspicious?"

Huddy nods, but he doesn't want to. "He might've been thinking, why would you be selling this sentimental thing? A ring like that's gotta be sentimental. Can't be much else."

She nods and stops facing him. "Maybe I knew that at the time." He watches her stare at her ring finger. Her head tosses back, a hurt swarms and reddens her face, a fresh bruise. "Would you have been suspicious?" She looks again at her finger, nudges it with her thumb, puzzled, like she's seeing the wrong ring, the incriminating one, and she can't force it off.

"Of a young girl, selling a ring like that?"

"Yeah," she says. "Of me." She itches again at her knuckle.

He can answer directly, but he doesn't. "Depends on the story that goes with it. Somebody comes in with an out-there story—"

"Whatever . . ." He watches her back straighten, as if she were trying to sit up tall over the memory.

He looks back at the TV, three people walking with no footsteps. Each person seems like they're talking to themselves, each word caught in a defective throat. "So what did Harlan think of the story?"

"He thought it was sad."

"'Cause you lost your family ring?"

She nods, and Huddy looks away. It's nice watching a muted show, every conversation avoided, every person unnamed. The miniature characters talk and threaten, but it's all some wordless calm. "He said it was a happy story, too. 'Cause it brought me to his good brother. But then *he* got sad."

Huddy doesn't want to listen to Harlan reacting three ways before Huddy's even felt the one. He returns to the TV, where there's no racket. On the other TV, though, Huddy detects channels flipping.

"'Cause he says you never believe any of *his* stories. He said if he walked into your shop with some old story about what he'd done, you'd be doubting."

"That don't make sense. You were *confessing.* Why wouldn't I believe a confession?" Huddy shakes his head. Some memory that was his and Christie's, their first day together, but Harlan's got not just involved but in front of it, and now Huddy can't see the meeting because Harlan's blocked it, casting his shadow. On the TV, no noise, as if people are talking in high notes only audible to Harlan's characters on his TV, who understand and answer back in muffled voices that get stuck in Huddy's shut door. His house feels like a large television, the divided rooms a single split-screen broadcast.

"He said you probably didn't believe my story at first, 'cause you don't believe nothing people say when they walk through your door. I told him I'd trust nothing neither, if I was you." She smiles, but her face stays afflicted. "But I hadn't really thought about that, what you must've thought of me that moment. Or what that man must've. I must've put the ring on, right before I walked in. Then took it off?" And she looks at Huddy, but he doesn't know this prehistory. Harlan's bent the memory back to some new beginning that Huddy can only guess at and Christie vaguely half-remembers. "Wait, that's not true. I put it on, but I knew it wasn't mine—it was her ring, and it fit fine, but it felt more like

stealing than when it was in my pocket, so I slid it off and kept it
there. I thought if I wore it, it would look less believable. But he
didn't ask questions. Either he believed, or he didn't care not to.
Story checks out, if you don't hear it? But I don't know why I went
looking for the ring again. I knew it wasn't there. Six years, come
on, that's dumb."

"You shouldn't've told this all to Harlan. He's always wanting to
hear the bad part. Part you don't want to talk about, is the part he
likes to hear extra."

"He didn't ask all this. It was after I told him, went to bed, why
I switched the sound off."

The TV characters keep talking into the next room, or maybe
they're fake-talking, mimes with mouths opening and closing,
silent to spy and listen in on secrets.

"You remember when you wrote your info down?" Huddy says,
and he tries to make eye contact. "On my business card. On the
back. Your name and number was on one side, me and mine on the
other." He's hoping to pull her to a better part, not the shameful
part. "I kept that card for a long while." But it doesn't work. Her
face stays in profile. The card won't remind or substitute, like an
invitation she can't yet accept.

"She didn't have enough jewelry, that if you took it, it wouldn't
count. I knew that, but I took it still. And I knew she'd be missing
that ring more, but that didn't stop me neither. When I took it, she
was in the house, the next room. She never went nowhere. Maybe
that's why she liked the ring. Thought she was in Africa, or just the
zoo. Somewhere else. But I took that away from her. When I took
that ring, it felt like I took everything." Her eyes widen, bits of the
memory reconnecting, her past relived. "And when they found out
the ring was gone, they knew it was me. They knew it wasn't my

sister. Or my brothers. No—they went to one of them. Billy. He was real mad at me, that they were also suspecting him. Took a long time to get forgiveness on that." She traces her thumb in a line down her finger. Then she rubs her fingertips against her palm, her hand now a fist. "Can't say how long it was before they knew it was gone, but it was fast—fast enough that I knew it was still in your store. Not your store, but, you know. But I wouldn't tell them where it was." The scene cuts out and the TV darkens, Huddy's vision emptying and then filling back with bright commercial colors. "Guess that elephant ring never walked back into your shop."

"Not ever," Huddy says. But then he recalls a monkey ring. This crazy guy, short and squat, five-by-five, coming in last year and showing him this ring, worn long along his finger. But it was what was hidden underneath that was the punchline. The man slipped off the gold ring—Huddy expecting some personal inscription— to reveal the monkey's penis lying flat against its belly, a ruby on the tip. The guy gave a hyena laugh and said that the monkey was humping his finger every day. So maybe Huddy's wrong about what he told Harlan, and all these made-up items, mink flyswatters and snakeskin goggles, are likely real. He should have known this, being a pawnbroker, that any and all odd items and ornaments somewhere exist. He tells Christie about the monkey ring and she smiles, and then she breaks out laughing, cups her mouth to not wake their son, but Huddy leans in and pulls her hand away and they share the laughter, and Huddy feels good for assisting, for flipping her mood, for kicking away her guilty story and finding another one, with a funny underside. If she ever tells of it again, he's got this different and better ring to crack her up. He pokes the air with his finger. She tips her palm over, as if the joke is right there in her upturned hand, and maybe any future thoughts of the elephant ring will trigger the monkey ring. Both TVs are going the same way, but now it doesn't feel like they're operating wrong but instead like the sets are paired up and connected, a high-end system, his house wired for surround sound.

"Did you buy it?"

"The monkey? It wasn't for sale. Just for show."

"But you would've?"

Sure. The right price. The ruby. The gold. Buy it real easy. Huddy nods.

"It'd be a good day if somebody walked in with an elephant ring?" Her head twists sideways.

"For me?" Huddy asks.

"I figure, since you won't tell me what a good day is, I might as well make one up. 'Cause I know you ain't trading marbles."

"Marbles and Hot Wheels watches."

"Who . . ." she says, but she doesn't say more, shakes her head to not care or worry. "So, today's a day when somebody brought you an elephant ring?"

"Today's a day with a hundred elephant rings."

Her eyes jump, and Huddy feels like he's just brought unnumbered presents. He stares hard at her, keeps looking, as if to tell her that she doesn't need to miss or even think about that sorry ring, when he's about to redeem it a hundred times over. That old ring got lost but their lives are offsetting, their future is getting raised. He sees both her faces at once, the younger one who pawned and defaulted, and the older one with this big win just up ahead with his expenditure and investment return. He watches her remember—but then she blinks, fast as if to forget the memory, and smiles, dimly but then brightening, so that maybe all of her just came back here.

He wonders, when he dreams tonight, if he'll see an elephant,

this decked-out elephant carrying a monkey, and the monkey spar-
kling, too. Maybe they're part of a parade or celebration. And then
he'll probably picture Harlan. Harlan's come from no direction, not
approaching but appearing all at once, as if he'd crawled out from
the elephant's underbelly, to flank these bejeweled animals. Huddy
watches the three of them move altogether, and Harlan sees the
shiny rings on the riding monkey's fingers, and Huddy waits to see
if Harlan will reach up high to try to slip one off. There he goes, up
close against the elephant—a little person next to this immensity—
one hand palming the elephant's side, readying himself for an
opening, the right unsuspecting moment, some coming commotion or activity elsewhere in the procession, or the sun a blinding
shimmer on the headdress, or the sun low and a concealing shadow
thrown. But if Christie changed, why can't Harlan? Except, when
Huddy met Christie, she'd already become another, already stopped
what she was one time. "Did Harlan ask where the ring went?"
Wouldn't it have been great if Huddy had found that ring and
brought it back to Christie on their engagement? He can't tell this
final thought's origins, if it came from himself, or if he was imagin-
ing Harlan saying it first to Christie earlier in the night. And since
he can't distinguish which speaker in his head, he decides it's both.

"No. He said, figured it was gone. Why you asking so much
what Harlan did and didn't do?" And she laughs again, this monkey
ring still tickling. Huddy's got her on some safari, where people
take down elephants and monkeys, and then wear rings as souvenirs mounted on their fingers.

But he's gone from the safari plunder. Huddy's in the gun room
checking the guns off a list. And Joe's in the truck laying the blankets. But you still need a third body, someone in the middle to walk
the guns out.

Eight

SELL HIS GOLD. SELL his gems. Sell his guns. Instant selling that he'll combine with Joe's bankroll to buy up the guns to sell them and swap out his Lamar life for the richer gutter of Summer Avenue. Huddy phones the buyers, tells them he wants money today. He knows he won't get full price—the cost of unloading is leaving money on the table—but right now he's a discount house that can never go negative.

He starts with gold, but here comes the diamonds with his old car to not draw attention, a hopped-up engine to drive away fast and a henchman stepping out the passenger side to guard the car during the interval between drive-up and getaway.

"That's some firepower," Harlan says, then returns his eyes to the movie below the loan counter.

The buyer walks inside the store swinging his beat-up attaché case. "What you got for me, Mister Huddy?"

"What I always got, reduced prices." Huddy pulls the bigger diamonds from the safe, a half-dozen higher-grade stones inside envelopes inside a cigar box, and he carries the box back to the showcase, which he unlocks to retrieve the smaller ones. The mounted diamonds sliding out of the envelopes and Huddy reading the price codes to see what years ago he paid and make sure he's not giving them now away. "Steam-cleaned 'em so you can get a fresh look."

"Appreciate that," the buyer says, the loupe and the Leveridge gauge tapping down on the glass of the showcase, and Huddy watches him lift a marquise and loupe it, his eyes strengthening ten-power. He sets the stone between the arms of the gauge to measure out width and depth. "Nice. Too bad these marquise ain't selling."

"Same with pear-shaped," Huddy says. "Emerald cut, too." He figures why not talk about two others falling out of fashion, when they aren't sitting here.

"Yeah, funny thing about womenfolk. They all want something special, 'cept they all want the same ring." And he picks up the round to show what that one brilliance is. Huddy watches him go piece by piece, a European cut and then another round. "Nice detail here," he says, a finger tracing the diamond-set shank. "Diamonds in a loop is classy." He sorts it with the pile he wants and Huddy'll wait to tell him he's taking all sorts. Mark it down, and down again, but it's still going out with you. "Kind of a hit-and-miss on this one," the buyer says after zooming in on a princess. Huddy nods. "Cut's real nice, but you got some real bad flaws."

"*Flaws* is such a mean word," Huddy says. "Especially when you talking about what she's born with."

"Well, I hate to be mean. Give me another way of saying."

"It's about *seeing*. Maybe you got an angel inside, sitting on a cloud."

"Ha! Well, that sounds pretty. But I ain't much for imagination. I just like clear stones."

"This clown sleeps here," Harlan says, and Huddy shoots a look at Harlan, who's up from the chair eyeing the parking lot and Del, who's eyeing the guardsman before turning toward Huddy's door and inching in. Sleeps here, crawls all over the merchandise like some insect you can't kill—you spray and think you stopped it but it comes back through the keyhole, some water bug you can't eradicate because now he's a goldbug, too. Del's arms stuck up high, except he's the one hijacking the day. Huddy sees the new hardware slung on his hip.

"My happy hunting ground," Del says to everyone and all the inventory. Huddy deciding whether his job right now is a juggler or a bouncer, and then his right arm goes sideways to pawn Del off on Harlan, but Del ignores the handoff. "Huddy, you gonna go with me on gold? I told you, I'm paying ninety-one percent of spot. Come on now, you gotta leave something on the bone. Just a little bit, so I can move it. Don't make me pay more or I'll never get to be a millionaire."

Huddy aiming for the correct incentive, some hush money, a kickback to kick him out.

"I figured that was your answer," Del says. "Which is why I'm asking today for silver. Silver coins. I'm hunting 'em cause I got the buyers lined up. These survivalists in Arkansas. Man, they buying up silver. And gold. They think Armageddon is right around the corner. They paying twelve and a half times the face value. Saying to me, What you gonna do when Armageddon comes, and I'm telling them, I'm gonna get my gun and get your shit! Gold and silver and hellfire. Man oh man, they scared about the third thing so they hoarding the first two!"

Get him to a corner, Huddy thinks, so I can go private in mine. "See you wearing something new. Let's put you a notch better. Let me talk to Harlan here about a setup."

"Good deal," Del says, hyped about the gift certificate he's gaining. "I seen you busy with the gem man." But Del doesn't distract him; he might be inside the store with the buyer, but the buyer's also inside the stones, and Huddy'll go internal, too. Del turns his back and Huddy's eyes keep on the diamonds and not on Harlan moving within earshot.

"He points, you say twenty percent off," Huddy says, without looking. Paying Del to leave and not jeopardize the deal that Huddy jumps back to.

"This one's beautifully cut," the diamond buyer says. "Not seeing no funny birthmarks neither."

The last stone, the measuring and assessing finished, Huddy stares at the two piles, uneven in the wrong way, but he'll call out these judgments. "What's your offer?"

"For these, I can—"

"Nope," Huddy says. "The whole lot."

The buyer shrugs. "That's a big commitment here."

Not really, Huddy thinks, adding the multi-values. I double my money and you double yours. And that gets me a quarter ways there. "Today, it's the wheat with the chaff." Huddy's hands point at both sets of kernels.

"I'm just telling you what the traffic will bear. These here," he says, at the pile of have-nots. "You got one that's drilled and filled. Another one, a purple rainbow shooting out at me. They gonna have to be dirt-cheap. I'll take 'em, but it's a giveaway."

"I understand. But what I'm seeing, it's all resalable."

"Then why can't you sell it?"

"I am. To you. Or someone else. I'm tired of looking at 'em. Gonna put this money all back in the business."

"Oh yeah?"

"'Course. Going all in on furs. Three-quarter-length coats. By the time I'm done, there won't be an animal left in the forest."

A smile, and then Huddy smiles when he sees Del going away. Not a word of jawing before, and Huddy looks at Harlan, who shrugs about his language, his mind blank about threats or insults over how Del got kicked.

"Let's say ten," the buyer says, and Huddy nods, and the diamonds switch owners and the money changes hands, the stones sliding into a new compartment and two packs of cash replacing the diamonds in the cigar box. Harlan sees this exchange, but he already witnessed a difference when he helped carry Huddy's guns from home, Huddy trying to make it some routine morning movement, a collection that circulates every off-day.

"What'd you say to him?" Huddy asks, after the buyer's gone.

"Thing is," Harlan says, "guy like that jams up pretty fast. I told him, if he don't see what he likes, don't fuck around. I said it polite. Made sure he was near to hear it. Even offered that cut-rate price you said."

"This all while he's wearing a gun."

"Well I'm wearing one, too. Push comes to shove, he gonna think about his house and his dog."

"That right?"

"Yep. And that's why I can help you."

"Oh? How's that? You braver? Or you just a mind reader?"

"No. I just ain't got a dog to go home to."

Huddy eyes his brother who's dogless and landless, but at least he's glad he's armed.

And Tom's armed, too, his next incognito buyer coming in, seems like everyone's carrying a piece today to the market, or *from* it, Huddy hopes: the collectors on the other end of the phone that he's calling on to come get his guns. Four buyers—a shotgun collector, a pistol collector, a big-bore collector, and a collector who's God-knows-what but has money. Huddy'll sell fifteen guns and want to make five thousand per buyer.

"Having a fundraiser?" Tom says, and now it's Harlan and not Del that Huddy doesn't want to have hear.

"Yep," Huddy says and Harlan's about to see what's clearing out of the cases, all the heavy, meaty chains, and even the light merchandise that barely holds weight, and somewhere between KayKay's necklace getting liquidated. Huddy eyes the parking lot, unlocks the cases, and starts stacking trays. "Grab the rest," he says to Tom.

"You cashing out?" Harlan asks, which Huddy ignores. Harlan's finding a home here, too bad Huddy's moving. He motions Tom to the office. He'd ask Harlan for help, but he's got a bigger haul maybe later.

"You said bring twenty-five," Tom says, "so I brought thirty. Whatever you'd like to sell, I'll take."

Ten-karat and fourteen-karat and eighteen-karat and some dental gold and a little bit of platinum. More gold to sell than diamonds, but the transaction takes less time; diamonds is an opinion, whereas the gold is on the scale. Huddy wishes he were getting jewelry value and not scrap value, but he's gonna be a big boy now, just get it over and get the cash and know that gold's bringing good money. He stares at the monitor, at the empty parking lot save for Tom's car and inside the store Harlan staring at the empty cases and then out at Tom's car, the reason for the emptying.

The gold separated and weighed and traded for cash, an in-and-out deal and the sold gold gets Huddy over halfway, and he can do the rest with guns. He watches Tom leave and then phones Joe.

"How's the fire sale?"

"It's going," Huddy says.

"Well, my funds are ready."

Two kinds of financing, Huddy would say, but he's happy to hear it. "How are we with the vehicle?"

"You offering?"

"Thing is," Joe says, which means he isn't. "They got my name on it. Company logo, and I don't wanna drive up like that."

"You think it'd look better if it said U-Haul?" Huddy saying. Or Wells Fargo, he nearly adds, but not with Harlan in range. Joe asking if they need a truck to say he's got plenty but can't be used. "Don't worry," Huddy laughs. "I'll get it." And when he does, he'll be driving.

"What's this?" Harlan says, gesturing at the door to a black man holding a liquor bottle, which Huddy sees is Barnes.

"Came by to say bye," he says, and Huddy saw a truck pull in earlier, which he realizes now was a deliveryman carrying *out* the merchandise. Barnes approaches and sets the bottle down. "Thought you might like some dessert wine. Taylor's. The port never rolled out of here fast. I'm getting my percentage on the regular stock, but the sweet stuff's been sitting, so the distributor says I'm stuck with it."

Huddy doesn't want to hear about getting stuck, about what never got sold, not on a day when he's unloading.

"Taking some Burnett's vodka home with me. You want a bottle?"

Huddy about to say no when he hears "Sure" beside him. "My brother," Huddy says.

Barnes looks over and back. "I'll get you two."

Huddy lifts his arms up, to say he ain't asking, because today feels all wrong for these gifts.

"Not supposed to give bottles away," Barnes says. "The law. Guess I'm breaking it. Don't tell no one."

"Me and him won't say a thing," Harlan says. "More you give us, the quieter we be."

"You might get some regulars coming around, asking where I at. Gonna send a few of 'em into a panic. But they'll just migrate over to King's Liquor. They won't miss me. Me—I'ma miss the people that paid cash." Barnes looks around at Huddy's shelves. He sees the empty cases and he frowns, as if the jewelry got hit; must not have been a smash-and-grab if the glass is still intact. "I'ma miss when it snowed, 'cause the customers always came to me, even before they hit the grocery store. Can't think what else. Anyway, I'll get you that Burnett's."

Huddy wants to say don't worry, that he'll be gone, too. He's leaving, Huddy is, and he shakes his head, because he's got more important things to think of than beverage policies, on liquor that Barnes is giving him illegally to drink.

Different gun collectors all asking why he's letting these choice pieces go, and Huddy gives them the same answer with different lines: Just thinning out, just selling down, just thought it time to reduce.

"You've been waiting on this gun for years," Huddy tells the shotgun collector. "Time for you to buy it."

"You never showed me this one," the big-bore man says. "Never knew it was here."

"Well, now you know I had it."

"You got any more?" the pistol collector asks.

"Oh, I'm sure I'll have something you like."

"Well, call me first," says the buyer who spreads everywhere.

Huddy puts the guns in cheap sleeves, watches the collectors carry 'em out and load 'em in their trunks. So that's it. He's made his bet. "Shop stays closed tomorrow," he tells Harlan, whose eyes sink. Without the job, he can't even buy an Egg McMuffin in the morning.

"Like to keep making money," Harlan says.

"How're your arms feeling?"

"They's good. Arms are strong. Legs are hollow."

"Got a decent shirt?"

"Like your outfit last night?" Huddy studies Harlan. Sits in my house watching how I'm dressed coming home. "Looking like you flunked debonair school," Harlan says.

"Yeah, well, the place we'd be going, there's a dress code. If I was a horse rolled in mud, she wouldn't care about dirty."

"Horse?"

"We *all* gotta be somebody else over there. A new look for everyone."

"All mean Joe, too?"

And Huddy doesn't say no.

"You tell big brother I'm helping?"

But Huddy just told himself, how could he have told Joe? This time, his silence won't mean yes.

"Yeah, well, he can't be somebody else when he been somebody else his whole life." And Huddy watches and knows Harlan can't help but ask more. "What's his end?"

He stares at Harlan, his eyes like flashlights shining out of the dark to search his brother's face. "You best drop that line. You best drop all of 'em."

"What's that supposed to mean?"

"It means, don't ask about any deal. Don't ask what Joe's getting or got and what you ain't, and what's luck or ain't and how you feel sorry. He went his way and you went yours and I went mine. I got a job for you today. For tomorrow. Hauling. And I need you on this. Let's keep it simple. You start feeling inferior, I'm asking some-one else."

"All right," Harlan says. But his head tilts at his middle brother to ask another question. "How 'bout you tell me what I'm hauling?"

Huddy shrugs. Just my life, is what you'd be lifting.

Harlan's head tilts again, down to the three bottles that Barnes delivered. "Thought he was some derelict, standing there."

"Wasn't."

"I seen. Nice what he brought you. Us."

Huddy shakes his head. "Barnes had a fire once. Long time ago. Not a big one, but still, he said the alcohol commission told him all the inventory had to go. Strict that way. They took it all to a dump. Crushed it, buried it."

"Okay," Harlan says, but he doesn't see the point, and he doesn't see why Huddy's scowling.

"You take 'em," Huddy says.

"If I take 'em, they getting drunk."

Huddy imagines Barnes next door, pulling the signs from the windows. "Get rid of 'em all the same."

For dinner that night, Huddy wants Sonic. They drive to North Parkway, and when the road becomes Summer Avenue and he doesn't hang the usual right onto East Parkway, Christie asks where he's going. "Thought I'd try a different one," he says, passing the Midas and the tire shops and body shops, crowded with wrecked cars, and then driving beyond the lumberyard and the self-storage lots.

"Closer than Poplar?" she asks.

"'Bout the same."

"Okay . . ." she shrugs. "Another Sonic. Let's get some fast-food variety." She half-laughs, as if Huddy's picked the strangest adventure.

He slopes up and down the overpass, and passes a crumbling trailer park that must've been built before the street expanded and took a tumble, then the thrift stores and antique shops, and then a pawnshop—twice as much competition here, but even more times the business supply. The Goodwill lot is still full at this hour, the street traffic is heavy, cars moving in and out of the wide turn lane. It's like Lamar, only busier, and it doesn't feel like all the cargo is going elsewhere.

"Longer, Huddy," Christie says, and she's right, they would've already reached the Poplar Sonic, but it's not much farther to make her suspicious, an honest mistake.

"Here we are," he says, after another half-mile, passing a car wash with soaped-up cars, and he turns left into the restaurant's entrance and swings around and parks in one of the angled stalls facing the street. He pushes the red button and asks Christie if they want the usual and she nods; he hears the squawked voice and he orders into the intercom.

"Cody'll just munch on our fries," Christie says. The sky is dark but the streetlights provide an outline of the shop across the road, and the name on the marquee is visible and unchanged: LIBERTY PAWN. He nods at it. Just like it should say, until it says him. He glances up and down the street. He imagines his future customers driving down Summer, his new business accessible from so many highway points. If you miss the Highland exit, just head on up to Graham and loop back. Soon he'll be able to buy in, and he smoothes his hands along the dashboard, as if he hadn't already bought this.

The carhop brings the food and Huddy makes the exchange. He hands the bag to Christie and pops the drinks into the cup holders. He feels like he's on a stakeout, planted here. The dashboard clock reads 6:07. It would be funny if he called Keller and said, "Guess where I'm at?" He doesn't have the number and Keller's already left—no car in the big parking lot—but the scenario still entertains him.

"What?" Christie says.

"What?" he answers back.

"This food funny?" She twists around to get Cody started on his milk and fries.

"Don't know. She must've given me a Happy Meal."

"Ha." She rolls her eyes at his dumb joke.

He searches the bag, grabs a burger, and unwraps it on his lap. He bites and says, "Mmm."

"Yeah. Tasty."

"*Real* tasty," he says, and she looks sideways at his cheerful voice.

"You auditioning for one of their commercials?"

He's not gonna tell her anything, and yet he's brought her here to see the promise across the street. He shoves several fries into his mouth. He's not gonna talk but he's not gonna stop himself either. "I think this is my favorite Sonic," he says.

"Oh yeah?"

"Ain't yours?"

"Gee, Huddy," she says, chewing, "I can't really say I like this exact food better."

He takes a sip. "Maybe I'm just hungrier. No, it's more than that. Maybe I should ask Cody. What you say, Cody, these the best fries you ever had?" He looks in the rearview mirror, where he can see Cody directly, now that he's facing forward in the purchased car seat. "It's a new thing for you, but your mama thinks she's eating clone food." He watches his son smile. "I think every other burger I ate is one thing, but this one here is another. Maybe it's the location. This here drive-in."

"Well, then, there's our preview." And she points at the sidewalk, at two black men, one with a skullcap, the other a bandanna, the bandannaed one wearing pants slung so low they're barely held to his ass. "Happy trails. Are those pants or knee pads? A couple more steps, they might even be socks."

Huddy studies his feet, watches him shuffle and sidestep. "Can't run fast that way."

"He ain't looking for speed." She opens her bun, pulls a piece of the burger and extends it back to Cody.

"If he came into my pawnshop and tried to rip me off, he'd just be duckwalking." Huddy's said *pawnshop*, but he's got the better slanted angle for seeing; he might even be the blind spot between her and his future store. If he leaned back, she might get a view, but why would she be looking for the Liberty sign? He wipes his hands on the napkin. "I like this street."

"It was something, way back when."

"Oh, no," he says. "It's good now. Might not be what it was, but in other ways, it's humming. Just gotta know which way to look."

"You think?"

"Sure. We're here."

"You brought us here."

"That's right. All this traffic. If I was this store, I'd be in the perfect spot. Right location. Busy busy."

"Well . . . good for them."

"Good for them. Good for us."

"Good for us?"

"Sure. 'Cause we can get to it. So many ways to reach this food."

"Maybe you wanna buzz the intercom and ask about investing." And maybe saying a word about money jolts her a bit. Because she stares down at her cup and then slowly raises her eyes over to him. "Huddy? Am I supposed to be following what you're saying? I mean, I'm following, but are you saying something else?"

"What you mean?"

"I mean, you eating this same old food. But you acting like a mystery."

"I am? The mystery meat." Everything out of his mouth feels funny to himself.

"See. There you go. Teasing again."

"Going. I'm right here." He grabs the box of fries, shuffles the ones from the bottom till they stand up straight.

"No you ain't."

"I'm right here. In the driver's seat."

"You ain't here."

He's not, Huddy thinks, he's right over there. He looks away, sees another carhop stationed and making change at a nearby car.

"This about what you told me before? You back in that bedtime conversation? Old monkey ring. Or, in your spare time, you just become some Summer Avenue expert."

Cody starts complaining about his seat.

"That's right. My wandering eye is this here street. Looks like the boss wants to skedaddle." He tips his soda cup to get the sweet remains from the ice.

"Hold it, Cody. Wait," she says. She pinches some burger roll for Cody, flings it on his lap. Then she switches onto Huddy, her hand touching his arm and pressing. "Tell me."

Her face urges him, her eyes not quite hurt. There's a break in

Cody's complaint, as if he too were listening. "That," Huddy says, pointing, and he tilts back in his seat so she can see across. He turns his head away so she knows not to study his sitting position, to encourage her to go beyond it to the dim nighttime shape. "You see it?" He's surprised he's just done this, but it feels more good than harmful.

"Pawnshop."

He turns back to her to see her gazing toward it. His finger presses the corner of the driver-side window, as if the shop were pinned there against the glass and not entirely outside. She looks around, her eyes opening, her thoughts clicking together, about the disguise of the dinner and why he wanted this particular food— this pit stop now arranged like a fancy reservation.

"Should be able to see it," Huddy says.

"I do."

"Because it's bigger. Now if I was just teasing, I'd only show you some small hint." He watches her mind seek and discover meanings. "Sometimes, a great view—it ain't always the pretty one." He feels like he's just brought her blindfolded to a place that isn't a majestic overlook or a high bluff or even a low bank along the river, and now that her eyes are uncovered she should understand why this trip is still worthwhile.

"This is your deal?" she asks. She says hush to Cody, but they both know he won't stop.

"I ain't saying anymore."

"But I'm supposed to connect this to what you were saying in bed?" He doesn't answer her train of thoughts, and she nods. Cody kicks and tugs to get freed, and Christie offers another scrap of food, but it doesn't work—it makes him angrier to be so misunderstood— and Huddy can feel the front seat tremble with his son's frustrated position. Christie turns to him and smiles as the noise takes over. "There he goes. On a timer. I guess we best get moving, Huddy." She gathers wrappers, collapses the bag. "Unless we like screams."

"Right idea," he says, and he drums the dashboard. "Let's bolt." He restarts the car, gives the marquee a final look. He feels like flashing his brights at the store, to signal Keller to come out from the other side, to give notice that his time is up. Or maybe Huddy should honk his horn, tap it repeatedly, like he's playing his own hundred-gun salute.

Nine

THERE IS NO NAME on the truck, but when Joe sees who's inside it his eyes grow like he's reading capital letters, an even wider expression of surprise than when Huddy last appeared at his door and Harlan didn't. And Harlan won't turn his face from the windshield to explain why. "Get in here," Joe snaps, his eyes lighting on Huddy. "You said we were telling no one!" Yelling before Huddy's inside the entryway, the argument without the security of a room, the door slamming behind him, and Huddy figures nobody's home.

"Yeah. Wives. And Harlan is—"

"Is what?" Joe's neck wrenching.

"We need three sets of hands." Huddy's voice as quiet as Joe's is explosive, hoping to meet up in some calm loud middle.

"Three sets of hands," Joe says, shaking his two. "This is a *two*-way deal. You got the math wrong. You're already fucking up numbers."

"You wanna carry two hundred guns?"

"Why can't *you* carry them?" His teeth grit, his mouth champing down.

"Because. I'm in the gun room. And you're guarding the truck. Harlan's doing the lifting." Joe shakes his head at the last name.

"You got someone you trust better? Maybe one of your ex-wives? Or maybe you wanna ask Lorie for a little help with a couple thousand pounds. Of guns. And all you do is bitch about who's working for you. This one's lazy, this one's suing, this one's stealing. Ain't never heard about no right-hand man."

"You never mentioned needing three on this," Joe says. "The whole time you talked, it was me and you. You sat at my table, you never said him."

"We can't leave the truck alone when the guns are coming or going. Are you crazy?"

"Crazy is what's sitting there right now. What you worrying over, someone walking in off the street? On Dogwood? Come on."

"I'm being careful. With the house. With the son—"

"Please. I trust him more than Harlan."

"You never met him."

"Exactly." He stares at Huddy, his eyes measuring. "This is your big chance. Why you chancing it?"

But Huddy thought the saying went different. The man who never took a chance never had a chance. Or maybe, He never had a chance because he didn't take one. Something about your big one-time moment. He won't correct himself or Joe.

"You just like him, borrowing trouble," Joe says, seeing one bad brother mirroring the other; the business barely begun and Huddy already needs to redeem himself. "He stays in the truck. He stays till we seal the deal. Signs on the dotted line, and then we fetch him." Harlan stuck in the driveway, just like he is now—Joe the mean parent keeping his boy in a room—a precondition Huddy should've thought of first. He looks up and nods. "When we get to the shop, when I'm on lookout, I'm watching him."

"Watch everything."

Joe shakes his head. "Harlan . . ." But it's too much at once and he can't figure out what part to bury. "He'll just run his mouth. 'You remember this?' No. No, Harlan, I don't. My whole life, what I remember—work. Twelve years old. Changing truck tires. Fifteen years old. Mowing. Pulling weeds with a butter knife. 'Cause some customer don't want no weed-killer and I don't care if she pays extra." Joe turns and leaves the front room to go deeper into the house, which means he's fixing to walk with Huddy into hers, and Huddy follows him into his office, where there's a briefcase atop the desk. "How we doing this?"

"The money?" Huddy asks. "Hundred-dollar bills."

"How we *bringing* it?"

"In a cotton sack."

"Do me a favor with jokes."

"A *business* envelope, okay? Three of 'em."

"Mine's in the case."

Huddy gestures at the desk. "I seen that."

"You wanna put yours in mine? Maybe it looks more right that way."

But—but Huddy doesn't like Joe ordering an arrangement he agrees with.

"My case, but you're holding it," Joe says.

Which is better, Huddy guesses, but Joe's still carrying instructions. "Hey," Huddy says, but he can't think of how to get in charge. He slips his cash out of his envelopes while Joe clicks the clasps and spins the case around to Huddy to consolidate. Fifty grand meets fifty grand—even money, but it ain't. Huddy sees the difference when the case opens and he compares the halves. The same denominations but Huddy's stacks are wrapped in rubber bands, while Joe's are held with bank straps, and Joe's money is new—must have requested fresh bills—crisp and edged and tight, while Huddy's stacks are thick and round, dirty and oily and finger-marked. "Looks like our money don't match," he says.

Joe shakes his head. "You got fifty K?"

"Yep."

"Matches fine," Joe says. "Money's money."

"I've always said that, what's green is green." Huddy got dressed up, laundered his shirt, but forgot to clean his cash. His hundreds look like more, but a messy more, taking up too much space to be worth the same small. Who cares, Huddy thinks, some high-low split with both players getting the pot. U.S. mint meeting city ghetto, and he unites them by sliding his commerce under.

"I don't want to go over there holding anything," Joe says, and he holds his hands up and away. "I ain't a builder, developer. Just someone from Old Germantown talking old times. Flowers and horses, right? That's my specialty. That's what I'm hoping she sees."

"What *you* hoping?"

And Joe considers, his eyes squinting, a fishing expedition that comes up empty. He checks his watch, some schedule they're late for, and Huddy follows him to leave and sees Joe's right arm push out against the air before he reaches the door and yanks it. He hustles outside but at the pavement's edge he turns back. "Weeds growing up through the floor. That's what I want to see there." Then he hurries around the front of the truck to the passenger side and flicks out his fingers, his chin pushing Harlan to slide over in the seat and be the one between. And Huddy takes the shorter walk to the wheel.

Quick travel, the directions a reversal from hers to Joe's before, this time starting out from Joe's rich neighborhood and passing other subdivisions of same-size residences and equal acreage and stick-treed greenery, and then cutting across a commercial dividing line and then an old railroad depot before houses resume, remote and neighborless, the yards loosening into deep fields and forest. Huddy is the only one to find this place, his two passengers first-timers to where they're heading. Nothing happens until he moves the three there. Harlan begins to speak but Joe's body jackknifes, so Harlan's mouth shuts and the only noise on the grand tour is Joe's angry breaths.

Huddy turns left into the driveway, both sides of the lane tree-lined and the road inclining so you feel you're going up into them. He parks and Joe hops out and Harlan slides over to go next. "Sit tight," Huddy says.

Joe shuts his door without looking back and Huddy steps away on his side, closes his cab door, leans in the window to peer at Harlan.

"Sure thing, boss," Harlan says and nods, but Huddy knows he's being seen with a black hat. "I'll wait for the signal."

"Should only take minutes. Three of us is too much, make her nervous."

"Say hello to the horses," he says, and his eyes fall to the floor.

"They's gone."

"Well, whatever's inside, then. You best catch up before he kicks in the door."

Huddy looks across the windshield to see Joe angling ahead but slowly, some investigator combing the grounds for clues, and Huddy the jailer about to grab the keys but then leaving them for Harlan to get radio.

He joins Joe and feels not disloyal to what's behind him but disciplined to what's ahead. He feels lighter, even with the weight of the case a small stone in his hand, or maybe because of it, too, and Huddy knows Joe was right to control it this way, to limit Harlan, to draw up a line that Huddy told Harlan not to trespass. Joe not advising now but Huddy listening if he does.

Back on the doorstep but this time with a brother beside him, the other not belonging. Joe tucks his shirt inside his cinched pants, his chest expanding, then tugs the shirt away from his skin. He combs his hand through his hair, and his head bobs a nod and Huddy steps forward and presses the bell, steps away, waits for the door to open for business. He follows Joe's eyes as they sweep across the façade and then turn to study the pillars up and down. "Like what you see?"

"Yep," Joe says, chin jutting. "Paint's peeling."

Huddy glances up at the balcony and sees paint pecked away from a second-floor shutter. Down at his feet, the cement of the porch step is cracked but also broomed clean. He hears the door open and he knows it will be the son materializing, which lifts Huddy to see what's there before it emerges, Kipp again, identical and advantaged, but maybe smaller, a houseboy on this second day, standing on a higher stair, but his eyes lowered to the cashbox. He smiles at Huddy, and Harlan's probably watching the trio merge hands. The truck in the driveway as if it drifted down a channel and Huddy landing ahead on this platform, where he's supposed to be and deserves. "My brother Joe," Huddy says and smiles back at Kipp for being only a doorman and not an attorney.

He steps in first, but his thoughts are behind him to what Joe's seeing but not as far as to what disappeared upward for Harlan. Going through the big rooms, the wide rectangles and long corridors, but Joe eyeing a different shape and design to things, trying to figure out how in late age you maintain all this. No signs of ruin or weeds sprouting, like Joe hoped, but Huddy now seeing in the yesteryear fixtures and furnishings some neglect—a dim chandelier with two bulbs not changed, a grandfather clock showing the wrong hour. Same wallpaper ungluing and above a chipped ceiling. The king-size grand piano and then they pass along the hallway, where Huddy views the close-up poses of the first family, of early kin and clan once here, young smiling faces on summer lawns and bodies adorned in formal suits and gowns, charmed circles grouped around white tablecloths, and the one person who remains here to gaze at her dressed-up relatives—this first lady now like the final chaperone of the dinner dance. An old woman in an older house, like centuries adding up.

Back to the hunt room, where he spots the widow same as last time rising, but now stiffer as if overnight she's been hurt, the chair arms like crutches to steady her standing. Huddy about to introduce when a voice nudges, "I'm Joe, Huddy's brother," and he watches a welcome hand extend quick and direct to meet, and Huddy smiles inside and shakes his head inward, too, at the way his own name was called and how it took Joe near fifty years to turn family man.

"Hi," Huddy says. If he were wearing the black hat Harlan's seeing, he'd cup it humbly in his hand.

She offers them drinks and Joe accepts and only after does Huddy see the full pitcher already set on a silver tray.

"Thank you," Huddy says, the glasses filled generously and passed and set down on horse-jockey coasters, and he wonders if Joe saw the pitcher or if he sniffed out the mint leaves the instant he stepped in, if he knew where to look or how to smell. She waves her hand at seats and takes hers, the same laced fingers resting on her lap. Four bodies arranged in a horseshoe ring, the brothers sharing the couch and the mother and son in facing chairs, and Huddy stares outside, at the horseshoe flower beds, which he realizes now are shaped that way, like being with Joe helps him decipher or maybe it's just being here twice. He turns back to inside, to the shelves and walls lined with horse heads and harnesses and a hitching post beside the foxhunt fire screen. Then he looks at Joe's profile, his eyes paying no mind to these objects, as if they were mere clutter or souvenirs to what he didn't collect or wouldn't profit from. He scrutinizes the architecture, assesses the borders and trims and moldings, then cuts along the walls and floor to study how the room was framed. "This is beautiful wood."

"Why, thank you," she says.

"Heart pine," Joe nods, and he lays his hand on the flooring.

"What did you call it?"

"Heart pine. Center of the wood."

"What a lovely word," she says, and Huddy watches a smile pull across her face. "Heart pine."

Joe nods and sips first. "Was it cut from out here?" he asks, and Huddy wonders if that's just an excuse to survey the land he wants to grab and scoop up, Joe's mind dividing the earth and racking up wealth, and Huddy figures he'll look out there, too, at the same unending hereafter.

"Well, I don't believe it was," she says, and Huddy looks at Kipp, who looks outside for cut pine. He shrugs when he doesn't see a mill or stacked logs.

"You don't find this wood available anymore," Joe says. "This is old-growth pine. You can tell by the growth rings."

"Well, you see the dogwoods," she says. "Mama planted those.

And that little Christmas tree is a giant redwood. Whoever lives here a hundred years from now can enjoy it." She pauses, the silence like a sigh, then mentions another family tree, how the yard man cut it wrong so the limbs don't go to the bottom. "It stands like a tree, but it's not supposed to."

"It'll fill in," Joe assures.

"Yes, in time, it will."

"But I know what you mean," Joe says. "The water garden I built at my place, I had to supervise every stone."

"Yes, your bother mentioned you had one," she says, nodding at Huddy. "It's hard to get good help."

Huddy settling back, happy to stay at the margins. The son has already answered yes, and the widow mixing with Joe keeps the answer there, like Joe keeping Harlan in the truck. Huddy imagines Harlan seeing the big yard and barn and knowing it's just two brothers feeding at the trough, and Huddy listens to Joe switch from trees to vines to flowers, talking about the irises and the azalea and crape myrtle, sounding as native as the plants, his eyes shining like he's not just admiring this place but remembering it. Remember when we played horseshoes, Huddy? Remember when daddy would cut the hay and we watched him bring it in? He sure loved to go out in the hayfield.

"It's beautiful land," Joe says, and the flattery doesn't surprise Huddy, but his feelings do, like Joe's not just talking about some green future but a past he hopes just as much to build—building fifty homes but finding one, too. Maybe those teenage years Joe was away he was sneaking into this pasture, camping out. Or maybe he dreamed about here when he was home.

"Thank you. It does need attention."

"Would that be a meadowbrook?" Joe asks, and Huddy doesn't

even know what that means, but he looks outside for water. Is there a pond here, too?

"A meadowbrook?" she says. "No." And Joe hesitates and, for an instant, he's found out, some loanword he got caught borrowing, and Huddy looks to Joe, who looks slight, sitting on the couch like he's standing small or fell through it, and Huddy stares outside to help but he can't locate where they're talking. "The meadowbrook is around the other side," she says, and Huddy guesses it's carriages. There's one on the near side of the barn. "I believe we are seeing a governess," she says, her response upbeat, as if you could never be certain of such things, a governess and a meadowbrook are such look-alikes, but what a challenging identity game it is trying to tell them apart from this distance.

And Joe squints back outside, as if it were just his eyes deceiving.

"The meadowbrook is driven in the horse show by a little Welsh pony," she says, as if Joe was right to talk about the one carriage even if he should've named the other.

"My wife has taken an interest in horses," he says, and Huddy thinks he's lying and he'd like to say it right now.

"Well, I'll tell you. To see horses grazing is just so calming. They're not like cats that want to curl around your legs. You can just love them at a distance."

And then Joe compliments the barn, and names it, calls it a pole barn or a pull, Huddy isn't sure, but the widow hasn't heard either because she's inside her head, contemplating horses or meadow-brooks or other loved ones, and Joe's word has leaked out at the wrong time and he can't say it again because Kipp is nodding, even if he doesn't know which word if any is right.

"I went to the first Germantown Horse Show," she says, "before it was called the Charity Horse Show. It was hosted at the football field of the high school, and they gave the overhead stadium lights to the football team, so I guess it was a charity even when it wasn't called one."

Joe must have been reading manuals on barns and carriages while Huddy hustled up his dirty cash. What Huddy'd like to tell the moneyed members is how much money is dirty. He could tell it to Harlan, Harlan would appreciate this fact, but Huddy remembered a cop saying if you sent a sniffer dog into any bank vault, they could smell out the drug money. Trace of cocaine, whatever. It's there, in every bank. Huddy forgets what the percent of the money was, that the cop told him was always there.

"That's a lovely board fence," Joe says.

Look what he knows. Not the carriage, Huddy thinks, although he sort of does, but everything else, the barn, the fence, the flowers, the trees, and probably every blade of grass and how they get hit by horse feet or darkened when the bodies leap over.

"The gates are in need of repair," she says. "But I suppose there's not much point in fixing, with the horses away now."

"You sure can't tell from here. But I'd be happy to do that, if you wanted." And he shrugs easily. Joe is here to buy the property and push it around with a bulldozer, but right now he's a preserver of the integrity of the land and what's man-made upon it. A healer come to mend and restore what's broken, and not to subdivide and chop. It's one thing to hide what you are. It's another to stand for its opposite.

"Are you in the building trade?"

"I am," he says and then turns away as if he's been immodest to say so, and nods at Huddy. Maybe he just spoke some marked words he forgot to mention being a tip-off. Sure thing, Huddy thinks.

Time to buy in. Huddy on the couch like he's hiding in a hole, but now he and the money won't be shy.

"We're ready to load up today," he says. "Has anyone removed anything?" And he looks Kipp square in the eye.

"Nobody's touched a thing."

Huddy nods and gently clears a space on the table, pushes a horse book aside to set down the case, and Kipp grabs a stack of magazines and places them on the shelf under.

"We agree on the list," Huddy says. "The price. I'm ready to count." The clasps click open, too loudly, like a malfunction. Huddy feels even with the money tucked in a case, being shown in a back chamber of this house, in a house set back from an exclusive street, a street so separate from the city, he could never be discreet enough.

"Kipp," the widow says, and her brow knits as if she's recalled some item of the family budget that doesn't add up, and Huddy thinks, There it goes. She may have traded in her horses, but she's still a horse trader. "What . . ." she says. "What was the gun that Pete wanted?"

"We already done that, mama." And he nods back at Huddy, and Huddy dips his hand in and distributes the cash, the stacks like bricks building out a row.

"Let's count along together," Huddy says. And Huddy counts out a thousand, and Kipp repeats the number, and Huddy says, "Agreed," and Kipp nods, and Huddy counts again and again till they reach ten thousand and he says the number and Kipp repeats it, and they push the stack aside. Counting thousands ten times and Huddy says, "Ten thousand," and Kipp nods and Huddy waits till he says it aloud, and then Huddy pushes the stack. Back and forth from Joe's paper down to Huddy's and back up again, and when the counting ends, Huddy knows what Kipp's gaining, even more to his inheritance, but he's unsure what her earnings mean.

The sellers in his store, the money's a magnet, but he's not there and she's not them, and she hasn't looked yet, just glancing warily around the room at her horse museum, the transaction sitting in her mind between a prize and a bribe. What Huddy would tell her is it's nothing suspicious, nothing smuggled in. Just the price of what's being offered, a rate of over a dollar a day for your entire laughing life. You could live near forever and still make that dollar. A never-ending allowance, a lifetime of pin money, so how could you call what he's done underpaying? How could his payment ever be low? Finally, she looks down, her eyes skimming the surface, a certificate she already possesses, a familiar skin. But then her brow unlines and she blushes. And almost laughs. And Huddy can't blame her. It's fun to look at. "My," she says.

When they step outside, the truck is gone. Until they look hard to the right and see it, pulled close to the house and turned around, the front of the truck now streetward. Harlan is in his middle seat like he'd paid a driver or like the vehicle backed itself in.

"We don't need a signature?" Joe asks.

"She's out of the picture. Got her money. I'll have her sign the list, if you want, after we take the guns." Huddy shrugs about a bill of sale, looks back at the house. "You had a good talk. Made a real connection."

"Connection?" His eyes narrow at Huddy. "You got no idea what connected is out here. I rubbed shoulders for fifteen minutes. If our granddaddy had hobnobbed with her daddy in one of them pictures, one of those grand old men on horses. Sitting around at the polo club. *That's* connected. You think having money gets you in? Money don't get you invited. And it's invitation-only."

"Joe, I'm just telling you what I seen. You did it perfect."

"Yeah?" And his face is open like a kid's.

"You bet. Two of you done walked a nature trail together." Huddy smiles and Joe smiles and they're sharing something mutual.

"You think she's selling?" Joe asks, almost mumbling it, and Huddy's surprised to be the one asked.

"Maybe," he says. "Maybe she don't know yet."

"That's typical," Joe nods. "You gotta talk them out of their property. Let's go get our guns." And he smiles again and Huddy's glad to hear such happy music.

They get Harlan from the truck and Huddy swings up the gate and the three walk to the garage, the door already opened, the middle car backed out to widen the lane for carrying.

"Kipp, this is Harlan," Huddy says, and he figures if he says both names, he can skip namesake. They shake hands and then Kipp moves back to the false-fronted door opening to the safe door, which leads to the gun room.

"I'll leave y'all alone in there," Kipp says, and he steps off to the side, and Huddy nods and brings his brothers through and waits for their reactions.

He watches Joe study the contents. He doesn't know guns, so maybe it's weight and what the truck's axle can handle. And Harlan's acting low-key and natural and then he says, "All of it?" and Huddy says, "Just the guns," and Harlan looks at his brothers and says, "Damn." Then he says, "You pay in Confederate money?" And he laughs and they both smile, but Huddy's not happy and not yet breathing because the guns are still here and not in his shop and he wants to move them so fast he'd throw them in the truck naked if they wouldn't bruise.

"We gonna load real neat here," Huddy says, his fingers tapping the air. "Joe, we got packing blankets in the back. Lay one down on the floor, and when you put the guns on top, space 'em out. Don't want nothing touching. Let's go ten across. You make a layer, throw another blanket over, make another layer. You making lasagna. Stagger the second layer of guns in over the first so they're not on top of each other." But then he thinks it's too much, and shakes off the last part. "Forget it, don't need to stagger. Just, no bruising, no rubbing." He turns to Harlan. "You carrying two at a time. One in each hand. No cradling. When we're done with the long guns, bring the crates from the truck. We'll take the pistols out in those." Huddy's got his list and his pen ready for checking, but he worries about the widow upstairs staring outside, finding a loophole, and the son lurking nearby, and there's too much of Huddy's payday in two guns, so he hustles over and picks the Henry and the Yellow Boy and they're coming out now.

"I thought you said I was carrying," Harlan says.

"I'm showing you. Just follow orders."

"I am."

"Don't talk neither!"

And Huddy rushes through the garage where Kipp is gone and he gets the cases he brought for rare guns, and sets the rifles inside, and walks them into the far interior of the truck. Buries a blanket over 'em. Then he steps out of the bed and hurries back to the gun room. Joe looks him over and says, "You alright?"

"Just get to the truck," Huddy says, and he points Harlan over to the first rack. "Grab two. Show 'em so I can read the serial numbers off the receiver. When I ID it off the list, you git."

Guns going out in twos, and when Huddy finishes with twenty, he steps outside to see, the butts of the rifles nicely spaced and stacked. He nods at Joe, whose shirt is untucked and his face looks warm and bothered, but Joe brushes him back to the room and Huddy goes there to get Harlan to bring more out. Huddy checking the list and Harlan doing his job right, reading off the guns and saying nothing else, moving down the gun line and in and out of the room, until he looks back at the empty rack where Huddy's first two came from.

"Something wrong with your eyes?" Huddy says.

"Nothing wrong, boss."

"Next two are right in front of you. You already passed that spot, so why you looking there?"

"No reason."

"What is it, Harlan? You wanna know what's special? You wanna know what I'm treating personal? Are you fucking kidding me? If Joe knew I was talking to you right now. This is *all* special. So don't look around for the one special thing to fuck up."

"Relax, man."

"When you get to the truck, bring the two crates sitting to the left."

Harlan leaves and Huddy walks over to the pistols cabinet and swings the glass door open. He hears Harlan returning with the crates and Huddy meets him halfway, grabs the top one from his arms and carries it to the pistols. He flips the crate and dumps the socks out. "One pistol per sock. Half of these should fit in a crate."

Harlan nods and looks back at the cabinet but doesn't move.

"What?"

"I guess you ain't gonna let me spin these things." Harlan eyes the first-generation Colt, and his face is serious because he knows the collection is, too.

"Not today. Couple days, I might let you have your cowboy moment."

"This man had some taste," Harlan says. "Sure treated himself right."

So Huddy whistles with Harlan for a bit, and when he's finished slipping the pistols in the socks and bunching the socks in the crate, he lifts one crate and Harlan the other and that's it, a gun room without guns, no reason to be here, and Huddy looks at the display photos of Yewell and he won't say goodbye because he's taking him with the guns. He'll say goodbye to her, though, but when he rings the doorbell and sees Kipp, he knows she won't, 'cause she's done with the meeting. He hands Kipp the list and tells him where she should sign, right below where Huddy's written, PAID IN FULL. SOLD TO HUDDY MARR. And Huddy waits at the door, watches the traffic on Dogwood. One car, then another, then a third speeding to catch up to the second or get away from what's behind. Kipp returns and Huddy's about to mention the ammo in the garage, in case she didn't know and wanted it out of the house. He could pick that up later and take it off her hands, but he figures Joe's the one that needs to come back, so he'll let his brother have his future day. Today is his own.

The packing looks good. The blankets are stacked high and the guns secured inside, ready to float to the shop. He steps into the cab and he can feel the extra weight, the load sinking the brothers lower in the truck. Harlan wipes his brow, and Joe's sweating fierce, red skin like he's been under the sun.

"Everyone good?" Huddy asks.

"Our brother here," Harlan says, "he breathing on one lung."

Huddy looks at Joe, who glances at his watch as if to read not a schedule but a pulse.

"Well, that part's done," Huddy says, but they're only halfway there, and he wishes it was Sunday morning or early on any other day, but if he can't get the timing perfect for part two, at least they can go in quiet.

"I'd hate to get stopped for a ticket right now!" Harlan says.

All the guns in the back, might as well bring out what's in front. Huddy reaches over, opens the glove box and pulls out two holstered pistols. Drops one in each brother's lap. Harlan swivels in the seat to strap the belt on, but Joe frowns at what's been placed there. He shakes his head, his brow creasing. Three baby brothers playing with cap guns. Then he unsnaps the holster, slides the pistol out and holds it in his hand. He blinks hard, clenches his jaw to strengthen.

Huddy drives west but feels like he's driving south, out of the leafiest street of leafy Germantown and shiny tall properties to low-slung homes and gray, broken buildings, deserted or looking so with switched-off neon, and down to his store, which feels like all the way to the bottom. Huddy's prepped his gun locker and his storage room, cleared space on his stout shelves, squeezing TVs and tools together or just dumping equipment on the ground. Tight space, but it'll fit. It's not late but the sky changed hours ago, pitch-dark by the time Huddy pulls into the lot—the Dumpster company has pulled the debris Dumpster from the blood bank, replaced it with a fresh one—and around the back, the lights sweeping across the weeds, the truck beeping in reverse like a distress call, a wake-up for the thieves. He backs in close, shuts the engine and the damn beeps.

"Let's go. Offload quick, no noise." He steps out, slides the gate up, grabs the top blanket.

The only different position is Huddy switching rooms. He stands by the empty shelves, waits for Harlan to come to him with guns. "Set them here," Huddy says, and he pats the blanketed shelf. "Don't stand 'em. You stand 'em, they'll fall." Harlan going the opposite way now, walking off empty-handed. If Huddy didn't need to do the load-in fast, he'd have sectioned his room, not just clearing shelves but setting up special areas for special guns. Group the '94s on a rack, put the regular guns with the general population. He'll untangle it all later. Tomorrow he'll sift 'em out.

He hears the gate slam behind the wall and before long Harlan walks in with the two cases, and Joe follows behind. Joe looks around and wants to but won't talk.

"Harlan," Huddy says, "go back to the truck."

"It's empty."

"I know," Huddy says, and waits for Harlan to know, too.

He throws up his arms, an angry customer who can't scratch up gas money, and leaves. And Huddy feels bad. He doesn't mean to treat Harlan like the village idiot, but right now he's not us.

Joe glances at the shelves and then down at the cases. "Who you gonna sell 'em to?"

"Don't know yet. Cowboy Hall of Fame."

"You serious?"

Huddy shrugs, "Just about."

"So what's next?"

"Got twenty-four hours to log 'em in. Which I'll try my best. But I ain't worried. ATF, they understand slow, but they don't understand mistakes. It's what I *do* log in that I gotta make sure is right. You put a dyslexic serial number in your book, you write something on the wrong line. You don't abbreviate Tennessee right." Huddy shakes his head. "You gotta be careful. We don't want ATF in here, because they'll find errors, double errors. They'll find a thousand things wrong."

"So be careful."

"Always am."

"And quick?"

"Yeah, I can do both. What'll help with quick is a second person for the log-in. You want it to be you or Harlan? Your call. Just walking the guns to me, reading off the info."

Joe nods. "Harlan can do it. And then you start selling?"

"Yep. Get 'em tagged, get 'em sold." And Huddy snaps his fingers. Sell the guns and get yours and mine and throw myself a goodbye party.

Harlan brings a gun and reads it and Huddy writes the specs in the book, the manufacturer and the model and the serial number and the action type and the caliber. The date and source are easy because they're all one thing. Huddy says the serial number back to Harlan, and Harlan says it again, so Huddy's having Harlan check with four eyes. The log-in can go fast, but the tagging is slower, because Huddy's gotta price 'em and every once in a while consult the blue book to make sure he knows how.

"These ain't your rock-low prices," Harlan says, reading off an inventory tag.

"I guess it's a new day in the pawn business. I'm going high-end now. And that's all I'm saying." A pawnbroker who for six months gets to sell more than pawnshop guns.

"Why ain't you tagging that AK?" Harlan asks, nodding at the gun that Huddy's set aside. What Huddy won't say is he's not tagging it because he didn't catch the extra notch on the selector switch when he bought the 47, and when he brought it here. Thought it was semi-auto, like the two others, but now he's examined it close-up and it's a Vietnam bringback and it's full. Doesn't know if it was Yewell's mistake or his, so easy to miss a third notch, but he doesn't have a license for full-auto, and he's not gonna take the time to get it, just eat the loss. Might as well drop the machine gun in the Mississippi, because he can't sell it and won't keep it here. And he won't call ATF to come get it, because they won't go away. Been a few years since he's been audited, so if Huddy hands 'em the AK, they'll say thanks for turning this in, and they're smiling but they're not coming in as friends, so now they'll ask to see his gun book, and now's not the time for that. What he says to Harlan is, "Just bring me the next gun."

"Sure thing," Harlan says, and he does. But then he says, "What you think can fool you more, a woman or a gun?"

"I don't know, Harlan."

"I think a woman can fool you, but a gun can't."

"You do, huh?"

"Why, you don't?"

"I think it's both. I think, with guns and people, if it's bad on the outside, it's bad inside."

"And what about if it's good?"

Huddy calling the collectors whose specialty overlaps with Yewell's, and even others who don't want the same thing but might buy for trading material because they know someone who does. Huddy talking, "Thought you might want to have first swat at this," and taking pictures and zapping them over email, reading classifieds in *Shotgun News* and gunbroker.com, and registering for the big gun show in Oklahoma City next month, which he knows will be a prime mover.

"How many you sell?" Joe says on the phone, and it's only been days.

"What?"

"You making my money back yet?"

"Can't start selling the guns for thirty."

"You said you'd make my money *back* in thirty."

"I'm lining up the sales. Calendar hits day thirty—boom."

"You were saying fast money."

"Thirty is fast."

"Huddy, I need that money now. I need the profit now!"

"What are you talking about?"

"Where do you think my cash came from? You think it's just reserves?"

"It was bank money."

"That's right. But not a savings account, if that's what you mean. That money was borrowed. Theirs, not mine. Took it out on a construction loan."

"Well, how the fuck would I know that? I don't know about your business. I don't know about your life." But as soon as Huddy says it, he realizes he's starting to, that the life and the business are all mixed up, one tangled-up fund.

"You saying you're betting everything. You saying you all in. Well, I'm *always* all in. My lots are sitting. And I'm paying interest on 'em. So stop sitting on the guns."

I'm not sitting, Huddy thinks. I'm only doing what's legal. He looks over at Harlan, whose mouth is open to understand.

"Where you at?" Christie asks, staring hard at Huddy, who's staring at the prongs of his fork, at the sliver of meat.

Huddy looks up from his plate to see a pointed finger twitching in a line to find him. "You trust Harlan?" he asks her.

"'Course not."

"Why's that?"

"When you ever trust him? Ain't saying he done nothing when he was here."

"When was he here?" Huddy wondering when his brother came from all the way out.

"What are you talking about? When he crashed."

"What—who are you . . . you talking about Harlan?"

"That's who you asking about."

"I'm saying *Joe*."

"No you—"

"I meant Joe."

"Well, Joe. He a different person. From Harlan."

"The person I talked to today—Joe—he was different. Different Joe." And a lot like Harlan. 'Cause, it turns out, neither brother been playing pay-as-you-go. Always knew Harlan would play like that, but now he's learned it about Joe, just on a higher debt level.

"Wouldn't trust him, if I was married to him," he hears Christie say. "I mean, seems like he's always in a fix with his wives. Kind of slippery that way. But you ain't married to him."

Not married, but still hitched, Huddy thinks. And what he sees on the video, when he comes in next morning and sees the two cases from his secure back room gone, is a brother. Not Harlan, although Huddy thought it might be. Harlan with his hands on every other piece, had to pinch his fingers against the cased two. Two Harlans, both inside the store at different times, one here now, one last night. But instead of Harlan, it's the other—inside the tape, inside the store, Joe's store, but he ain't a picklock because he has the keys, and he ain't a burglar because he owns the building, and he ain't even a thief when he's stealing from a deal where the first money was his. Huddy watches Joe stab his key into the gun locker, like some after-hours workout, watches him walk inside and disappear and reemerge with the cases. It feels like watching a body scan, Huddy's own X-ray, the key cutting through layers of his skin, the guns two bones Joe was carrying out. Harlan hears Huddy cursing and asks, "What?"

"Come here, Harlan," Huddy says. "I wanna show you what a bank run looks like." Let's bring my bad brother over here to show him what the good brother's done. Let's make it so all three brothers are here.

Ten

NOT JOE AT THE door and Huddy'd like to push past her to get to him, the same way Joe cut straight through his shop, but instead he says, "Evening." When he rang the bell, he wanted to ring it over and over, the noise repeating, until a body appeared in the doorway with their hands held to their ears. "Need Joe," Huddy says, and Lorie stares at Harlan beside him, Harlan not an onlooker stuck in back now but up front in the door light with his brother, the two of them lined up tight together.

Huddy watches her mouth move to tell them he isn't here, but she's not used to this lie. "Okay," she says, and her mind searches for a problem at home. Then she smiles, a smile Huddy takes as, You brothers keep pestering at night with your games, but it's time to stop. "He's busy with the garden."

Huddy shrugs. Guess there won't be a tray with drinks. "Won't take long," he says simply. "Need to ask something." Just, *Where are they?*

"That right?" she says, but it's not a question, and Huddy sees her head shake a little because he should know he's an intruder and doesn't belong here.

"Yep," Harlan says, "something he done to Huddy."

Which is okay, Huddy knew he was bringing Harlan's mouth,

didn't bring him for quiet, and he figures he'll match his voice. "Need to ask about some guns," Huddy says, and talking too much feels better.

"Guns?" she says, her voice scraped with fear. Her eyes shift to Harlan. She touches her neck. Her cheeks flush like makeup smudging, her mouth opens in a puncture.

"His and mine," Huddy says, pointing inside the house and then turning the finger around on himself. "Not us," and he flicks his finger between Harlan and him. "Me and Joe's guns. Our guns."

He didn't ring the doorbell repeatedly, but now he's got a better alarm, a word that for her is both warning and warfare. He watches her eyes blink.

"I'm just here to help patch things up," Harlan says, grinning.

A gun: not just harmful but criminal, a shot and the blood spray and a splayed body dead on the floor. Their hands are empty, but she worries what arms they're concealing beneath. Nowhere for her to look off or see past, the two of them filling the doorway, Huddy feels like bringing Harlan is like bringing a crowd, not just a second man but others added onto him, midnight prowlers circling the house, hugging the corners and dark walls—that's what her scared face tells him, no word or sound coming out of it.

"You want us to wait here?" and then the memory of Joe, his keys in hand to let himself in, and forget about permission and the proper time to enter when Joe's already barged through. Huddy had only seen the video once but Harlan watched all morning, rewinding it in a loop and doing play-by-play, "Here he is at the counter and where'd he go and now he's back with presents. Now *that's* the way to shop." The camera catching Joe's wrist and the Rolex he took years ago, as if he'd worn it last night to justify his claim—and so Huddy, when he saw Joe's stride without a pause or second thought, would understand Joe was acting ordinary, doing what he'd always done with valuable possessions and therefore regular and right, the guns just another giveaway. Huddy leans close, puts his hand on the door and says, "Let's all go. Me, you, and Harlan." The way he buried Harlan at Yewell's, kept his name down, too, but resurrecting him now. He claps Harlan's shoulder. She hesitates, eyeing them like thieves or thugs who whisper their crooked plans at her door, when it's what's behind her that helped himself and stole. Her suspicion and fear pleases and angers Huddy, but Joe isn't worried, or else he wouldn't be back there letting her play doorman. Huddy didn't call him today, because he wanted to read his expression—plus Huddy needed time to change the locks and the code.

She retreats and he steps forward to find. Inside the house, his eyes searching the belongings and the rooms, but he won't detect and recover what's half his. No changed arrangement, the same clean order not affording any clues—he'd ransack and dismantle the furnishings, overturn cushions, tear out linings, but Huddy knows Joe stored the cases better—so he's just walking in to go out again, sliding the glass door to set out for Joe. Can't win hide-and-seek with the guns, but he'll win against Joe. Huddy sights him in the middle distance beyond the pool, but not far off and unseen like before in a back corner. Still obscured by interlocking branches, but they're only part of what's screening him. Joe looks crouched, lower, as if he'd taken cover in the bushes, or sunk in a bunker or burrow, and then Huddy remembers the pond and realizes he's inside the water. They march toward him, past the pool and its green glow, and Huddy grinds his teeth because he doesn't have a jackhammer to break up the ground. Filing through the garden path, his prior footsteps retraced, and what was special at first visit is familiar on return. This big spread smaller for seeing the vastness at Yewell's, even if the land between Joe and Huddy was still large and his envy was the same or grown. The blooming flowers, once bright and bunched straight, now paler and wilting. Petals of dying colors, limbs half-bare and some leafless, but the trees aren't cleared—Huddy swats at a branch that nearly brushes his face, snaps a stick under his foot, which stops her, and she turns back and he sweeps his hand at the ground as if he were confused by the breaking noise, and she turns forward and quickens her step, to keep ahead and away and escape to Joe, her shoulders stiffening so her body looks frail, and Huddy's happy to tail faster. He hears Harlan kick gravel behind him. Sees boulders that he'd like to roll free in a rockslide. Hears his own feet crush along the footpath. Crossing the bridge, the thin stream flowing underneath, the path curving and Huddy wishes he had a blade to hack through the brush and make his own short way instead of following the snake-lines Joe ordered and angled.

"Joe!" Lorie calls out, her voice tensed with fear but also open-ing into anger, a better method to hail Joe's attention, not to cry his name but curse it. Huddy advances to the water's edge to stand over Joe, in waders, knee-high in the water, the rest of him sticking up like a stalk, but after seeing the three approach, he won't quit working, too many things to do. Three five-gallon buckets of pea gravel, spaced three feet apart and running the length of the pond, PVC pipe driven down into the buckets, and Huddy not seeing a white flag flying from any pole. He stares downward at Joe, as he tests the buckets to make sure they're set stable. Behind him, the waterfall gushes on the stones.

"If you hiding," Harlan says, "you gotta go all the way under. You only half in."

But Joe ignores him. Harlan's been away three years and he'll disappear again, so Joe won't acknowledge him just to say farewell. Couple of years from now, he might sit back and remember what his brother was. As for Huddy, Joe's got no interest in explaining his day-old intent.

So Harlan tries again, because he's here, even if Joe pretends he's no one. "If it ain't Joe, then one of them fish swole up," he says. "Or maybe it's a turtle. It looks like a turtle but it's dressed like a duck."

Still a blind eye to Harlan, but he raises them to Huddy. Or maybe he's saying he can see Harlan through Huddy, as if one fell into the other, their lives mixed up and run together. *He's you and you him*, is what Joe's stare says, and Huddy thinks, He ain't me, I ain't two—and you ought stand there upside down. Not a turtle, not a duck, but maybe Joe's a bat that just needs a branch to dangle from. Huddy scans the bricks and the netting and the pipes and the hand truck holding the gravel bags. "I don't see a hook to pull you out."

"Joe," Harlan says, "why don't you come up to street level so we can talk?"

Come up from the pit, Huddy thinks, or I'm climbing down. Either way, you gonna listen.

But Joe stays busy. He wades forward to the edge and grabs the joist, two pieces joined in the middle with a T, with elbows at the outer ends. He carries it into the water, holding the long pole out like a tightrope walker, and positions the T-joint over the center post and taps it down with a rubber mallet. Then he steps lightly on the algae to do the same with the elbows, Huddy watching Joe assemble the beam like he's moonlighting in some underwater smith shop.

"I bet them rocks slicker than owl shit," Harlan says.

"Everything alright?" Lorie asks, her voice careful, her eyes quick and alert, and Joe laughs at her concern and at what's confronting him. Two against one, and the one defenseless in the water, but Joe's sure of his advantage, bringing Harlan is a tactic that hobbles Huddy, and strengthens Joe. Down in his hole like a ditcher, but his position always topmost.

"They taking up my time, so they must be here to help me." He glares at Huddy.

"Help you what?" Harlan says. "You been doing your work solo. 'Sides, what you on now, you a clamdigger?"

Lorie's puzzled face, every line of Harlan's a trick question, but when Huddy glances at Joe, he sees only certainty. Nothing wrong or off-limits with what happened or went missing, except Huddy screwed up by not opening the shop and holding the door for his spree.

"Leaves falling early this year," Joe says. "Gotta build my roof."

"They talking about guns," Lorie says. "What y'all involved in?"

"Collectibles," Joe says. "Huddy thinks they belong in a museum." He looks off, here and there, settles on some midpoint between the brothers. "And I think they belong elsewhere."

"What all's going on?" Lorie says, hands on her hips. "What is this business? And y'all need to finish it."

"Sure," Harlan says. "Where you want these bricks?"

"Do I need to call the police?" she says, and Huddy watches the word speed her nerves. "I'm calling. This is harassment."

"You don't call anyone," Joe says, and he gets out, the shallow water sloshing and breaking apart, dripping down upon the stones. Slips his gloves off his hands. "I'm gonna talk with Huddy about these souvenirs, and then we gonna roll out this net. That's it." The gloves slap on the ground. "They ain't here but to cover up my pond."

"We looking for a couple boxes," Harlan says.

"You settle this," she says.

"You ain't seen any new boxes, have you?" Harlan says again. "Hate to ask twice, but Huddy's business is *unsettled* until he finds them." Joe's eyes lock on Harlan. "Maybe you buried 'em," and Huddy looks at the tools and can't find a shovel.

"He your mouthpiece?" Joe says to Huddy. "He opens his mouth, you both sound stupid." Turns to Lorie. "We're good here," he says, and his chin raises to wave her off. She doesn't move, and he nods. "Go on back." She stays on Joe, then looks at Huddy, then almost to Harlan, and they wait for her to do what Joe tells, to leave them alone for the next part. Harlan smiles at her going away. "Don't you pick up the phone," Joe yells, which Huddy hears as the start of the next divorce, and they pause till she's halfway to inside, Huddy's eyes following, then narrowed at Joe. "I'm late putting up this net, and the leaves mess up the water's acidity. I put some salt in, to help the fish survive. Salt's good for the fish, but it can kill the plants. What helps one don't always help the other."

"Where are they?" Huddy says.

"You best not've come over here with him, thinking you getting something back."

"That's right," Harlan says. "Time to surrender what ain't yours."

"Yours?" Joe says, flicking out a wet arm. "You got nothing yours." He turns from Harlan, trades stares with Huddy. "Locked up."

"Already *were* locked up." And now they're gone. Behind some wall, or inside one. All the closed-off places that Joe owns and constructed. Houses and rooms and offices—locations high up and underground. "Two-way deal, remember."

"Two-way—sure. But I went first so you could go second. So more like one-two."

"Did you sell them? You best not sold 'em," Huddy says.

"That's the thing. I could've, right? Did some research. Turns out I don't need you to sell 'em. Don't need a license. Not if they're older than—what's the year?"

1898, but Huddy's not giving dates.

"You didn't tell me that, Huddy. All these fine points you made about how old and special they were. What'd you call 'em? Famous? Historical? This gun tied to so-and-so? But you should've just said they were antiques."

"So that's what this is? You take 'em 'cause of something I didn't tole you?" This sneak raiding the shop and he's telling me about lessons and secrets. Joe knew he'd be caught on video, but that still didn't make his act not a lie.

"Well, since we're sharing the whole truth," Joe says, "no, that's not it."

"You know shit about guns."

"What's to know? Bought 'em here. Sell 'em that way, too. I figure I can just go over to the Hunt & Polo Club and find a buyer. My banker, he collects guns. You said yourself—you never seen guns like these. Well, me neither. These guns are as far from you as they are from me. Except I live here."

"So you a gun dealer now? I'd suggest wearing one, if you are. And if someone breaks in here, you better show 'em more than your ADT license."

"You threatening?" Joe wiping a wet hand across his mouth.

Here we go, Harlan thinks, can't fight over guns without a gunfight. Two casualties in a duel, except the third brother would never know from the one brother where the guns are hidden, and he wouldn't know from the second what to look for. Unless they used the guns they're arguing over, ten paces and turn and draw and they both hit dead center—one-two—and drop and Harlan steps through the powder to pick up the pieces, the guns like blown-off bones from the bodies. Only right now, it's a standoff to be settled with fists, and Harlan's here to overwhelm, to turn a fight into a beating—not that he knows this from Huddy, Huddy didn't even say destination, but Harlan knew without word or signal what they were tracking down. Huddy's face red-hot, his clenched hands ready to sock hard at Joe's mouth, drop him to the ground or back undersea, but then he collects himself. He's wanted to wring some-body's neck every day of his pawnbroker life, had years of practice with restraint.

"Fine," he says, shoulders shrugging out a truce. Pulls back to a better punishment. "Go sell the guns. You do it right, they'll bring fifty thousand. And you better, 'cause your fifty's done. I'm doing the rest."

"Ain't." Joe frowns, looks dumbly at Huddy as if he'd already given this same answer and why can't Huddy get it? "That wasn't the deal."

"Wasn't the deal!"

"Deal was sell the guns and split the final number."

"That was before you took them pieces. Ain't halves anymore."

Harlan with zero, listening to his two brothers, two partners with equal portions arguing about equal shares, half and another half, and not a cut left over at the end.

"What I took was my collateral," Joe says.

"I told you, your collateral was me."

"You don't decide." Joe points and then his eyes shift two ways, to size up both of them. "And no brother is ever gonna be my collateral." He looks twice, face to face, his lips twisting in a sneer. "I'm holding these guns. Holding 'em 'cause I need more coverage than my collateral being you. What I got is first-dollar coverage. You want 'em back, start selling the others. The timetable is now. Or I'll close up the shop. What do I care? You must be crazy if you think I'm gonna invest fifty thousand dollars and have you tell me wait. You don't take my money and take charge. Fifty thousand, that buys me yes—and yes again. We still dividing the total. I gave you fifty 'cause I'm getting more. Never about breaking even. And don't tell me about no waiting period. It's over."

"Waiting is what's legal," Huddy says, but all Harlan's hearing is that thousands number Joe said and repeated, and Joe squints to see that line between what's legal and not.

"This thirty-day thing, it's a gray area. Postdate the damn sales."

Huddy shakes his head. This isn't collateral but blackmail. "ATF comes in when these guns are in my book sold—sold, but they're not in the store—I'm done."

Joe shrugs. What Huddy just said changes nothing. "You were the one that wanted to be a pawnbroker." His shoulders jump. "That's your problem."

Huddy thinks, He takes my guns, our guns, guns that were his and not his, mine and not mine, and now his expense is protected and I'm the only one risking penalty and loss. Took his part of the deal and now he's dealing me.

"My problem," Joe says, double-tapping his chest, "is I just finished this subdivision and the market bottoms out. Don't give me hypotheticals about how you might get hurt. ATF comes in, whatever. I'm getting hit right now. Interest bill due every month. Taxes due. Insurance. I got more problems than you. How about you, Harlan? What's your problem?" But Joe answers it himself— Harlan can't have a new problem when he's squandered his life from the beginning. Harlan's failure, it started too far back to remember. A long time ago, before adulthood, Harlan took some wrong turn, walked through some wrong door, and was done. Fell down in a ditch and the lid closed tight over him, and you could pry it open, but it's too late for saving, so why spend energy on a dead thing?

Harlan sees the wealth and the luxury and feels numberless. How is this hard times? "Man, I wish I could be *this* broke. All this, and you broke. *You*," Harlan says, and it sounds like not only a laugh against Joe, but a brag about himself, Joe fallen means Harlan's risen a level. If Joe is broke and so is Harlan, then all this bankrupt excess must be his somewhere, too. Or maybe Harlan's seeing a game of seesaw, if Joe goes all the way down, then Harlan must swing up.

"I ain't broke," Joe says.

"You're just leveraged," Huddy says.

"What's that?" Harlan says. "That mean you out of money? You talk to Huddy here, he come up with a payment plan. Or maybe you wanna liquidate some things. Sell these decorations. Sell or pawn, he'll set you up both ways."

Joe looks around, his eyes crossing the garden, lost in the path's windings. He squints at the big dimensions of the house, at the brick façade, then high up to the second story where the bedrooms blur in darkness. He shakes his head, bites his mouth. How did this happen? How did he get all the way out here only to be on the brink of where he started? Worked and overworked, drove hard and far on a self-made road that seemed straight and suddenly doubled back. "Highly leveraged," he says. "Full-bore taxes on completed homes that no one's buying."

"Filthy rich and dirty poor," Harlan says.

"You ain't been but one," Joe says, but it's a different sound, and Huddy's surprised to hear it sputter out from him, Joe's mouth a choked vent that won't fully open, or his anger too deep inside to get out clear and across to Harlan.

Huddy looks back at the house, doesn't see any boarded-up windows, just glass unbroken and clean. "Give me one now," Huddy says. "One of the two, and I'll start selling."

"You got plenty to sell," Joe says, his voice restored.

"It's about you taking what wasn't full yours."

"I already told you what it was. People like me are going *under*. People with more."

"And I'm telling you what it was, too. I know when my pocket's been picked." At the kitchen table, Joe's delayed thinking—it wasn't confusion but cunning. Huddy thought Joe couldn't read the gun list, but he was just scheming ahead to the timing of his con. "And I don't like this now-or-never shit. You talking like you bought me."

"I own the store. I bankrolled you—then and now. Propped this deal up till you got your half scraped together."

Huddy shakes his head, 'cause he is and *isn't* in Joe's pocket. He was, but he won't be. "We sat at your table and you worried over all the ways this deal could go wrong, and now you making it wrong."

Joe's shrewd face tells Huddy that he both agrees with him and who cares? "Sell twenty, you get one."

"Twenty to get one, twenty to get the other."

"Get the other at the end. A fair compromise. Which one you want first?"

"You pick," Huddy says, blank and neutral, both guns are his favorites, both are nothing, and Joe smiles at Huddy not naming the one or bluffing with the other. "Don't worry," Huddy says. "Whichever you keep is the one I'm wanting."

And Joe laughs into Huddy's dead stare. Then he checks his watch, gestures at the ground. "Like I told Lorie, y'all helping me with this net. Roll it out."

Harlan looks at Huddy, who shrugs yes, and Harlan shakes his head—came here to get payback and instead Joe gets helpers, free hands—and nudges the net with his foot. Joe grabs it himself and unfurls it more. They take positions, Harlan staying in place and Huddy moves away and Joe past him to the other side, so they stand around the ring, all gripping the edges of the net in their hands. Joe nods and they swing their arms and send the net floating and it settles down and catches on the beam. They bend and stretch the edges to the ground, the net tight and transparent, the water closed up but not disappeared beneath the scrim, like blood seen through skin.

"Don't pull too hard," Joe says, calling across. "Tension's gotta be just so. Harlan, you pulling too hard."

"I ain't."

Joe points at the peak. "You getting the pipe out of whack."

"Well, maybe that's a problem with the pipes. Maybe they sitting in the buckets weak."

"Gravel's stabilizing 'em," Joe says, slowly, and Harlan looks across the pond, then at Huddy, and Huddy reads the face: Does Joe ever stop telling what you done wrong? "Don't make me build my rafter again," Joe says. He walks to the brick pile near Harlan and stacks three and carries the stack to his side. He sets them on the ground, a small tower, and takes the top one and wraps the netting around it. "Every couple feet, roll the bricks up in the net."

Harlan tugs again and the brick at Joe's feet tumbles forward, teeters at the rim, like some clumsy trick where what's supposed to stay in place doesn't.

"You trying to hit my fish. I know you ain't trying to whack my koi."

"Checking how it holds up to wind," Harlan says. "Straight-line winds'll rip this thing right up. Take this whole thing off. Fish might blow up with it. Poor fish. They leaving the ground. They hearing that wind coming overhead and they eyeing the net and they know it ain't holding. Ain't trying to kill your fish, Joe. I'm trying to keep 'em alive."

And when the last brick's been rolled, the ends weighed down, Harlan reaches inside a gravel bag and picks a pebble and skips it at the net and the pebble bounces off the tented surface, lands somewhere else with a quiet tap. "Tension seems right," he says, which Joe ignores, a harmless throw, forgotten. He concentrates on the rigging, the buckets centered in the pond, the poles upright under the net, the bricks lining the rim. He frowns, frustrated but then pleased—whatever is wrong is just a minor nuisance or fault, like the cover's been put on backward when both sides fit.

And Huddy waits for the wind to come and shed leaves down upon them.

Eleven

HE GETS GOING, SETS up appointments. Chats over the phone about models and ranges of years, emails photos for first looks. The visits will be one at a time, two per day—a more crowded schedule will cause too many mistakes—ten or twelve guns displayed per dealer. Not gonna show everything to one and have his collection get creamed. The dealers can name their price, set their stakes, but Huddy won't let the game be dealer's choice. He's holding the guns and he'll watch their surprise that he's holding them, watch their hair stand up. They'll come looking for bargains, thinking Huddy specializes in lawnmowers and electronics and jewelry and guns and guitars and tools, and they're right, he can't know as much as the pros, can't have their knowledge, because he's never handled this kind of collection, but he knows enough of what he's got and what it ain't. No alterations, no re-bluing or re-wooding, no extra holes, nothing touched up and ruined. Nothing out of place with these guns, except for them being here. All these rare originals in a secondhand store. Never sold guns like these on Lamar, and the dealer's gonna think he's in Tulsa at a table at a major show, so they're both gonna feel elsewhere.

"I've always seen this gun at eight," the first dealer says, and Huddy thinks to point out the finish, but he nods, eight doesn't sting. Huddy shows twelve, the man wants all of them. Probably buy them to sell eleven and make enough to keep the twelfth. The man not blinking, so Huddy won't either. He makes his offer and Huddy pushes it up, and the man knocks it down a notch. Two happy hunters, so easy to sell real guns, the dealers bringing big cash to get 'em. Huddy's been grinding away all these years, hitting singles, and he'll never own this stuff again, but his consolation is a pile of money.

Harlan sees the cash get counted, sees Huddy's pocketbook getting thicker. He watches Huddy log out the first batch. "You ain't postdating 'em?" he asks, after the dealer departs.

"Why, 'cause Joe said to?"

Harlan shrugs.

"I entered *today* 'cause that's when they been sold. Unless something pops up stolen, no one cares. Year from now, feds just gonna slap my hands when they see this book and these hurry-up sales. I pay a fine, or pay a lawyer to get me out of paying it. Joe don't tell me how to do my gun book."

But Harlan shakes his head. "Postdating it seems better. Leave it blank, fill it in later. What's the difference? Two weeks?"

"I ain't fudging my book. That's federal. I'm up and up with ATF. They come in tomorrow, instead of a year, they look at my books—"

"Nobody coming in here except the buyers. You wait two weeks, you write it down then, you ain't done nothing wrong. You write it down now, somebody comes in tomorrow or next year, you caught. So what if it's small-time? You get busted the second way, not the first."

"We gamble different. The waiting-period law is a local law, and not federal. I'm choosing what's less wrong. I ain't messing with federal. Any of these guns were stolen, they ain't off-the-street stolen. They thirty-years-ago stolen. Police won't care about that, they just wanna catch crooks *now*. And they ain't gonna check my book, because that's federal. Bookkeeping is federal. So I'm keeping my book straight. Yewell—was almost a dealer himself. Like buying from a wholesaler. He ain't some unknown on the street. Hurrying these sales won't look as bad, 'cause it's like I was just buying from Sears."

Harlan doesn't understand. Is time against Huddy or not? "How's that dealer get to know so much?"

"You hear me ask him?" Huddy says, still annoyed that Harlan agreed with Joe. "Only thing he tells me about is his money."

"I bet his daddy got him started."

"Or maybe," Huddy says, "it's something he learns himself. He buys a gun for forty-five bucks, takes it to a gun shop, sells it for fifty. Now he's hooked. That was fun."

"When you talking about, this fifty?"

"Forty years ago. First gun—I don't know, I'm not counting years. Saying, he makes five bucks, so then he's nosing around garage sales, reading every manual and magazine. Homes in on Winchesters. You can make a lot of money specializing in one thing, if you pick the right thing."

"Or maybe he was just too stupid to learn more than one."

"They have a crazy interest in it, Harlan. The Western lore, and the mechanics. They study every rare feature. It's money, but—"

"Why couldn't *I* have an interest in guns?"

"I'm talking about them."

"Dad liked Westerns."

Huddy shrugs. "So did everyone."

"He knew guns, but he didn't stick around long enough to tell it. At least, not to me."

"Can you talk about something that hasn't happened yet? Where are you, 1926?"

"I'm asking about this dealer. Today. Maybe he takes some rifle that's been in the family. So that's his running start. He sells it, and that's how he makes his first dollars. Some hand-me-down that however you sell it is money. Your own flesh and blood saying go ahead, take your cut. Blood money."

"That ain't what blood money means."

"Means to me," Harlan says.

And the next day, when another dealer comes in asking where these guns came from, Harlan says again, "Me," like he's spent all night alone in a room, waiting to repeat the word. Huddy skips the lie and the crack, but the dealer turns to it.

"Nah," Harlan says, "I don't collect guns. I collect bullets. All kinds of bullets. Every round."

The dealer turns back to the Model 92, eyes the beautiful peep sight on the rear. "Most of these Trappers went to Alaska."

And now one made it here, Huddy thinks.

The dealer names a price, shrugs, if it works, it works, and after a quick back-and-forth, it does. Next pocket of cash comes out, another roll of hundreds Harlan sees pass into Huddy's hand without profit sharing. Dollars ringing, and the phone, too—but Joe's gonna have to drive here to get into Huddy's business.

"You must've got to something first," another caller says. "You got Yewell's collection, didn't you? I called about that, but I never heard back." The following days, the phone rings more, not just Joe, but the word spreading around town and beyond, a network of collectors, a caller from Texas wanting to know how many are left, how many people have seen them, and has Huddy been allowing these folks to pick and choose?

The phone again and Huddy answers, and it's Mister Keller saying, "I heard what you got."

What I got is for getting yours. "I hope you ain't changed that marquee yet."

"Lemme take a look outside, make sure my wife ain't set up the ladder." Keller pauses—Huddy has a strange feeling of being seen from his Sonic stop before—and then says, "Nope, ladder ain't up."

Huddy laughs with relief. It's nice hearing Keller in here, even if it's just a voice through a line. If Keller's voice is coming to him, then Huddy must be that much closer to moving there. He can't wait to switch that Liberty sign over. "Just give me a bit of time on this collection. You ain't getting any other offers?"

"Just you. Of course, I can't stop others from asking, but no one has. It's just us."

Which sounds good, until Huddy recalls Joe and him saying the same thing, before Huddy brought in Harlan.

"I hear you got Yewell," the next visitor says. He picks up an '86 and starts picking it to death. "Looks good on one side," he says.

"If it was that way on both," Huddy says, "I'd have to ask for twelve." The dealer nods but he keeps finding flaws, blemish here and bluing's missing there, and Huddy knows he likes it, so he says, "I wouldn't buy it then."

The dealer wants the gun, Huddy thinks, but he wants Huddy to know his interest is complicated. "What's a gun worth if people are squirreling their cash away? And all the guys who want these guns are my age, and we're dropping like flies. The younger ones aren't collecting Winchesters. What are they doing? Paragliding, dope, girls, cars. Most of the guys I know that'd want this gun, they're six feet under."

Sure, Huddy'll listen to a bullshit story about a soft economy. It's a true story, but it's still bullshit. And he'll feel sorry for all the belowground collectors who wish they could come up for one more Winchester. He'll even feel sorry for this dealer as soon as he stops hoping for a deep discount and comes up to the ticket price.

"You know," Huddy says, "I hear what you're saying, but it's always happened before. Always somebody driving the price up. Those software kids, whatever, they'll be there. There's always gonna be extra money, and people gotta collect something."

Huddy gives him quiet. And it's quiet from next door, too. No material banging in the Dumpster, no demoing devices, no compressor firing up—all of which means the bank is phasing to completion.

"My first bullet was a BB," Harlan says. "A BB that Huddy here shot into my leg. I dug it out and kept it and I've been collecting ever since."

And on top of Harlan's noise, here comes Del sticking his nose in. "I hear you hooked into some Winchesters."

"Don't have anything," Huddy says.

"That's not what I heard."

"Don't care what you heard."

"Huddy's been to grandma's house," Harlan says. "This ain't no bargain-basement stuff. Can you go top-of-the-line?"

"Will you shut yer mouth," Huddy says. Del interfering, Harlan encouraging. The two of them would make great decoys, if they weren't distracting the sale.

"I'm asking if Del's got real dollars."

"You know I do," Del says, "that's how I been buying my gold." Huddy watches his face whip around, his nose sniff like a bloodhound.

"This is appointment-only. Ain't public viewing," Huddy says, and he gestures at the dealer who's still having his doubts, and Huddy's about to ask him why he's here if he's just degrading.

"Come on, Huddy, I ain't public."

"Call me later, come back, then you private." And Huddy'll arrange a fake showing. Show Del a bunch of used and abused rifles, and when he starts begging to attach his hands to others, Huddy'll say, "Buy these first."

"Well, I guess you can ask anything you want for this," the dealer says.

The negotiation started bad, but Del and Harlan teamed up to destroy it, so when the dealer leaves—fine, Huddy thinks, you leaving with a hole in your collection—and then Del, to make his private call, Huddy tells Harlan, "You talk like that again, I'm tossing you."

And later, when the next dealer comes in, Harlan walks to switch places.

"Where you going?" Huddy says, Harlan at the door, hurrying, jacket bunched in his arm.

"KayKay," he says.

"I need you to close."

"Just bark and I'll come," Harlan says, and he opens the door like a breakout.

Huddy wants to think more about Summer Avenue, but for some reason, his vision failing, he can't see all the way to his prospects with Liberty, but instead only to the progress and timeline of next door. Done with demo, the work crews are probably rearranging walls, patching concrete, redoing or adding bathrooms, putting up utilities. One day, a big crane will slide in the drywall, but not before Huddy's sliding out. When the painters and carpeting and furnishings arrive, he'll be gone. Huddy nods at the finished project, as if he were the health department confirming every-thing's up to code and been given the final seal of approval.

At closing, Harlan's still bailed, and a cop car appears, eases up, parks, and it can't be about some stolen chain, because the jewelry's gone. Maybe a tool or part. Huddy doesn't recognize the cop step-ping out, unless it's a new face from pawn detail. Or maybe he's just another Winchester collector, hearing about Huddy's new guns, and Huddy'll have to go low on the price, keep the police happy. But pawn detail almost always calls first, and if it's not a collector, maybe it's just some information Huddy needs to give. He braces for what else.

"You Huddy Marr?"

Huddy nods, his hand waving up in a salute.

"Sergeant Corley, Project Safe Neighborhood."

He doesn't know what that is, the officer not holding any claim or report or other bad paper. "What can I do for you, sergeant?" Huddy watches him survey the hardware, the instruments hanging on the wall.

"Picked your brother up."

"Which one?" Huddy says, but he knows, wonders if it's some domestic bust-up, or after the quarrel, some stupid brush or acci-dent. Huddy jumps ahead, tries to frame his next answer. Works here, some part-time hours, Huddy'll vouch that much.

"Harlan," the sergeant says, and his lawful eyes scan the gun racks. "We get a phone call. Somebody hears gunshots, out by the Wolf River. We drive out there, find your brother stashing an AK-47 in his trunk."

"Wait . . . wait a minute," Huddy says, turning to the storeroom where the AK's supposed to be, even if it shouldn't, and he knows the sergeant just saw him react. He looks away from the door, outside, sees only a shadow locked up in the caged backseat. No matter how Huddy's eyes widen, he can't detect Harlan through the dark windows.

The sergeant says more about Harlan, the weapon was fired within the city limits, and Huddy knows his part's coming, the sergeant is talking about Harlan and automatic fire only to move upward. The police are here because the subject is him. "You got papers for an AK?" His voice is calm, which means Huddy can't calm him down. "You got a license for full-auto?"

"Look here," Huddy says, blurts it, and the cop's head turns sideways at Huddy's wrong statement. Every word is wrong, every explanation or apology, every pleading tone. I been meaning to call, I bought that gun and I made an honest mistake, this extra notch, and I didn't call because if I call, they come in and look everywhere, and I was gonna get rid of it, would've thrown it in the river if my other brother didn't sneak these other guns out that made me think of them. Both my brothers been sneaking out guns. Arrest them, you already got one, get the other, but don't come between me and what they've been taking. Take everything off these shelves, this whole showroom is your buyoff, but let me keep what's in back. Huddy swallows, breathes. He just needs a month to be left alone, to bank these guns. How does he change the cop's direction, move him backward and out of his life instead of coming forward to take it away. He shakes his arms, at what clings to him. The gun, he should have dumped it in Joe's pond. Better than the Mississippi, he should have slipped it right there before they threw the net. Joe wanted guns, Huddy missed a chance to give him one more.

The sergeant looks again at the racks, longer, scrutinizing, his eyes disbelieving. Huddy sees the racks are half empty, and what's missing somehow incriminates him, the blank spots are spaces where guns should be secured, and instead they've been slipped out, used for target practice in deserted city woods bordering the backyard of scared neighbors, near driveways chalked with hopscotch games.

"How do you have access to it?" the sergeant says. Why is a gun in a pawnshop if it's not gonna be sold? Was Huddy gonna black-market this gun? The sergeant studies him, a guilty offender, which Huddy is because the crime has already been committed, the evidence is the weapon that's already been collected.

Huddy shakes his head, because this can't be worked out. The gun isn't in his book, which is good but bad. Harlan wouldn't say he took it from here, but that don't matter. Whatever Harlan said or didn't, what Huddy says now or doesn't, it's ugly every way. Mouth closed or open, the police will pore over his shop, search out violations, try to separate him from his guns. But I won't roll over and play dead. I'm coming out of this wounded, and I'll find a way to heal up.

The sergeant waits and Huddy weighs his choice: Confess and get jail or lie and maybe get off. There's no light punishment, no minor charge. Because of Harlan's mayhem, Huddy won't get spared his negligence. They'll do more to Harlan, but it's still too great an offense given to him. So Huddy starts backtracking, before he's admitted possession, his mind reversing, the *not* logging in of the AK didn't happen, the gun was never at all here. Huddy cannot get hung on a gun that he intended to drop in the river. Harlan took it, to the wrong river, but the gun's gone, so Huddy's not involved. The sergeant has apprehended Harlan and now he'll look to snag *him*—a hook caught in, tugging on, Huddy's flesh that he needs to remove without the cop detecting a lifted finger or a telling gesture to slip the curve free.

The cop confiscated the gun but he didn't witness the taking, and Harlan will tell his story and not get turned. Huddy knows this because, unlike the policeman, he was there when they were brothers playing in Shelby Forest (knew every corner of those woods), rock fights and setting small fires, no one around and then a game warden crossing the open field, Harlan about to run when Huddy quick-grabbed a fistful, the warden at the near edge and cutting into the woods and coming toward them, and Harlan struggling to get away, Huddy clinching for Harlan to go nowhere. The warden approached and they waited and didn't move as he surveyed the dark spots on the ground. "What's happened here?" the warden asked. Arms at their sides, sleeves touching, hand-me-down shirts that were secondhand when Joe first wore 'em. The truth at Huddy's lips—his mouth full but blank—when Harlan stepped ahead, Harlan younger but faster with false words. "We was playing over there," Harlan said, pointing away to a far end, "and we smelled smoke so we run over." The warden high above them, but Harlan somehow equal for standing tall over burnt twigs. Huddy watched a ten-year-old and a uniformed man in a staredown. And the warden shifted to Huddy and asked again and even though Harlan's campfire lie was nonsense and Huddy felt responsible, he repeated it. Because he couldn't let his little brother outdare him, and the truth wouldn't correct Harlan but make a mess of where he'd first stepped, even if Huddy felt lesser for saying what Harlan had said before. Huddy had their mama's lighter in his pocket and he needed to explain the reason before he was searched—maybe say they set this one fire, after they stamped out the others—because the warden saw through their words. But the warden frowned and breathed heavily and shook his head at the blackened piles, just burns on ground where property wasn't built and nothing grew.

The questioning ended. The warden switched authority figures. Kids being kids, and it was time to minister, to teach an elementary lesson. "Boys," he told them, "when you done something stupid, the easiest thing to remember is the truth." He opened his hands, showed his palms. "So you can always pull the truth out." Huddy listened to the message and hid his eyes—he wanted to say he had another brother on the other side of him—and then he gave a weak nod which Harlan missed from the corner of his eye, but Huddy hoped would mean an apology for harming the nearby land. The warden nodded back at only him, which was visible to Harlan, and Huddy was thankful for getting favored, for the man registering his difference. But he was ashamed for surrendering an apology he couldn't help, as if he'd said sorry outright. The warden waved a fatherly hand to grant their release. And Huddy and Harlan walked the same path out of the woods and then ran loose across the field and back home, and Huddy felt like they'd been sentenced and were up against a wall when a guardian gave them a reprieve, and Harlan laughed at being let go, amazed at beating a grown-up who knew the truth but couldn't get them to say what wasn't seen, a game of hide-and-seek where your secrets never surfaced, and your denials always deceived.

The sergeant only knows Harlan once, a few hours of one day, but Huddy knows other incidents and history, his beginning lies, knows what he'll say now as if it were an old episode coming back, a memory safely remembered. He trusts that Harlan will lie, depends upon it, and he'll use Harlan's version to cover his own mistake. Huddy will give not his own story, not some other side of it, but Harlan's.

"I got two AKs here," he says, matter-of-factly, looking back to the place he got caught prior, "but they're both semi-auto."

"Let's go look," the sergeant says, faceless, and Huddy watches his arms unfold.

Huddy takes him inside, through the double doors leading to the darker storeroom, down an aisle flanked by shelves crowded with hardware and cheap sets, equipment and instruments, other people's things or Huddy's or soon to be, the cement floor lined with oily machines, and then to the gun locker. He keys the hockey-puck lock, swings open the heavy-hinged doors and steps to the gun racks and stands at attention. Two AKs side by side, the third one off the books and off in Harlan's hands, Harlan not knowing it was full-auto until he fired it, touched the trigger and got a burst, the recoil carrying the gun upward, went from shooting straight to shooting up at the sky. Dogs barking, the Wolf River filled with echoing combat noise, target shooting that sounds like a military operation, and Harlan's legs wobbly and his eyes twitching, but his thoughts now clear on why Huddy didn't log it in. *You paid for it but you can't sell it, so let's see what I can do.* Reloading another magazine and squaring his stance, his legs spread and shoulders leaning in so he's steady on the gun, bringing the weight to him, the can he's just finished a long-range target on a tree stump, Harlan squeezing and the bullets burying into the dirt behind. Another beer, another can set up afar, more lightning rounds blasted, and Wow, this weapon, all that energy pushing through it, the next magazine emptied and Harlan's indestructible, the power in his hands, the stump drilled and the target hit and zinging, the gunfire rattling through the deep woods and volleying out, a dispatcher answering distress calls about what must be the local militia engaged in training exercises, a mother crying about her kid on a river-rafting trip, a veteran sitting quiet on a lawn chair and he hears rapid fire, perfectly timed, and it's wartime again, the surrounding miles in ringing earshot, there's a shooter in the woods, a machine-gun psycho in a city park, an artilleryman gone AWOL, but Harlan's mind is remote and soundproof.

Two AKs on a full rack. Nothing absent, so the gun couldn't've been stored here. The configuration encourages Huddy: the rack a complete story with no missing pieces. Just repeat it. The sergeant's eyes move across the lineup.

This here's my brother's gun, but he don't know I got it. He don't even know it's his.

Huddy hears Harlan as if he were hearing himself.

"These are my AKs."

"What about what your brother was firing?"

Huddy shrugs innocently. That third AK is a mystery. He's only sure about two, and two's his limit. "These are what's mine." He knows he's crossed a line to walk back to Harlan, and the sergeant is even more suspicious because he's interrogated Harlan before coming to him.

"What are you saying?" the sergeant says, after peering at the guns.

He's confirming that Harlan took it before it came into the shop, because that's what Harlan said. A loyal thief, he'll steal a gun and surrender it but not a brother. Caught red-handed, the gun leaving Harlan, the sergeant's hands taking hold, and Huddy is seized by fingerprints. Panic inside him, but don't signal outward. His shoulder blades squeeze, heat surges across his face. He stares at a corner, fixes himself. If they ran prints, he can say his touches came from the gun-room inspection.

"He helped me load the collection in. He must've slipped the gun out for hisself. Before it came here." One added word to change the sequence—Harlan took the gun *before*—to avoid incrimination. A lie, but more than half-true, completely true minus the one word. He's matched Harlan's account, told an accurate lie. He tries to read the sergeant but there's no impression, the stubbled face not moving. "My brother may have been upset about me and my other brother buying them."

"Your other brother."

That's right. Huddy gives up the name. He watches the sergeant take down the information on his notepad. He wishes he could add a brother to every answer. Ten, fifteen brothers—older brothers and new ones till his own name hid inside them like an alias, and what he'd done wrong couldn't be found. "He may have been angry about not getting a share."

"Harlan."

Huddy nods because he is telling the truth. Watches the sergeant write another note.

"And so he walked off with your gun. Without either brother seeing it."

Huddy spreads his palms in both directions, at the other racks and the number of guns all over shelves and different levels and along every plank. "It was a big collection." He nods again, another correct answer.

The sergeant turns behind him and his nostrils flare, as if the mowers on the ground were doused in gasoline. He steps out of the locker and scans the room, the property everywhere, and then he looks past the personal items on the long rows of shelving, to the walls, the length and width and corner edges, surveying dimensions and angles up and down as if he were measuring the floor plan. "You won't mind if ATF conducts a compliance investigation." It's time to pass the case up to the feds.

"Of course not," Huddy says, he'll cooperate fully, because if he objected they'd push harder, and the audit would feel like a raid.

ATF isn't here yet, but Huddy feels them so close he wouldn't be surprised if the sergeant could wave agents in from the back wall. They're waiting for their directive, poised to take over. They've already read the report that the sergeant hasn't written up yet. Huddy's mind pulls backward to Harlan's arrest and forward to the audit, his mind in two places but his eyes only in this small locked room.

Twelve

HE ARRIVES AT THE end of dinnertime. He drove here, but he feels like he's been dropped off. He's home, but he's still over there, separated, and he walks through one room to get to another, to stand beside the table and see what his wife is having on her plate.

"Da," Cody says, and Huddy smiles, his son saying almost words.

"Hi," he says.

"Ieee," he hears back, as he heads to the kitchen, fills his dinner plate at the stove, sets his pistol atop the fridge, grabs a beer below, and rejoins them.

"Did my brother call?"

"Which one?"

The one that got caught, he thinks, but he just says, "Either." He could call Joe to see if he's learned about Harlan, but he's talked enough brothers today.

"Something wrong?" she asks.

"Why?"

"You ain't sitting down."

He sits across from Cody, who's strapped in a high chair, Christie in between. After lying to the police, maybe he should rehearse his lines for the feds. Or maybe he should relieve the pressure of the truth, make it easier to lie all day tomorrow. He cracks the can

204

open, considers which talk. And then he tells what Harlan did—he watches her fork pull from her mouth in disbelief—and what he didn't do, and how Harlan's lie will be his alibi.

"He fired one of your guns in the Wolf frickin' River?"

"It's an all-time fuck-up."

"Ah ba ba." The baby points at his food, at some complaint or demand.

"What's he saying?"

"Beats me."

"Abba-dabba," Huddy says.

"Something like that."

"Ah hop," Cody says, his tiny arm stretching across the tray and the food beyond reach.

"That means he needs help."

Huddy rises and edges the fruit chunk over.

"So where's the fuck-up now?" she asks.

In a box. And if Harlan wasn't put in a cell or cage or wherever he's stuck, where would he be? Not back at the pawnshop. He's test-fired a machine gun that Huddy can't sell—might as well take it to a gun show, sell it out in the parking lot to a buyer who, surprise, is undercover. Win the award for stupid, except he's already won it for the woods.

"What are you gonna do?"

"I told you," Huddy says, and he eats his meal. "It's Harlan's problem."

"How's it just Harlan's problem?"

He doesn't answer, sips instead, clenches his mouth so it's airtight.

"Boo," the baby says, his lips pursed.

"He's trying to say *spoon*."

"I figured," Huddy says, and he nods at the clutched utensil.

"So you're gonna break the law?" She eyes him, then their son, but Huddy doesn't, just her.

"There ain't no point cooperating. It's paying for something I didn't do. They want me to tell the truth so they can take my guns—and they ain't once gonna ask for no asking price. Well, I aim to sell what's mine."

She gets up, removes her plate. He takes a bite, and another and he's so hungry he devours half his serving, and he's already planning for seconds. He tears the meat from the bone. He hears food scraped into the garbage, hears the sink run, the dishwasher tray sliding out, the door banging shut. Done with cleanup, but the floor creaks as she paces. He chews, swallows. Needs more. Cody smears his leftovers, draws arcs and circles. He says words and fake ones.

She returns, wipes her hands.

"He's talking up a storm," Huddy says, but now it's her turn not to look, to only talk at him.

"Did I ever tell you about my cousin Bobby? The car thief?"

"No," Huddy says, studying her features. He watches her focus, her face serious but also relaxed.

"He had this scheme. Steal cars, drive them from Arkansas to Florida. He was hooked in with—I don't know what you'd call it. Some syndicate. Crime ring. Anyway, it was big money. And he decided he was gonna make seven hundred fifty thousand, not a million, and that's how he wouldn't get caught. 'Cause million was the first number he thought of, so when he lowered it to seven-five, he knew he was being safe. As long as he didn't get greedy for that extra money."

"What happened to him?"

"Nothing. Happy ending. He stopped at seven-fifty. Living on a houseboat is what happened."

"That's a sweet story. Call that a cautionary tale. The moral being, go for less. Break the law smaller. Don't try for an even million—but just about."

A baby arm swings, the sippy cup knocked off the tray. "Uh-oh," he says.

"You told me it before," Huddy says, after Christie bends down to pick what fell.

"Yeah? I thought so. It felt familiar. I was looking at you, wondering if you'd heard it. Why didn't you say?"

Huddy angles his head, gestures at his motive. "I wanted to see how you told it."

Later, after Cody's bedtime, after watching TV in the living room, Huddy turns off the bedroom one and faces her. "How long did he steal cars? Your cousin?"

"I don't know."

"Say it like you did."

She sits up to understand. "You mean, make something up?"

"Tell me how long he stole cars."

"A year," she says, but her eyes lift in a giveaway. He shakes his head at her body language. "What'd I do?"

"Not much. You just looked like somebody else. Or trying to be."

"That's what you have to do?"

He shrugs, sees her doubt and fear, her arms wrapping her stomach. The door is closed, the blinds drawn. The back porch light, set on a timer, casts shadows on a window. Dirty clothes tumbled in a dark corner, stray papers on the bureau, disorganized. A phone on a nightstand that if you stared too long, would ring.

"Don't," she says.

"I'm already."

"Well . . . don't," her voice nervous, stammering.

"The alternative being?" He stares ahead, at the red light on the TV indicating Off. "Maybe I could tell 'em that Harlan wanted to join the Army. He went to the woods to enlist, but nobody was there. I already told you, it's too much blame. 'Sides, they won't find anything."

"They'll surprise you. And then they'll find it. You'll get in more trouble." She shakes her head hard, as if she were answering a list of questions.

"I didn't steal a thing. Just bad bookkeeping, but they won't penalize me for that. Now I'm liable for what Harlan done." He's tired of defending himself for Harlan, or what he forgot to do himself. He wants to answer differently, *be* someone different. *I stole cars for one year.* No, he changes himself better. *I never stole cars.* Ain't responsible for cars getting stolen.

Outside a dog barks at a dog that's barking from inside the next house. They listen for a noise from the crib, a thump or cry. The barking dies down, stops. The commotion out front is nearer to the baby's room, not enough to wake him, but they both lie still. He gives a second look at the red dot.

"I'll tell you something else about Bobby," she says. "About his wife. She moved to Florida because she was part deaf and she always wanted to live by the ocean, because water was the only nature noise she could hear. Couldn't hear the birds, but water came in fine. So now she's on a houseboat and she gets to hear it all day."

He's watched her—noticed a small eye-shift on a mostly sign-less face, and her voice sounds sure, her words authentic. "You just made that up," he says, but he's guessing.

"It's true." She stares right at him.

"Yeah?" He tries to glimpse what's invisible.

"True story." She blinks. "Just not about him."

"Who about?"

"Someone I used to work with. *Her* cousin."

"She married someone on a houseboat?" Because he can't follow where she is, what she means.

She smiles at his confusion and her own act. "No, my cousin's the one that lives on the houseboat. Her cousin's the one that's part deaf. Bobby's single, far as I know."

"So . . ." He's stuck between stories. Or inside one story that's inside another one. "You just came up with that ocean bit?"

"No, Huddy. That part's true. She lives on the Gulf Coast. I was just telling different water."

Huddy laughs at her adjustments, the switched geography, the borrowed lives and different sources. "Different parts of the same. Of course, that depends on which coast that houseboat sits on."

"I guess I don't know that either. Suspect it was somewhere in the Keys."

"Oh, I know which side," Huddy says.

"You do?"

"Sure." He knows this part by heart, can say it honestly. "The right side."

He lies back, exhausted. He imagines he's in a car, stealing through darkness, the headlights broken and no traffic and the road so dim he can't see past the hood, and then a light brightens behind on a highway shoulder and flashes in closing pursuit. His eyes open, his mind comes back. Her hand covers his, he feels its weight, and she stares up at the ceiling, then over to the glowing window. Another barking fit, inside and out, from the window and the street, the same dog and a different one. The noise passes. He rests again. He sees himself, in the next vehicle. Floating offshore, a deaf man on a houseboat. And the questions are called from a distant island and as silent as the water all around him.

"Hey," she says.

He's almost on a boat, then not. A voice, a light scratch on his skin. He opens his eyes and he's not away. No water, no wind, just himself.

"Don't go to sleep."

"No?"

"Not yet," she says, and her body curls sideways.

"I wasn't sleeping. I was *dreaming*, but I wasn't asleep."

"Oh, yeah?" She smiles.

"I don't fall asleep till the middle of the night. Not till I've been dreaming for hours."

"Now *you're* the one confusing."

"I'm just playing," he says. "Or maybe I'm sleepwalking." His eyelids drop low, a zombie hand comes out and she swats it laughing. He tries again and she lets him touch. She pulls him close, clutching. He kisses her, she breathes on his neck, seizes his shirt, and now it's early and they're both awake.

They drive up in two unmarked Chargers. Nine A.M. sharp to meet him at opening, but he's been here hours, earlier than ever, but it's never felt later, because he can't go backward, reverse yesterday, rewind the month, redo the log-in when he first saw the selector switch and wrote nothing, called no one. He's never been to the shop before six, but he woke up near five with a problem in his head as if he'd dreamt it from the dead of night: Joe took two guns, but Harlan took one. The imbalance of the theft, he couldn't imagine Harlan taking less, worried Huddy through the house and out the door—speeding over, he remembered Harlan wanting to spin that Colt in the gun room. But when Huddy got inside the shop and the locker, and pulled the wooden tray from the top shelf, he saw the Colts all there, the pistols flipped to face each other, trigger guard to trigger guard, right angles undisturbed. But his heart still raced—there was something that Harlan or someone else had done with guns that he didn't know about. He checked his watch: enough time for an inventory. He grabbed his gun book beneath the loan counter and returned to the racks and shelves and started counting (trying to rush carefully so the ledger lines wouldn't blur and jump), the contents of the locker and then the various safes, and when he finished, the totals matched. At least there were two questions Huddy wouldn't get today: "Where'd that gun go?" and "Where'd that gun come from?" None too few, and none too many. Even the absent AK corresponding, invisible in two places. His mind, for an instant, at rest. He nods, tells himself he knows everything. Minutes before nine, the morning hours feeling like a footrace, and he goes to the bathroom, splashes water, unclings his shirt. He readies himself at the loan counter. A chair but he can't sit. He searches the *Appeal* and finds the article, not on the front page or even the front of the local, but tucked inside, at the margin, a small brief beneath the CRIME REPORT heading, with no information that the police didn't say prior, except for the final sentence: *The identity of the shooter was not immediately released.* He's surprised that Harlan is unnamed, but he's more surprised that there isn't a photo, since he'd already pictured it in his mind.

Three agents. Two or more is trouble. Never dealt with this much manpower before, which means this team isn't assembled for compliance but for criminal. Huddy knows this ain't no knock-and-talk assignment, *We have a problem, can you clear this up?* They'll close him down for the day. The dress code isn't street clothes like previous visits, but slacks, white polo shirts, jackets. Like aggressive auditors. They look somewhere between accountants and him. Huddy half-recognizes one of the agents from the last inspection. The same man but in different clothing, and he now plays a lesser role, as assistant to the lead agent, who's the oldest and flashes a badge and says, "Good morning, we're from ATF."

Huddy ready to be a kid, Yessir, yessir.

They cross the room, the lead agent in the middle, the others alongside and a step behind.

"We're gonna need to see your bound book and your 4473s."

Huddy nods, sure thing. Check my pockets, check my house, ask me my favorite color.

"We're gonna secure the area." His finger moves left and right, his voice important enough to shut down streets.

That's okay, too. Go lock my door. Staying open isn't an option anyway. Alone with them, he won't be able to hardly function, and Huddy already postponed his appointments.

He opens the file cabinet and removes the stack of sold forms, and hands them over the counter to the youngest agent, who looks straight out of the military, a fact-finding rookie who'll write Huddy up for everything, justify his pay. Huddy hands the gun book to the one he sort of knows. Doesn't say, "My books have always been straight with you," because being on good terms means nothing. Last audit, Huddy offered coffee, which the man rejected, "No thanks," his voice polite but firm, but this time Huddy won't say coffee. Today, coffee is bad conversation, a drink is a bribe. These three won't take a glass of water. Packed their own lunch, their own beverage, and all they want from Huddy is a chair, a table, a light. And Huddy doesn't need coffee either, the adrenaline like a third cup in his veins, but he'd sure like water, without them sensing his thirst, because his mouth is chalk-dry.

"We're gonna do a count of the inventory," the lead agent says.

Huddy swings open the counter door, brings them back, let's all go where the guns are. Can't be on their own with his toys. A small office beside the locker, and Huddy shows them to places where they can work. He retreats, positions himself close enough to be of help interpreting or finding, but only if they ask. The youngest agent takes the yellow sheets to the table, sets them down beside his pad, where he'll write up errors. Forgotten dates, forgotten signatures, middle names only initialed, the state abbreviated where you're supposed to write Tennessee full. The two others gang up on the physical inventory, the oldest one counting the open entries in the book, the middle one counting the guns in the inner room.

"Where else do you have guns?" he asks, when he's finished there, and Huddy opens the back safe, walks to the showroom to open the front one (which he'd relocked moments before, to hide his nervous inventory just ahead of them), and declares his counter gun and his carry gun. And then it's simple accounting, guns taken off racks or out from safes, chambers checked and the guns carried over and placed beside the book. Match the stock number on the ticket to the stock number in the ledger. One agent hash-marks the open entry, the other flips the gun tag over. The biggest noise is the sound of paper turning. Huddy tries to keep busy, kills time by pulling merchandise for sale, pricing stuff out. The phone rings to the answering machine. Maybe a brother calling for bail or information, but Huddy can't supply either now.

A knock at the door, and Huddy walks up front and sees a pawner and he yells to him from the middle of the room, "We're closed." He hears a muffled reply, and he shakes his head and hand, not to say or hear more through glass. The mail lady can come in, but the rest of the outside world stays on the street. He turns around to the loan counter, where the newspaper is hidden, and he's not gonna search online for an update. He imagines Joe hearing the story somewhere and not knowing his involvement—unless Harlan called him to get out of jail. Otherwise, it's just some crazy, anonymous AK shooter, a danger to the community that's not his.

Huddy walks back to the larger room and sees a problem form already set aside, the agent hunched over with his elbows on the table, scribbling a sentence at the top of a clean pad. There's no way you can keep years of forms without errors. Huddy doesn't necessarily mind if there's a few mistakes (not a lot, but maybe enough so they can yell at him for that, make his life hard *that* way, feel good about making a showing)—as long as they're small ones. Clerical errors that are easily fixable, *Call this guy, he needs to come back and sign here.* But Huddy doesn't want some important box left blank, a forgotten X or one X-ed wrong, *Yes, I'm a fugitive from justice.*

"When was your last audit?" the agent asks, and they already know the answer, so he's asking the simple question to register how he talks truth and see later how he deviates.

"Three years," Huddy answers to all of them. Paper moves on the desk. Huddy imagines renaming himself or saying a different house number to throw the whole test off. He can't help but think of Harlan's name game.

The young agent nods. He doesn't smile, but he's not mean. If it were up to him, there'd be no gun dealers, but it's nothing personal.

The answering machine records another message.

They break for lunch. Huddy drinks water, and waits for them to exit the lot before playing messages. A loan question, and then Joe: "Huddy, give me a call." He figures he's heard from Harlan, or about him. Other voices, a merchandise question and another loan, and then a hang-up. Huddy checks caller ID and sees the name and number is Joe again. He feels too monitored to check the Internet, flips on the TV, the news at noon is past crimes and headlines. He picks up the phone, but hangs up. He knows they haven't tapped it, but talking is complicated. If he tells Joe about ATF, those two collateral antiques will go deeper into hiding. Although, if Harlan called him, the guns are already more gone or even sold. He remembers his food, the meat is leftover dinner, but he's too panicked to eat. A car rolls up, parks, the driver sees the switched-off signage, reverses, drives off, straight into the center lane and then turning left in the opposite direction of the agent's cars, but all three seem connected somehow, like some operation splitting off to reattach later. Huddy walks to the locker. Except he's done the inventory, so there's nothing else to examine. Bathroom again. He returns to the counter, sees a face pressed to the window, a visored hand against the glare, but Huddy shoos him. The man lifts grocery bags from the curb and walks away, the plastic handles twisted in his grips, the bags tilting his body with each step. Trucks rumble down Lamar, and above the trucks and across the street is a vacant billboard that Huddy can't read from this sideways angle, but he knows is spray-painted with SIGN FOR RENT. He looks down from the sign to the semis to the itty-bitty man, who looks as if he's shrunk and lost weight in the time he cut across the lot. Huddy swallows more liquid. The trucks run past the man like movable walls. The man is up against a wall, then he's not, then he is again. The lunch hour is almost finished and Huddy should eat, but he still can't. The story could reach Joe in multiple ways, and Huddy sees it happening simultaneously, turning on the TV and the phone ringing while reading the paper. Get off the phone and check the computer inside the phone and it's released there, too. Huddy looks at his own phone. No word from Harlan—away like he was in Florida, but this time Huddy knows the exact location, 201 Poplar. Huddy unwraps his cooked food, rewraps it, covers up the smell.

They reappear. Just one car pulls in, two agents get out, and Huddy sees which one's missing, the youngest, which might be fine since the yellow forms are completed and he could be typing up his findings. Huddy cannot think about loose ends. He needs to concentrate not on everything, because he'll get lost in too much thought, but only the shut spaces of these two rooms. Huddy has a simple story that he can tell endlessly. The phone rings three times and he answers it, to hear someone else's voice besides his own.

"Bluff City," he says, and a man asks about phones. "I'm sorry, we're closed today."

"You closed but you there?"

"That's right," Huddy says.

"The one I'm at, the phone, it ain't mine, so I'm needing one myself."

"Call tomorrow. I don't really know. You'll have to check back."

"Just come by?"

"That's right. Call."

"How 'bout brushes?"

"Huh?"

"Sir," Huddy hears from behind the double doors.

"Paint," Huddy hears in his ear.

"I don't have paint."

"Naw, man . . ."

"I have—" Huddy says, and he hangs up and follows the voice, approaches the desk, where the agent presses a finger to the ledger.

"Where is the original paperwork for the guns you logged in on the eighth and ninth?" Yewell's guns, the widow's name written more than a hundred times, her name atop her name again and again, like reading a one-name directory, a two-word book. All the names collected there, but the agent only cares about what's seen over and over.

"I don't have the paperwork." Huddy nods because he had to trash the papers last night, after the sergeant left.

"Do you normally destroy documentation?"

"I discarded the paperwork once I logged them in. That paperwork was just a duplicate of what's in the gun book."

A gray area and the agent shows no emotion. He doesn't say which way he understands. Doesn't shake his head or accuse Huddy of wrongdoing, and doesn't signal he'll accept the conduct at face value. The action is lawful, even if Huddy won't admit it's right. Instead, he thinks of her. She'd hate to know her name was all across his book, especially with how she wanted to get rid of the guns. She never wanted to touch that list, so why save it? Huddy's heart accelerates. He waits for another request, to help find some numbered gun, *Where would this one be?* But the agent doesn't ask. Huddy grabs a toolbox off the shelf and starts for the counter, even though the item is still in pawn. The phone rings once and he goes to answer it and sees a second parked car, the third agent at the door. He picks up the phone, says, "Hold on," replaces it for the door, lets the agent in. The agent doesn't look at Huddy—but he hardly looked at him all morning—but he doesn't carry a report. Huddy gets to the phone again.

"What the hell's going on?" Joe says.

"I'm afraid we're closed today."

Silence for too long, and Huddy's about to interrupt it when he hears, "I just talked to Harlan."

"I can't tell you that. You're gonna have to check back."

"Jesus Christ," Joe says, his voice between a hiss and a whisper. "I'm hanging up," he says, and he does.

Huddy returns to see three guns moved from the racks onto the table, the two AKs and one AR-15. "Sir, we're gonna field-test your AKs. So those will come out today. Your AR—" The agent lifts the rifle by the stock and the handguard. "We'd like to field-strip it here." He waits for Huddy's okay, but he doesn't need it.

You run my industry. Pointless to say no, they'll get a court order authorizing what they're asking to inspect now. Huddy wants to let them take apart this gun since he's without Yewell's papers. He stares at the many holes in the handguard.

"Big-brother caliber," the oldest agent says.

"That's right," Huddy says.

The agent nods. He's the nice one, but he's not his friend. He presses the pin, the upper receiver swinging open to view the trigger assembly, and set inside the lower receiver is a lightning link, a thin metal strip that converts this legal gun to an M16—and for Huddy, makes possessing it a felony. His eyes water, his head shivers. He's never been more scared by a smaller piece of material. It lies flat, dropped in over the disconnector hook, but it looks enormous, bigger than the gun it's set within. "Wait," Huddy says. If they'd just give him a moment to modify this illegal gun back, dismantle the link. Countless people double-crossed him and inserted it—these agents when Huddy answered the phone for Joe, yesterday's sergeant, Joe, Harlan (he took one gun, so he must've messed with this one to make two), dead man Yewell and the gun owner before him or the amateur gunsmith before them both who tinkered in the basement, Yewell's widow and son, the customers Huddy turned away today at the door, or the one who came in two days ago wanting to sell him phone lines, garbage bags. A whole system that sabotages.

"I never tested it. I would never have sold it before test-firing it. It's logged in my book as semi-auto."

"It's logged in your book wrong." The oldest agent looks at him like he's old enough to know better. "You are in possession of an automatic weapon." Which is what the sergeant would have said to Harlan yesterday.

He can't stop the agent from writing down the violation. Now Huddy has two automatic weapons to answer for. He feels like everyone and no one put it there, like it wasn't here until all of a sudden it was. Like a magnet flying in.

"I'm gonna need you to open the front door."

Huddy doesn't want him to leave, but he can't stop him, not even with all of these guns. The agent walks off and Huddy follows him through the room and to the entrance, passing him only when the agent steps away for him to unlock the door. He watches him walk out, into his car to contact his superior and report the new evidence. Out the door is one man, behind another door are two others, and Huddy waits between, alone in a showroom with empty cases, an empty gun room. These three might sweep up what's in back.

"His list said semi-auto," Huddy says, when the agent re-enters, but the man won't answer him. Huddy needs Yewell here to explain it. Two mistakes or two disguises? Why would Yewell have two full-autos? Were the guns disguised or was the disguise Yewell? *I wanted to have 'em just to have 'em. Never shot these guns, they just complemented my gun room nice.* Yewell talking to Huddy, but how does Huddy know it's him? And how does he explain to strangers a dead man's secrets? Yewell entered them in his gun list as semis, so it's oversight, or an oversight on purpose. Huddy says his line again about the list, says it the same way, and repeating it makes it pleading.

"How do you know that?" the agent says, only after he's passed through the double doors and rejoined his team.

"Because that's what I wrote down in my gun book."

"And everything you wrote down in that book is what was on the list. Except you don't have the list."

They all face him. Huddy shakes his head. And as soon as he does, he knows they do, that they've tracked it back to her. He watches the lead man reach inside his pocket. Like a magic trick how it got from the youngest one to him, although he probably handed it over when Huddy switched rooms before, when the phone rang with Joe. He imagines the widow inviting the agent in, sitting him down just as she did with Huddy in the same hunt room. The agent called so she's expecting him, prepared tea to sip, along with another copy of the gun list, again centered on the table. He smiles when he sees the list, and she smiles, too, as if the pages were a favorite recipe.

"Okay, that's *her* list."

"What are you saying? Are you saying it's not the same? You saying you have a different copy?"

No, he says, but not aloud, because he's already talking to his lawyer. He can't speak, because if he does, he'll stutter.

"That she added something? Because I'm having trouble understanding how your brother could fire an AK that only existed on paper."

"It's the same." His copy was her copy. Huddy shakes his head at his own inconsistent statement. What he means is that maybe Yewell himself had two lists, a phantom one where he recorded them as full-autos. Yewell's list was wrong, just like Huddy's book is wrong, and both of them know it. But Huddy shakes his head at that, at Yewell. The dead man telling me things is just me. "I'm saying, I logged in near two hundred guns. You seen this big pile. I might've missed one."

"You missed *two*. And missing an AK?" The agent's eyes pop open, as wide as Huddy's when he saw the link. "You got three AKs. You telling me you take in two hundred guns—Winchesters and Colts and *three* AKs—and one goes missing and you don't notice it? That's like a bunch of handguns and a rocket launcher."

Huddy wants to sit down, but the chairs are taken even when no one sits. "My brother logged in the guns with me. If he'd already swiped the gun, he must've checked off the gun when we were doing the inventory, so I thought I'd already booked it."

"Look. We know you're lying. You know you're lying."

And Huddy can't even shake his head. He wants to say nothing's ever popped up with him, that he's only done something sloppy. But the guns are neatly racked, so it can't be that. "I'll need to talk to my attorney."

"You do that," the agent says. "And we'll go write up the case report. And we're freezing your inventory. None of these guns move."

Thirteen

HERITAGE COVE HAS A brick wall that steps with the gradations of the land. Huddy drives through the dual entrance and passes the stone guardhouse, and views the overblown properties, the upscale many-gabled mansions and the terraced beds and the long, well-kept lawns with Sold signs posted at the edges, but before he can feel familiar resentment, he sees a fountain with water not playing, and other markings of what's wrong at this well-to-do place. Just beyond the sold houses are even more completed, darkened homes with For Sale signs, the windows without drapes or curtains. In a driveway of this vacant, finished section sits a car, a Lexus, Joe's, and Huddy slows and sees a shape in the lit-up front room, the interior unfurnished, like staring into a cold house with dead eyes. Joe called the meeting, directed him here, but he doesn't get to pick the time, not after Huddy's been commanded all day, so Huddy keeps moving, travels a half-mile farther, he'll assess the entire premises, make Joe wait longer inside.

He circles a landscaped roundabout, sees unnumbered houses framed and roofed and weathertight, with manufacturing stickers on the windows, a cement mixer at the curb, some scaffolding beside an unfaced exterior, brick ties sticking out of the house wrap, and cubes of brick strapped and stacked on the ground. And then the buildings drop down to foundations, with sawhorses and a Dumpster and a backhoe, with wire mesh and rebar lying in the dirt. A second roundabout has only a big stone in the center and nothing planted, and then there are more poured slabs, as if the structures had collapsed, were flattened by disaster or demolition. Joe began at the front, but this partial construction looks older, not merely delayed but forever left unassembled. The cement slabs resemble giant tombstones for the families who lived here long ago, or those who will never live here now. Huddy coasts to the end, where Joe still hasn't broken ground, and surveys For Sale signs on empty lots and wild grass a foot and a half tall. He parks at the last circle, engine running, and stares at the patch of weeds and neglect, the overgrowth like an away-going crop, a final harvest on an old field. Huddy will lose big, but Joe's misfortune is greater—a confusing consolation, that he's been outnumbered, that he can't compete with Joe's steep losses. After work, Huddy had phoned his lawyer to tell him about the AK and the AR and his bad statements and his bad gun book and the recovered list, and the lawyer went silent before saying, "They have proof of all of this?" and then it was Huddy's moment of silence, in which he could detect the sound of the evidence sticking.

The guns will be lost. Soon. He'd be charged, and they could stall with four thousand pages of paperwork, and request a hearing, but the government would never yield on the violations, and he'd never convince them that his actions were defensible. He might be facing prison, or, more likely, the leveraging of prison to get him to forfeit the guns and surrender his license. He said as much to his lawyer, who paused before acknowledging that he could imagine the U.S. Attorney's office signing off on that type of deal. "That would be a way to avoid prosecution," the lawyer said, as if Huddy had just outsmarted them and won a split decision. "And we'll fight against a fine," the lawyer added, as if Huddy shouldn't underestimate the extent of their plea bargaining, but all Huddy heard was the added fees for arguing the fine's dismissal. And now Huddy has to re-enact the day's events and the eventual pleadings, to hear about Joe's worries and what's life-threatening to him, when the agents' discovery wasn't only inside that gun but inside of Huddy's skin, like they'd cut him open in his sleep and stitched him up before waking, and then cut him again to show him what had been hidden there.

He rounds the horseshoe bend and circles back, Joe already exiting the house and down the steps before Huddy's rolled to a stop far behind the Lexus. Joe slants along the path and into the bending driveway, his hand shielding the headlights' glare. Huddy switches off the engine and gets out and when he looks at Joe, he sees it wasn't just the lights bright on him that made him seem crazed. "What happened?" Joe asks, and Huddy might ask the same of Joe, the sawdust in his hair, the golden shavings on his shoulders, powdering his flannel shirt, the dirtlines of salt and dust on his neck. "What the hell were you doing? You seen my car. You keep going?"

"Missed it," Huddy says. "Too many houses in the dark."

"This one's lit!" Joe says, and points behind and walks off, and Huddy watches him corner the hedgerow and disappear into the downstairs light. He follows him, slower for Joe's impatience, loping around the clumps of bushes and into the open house, his feet loud on the stone entrance. He gazes ahead at the flight of stairs that looks shiny and unclimbed, and steps left into the empty living room, Joe already deep across the wide-planked floor, and Huddy moves forward, hearing the hollow sound of the hardwood, and without any furniture he's unsure where to stand, so he stops midway. The dining area is only a chandelier hanging. The interiors seem not just empty but abandoned. The windows are closed. Huddy inhales the uncirculated air. The brand-new house, freshly painted, already smells stale.

"This your new office?" Huddy says. He eyes Joe in this clean room and sees more of his changed outfit and harassed condition, the dirty pants, the right knee torn, the toes of his shoes discolored. The gray undershirt is filthy, striped with the same horizontal grime as the neck. Huddy half-recognizes him. It's like he's the teenage Joe after a backbreaking day, even while he looks overage for the job—been decades since he's done this hard work.

"How did Harlan get a machine gun?" Joe says, his anger rising up to the vaulted ceiling. "You fucked this deal."

"*He* fucked it." Huddy looks around unobstructed, seeing all the way through to the kitchen and out the back. A living room with no pictures, a dining area without chairs. How strange, to move from a day with ATF delving everywhere to a night with blank spaces and no shelves and no possessions to uncover or find.

"He didn't say a word," Joe says.

"Where is he?"

"What did you tell them?"

"It's what they told *me*."

"Which was?"

Huddy gives a recap, except for the AR and what was housed there. "They ain't brought charges yet. But it's coming."

"Who's your lawyer? Forget it, call mine."

Huddy shrugs, I'll call as many lawyers as you want me to. "They froze the collection. That's just today."

"How can they get the guns? Harlan . . ." his arm outstretched to signal who should be implicated, who shouldn't. "Why is it touching us? Why's it touching *me*?" He slaps his chest, yanks his shirt, aggrieved at the collateral damage. "You didn't say nothing about machine guns! You talked about collectibles. I knew he'd do something stupid. But you? You must be the smartest stupidest person I know!"

"He stole that gun, 'cause you took yours first. You started it."

"Me? No, you, Huddy, you!" The words tearing out of him and Huddy tears back.

"You! Pushed it downhill, and I'm at the bottom with my hands out catching all the shit you rolled onto me."

So mad and Joe's hands come out to spring, and Huddy quick-pivots with a hand going straight to his pocket. Joe stops, startled, legs faltering, mouth open. His fear in a moment returns to anger, and he stares in confrontation. Glares at his trigger finger, shakes his head at Huddy's violent self-defense, at the gun worn under, here in Joe's house. "You little thug."

Huddy nods at Joe's critical face, but he's already been accused too much, and he's already been hit. His hand stays there. "You walking the wrong way."

"My thug brother," Joe says, his face sneering, revolted. "Guess I should expect as much, with where you work, what you do."

"That's right. Now move back," he says. "You need to get yourself normal. You come at me, I'm gonna sit you down on the floor."

"Normal," Joe says, and he steps away, carefully. "I feel so normal it'll scare you." But his voice doesn't threaten, is wrong for scary, too weak, surrendering. "Sure scares me," he mutters darkly. "You'd pull that? You serious—you gonna shoot?"

"You going for my throat?"

"For a headlock!" he cries. "Jesus Christ."

But Huddy can justify his instinct, after being challenged unevenly. "I seen you. Weren't no headlock." Looking like he could break through a door. "Knock the fuck outta me." Knot his head, so he'll put a bullet in his foot.

Joe frowns out his residual anger. Screws his face at the explanation, at his own blocked aggression. Thought they were scuffling, a hand-to-hand fight, and his underhanded brother outfoxed him—no way is Joe holding him harmless. Still, he nods a truce. He rotates his shoulder, stretches his back, flexes out his sore right leg. He winces, the aches and pain of a twelve-hour day spent balancing doors, crouching down on his knees. "He told me the gun was never logged in. How's that, Huddy? You find something bad and just ignore it?"

He's right, Huddy admits his guilt. He didn't need to dump the AK, shred it, cut it up. Just say, *Come get this gun.* They might've done a spot check, they might not have checked the AR, and if they had, the trouble wouldn't have been compounded by lies. He'd apologize, but only to himself. He looks back at Joe, who's still extending his hurt leg, and Huddy feels sorry but then resentful, because he's also afflicted. "You got your money out. Go sell your two prizes." But he knows the guns won't recoup the expenditure on the houses and the lots.

"I sold one. The other, it's tied up."

"What's that mean?"

"Posted bail. They got him on federal charges. Took the Yellow Boy down to Poplar."

"Bullshit."

"Go down there. Across from the courthouse. They got a two-in-one operation, part pawnshop, part bail bonds. You just switch counters, paperwork. They didn't need nothing but the gun.

'Course, they put on a lien on it, so I can't get it back until the case is over." Joe looks around, bewildered, lost in an empty house. "I can't afford frozen. Frozen means time runs out. Lorie's gone back to work. I'm back to installing doors. Long hours, upgrades, repairs—but I can't offset the losses. Just wake up owing more. Can't sleep, 'cause there's no off-hours on the debt. Every hour is the same—midday, midweek. I went from planning early retirement to never retiring, and now I'm just trying to save my own home. I'll be damned if the bank's taking that."

Huddy raises his hand for Joe to stop, slow down, his labored breath relentless and outspent. It's hard to look at this panic and pressure, so Huddy turns aside, listens for Joe's breathing to lengthen and normalize. He examines the construction. The surfaces fit perfectly. No gaps in the casing joints, no wide seams in the floor, no taping lines in the walls. "I can't believe no one lives here," Huddy says. How does a big, new Germantown house with no mistakes stay vacant? He exchanges half-grins with Joe, lifts an appreciative hand to pay tribute to his brother's design. It must be an accomplishment to make something this solid, to build something that won't come apart and destruct, to feel such pride of place, even if it breaks you.

"Upper-end homes," Joe says. "When no one can afford upper-end. Looks like I built the wrong product." His hands form an empty bowl and he splays his fingers to show the money sifting through. "Maybe I should take out the chandelier? Maybe I picked the wrong doorknobs? Go less neutral with the walls? You think if I switch out the doorknobs, darken the floor, I solve my problem?"

Huddy shrugs at the alterations, the retouchings and different colors. "Up the road looks good. Sold some."

"Real bullish up at the front. The first offerings went quick, then ... it slowed. Then ... Like a spigot turned off. But you took a look, didn't you? You seen what's out there."

Huddy can't see beyond the windows, but he knows there's nothing hidden in the darkness. No people, no trees, no activity, no noise. Not some hushed suburban evening but a street gone mute. "Ain't your fault it's a dead market."

"Dead market? Smell of death, alright. The owners, the few I got, they complaining how I won't bring in mowers, keep the entire place neat and clean. I'm like, go talk to the bank. They're past renegotiating. They're doing a cash call. Calling the loan. I'm hanging on for dear life. Bankruptcy, receivership ... All that fine print you don't read. This wasn't supposed to be a gamble. I built the houses they wanted built. I was punching out fifty houses a year, and people were paying before I finished painting the baseboards. Selling faster than you could build them. Come in on a Monday, you'd have multiple offers, three, four contracts on my desk. And now ... I can't get out from under. I'm upside down. I can't *work* my way out of this." He wrenches his arm from a sleeve, sets a hand on the mantel ledge to steady himself. "I did it right. These other builders—I didn't go down to Florida and play. Get crazy with money. I've stayed on every job. Walked it every day. It's insulting, when you build something like this, and you don't get a single person to rag you on the price—you can't even sell it below market. Can't even fire-sale it. I know what's in this house. How do you do everything right and it's wrong? I don't know, Huddy, you think I should try arson?" He looks up at the beamwork, a place to set the spark.

"You serious?" Huddy glances at the fireplace, with its one fake log.

"Am I serious about full replacement value? Now why would I be serious about that? Except I'd only get away with it once. So I guess I'll have to be serious about killing myself." He looks above again to the ceiling—a place to suspend the rope. Huddy shakes his head, won't imagine a strung-up brother. Joe turns, scrubs his face, drags his fingers across his skin, tracing a raked outline. "I can't believe they froze the guns. I'ma talk to my lawyer, we gonna unfreeze those guns. Government agents, who's paying their salary? I am. You know, some thieves stole my compressors? Scum driving around. They vultures, circling this place, and they on it like a dead cow. If I catch 'em . . . Only person who's gonna steal from me is me."

He removes his hand from the mantel, squares himself on the wall, crouches and sinks to the floor. Huddy stares at slumping Joe. He feels foolish, left standing while his brother sits, as if Joe had stepped down into his backyard pit, so he finds a spot against the other wall. Their bodies fold at right angles and face each other. But now Huddy feels sillier, staring up from the ground at a bare room, the two of them sitting without chairs when a moment before it was just Joe. Joe scratches his hair and the dust falls, collects on his sleeve. "Ain't I shaggy dog?" he says, and he shakes out his shirt, and Huddy thinks, You look like an honest day. "You gotta come up with a Plan B," Joe says, and Huddy is almost flattered that Joe would defer to him a second plan, even if he doesn't have one, and even as he mistrusts the flattery, which is confirmed when Joe inserts, "squeeze more from the shop."

"How I do that?"

"You tell me," he says, only curious. But then he adds, "Maybe roll the dice a little," and he nods, chin nudging, a small favor, nodding again, already decided. He twists his wrist, as if Huddy just needs more flexibility to generate cash. "Don't tell me you always been by-the-law legit."

ATF accuses him of being a criminal, and now Joe's accusation is he better be. Huddy laughs.

"Something funny?" Joe says.

"Oh, I don't know. Sure, Joe, I ain't been no poster child. Some controlled instances, but I never gone overboard. You want me to put some kind of word out? Maybe I should read *Break the Law for Dummies?*"

"Don't lecture me."

"I'll have every hoodrat bringing me shit, and two months from now, one'll get caught and his new best friend is a detective. I ain't getting rolled by some crackhead with a case of iPods."

"Nobody cares about some pawnshop on Lamar."

"Except now they do." The sign in his shop that says, SMILE SHOPLIFTERS YOU ARE ON CAMERA, but now the sign is flipped. "You ain't getting the part about me being monitored. ATF already swarming my place. I'm a target. Whatever happens, cops'll still be stinging the area. Ain't getting my ass burned on parking-lot buys."

"So have 'em bring the stuff somewhere else."

"Like, my house? Oh, that's miles away, I'm safe there."

"How about I *offer* you a house?" Joe says, his voice uncertain, hedging.

"What, to stash?"

"To have. After," he says, and he waves his hand to present the property rights, and his voice is secure. "You get me out of this mess, the last one's yours." He points a finger, a confident line aimed straight at Huddy's reward.

"You'd sign it over?" Huddy asks, and he air-scrawls a signature.

"Exactly."

Huddy aims two fingers back, extending his index finger and raising his thumb.

"What's that?" Joe asks.

"That's my bullshit detector."

"You know—I'm getting tired of you pointing guns at me."

"And I'm glad there's a wall behind my back. You think for a second I believe one of these houses is mine? And how do I take that promise to the bank, after they foreclosed? 'My brother said it was free. He said if I stole enough, I'd get this freebie house.' I suspect they'd reject them terms. 'Sides, I already got a house. You ain't never been there to know."

Joe's back is stiff against the wall, his hands stacked in his lap. His face holds still, like a mask of his real face. In this blank room, there are no plans and no obstacles to them. Huddy eyes what statement is building, sees a hand come up and squeeze the side of his skull. Then Joe slides the hand over his mouth as if he were smothering himself. All the times Huddy's driven over to Joe's house to urge and beg, and now he can not talk and just wait and outsit him because it's Joe's turn to devise. He watches Joe's fingers touch together to form a cage, which he sets around his eyes as if to compress his mind, and he stares through the cage as if staring through a circle, a zero. "Maybe I got something," Joe says, and he wrings his hands, his fists tensing, opening and closing, little squeezes. "This neighbor—not here, where I live. She and her husband—filthy rich. Lake house, yachts. Four-wheelers to play in the mud. Stupid money. Went to a party at their house. Platters of filet mignons. Should see her. Full mink, cowboy boots. She's wearing four bracelets just to upstage the other wives. The two of 'em: Clampetts got rich. Well, they've been having money troubles. Like a June frost—gone. So this lady, I run into her last week, and we get to talking about times is hard, and she asks me if I was wanting to buy these Christmas gnomes."

"Gnomes." Huddy's whole day with ATF, in his records and all up under his clothes, and now it's ending with a nickel-and-dime story about gnomes. Tried paying in for guns, and now let's chip in for gnomes and eke out a profit. Today, Huddy just can't hear a small-time scheme.

"Says she got like twenty of 'em and they're worth fifty apiece, but she'll sell all twenty for a hundred, and she's telling me about the bank and how dumb her husband's been. All this money, but her husband's just been pyramiding. She don't say it, but it's how. Now, she don't want nothing to do with a pawnshop, but I figure if I buy this stuff, funnel it to you, and you sell it—"

"Gnomes?" He looks at Joe, propped up on the wall.

"It's a hell of a lot more than that. She's just *starting* there. It's name-your-price. And she ain't the only one who's down to the nub."

"Fine, go crumb this lady." Huddy rubs his fingertips. "Right now, the retail market ain't too strong on gnomes."

"Will you stop saying *gnomes*?"

"Why not? Sounds like these are premium gnomes!"

"Just stop."

"Are they twenty *different* gnomes, or they all the same kind, or maybe somewheres in the middle—like, five sugarplum fairies and five Princess Whatevers? She got a Santa Claus fairy? She got Father Time? She got any bells on the feet? And have you *seen* these items? 'Cause condition would be important. If she's kept them in mint, that's one thing. Maybe she preserved them in plastic? But, the way you describing, she probably been sleeping with all twenty. And a bunch of 'em been falling on the floor, and a few of 'em been chew toys for the poodles. I'm asking cause, money-wise, I'm at zero."

"And I'm at minus zero."

The bad tallies, the claim and counterclaim, echo in the air. The room is smaller with nothing in it, but their discussion is bigger for the same reason. Huddy feels double sensations, closeness and distancing, far apart at opposite ends but identical in their positions. "Why are we talking trinkets?" he says. "Why are we talking *cost*?" Everything is out of the room because everything is inside them, all personal effects emptied so he and Joe can focus on one essential fact. Huddy's eyes narrow. The room is only hard edges. "I'm at nothing. You're at negative. We both out of pocket. Unless there's some number I ain't crunching. Far as I'm concerned, anything we buy, we overbuying. Unless we buying it free. Unless we use *play* money."

"I ain't a criminal," Joe says.

"Ain't one either."

They stare deadlocked.

"I don't care what you are," Huddy says. "I'm talking against payments. You best stop asking me to open my shop to thieves. You're the one trying to buy time. I'm just saying—maybe you should steal it."

"I'm not a criminal." Joe laces his fingers and Huddy studies his interlocking hands.

"That's what I tried telling ATF—about me." Huddy gestures at the surroundings as if the contents were lifted, the entire house burglarized. "Maybe for just a little while, we are." He can't decide if he's in a crime scene or a hideout, a place where things have been taken from or later taken to. The police, ATF, and now his brother all suspect him of lawbreaking. Okay, the little daily maneuvers:

Someone brings you a fifty-dollar Sears gift card and you know it's stolen and you buy it for twenty and sell it for thirty-five, and they bring you another card the next day, and you take it or don't, but either way you stop. And when a young man brings in twenty memorial coins, with the impression of his grandpa on the front of the coin, do you ask, Did you steal this from the old man's funeral or from your grandma's safe? Or do you listen to the bogus inheritance story and ask how much? And when this family thief returns with another stack of death benefits, do you cut him off then? But Huddy's never been so bad as to buy fifteen engagement rings from some fella saying they're all mama's engagement rings, when mama ain't been engaged but once. And Huddy never was the broker who had thieves working for him, who paid addicts for stolen goods with drugs he kept in back. Or like another broker, who intentionally scrambled the serial numbers when he'd fax the merchandise list downtown. Huddy's crimes have always been about omission, just little cases of daytime blindness. But why not, for a quick fix, be the lowlife people think he is? Especially if he gets to tell his brother, as they sit in one of his unsellable houses, that he's one, too.

No table to gather around but Huddy feels like they're hunched together in a corner booth, and without the table, Huddy can see all of Joe, no body part hidden underneath. He suddenly realizes how visible they are from the street, but no one's looking in. They're in a subdivision that feels like a clearing, on a site without a street address, in a house that's not a home. It's hard to feel like their words have any substance, that their crimes could occur in any real jurisdiction. Hard to feel like yourself, much less like anyone, in an empty location. Nothing hanging on the walls. No clock with ticking hands, as if any time—five minutes or all night or into a second day and onto next week and passing through a different year—is this same hour. No one else is in the room to say, "Stop."

"Harlan ever tell you what he done in Florida?" Joe says, which to Huddy sounds like another world, as far off as the future undetectable crimes he just imagined. He shakes his head, but he already knows why Harlan's been named. "Shed burglar."

"When'd he say that?" Huddy says. He's hearing about Harlan's past exploits to learn how best to exploit him, to put Harlan's illegal actions into practice. Joe wouldn't mention Harlan unless he'd already made that decision.

"Today."

"Piss-ant burglar." Huddy's pictured Harlan out in the woods, and now he's a sneak thief, busting doors, smashing glass, slicing through screens. "Get caught?"

"Petty-theft conviction. Misdemeanor."

"That's why he left Florida?"

"Sort of. Did time, got out. Stopped doing sheds. Got to stealing credit cards, taking 'em to a gas station, say, 'I'll fill up your car, you give me twenty bucks.' He'd do it three, four times, go to another station. I guess he got to feeling awful. Came back to Memphis."

"Lassie comes home."

"Says he was a good thief before he got busted."

"You believe that?"

Joe shrugs.

"He tell you that, or you ask him?"

Joe doesn't respond, his eyes shifting away, and Huddy'll count the answer as both, hearing one of Harlan's brags secondhand from Joe. Huddy adds up the grains of truth. Or maybe Joe, in paying the bail, is entitled to a full confession, and now Huddy will confess to what else is true, just a small amount, almost weightless.

"Gold," Huddy says. "No electronics, nothing bulky. An ounce of gold, sits on your finger. You can turn it quick. Always have a buyer, and the buyer is the fence. No paperwork, no inventory, no serial numbers. Not after you hit it with a hammer. Engravings come off with a torch. Mash up all the gold chains and rings. There's your quick untraceable cash. Start bringing gold."

Joe stays silent, and Huddy talks to mean the same wordless thing. "I'm already caught today. Got my hands full with ATF. I ain't going near a crime, and the crime ain't going near the shop. I'll move it for you, but I ain't getting tied. I'll sell, but not steal. It's time for you to get brave. You a big keyholder, Joe. I already seen you with mine. Start using some others. You probably got master keys to all of them houses you built. And the alarm systems, I bet you got a bypass code. Looks like you just found a way out. Or in."

Joe shakes his hand, nullifying, impossible. "You're wrong, both ways. Sure I've got bypass codes. Except the alarm company would know the numbers I pressed to disarm the system. As for keys, the master gets disabled on first use. The doorknob re-keys it."

"Looks like we're stuck at zero. Or minus."

Their eyes meet. Neither brother can give ground because both are backed against a wall. Huddy looks around. It's the first vacant house he's been in where a person hadn't left to make it empty. The first house he's been in that's all gone just because it's new. "The last house we were in with nothing, it was mama's, when we cleared it together."

"So what?" Joe squints his eyes as if he can't hear what Huddy's saying, then shakes his head as if it were said too loud. "Jesus, who cares?" he says, as if Huddy'd said it a hundred times.

Huddy laughs at his exasperation, a joke about Joe's mind and the direction it won't work. Can't do family history, can't do the past. No old days, no *then*. No remembering, even if it's recent. But looking at Joe, in his grubby jeans, Huddy can see him smaller at fifteen, like he was wearing an old disguise that he thinks no one will identify because he's grown into someone else. Teenage Joe and his dead mother—it's like Huddy's returned to a new place, not a complete reunion, not seeing both parents and not every sibling but enough of a homecoming, the rooms cleared like furniture pushed back for the evening dance. But Joe doesn't care about remembrance, so neither will Huddy. Joe was there, Joe wasn't there, same difference.

"Eight hundred square feet," Joe says. "Our home. That was the size of it. That metal roof. It was so loud when it rained, it sounded like trains going over us."

"I remember that," Huddy says. "Like airplanes."

"We were gonna be put out on the street," Joe says, and Huddy remembers that, too, their father splitting, and they borrowed some money from their aunt, but mostly it was Joe keeping them inside. There was a house up the street that had been demolished and Joe picked through the ruins to salvage bricks for resale, took a hatchet to chip off the mortar. Another time, he collected newspapers by the pound to bring down to the paper plant. All the ways that Joe cleared money.

"I remember," Joe says, "a renovation. Here, in Germantown. This was when I was starting out. I was moving up. I hadn't done houses yet, but I was close. And the owner comes over, he was a real society type, and we got to talking, and he asked me, 'And where do you hail from?' Just like that. *Hail from.* I thought I'd spiraled off into outer space." He shakes his head, both at the story and the reminiscing. "The thing about Germantown," Joe whispers, but in this room even a low voice is raised. "Most everyone got security systems. But half of them feel secure enough not to turn them on. They got the alarm sign in the yard, but that's it. This house is protected by a lawn sign. And the old-timers, they still unlock their doors. They think it's 1950."

"Like the widow Yewell."

"Somebody like her. But not her." He brings a hand to his head, scratches his hair, his hand circling like he was spinning his mind, until he stops and says, "Harlan," and Huddy thinks he knows what he means. "He owes me for the bail. And I'm gonna hook him in with a big lawyer, who's in tight with the DA. He'll cut his time."

"You'll have him commit crimes to get a lighter sentence?"

"Backwards, huh? 'Cept forwards is going broke. Don't tell me what's fair. I ain't hearing from a loan shark about fairness. If I did what you did, it would tear me up. I'm saying, Harlan, he'll be on board with this."

Harlan worked for Huddy, and now he's been passed on to do contract work for Joe. Huddy forgave Harlan's debt, but Joe will make sure he redeems the bail. Why does Joe get to set Harlan's amends? Where is Harlan? Here, nearby? Kept upstairs in a bedless room? Huddy listens for footsteps, a creak of a door half-opening. He looks to the window for a face to show, turns to the doorway for Harlan to cross the threshold. Maybe he's skulking in the street, or hiding behind the roundabout rock.

"And this big lawyer, this plea deal, Harlan gets less by telling more?"

"Are you crazy? And lose the guns?"

But the guns are almost lost. Sitting level with Joe, and Huddy thought it was a clear conspiracy between the two of them against Harlan, thought Harlan was theirs, and now it's Joe and the lawyer and Harlan colluding against him. Huddy is in the room, but he's the odd man out. First-born and last-born, with Huddy in the excluded middle. "I think I'ma stick with my lawyer."

"I'm not gonna play him against you, 'cause I'm in with you."

"How do I know you're bringing me all the gold?"

"How do I know you're bringing back all the cash?"

He eyes Joe, who eyes him back with mutual suspicion. "I guess everyone's siding with everyone." Mirror images, with Joe trying to make money on both sides. "As long as we don't trust each other equally, we're okay."

A shaky deal with no agreement, not even a hands-free nod. Joe's arms stay folded and he adds to what wasn't finalized, to what he might not deliver. "I can't do halves on this. It's gonna have to be two-thirds, one-third. 'Cause my risk is double."

"Your risk? What role you playing? Maybe you ought split your thirds with who's risking. Fifty-fifty. This money ought be shared three ways."

"Okay," Joe says, but Huddy knows how he'll divide the difference, a high-low split with his third worth more. But Huddy won't negotiate percentages for an absent party, and he won't demand evens. "He said the way he did sheds was fast. Four or five in a night. Full speed, then wait for things to quiet down. Full speed again."

His voice switches, and Huddy realizes Joe wasn't just repeating Harlan's words but attempting an impersonation. "Stash it here," Huddy says. "No one's worried about you."

"I'm worried about me," Joe says, back to his own voice. He looks around to comprehend how his open house can become a hiding place. He stretches his face, as if that mask that Huddy imagined fit on too tight. He taps his jaw. His cheeks are red, his eyes bulging as if sitting by fire, too close to burning air.

"I'm worried about you, Joe. You worried about Harlan?"

"Harlan's not worried about Harlan." Joe looks off, disowning. "Yeah, I'm worried." But not for Harlan's punishment but his experience, about whether he's competent enough to be a professional thief. "You?"

"I think you better slap a GPS on him. Brand it on his butt."

Joe tugs his arm to check his watch, frowning at the time, but Huddy knows it's not impatience but fear. Joe's not delayed today, because today is over, tomorrow is beginning, and he's already running ahead breakneck.

"Harlan," Joe says again, and for once tonight, the meaning can't be apprehended. The name could be used as assurance or warning or grievance. Huddy's only sure of what it's long stopped being—a shared joke. Joe glances overhead, and Huddy can't perceive that action either, if he's confirming that Harlan's up on the second floor, or if he's praying to a higher power—for forgiveness or assistance or answers—or if he's scared of all that could fall upon him, or if he's saying, *Look at me, Huddy, hanging on air.*

"Harlan," Huddy says back, his eyes not going vertical but straight ahead at Joe, as if Harlan were right there, in between. Huddy sees through him and then beyond to Joe, who appears to look back but only gazes inward, his body freezing.

"No," Joe says, like he'd just flinched awake from a nightmare, and then he shuts his eyes as if he were entering another one, some picture of Harlan tripping alarms, being chased. Or maybe it's his own arrest, Huddy can't say. Joe draws his lips together, his eyes open and squinting to study what's dreamless before him, which is just as confused, and he glances at Huddy for understanding, but Huddy can't explain it—can't find any reason in a voided room— how his life ended up here.

"You want to know how to make a million?" Joe asks.

"How's that?" Huddy says.

"Start with ten." Joe covers his neck, but Huddy still sees him swallow. "Let's get this *over*," Joe snaps, and his face seems to Huddy both sad and ferocious. Huddy hears the bad rhythm, the heavy, overworked sound, of Joe breathless again.

And with the conversation settled and with no interference—nothing in the way on the walls and every wall the same nothing, no centerpiece on the floor as if the entire floor, including the two people at the margins, were in the center—Huddy doesn't need to close his eyes to any clutter. He can envision his entire inventory, his mind running through his stockpile to furnish a useful accessory, like a police radio, left by a cop with a drug problem, who pawned it, got fired and never reclaimed the device.

"You're gonna need a scanner," Huddy says, and they both sit still and don't talk at all, as if they were already listening but not yet hearing outside voices.

Fourteen

BUT BEFORE ANY GOLD comes in, the guns come out. A car appears, a man exits, enters Huddy's store. He wears a suit, a badge, a gun, and he identifies himself: Shelby County Criminal Investigator. He asks if he's Huddy Marr, and Huddy wonders about the cost of saying no. For an instant, he thinks he might get off lighter, that his lawyer knocked the charges down, the U.S. Attorney's office dropping it into the county's lap. Federal got bigger fish, and Huddy wants to be small, and maybe this has all been a scare.

"Mister Marr," the man says, "the state is prepared to send to the grand jury a statement with the following charges." He places a large sheet of paper on the counter, but Huddy is unsure if he's supposed to read the paper or keep hearing the man, so he listens to the litany. "Two counts of unlawful possession of a prohibited weapon. One count, false statement to law enforcement. One count, tampering with or falsifying official documents and evidence."

Which means the charges haven't been lowered, the federal laws mirror the state, the county DA treating him like he's big enough to reduce him to nothing.

"Four charges. If you're convicted of all four counts, you're looking at a minimum of twelve years. We're offering you an opportunity to play right, but you'll catch these charges if you don't play. We will refuse to prosecute on the condition that you give up all your guns and surrender your license. And you agree to contact Memphis Burglary Bureau if an individual is looking to drop off stolen merchandise."

Huddy avoids the man. If he never looks up again, if he only looks down at the paper but never touches it, maybe the charges can never touch him.

"That's the offer. Today. Right now."

Huddy shakes his head. The man can stay, but the paper doesn't belong here.

"You won't cooperate?"

No, the man can't be here either. "I don't know who you think I am."

The man points to the paper for his list of answers. There is nothing more to understand.

"I'm not some undertrader. These gun charges—"

"Sir, I'm only gonna run it down for you one more time. We're done talking." He repeats the charges, fast and emphatic, as if they've been memorized for years. "And you agree to apprise us of other criminal activity. Do you accept the terms?"

What about if Huddy knew of a plan in the works? Would he get his guns back? Keep them? But he can't get credit for what he's agreeing to do.

"No jail?" Huddy asks.

"As long as you play ball."

He waits for something—a thought, a call, a signal. He is silent a long time. The wall clock reads 9:22 or 23, an in-between number, misaligned, as if this moment were happening too early or even more late. If this paper is on Huddy's counter, why isn't it for sale? His mind narrows. Then he nods.

"I'll need you to open up your gun safes," the man says, and he gets on his phone and Huddy sits and buries his face and before long two more vehicles appear, one identical to the investigator's sedan, the other a white panel truck with gold lettering. The truck swings around and backs in next to the parked sedan, the other sedan parks on the other side, boxing the truck in between. Four men step out of the two vehicles and slide open the truck and remove Anvil cases and carry them into the shop. The investigator meets them inside the door and they huddle together and then the men walk to the back room and grab the guns and tie-wrap the cylinders, the guns go in a box, the box goes in the Anvil case, a receipt is attached to the case with the serial number of each weapon inside. Two men grab handles and carry a case to the investigator, who stands near the counter writing out the serial numbers. Huddy looks away, but the monitor shows the same image, as if the seizure is happening twice at once, one real and one recorded—but it should be happening a million real times. He'd switch off the recording, erase the footage, if it would help him forget this wrong moment, but it's already his worst memory. The cases go out to the truck, the gate slides up and then down, the men return to the store with more cases and disappear into the back and emerge again. Huddy wants to leave. He doesn't want to see this awful procedure. The men convey the cases, pause before the investigator for the writing, and walk again. The investigator provides Huddy with a copy of the manifest, three eleven-by-seventeen pages, all the guns listed, and Huddy can't take his eyes off the pink pages. *Confiscated by Shelby County District Attorney's Office, Criminal Investigative Division, File Number*—ten digits, far bigger than the profit Huddy would have made. *You want to know how to make a million?* Did he hear this line or think it himself or say it aloud? The investigator turns his back and leaves. Huddy stares at the gun list and wishes he were seeing these numbers for the first time, that he was back in the hunt room with the widow, starting the acquisition, his initial sight of those fine makes and numberings. He has a sick thought that these agents are working for her, that they've confiscated the guns to return them to her—perhaps the son has arranged it—to rest them back on the racks in Yewell's gun room, which sits inside the treasure house, as if Huddy's bid and purchase weren't nothing but a break-in. When he closes his eyes, he sees the investigator handing the widow the original white copy of the manifest. He sees Kipp spinning the wheel. He opens his eyes and watches three cars drive off in a line, and it's surprising that they turn left, away from Germantown, because he'd already completed the neat circle in his mind. It's the quietest robbery ever, no smashed glass, no taunts, no roughing up. Nothing ransacked, everything standing. Never once rubbed his face in it. He's never been so politely bullied.

He stares at the duplicate pages and calls Joe. "The guns are gone," Huddy says, and he's phoned because he doesn't want to hear more face to face. "I'm out," and the silence means Joe knows it's more than the guns. No scanner, no selling.

"Me, too," Joe says, but Huddy doesn't believe him, he hears it being said to a third person who's not listening in.

"Where's Harlan?"

"You lost the guns. Got no right to find anyone." The phone shuts off.

Driving home, he sees a dead animal on the road, but on closer inspection the carcass is nothing but a wet, mashed-up cardboard box. He tells Christie that it's done, that he's not going to jail, and when she asks about the guns, he turns away from the center of the bed and repeats to the wall that he's not going to jail. He doesn't mean to snub, but he just wants to be shut of the day. Except, he keeps thinking of the widow—as if each eye-blink trips a silent alarm in his head. He can't help reconnecting the confiscation to her. She graciously thanks the men for the recovery, the pages a valued want list, while Kipp excuses himself to recount the guns.

It's quiet and Huddy keeps to the bed edge. He can feel Christie deciding what to do with his ignoring. And then the mattress jostles as she shoves her weight out, her feet down on the floor and away. He pushes out, shuffles along the narrow aisle between the bed and the wall, through the hallway and follows her into the living room, where she's at the front door, and he thinks she's turning the key to go outside—he's about to say, "Wait"—but she's just double-checking the deadbolt. He hears metal click against metal. The sound is thick and solid. Not a safety lock, but it still feels pickproof and secure.

"I'm glad you ain't going to *jail*, Huddy," she says, and she falls back on the couch. He stands before her, his toes touching the scatter rug. Her hand rakes across her face, and then drops to her lap. "Now, you wanna tell me where you *are* going? Maybe fill me in on *that*."

He presses a hand to his forehead to stop the pounding. He tries to answer, but his day's been too full of demands and penance.

"Are they shutting you down?" Her eyes squinch and study him as if she were reading a page of rules to find the exact penalty.

"They ain't running me. But they cutting me down. A lot."

She looks older, Huddy thinks, or an older version, like when she first walked into his life talking about her younger self. He can't help but picture her again before and now.

"I'm losing the way I run it. But there's different ways to farm. Guess I'm about to learn another way."

"Harder?" she says, and he nods. "I guess no Summer," she says, and it isn't until she gestures in a direction that Huddy realizes she means street and not season. "Maybe you stop farming, then. Sell cars. Houses."

Sure. He even knows where he'll start, a whole mess of over-built houses. Good money there. "Not neither. Them markets done a swan dive. Buyer's market, but no one's buying."

"I'm just trying to talk up some facts. You talking about farming."

"Look, I just need to find out where I'm headed. Soon as I figure which way, we'll be fine. I'll get moving again." He shrugs his shoulder, to signal a minor adjustment, some small change, but it looks like a tick he can't control, and it only increases the annoyance on her face.

"Funny you should say that. Moving."

"What's that mean?" He looks back at the deadbolt, thinks of the snicking sound of the lock, along with her fiddling hand that he thought was for leaving the house.

She folds her arms, her body hunched and coiled. "All this talk of Germantown."

"Germantown?" he says, surprised but relieved, since he thought she meant going, even if she's never said so before. "I thought you was pulling the pin."

She frowns, because she doesn't want to discuss what she's *not* doing. He watches her arms tighten against herself.

"You wanna live out in Germantown?" he asks.

"Wouldn't mind living in a bubble. But no, not there. Farther."

"Collierville."

"No," she says, louder. "I mean being gone from Memphis."

"Thought you like it here. Thought you were alright with it."

"I am. And if you said, 'Let's move tomorrow,' I'd say, 'Let's go.'"

"You need more house?" he says, and he gestures around the bungalow spaces.

"House is enough. I might like this enough ... *elsewhere*. You like hearing gunshots?"

"That's over there. Other side of McLean. Always," Huddy says, and he extends his arm fully to push the trouble far out—go past McLean to another world—even though the crime is near, just a couple blocks, same street, a half-mile. Still, his eyes pinch to insist the trouble is concentrated there.

She throws her hands out right and left. "North and south ain't any better."

So what, he wants to say, about the surrounding area. This long street is fine, and he's pretty sure that every respectable city neighborhood borders on a ragged edge.

"It's stuff spilling over," she says. "Matter of time before what's there overtakes what's here." And then she tells him about the neighbor who's been pruning his bushes so he can see his driveway better, keep an eye on his car. Because he's had two break-ins already. Another neighbor, who lives on a corner lot, thinned his trees to watch for activity along the side street, because a pedestrian got pistol-whipped and robbed. "He told me *another* neighbor was pulling her hedge for the same reason."

Huddy's never heard of this, people unplanting their land for safety and sightlines, shedding limbs so nothing hides behind. He imagines this street of shrinking trees, cut down to a clearing, this old neighborhood now an open field. Or maybe, Huddy thinks, instead of trying to see everything, how about just grow gardens made of thorns. The street could have its own anti-theft garden club—roses and nettles and cacti—prickers as if the ground were topped with barbed wire, and then every burglar or robber would get snagged on vines when they attempted to rush out from the street or climb up to windows.

He can't take his neighbors' fears seriously, even if the threats are real. Their actions, their in-house stakeouts, spook him more than the assaults and disturbances. If this neighborhood of tree surgeons is worried that their borders and hedgerows aren't safe, if they're concerned about protecting their property and themselves on a walk, he might suggest stronger defenses.

"Another neighbor says we ought form an association and document all the incidents, so the police will know to patrol more."

Any other day, Huddy'd be glad to hear about an extra sweep.

"People drive through here crazy. 'Member when that car flipped over?"

He does. Screaming tires and a loud crash in a small hour that woke them and sent them outside to see the smash-up, a car flipped over and the engine still running, the driver's-side door open with no driver. Cops chased the suspect across yards and tackled him in the neighbor's driveway. Smoke billowed, and a cop asked the crowd for a fire extinguisher before the vehicle sparked. It reminds Huddy of another story, another chase a cop told him of. A late-night traffic stop, the driver ditching out, and when the cop found him, the guy was hiding in a backyard—not just hiding but buried into the earth, he'd climbed down into the garden and thrown the dirt back over him, except his eyes were poking out, and the cop, shining a flashlight, caught these sparklers staring back at him.

Huddy knows right now to keep this creepy story to himself. Instead he says, "This stuff happens once in five years."

"Flipped cars, maybe. But not the crime. And how about the panhandlers? That's a daily thing. Going door to door."

"They just knock, go away. You don't even gotta answer."

"They walk up . . . After a while, it's like they live here more than I do. We ain't raked the leaves, so every day somebody comes to the door asking to do it for money." Which is true with the panhandlers: the branches shake and the doorbell rings as soon as the leaves fall and reach the ground.

"I'll get to the leaves," Huddy says.

"That ain't the point. It's our yard. Half of them don't even ask to do work. They just poor. They come up to our house at night, even. Maybe we put up a lawn sign, says, 'We're on it. Stop asking.' "

"Or just 'No Panhandling.' "

"Or we could get a dog. Some of the dogs on this block, I can't believe they ain't tore the door from the hinges."

"Maybe the neighbors could ask the panhandlers to prune their trees, too."

She doesn't laugh and he doesn't blame her because nothing's laughable today. "Huddy. We've lived here all our lives. It ever feel like spending your whole life in the same place is wrong? I don't mind it, as long as I'm the one choosing. Take away the choice and I'm stuck in West Tennessee. I mean, are we attached to here? If not, maybe we try something new. My sister, she's lived other places. Dallas, Nashville, Missouri. Been like a tourist her whole adult life. Ain't saying it's made her happier, all that change. But she ain't homesick, neither. It's when I think about how I never left—I start thinking this might be all I'm gonna see. Then I start dreaming about it."

"Dreams?"

"Yeah. Wake up and I've been in Louisville. I hear Louisville is nice."

"Where else?"

"California—I always had a thing for it. Used to think about New Orleans, but that won't work no more. Middle Tennessee would be good, for country living. Wouldn't mind living in a good part surrounded by good. Or surrounded by nothing. Farms, fields. I don't know, I like it here, it's a regular house."

"Might take a long time, to make a house change. Longer, now. Bad time for everyone, for relocating. The whole country's stuck where they at, so if you haven't gone to where you wanted—got no choice but to overstay here. The ones that *are* moving, they ain't got no say in the matter." He looks down at his wedding ring, and when he looks back to her, he says, "I lost fifty thousand dollars today."

"Jesus Christ!" she says, burying her face, her voice deep and echoing inside her cupped hands. He listens to her blow heavy breaths into her palms, and he watches her eyes open but her hands stay veiling, as if she were staring out at a movie's scary parts. She opens her hands to the side of her face, like shutters flung, and holds them there, as if she were shielding her eyes to better see the sum. He sits beside her on the couch. She looks straight ahead and then around, to survey the items contained here, the secondhand TV, the mismatched chairs. No signs of splurging, which makes her both mad and afraid. "Where'd you *find* fifty thousand?" She turns to him, sickened and confused at the spending, the lost money from an unseen source, squirreled away and then stolen out.

"Scraped every surface of the store. Scraped it clean."

"What about the house?"

"Didn't touch the house."

She smoothes fingers against her eyes; pinches the bridge of her nose, sniffs. "Damn, Huddy, that's some fucked-up sweepstakes." She shuts her eyes again. She sighs, exhausted, and doesn't speak, and it almost looks like she's sleeping.

He struggles for an explainable statement. Except, to talk about his surefire plan is to talk about how it wasn't. He looks at her flushed cheeks, then turns away, to the fireplace, the chimney, thinks of cash going up sooty walls. The money he might've earned—the number sounds uncountable, irrational. It's as if he expected to purchase a million-dollar gift at a dime store. When he closes his eyes, he thinks of the neighbors hacking trees, cutting them down to stubs.

He returns to her, watches her think in silence, her hands stacked in her lap. "I guess one way to look at it is, fifty thousand to keep you from jail."

"That'd be *one* way. One way of saying I got skinned." He shakes his head. "I missed something big."

"Missed jail."

"That, too."

"You missed something, and it missed you."

"It don't make it feel even. Way I'm seeing it, I feel like I've been pushed out. Or kept in. Everybody's just standing around a circle, holding me right here." He sees everyone standing about him, taking up their positions.

"Who's everyone?"

"Cops. Feds."

"Brothers?"

He shifts side to side. Then he nods at the scope of the scam and investigation.

"Well, you saying you got skinned. Maybe not all of you. What's left of your skin—you *save* it."

He nods.

"You do that?"

He nods again. Sure, it's history. He better.

"Let them people go about their business. They over with you. They gonna disappear and the next bad part happens elsewhere. Let that circle of yours go circulating. Gang up on someone else." Her face is severe, and he stays on her eyes which won't blink.

Two days, and then Huddy reads an account in the paper, a string of break-ins, the Germantown police on the lookout for a serial burglar, cash and jewelry taken from five residences. Doors unlocked, back doors pried open, no sign of forced entry, and Huddy pictures Harlan turning handles, bumping locks, mule-kicking doors. Rings and chains from a jewelry box, cash from drawers and counters. Huddy calculates the melt value. There are no reports of suspicious behavior in the targeted neighborhood. Residents are reminded to secure their homes.

The following week is quiet, the second part of the pattern, the lull between strikes, Harlan prowling and casing and laying down in the dark. Huddy sees Harlan's eyes through the eyeholes of a mask. Another series of home burglaries, this time in adjacent counties, Harlan dipping across the state line to hit Olive Branch and Southaven. Engagement rings, family heirlooms lost. A crime spree, the police matching the methodology. One neighbor heard broken glass and phoned the police, who arrived to find a smashed sliding door. Another resident spotted a white male walking down the street, in the late-morning hours, but could not provide a detailed description. Unnamed and unrecognized, but the stranger

is so blatantly Harlan that Huddy's surprised the writer didn't identify him. Caught, or beginning to be, the blanks filling in, and
Huddy is happy to sit on the sideline, relieved to have stepped
aside, thankful even when he imagines a broken promise, a hypo-
thetical scenario where he didn't back out and Joe still doesn't
bring the gold. But why does Joe have to use Harlan to recover his
debts? Huddy wants to discuss this dirty work, he even wonders if
he's obliged to intervene. Joe selling the stolen gold, but not in a
store, where he'd get ID'd. Of course, with half the city on the gold
bandwagon, he could go around the stores, and then Huddy realizes that Harlan's remembered a name, and that Joe has his fence.

He unbelts and steps out on the passenger side, and the driver stays in,
eyeing the mirrors to catch what's approaching behind. Del's driver
and the poorer clothes could mean hidden wealth, but he won't act
poor-mouthed when he reaches Huddy. Huddy watches him walk
through the open door, smirking like he's just gained illegal entry,
striding forward like he's been ushered in. He surveys the emptiness
and grins as if the tables have been turned, as if the merchandise had
accumulated elsewhere, stored off in Del's trophy room.

"Damn," Del says, "did I miss the closeout sale?" He shakes his
head at Huddy's mismanagement. First it was jewelry, now it's guns,
and where are the customers? Every time Del walks in here, the
shop's been reduced. He breathes an exaggerated breath, puffs up
like he's become the full set of himself.

Huddy gives a luckless shrug. Oh, well, deals just blow up sometime. It's funny what's happened. Downright comical, so rub it in,
Del, but stop smirking. All the times the loan counter has been a
barrier keeping the customer from rushing, but now it's so Huddy
won't lunge across.

"First time you ever called me," Del says, and crooks his face. Throws his bag on the counter.

I'm not the only one calling you, Huddy thinks. Already feels like Del's been here all day—get him out as soon as Huddy gets his answer.

"Last time, you wouldn't even show me them Winchesters."

"Winchesters?" Huddy says. "That don't sound like me. When you seen anything here but ugly guns?"

"I heard about them Winchesters."

"Come on, Del, you an honest man. You know my racks is filled with nothing but mudpuppies."

"I heard they got taken," he says in a voice that from anyone else would sound sympathetic.

The gun room looks like a basement room in one of Joe's blank houses.

"Who'd you hear it from?"

"Everywhere, Huddy. Automatic weapons! You an arms dealer?"

And Huddy wants to say what he's heard about Del, too, not from a news source or any person, but all from within Huddy himself, didn't even need to ask a brother, but he holds off.

"Truth is," Del says, "I don't much do the pawnshops anymore. I bought this Tucker saddle over on Austin Peay. I hate horses—but not a hundred bucks. I'm going more with auctions. Bought a champagne bucket last night. Made a phone call, sold it before I'm out the door. And I've been busy with the gold. People are just calling me up. They burning up my phone. This one fella, he works at a nursing home. Somebody falls asleep—bang!"

Huddy stares at Del's popping mouth.

"Got someone else, he's over at the county morgue. Stealing from corpses, now that ain't right. And let's not even talk about cops and crime scenes. First responders—now ain't they lucky? Me, I been doing them gold parties. Them ladies, they're trading in their jewelry and they can't believe how much money I'm giving, and I'm like, Lady, you don't know the *half* of it. I hate to be your competition, Huddy, but the secret's out."

Huddy shrugs again. "Weren't you, it would be someone else getting a share."

"I'm jumping in at the last minute, so I'm trying to catch up on what I've missed. In a year or two, I'll be gone. Day the bubble bursts, I'm done."

"Let's hope the day before."

"Ha! You got that right. Let some other latecomer take the hit."

"Get as much as you can, as quick as you can."

"You know it," Del says, still laughing.

"Last in, first out," Huddy says, and Del nods, but he's ready to laugh at something else.

"Tell you, Huddy, it took me years to figure, there's only two things worth anything—gold and bullets. The second protects you from losing the first."

Huddy looks at the sidearm, then gestures outside. "That your extra bullets in the car?"

"Him? Yeah, he's an idiot. Borderline bogus. I think he's an escaped mental patient. Hope he can shoot straighter than he drives. But you said I needed a hired gun. Me and him, we're having a salary dispute. I told him, 'Only thing that's keeping me from owning a hot rod is your pay.' Hey, how much for this?" he says, gesturing at the weight bench.

"Price is on the sticker," Huddy says.

Del squints, half-steps to the object. "Thirty. You chop it to twenty?"

"I can do twenty-five."

"A little give-and-take. Something always gotta come off!"

"Already off. Priced at the off-price."

"Let's say twenty-two. As long as we price-cutting. You know me, Huddy—every corner, I whittle."

"I could do twenty-two. That's my minimum. Sure, Del, I know you."

Del puts his hands up and leans back from the offer, as if any price is too pricey, any deal a forced sale. "Yeah, well, we'll see. I need to get in shape. All I do is sit. Drive around. 'Sides, we're here on business. I'm hot to spend my money elsewhere."

Huddy stares at Del, then behind his back at the car, then behind the car at the lot and street. "I forgot what your rate was. I tried remembering, but I didn't want to guesstimate."

"We never set one. We were between ninety and ninety-five, and I said I'd bump it past whatever your man was paying, but you never says what that was."

"Okay, so we're doing ninety-two five."

"Now I didn't say that," Del says, raising his palms. "I said we were somewhere *between* ninety and ninety-five, but I didn't say it was halfway."

"So ninety-two."

"No, my limit's ninety-one."

Huddy concedes, and as soon as he does, he can see that Del wishes he pushed it down to ninety. He looks at the blades and sanders—the number ninety-one a dullness he'd like to sharpen. Del waits for Huddy to reach for an envelope or a drawer, but Huddy does nothing, keeps withholding, eyes staying on him. "Well, what you got?" Del says, puzzled that Huddy hasn't moved, and still annoyed at that bad bid, that missed single concession. They've just negotiated the price, so where's the offering?

Huddy's arms outstretch to the gun room on his right and the display cases on the left, as if to say, *Can't you see nowhere?*

"You called me down here, just to ask rate?"

A truck horn sounds on Lamar, and Huddy watches the gunman glance up at the rearview, then the side-view, then twist his neck for the blind spot. "I don't like talking rates over the phone. I might mishear you. Sometimes, what you hear over the phone is different face-to-face. And you can't *see* nothing. One time, this customer calls me and says, 'How much you pay for my guitar?' And I say, 'How 'bout you hold it closer to the phone so I can see?'"

"You said you had gold, Huddy?" He glares, his greed for what Huddy possesses edged with anger for what Huddy doesn't.

"I retested it. Turns out, it's bad."

"So why didn't you call back?" Del says, but Huddy won't provide apologies or explanations for wasting time, and he'll keep delaying with talk until he snaps the trap.

"The bracelet just jumped right up on the magnet. And I got this ring, but it's heavily plated. Thought there was gold in there, but it's not gold. I wouldn't want you to buy this stuff from me, and then it don't assay right. All trash and brass. Gold-fill, and I know you ain't fooling with costume jewelry."

Huddy glances outside again. The gunman is no longer watchful. Not at the mirrors or over his shoulder. Instead, his neck tilts forward, like he's fallen asleep, or eyeing his lap, probably texting. "So I thought we could do something else."

And Huddy reaches inside his pocket, for a piece of paper, which confuses Del—he's still angry but wary now—because it's not an envelope. Unless it's a paper trick, the piece can't hold much gold.

"And then I thought I had some pearls to sell, but they just synthetics. Everything I thought I had is something else. Now, my brother Harlan was working for me. You think he swapped out the good stuff?"

"Wouldn't know," Del says. "How would I know?" He stares at the folded-up paper.

"Well, how 'bout speculating? You think I got cheated? Or maybe my brother Joe, he owns this place—you might know him."

"Don't neither."

"My business partner? My brother? You don't? Skimming off the top?"

"Wouldn't know."

"What wouldn't you know?"

"Your brother."

"Which one?"

"You talking about both. I don't know neither."

He looks back again at Del's driver, who's still texting, dozing, curled up with his phone, inside it, the noise on Lamar no distraction. A man passes along the sidewalk, behind the car, and Huddy glances at the driver, who's not training his eyes on any mirror. Huddy follows the man to see if he veers into the parking lot and becomes a threat, but he moves away, trailing past the store windows and disappearing. "Well, I know you know Harlan. 'Cause he was here the last time you were here." He thinks of the unnoticed man in plain sight.

"Okay . . ."

"You don't remember the one, maybe you don't remember the other."

Del looks outside to his protection, the car right there but the man inside way off. Maybe you should call him, Huddy thinks. Maybe you need a second guardsman, someone to guard the car, and someone beside you for confrontations. Or even a third guardsman, a second one to sit inside the car and keep tabs on the first. Huddy watches Del calculate the added support. The paper in Huddy's hands, and he unfolds it to show a photograph of Joe from the *Memphis Business Journal*, pulled from the Internet, since Huddy doesn't collect family pictures. Huddy's eyes not going back and forth, not one to the other, but only point-blank on Del. It's like Huddy, with his paperwork, gets to be ATF, and Del has to be him, and let's see how he tries to lie.

"Yeah, sure," Del says, and Huddy's surprised to hear it outright. "This guy calls me up, I go meet him."

"He's my brother. Joe. Then it's me, then it's Harlan," Huddy says, and he wants to match the unexpected directness of Del's answer, but he just sounds defensive.

"Joe?" And Del looks back at the picture, confused. "Said his name was Hollis."

"That's his middle name," Huddy says, unsure why he's covering the falsehood. "Goes by it sometime." Joe and Hollis, one and the same. Along with Hank and Huey and Howie. Full false name: Joe Hollis Hank Huey Howie Hiram Marr.

"Well, he didn't say he was your brother. He didn't say much of anything. All's I'm doing is answering my phone. Just cash-and-carry, just throw it down, goodbye. Hell, Huddy, if I had the smelter, I'd melt it, too." Del looks off, almost embarrassed, for both Huddy and himself, then at the merchandise, which seems embarrassing, too, just discards, odds and ends. "You and me, we both buying cheap. We both got numbers in our minds, and we squeezing, but we ain't cheating. I don't mean to get between you and family. Must've had a falling-out."

"Guess so." Huddy tries to add up his brother's names but loses count. He shakes his head, because Del's more credible than either brother, Huddy trusts him more than himself, for the way he told the truth. He was sure that Del would talk the wrong way, when he was role-playing Huddy.

"He don't seem like you. I'm saying that now, I mean, even if I'd known he was your brother, I wouldn't have thought it. I got a sister like that. People see us together, they never guess relation. She inherited one side, and I took after the other."

Huddy has learned something, watching Del give his straight answers, so maybe he'll ask what else and how much he knows, see how informed he is. "You scoring big with this gold?"

"Yeah. Sure. Big enough. Bigger than I was. It was bad before." He nods humbly. "On a shoestring. But the gold—"

"If you were me, what would you do with this place?"

"Asking me?"

"Guess I am."

"Move it, to where people live."

"Trying to."

"I mean, things are sliding everywhere, but they really sliding here."

"I know."

"I'd close it. Or, why you bothering with the pawn angle? What's your default rate?"

"Like, ninety percent."

"Ain't really a pawnshop if it's ninety." But it's not an insult, a thoughtless remark, and the voice is friendlier for being honest. "The loans—they just slowing you down, if they just defaults. You already like a buy-and-sell shop, except you a slow one. That storeroom, that's money sitting back there. But no one can see it. Maybe you should be *all* floor. And get your stuff online."

"Some of it is."

"Get all of it. Do the auctions. Hell, I go to three a week. Buy all over, sell all over. Spread the joy all over town. Go chase the money. Don't be stuck, be mobile. The whole city is your bargain counter. And the guns—what happened? You lose your license?"

Huddy nods, which becomes a shiver.

"That's, like, twenty-five percent of your business."

Something like that, he shrugs, and he peers at Del to find some changed impression, some unseen image, but it's the same face.

"Damn, Huddy, that must've felt like a thousand kicks to the head."

"Hurt," Huddy says, wincing, and Del nods, and Huddy returns it, one peddler to another.

"Your brother calls again, I won't answer."

"No, you take it. Do the deal. Sounds like you've found the golden goose."

"This gold thing. I wish I got in earlier. I think it's my last shot. I'm rubbing sixty. Just some old goober. How long this gold run gonna last?"

"Gold market's like any other—up and down."

"Lately it ain't been but one. It's probably peaked, though, don't you think?"

"Every time I think so, it notches up."

"If it goes down, if it *stays* down, I guess I just branch off to something else. But the next thing, it ain't gonna be like this, is it?"

"Be different," Huddy says.

"Worth less, I bet. I wouldn't even care what the next thing was, if this one lasted long." He taps his hand on the counter, and Huddy hears the wedding band clink.

"The golden age," Huddy says, and they exchange smiles.

"You get some gold, I'll give you ninety-two," Del says. "Bank on that." And he collects his bag, and Huddy watches him measure his goodness against the point he gave away, and then he walks but stops, as if he were second-guessing his value judgment. "You wouldn't happen to know what boom's coming next?"

Huddy shrugs.

"Listen, you ever wanna go to auctions with me. I sell stuff there, too. You'll be my ghost bidder. Drive the price up. Heck, we'll both be each other's plant. Bait everybody else, get them hyped up."

But Huddy won't play any more games with Del.

"You do this buy/sell, we should partner up." But then Del waves off co-ownership. "Thing is, I don't want nothing with a front door, or a roof on it. I hate paying taxes. I just as soon not exist. Who's the guy with the black bag? I ain't real nothing. Who was that masked man? Don't know, but he had cash. Goes by the name of Buyer Number 473. Ha!"

"You're parked the wrong way," Huddy says. He directs him outside, and Del looks but doesn't see it. "Quick exit. Turn your car around. And you ought switch places. You be the driver."

"Lose my chauffeur?"

"I'm serious. You drive, the shooter shoots. A lot harder to drive and shoot at the same time. And you might want to get a better bodyguard."

Del studies the tilted gunman, weighs what's necessary. "Yeah— he rode the short bus to school. I don't know, Huddy, I gotta pay for better. Maybe I just stick with him, but he's gotta pay for gas. That way I'm getting what I paid for. Don't worry about me. Shots fired, he'll be my bullet sponge. Give me time to fire back. I'm always a breath ahead."

He continues toward the door, his steps short and anxious, and the gunman is still wired and asleep, and the two of them look like easy pickings. And then Del, as if he were pushing back at Huddy's thoughts, gives a quick vigilant check of the vicinity, and the gunman jumps to attention, his back straightens, his eyes on Del and then shifting left and right. An alert tandem, but Huddy's thoughts linger on the prior watchless moment, enough to wonder if Harlan's target may be bolder than a house. Del's just told Huddy what Joe's been doing, and maybe he's signaled Harlan's next attempt. It's time to find a fugitive brother.

Fifteen

HE PHONES HARLAN, BUT there's no answer, no rings, just silence and then a beep without Harlan's recorded voice, and Huddy hangs up. He recalls that KayKay pawned items years back, right after Harlan departed for Florida. Harlan can remember Del's name and Huddy will track down KayKay's. He types in KayKay but gets nothing, and then he realizes that KayKay isn't her real name, or the echoing of her first, but the sounding out of her first two initials, Kaley or Kaylie, and another K. He tries them both, gets no records. He pronounces her nickname again and hears Caitlin, and he types Katelin and Kaitlyn, and draws blanks, and tries other spellings and gets one for Katelynne but the middle name is Lee, and then he thinks of Kelly and tries it, gets two hits, but the middle name for both is a man's. Tries Krystal and one name appears with no middle name, and he's about to dial it anyway when a last name pops up in his head—Stokes—and he types it, and up comes Kaylee Karly Stokes. He looks at the full name. It feels like he's found a missing person, and that he knows her better than Harlan does. He calls the phone number, and the computerized operator tells him the number is not in service, and he searches the white pages online, and KayKay's name comes up. One result, and Huddy stares at the screen, at the last column: *Associated people:*

unknown. He clicks on her, expecting unlisted or the disconnected one he's just called, but there's a different number, and he dials it and it rings. A pickup on the fourth, and then finally a real voice on the line saying, "Yeah," and it's hers.

"It's Huddy. I'm looking for Harlan."

But she doesn't answer and he doubts the voice he recognized—maybe he's dialed a wrong number—until she says, "Me, too."

"He ain't there?" Which he knew, but he thought she might know elsewhere.

"Not no more. Last time he called, I was asleep."

"He say where he was?"

"Ain't said nothing. Just hello on the machine. You talk to him, tell him to call me when I'm awake." Her voice is slow and smothered, as if she were again asleep.

He won't call Joe to get to Harlan. If Harlan isn't staying with KayKay, and he can't be at Joe's, there's only one place left, which isn't a place at all. He drives back to the trouble spot, through the double entrance, past the retention basin with the dead fountain, past the common island. In the daylight, Huddy sees more upmarket features, bay windows, Palladian windows, double turrets and copper cupolas, bird boxes in the gables. Every driveway hooks and curves. One-of-a-kind homes, customized, but patterns emerge in the layout, the same houses but turned at angles so it isn't box after box. Different façades, varied elevations and colors, but maybe the floor plans are identical and flipped. Costless tricks to make a house look custom.

There's no car in the driveway of the previous meeting, and the three-car garage is windowless. Huddy parks, walks and knocks, but there's no answer. He'll go door to door to all the pockets of finished and framed houses. He drives and knocks and peers through windows and waits in doorways, returns to his car and reverses and pulls in elsewhere and backs out again, up and down driveways like a deliveryman bringing phone books to new addresses, to unarrived residents, like a salesman who can't drum up business, like a disoriented messenger, until he tires of searching one by one, and he speeds past trenched land and onto the next built pocket, where he stops in the middle of the empty street.

He climbs out and he's about to call to a half-dozen houses within shouting distance when he hears gunfire, the sound of a .22, popping again a few seconds later, and again. Too quiet for a nail gun, Huddy thinks, and no compressed air escaping, and then he remembers the stolen compressors, and maybe Joe owns a battery-powered gun. Maybe the electrical isn't switched on inside, or maybe Joe just wants no engines, and to keep the work quiet, even with no one living next door. More firing inside, and no other noise outside, and Huddy listens and follows the noise in a diagonal, and he knows who's holding the gun. He approaches the filmed window, clouded by sun and work suspension, and he presses his face but Harlan isn't visible. A ladder and the sound of shooting right inside the room, but there's no body materializing. It feels like some deception, as if Harlan is there but vanished, as if Huddy were staring into a dark well, except the room is lit by an overhead light. He steps from the windowpane to the front door and turns the knob and enters and looks sidelong to the right and in the oversize room is Harlan, his back turned, crouched down on the floor, under the window that Huddy just gazed through. The shooting is louder, and Huddy waits for him to clip the gun to his belt and rough-measure the wall, and then Huddy identifies himself. "Harlan," he says.

Harlan scrambles, tool belt clanging, but he turns enough to the naming, and halts. He faces Huddy, relieved and suspicious, unsure if he's still scared that it's only him.

"You think I was someone else?" Huddy says, and he walks through the warm air and across the plywood.

"Didn't know," and Harlan studies him, as if he still doesn't. "What you doing here?"

"Ask you the same."

"What, I look different, 'cause I'm working?"

The same, Huddy thinks—as Joe, with his gold dust in your face and eyes, the dust all over you. Whenever Huddy sees his brothers here, they always look different, younger, older, the same. "Thought those were warning shots," Huddy says, nodding at the gun. "First ones. You camping out here?"

Harlan nods. "Got my bedroll in the master. You know why nobody can't live in these houses? Because they're already occupied. This is the family plot. I'm the night watchman, walk the grounds, and everybody's here. Mama's in one, and daddy's in another. I been over to them's houses. You 'member daddy telling us how he'd go up in the attic? When he was a kid, he'd go up there at night and kill pigeons. For food."

"No."

"Whatcha mean *no*? You was there!" And what looks different is his eyes.

"Wasn't," Huddy says, but he remembers he was, but not right now—that time isn't in him.

"We talked about it after. Dad the Pigeon Eater."

"Okay."

"Bet you don't remember rats in the pantry, either."

"Is that dad, too?"

"That was us! We'd hear 'em knocking over pans."

"Guess I dropped it somewhere along the way."

"You as bad as Joe."

Huddy stares at a floor wrapper, a few sandwich bites uneaten, a thick bread end, along with a soda bottle almost dry. "He bring you that?"

"Why you here?" Harlan says, and Huddy says he tried calling and then he asks the question back. "Keeping busy with house-work," Harlan says.

More like house arrest, Huddy thinks, his eyes swiping top to bottom. The drywall and doors are up. Harlan's run the crown molding and hung the door casing, and now he's shooting base clockwise. An A-frame ladder is pushed in a corner. A battery-run chop box is dead center on the floor, with a bundle of wood trim stacked nearby.

"That ain't all you doing," Huddy says.

But Harlan doesn't show the smallest of double takes on his guiltless face. He pushes the tape out toward the next wall and pulls it toward the cut. Transfers the tape measurement to the board. Goes over to the chop saw, feeds the wood in, sets the other end on a wooden block he's rigged, the saw and the block both on the ground so Harlan can stay at floor level and work faster. He swings the blade to make a forty-five cut, and Huddy watches him cut it on the line without pausing, not slightly long but trusting the tape, trusting his skill. Every time Huddy comes into these houses, he admires a brother's craft. The saw grinds and whirs to a stop.

"Buddy of mine in Florida," Harlan says. "Worked with him. He lost his thumb bad on the saw. Cut it way down and they couldn't salvage it. And you can't work with no thumb, so the doctors— they took the pointer finger off and moved it over to the thumb. He's got this four-fingered hand, but it's like five fingers 'cause he's got his thumb back, even if that thumb was his pointer. That thumb has learned how to become a thumb. When you see that hand—that pointer sticking up where the thumb should be, and the stub where the pointer ain't—it'll freak you out."

"So he can still do sheds," Huddy says, "if he's your work buddy."

"Well, I've done a little of this and that. I'm mostly ex-something."

"Joe told me about his backwards plan. Working off the bail."

"I'm already looking at jail. Get busted, it'll all be the same time. They'll just run 'em together. What's that word?"

"Who told you this?"

"Joe. Said his lawyer would make that happen. Money equals justice."

"Except he's broke."

"That's just on paper. Out in the world, he's still rich. Thing is, it would've been better if my charges were state. Lawyer says. He's still gonna whittle it down, but—so much for get-out-of-jail-free. And I'm not built for prison."

"Yes you are. I hope you pushed that AK hard. I hope you killed that trigger, for the time you're getting."

"I ran the hell out of it. And when the cops came and grilled me, they told me that I was looking at five years versus six months. Six months—that's *your* life, on the dotted line, they was wanting me to sign away."

Huddy looks back at the wrapper and sees it as a tray slid beneath a door. Harlan lines up the board and holds it in place and shoots the nail into the stud and the board pulls tight. He slides and shoots again, and releases his hand, and eyes the board and frowns. He takes a knuckle and knocks the wall, and hears the stud and reshoots it. Releases his hand again and sees a better fit. He keeps going across the floor, flowing with the studs, shooting the base. When he finishes, he turns to Huddy and sets the gun on its head. "It was stupid, what I done."

Not as stupid as what I done after you. And before. Huddy nods at his own mistakes.

"Joe says I do enough for him, he'll give me this house."

"That right?" All these houses in the bargain.

"Think I'd work on it if it ain't gonna be mine? Pride in owner-ship. I'll say this, Joe knows how to incentivize."

Must be what Joe meant by multiple offers. And we would've been almost neighbors.

"I don't know, Huddy, never thought I'd live in Germantown. Side by side with the Cotton Carnival crowd. I told Joe, I want all the fancy features. All the trappings. I want a froufrou house."

"Lying."

"It don't mean the rest of what he's saying is."

"Who, Joe? Or Hollis?"

Harlan stares unblinking, returns to measurements and cut-ting. "I always said he should be H-something." He grabs the upended gun.

"So you fixed his name."

"If daddy named him wrong, I'd name him right. Now, three of us, we whole blood. Joe, he wasn't named after no one. Now he's named after us." He doesn't speak spitefully, only to set the record straight.

"You renamed Joe, and you remembered Del." Huddy naming names, but none trips up Harlan, who keeps moving efficiently from the wall to the saw and back, shooting the trim and tapping the studs.

"I tole Joe, don't you think Del suspecting when the person he meets ain't sound like the person on the phone? 'Cause Joe won't touch the phone. He don't want to touch the deal either, but he don't trust me on that. But Del, he don't care. If it's smoking and on fire, he'll buy it. Either he ain't hearing the difference, or he don't care to. Maybe we sound the same. Me and Joe. Same enough. Then again, only voice Del hears is hisself."

Huddy follows the threads—Harlan impersonating Joe to say he's Hollis. "He's probably cheating the weight." Which to Huddy seems fair, if both brothers are playing impostors.

"Ain't me he's cheating." Harlan looks as uninterested in discussing *now* as Joe is with *then*, as if recent events were as vague as Joe's memories. But then his eyes glimmer, just like Joe's when the old tin roof surfaced. "You should see Joe after he's done the deal. He looks like he's gonna pop. Like his own sick twin. Telling you, his heart's gonna vapor-lock one day. I told him, your wife better know CPR, because one day she's gonna be pumping on you. This hooking-and-crooking thing, it ain't for Joe."

"It's for you."

Harlan can't decide if it's an insult or a compliment. He moves for the tape measure, but stops working, his hand at his side. "I guess it is. I'm running out the house. Five blocks from the car, where I parked it, and I hear the police. No siren, 'cause they're running stealth, but that big engine roaring. They're quiet, see, trying to be, but they're turbo-loud. I'm hiding in bushes, ducking under cars, and I hear them horses, and they pass me, and then I'm back on my feet running. Hear that sound and I know they're coming for me, but they don't know it's me, and they don't know I know they're coming . . . I'm on the ground but it don't feel like it. I feel like I got a hundred brains. Seeing if mailboxes is full. Newspapers in driveways. Outdoor lights on in the daytime. Get inside, I've got dog biscuits in my pocket."

"I know what you're planning."

Harlan ignores it, measures and marks the wood and slides over to the chop box and cuts square.

"Does Joe?" Huddy says.

"Whatcha mean?"

"You're fixing to rob Del."

Harlan looks at him.

"Getting gone."

"Well, I guess you a mind reader. No, Joe don't. Or else he does. He's ahead of us in lots of ways. So maybe he knows what I think I just know myself. 'Course, I can't ask him if he knows 'cause then he'll know. Then again, if *you* know, that must mean he knows. 'Cause Joe always been first. But he sure didn't know how to build this place."

"Couldn't know about a recession."

"This ain't nothing but greed taking over."

Huddy looks outside. Across the street, a bunch of plumbing stubs stick out of the ground, and he thinks of Harlan's maimed buddy, his transplanted finger. Huddy couldn't have seen these stubs the other night, but he imagines they weren't here last time, that the development has regrown, sprouted up on second sight. "You know Del's got a bodyguard." Which Harlan didn't, because Del was alone in Huddy's shop, and Huddy watches his face tense. A split-second whitening, maybe the face Huddy wore when the policeman showed up to ask about the AK. He doesn't mention the tilted head, the fearsome cell phone, because the distracted man is still armed, and Huddy wants to talk Harlan down, to show he's weak-handed. But Harlan just shrugs. Strong-arming Del would have been too easy, and now it won't be. His shoulders flex, some imagined bumping or struggle, because he's already made a decision, and Huddy's only complicated it before helping him overpower.

"I got a gun," Harlan says.

"Better not be one of mine."

"Street gun," he says flatly. "Any old street."

Huddy eyes Harlan's equipment and the robbery seems not sinister but ridiculous. He's dressed as a trim carpenter, and maybe the caulk gun is the stick-up weapon. Maybe he'll slap them with the tape measure, poke them with a utility pencil, bonk their heads with base scrap. Not even the nail gun looks dangerous. Huddy pictures Harlan not wearing a mask but safety goggles, as if a work costume makes him unsuspecting. But it can't. Huddy gazes at him, and he's regular Harlan, same old, and what he's about to do is what he always was, except he's a felon now, so he's himself plus a look-alike, identical and transformed. "You really stepping up to armed robbery?"

"Well, let's see," Harlan explains, as if Huddy had asked only something technical. "I want his bundle. And he won't want to hand it over. And we ain't gonna play tug of war."

"Why?" Huddy says.

"I'd rob you, but you ain't got enough money."

Huddy keeps asking.

"Don't ever ask me why again." Harlan turns aside, to find a lawless reason beyond himself. "Del's a slug and anybody that can stick it to him needs to stick it to him. You said it yourself, he's cheating. He'd steal the gold out of your teeth. There's bottomfeeders, and there's bottomfeeders with money, and that second one is him—and now it's gonna be me."

If it were me, Huddy thinks, I'd do it on a Friday, late. End of day, end of the week, he'll be in a Friday groove, not looking around as much, thinking of the weekend.

"What?" Harlan says.

"What?" Huddy says back.

"Your face was saying something."

"I don't give a fuck about my face." And Huddy won't say what he was thinking, won't give a set of instructions. He isn't a robber, he isn't Harlan, and Harlan's not him. "You think no one's gonna suspect you? You think you gonna wear a mask and it somehow ain't you?"

"Fine," Harlan says. "It's me. Or maybe I'm Joe. You think he knows, but he don't."

Unless I tell him, which is why Harlan's telling me. Not out of loyalty to Harlan, or spite for Joe, but enough of a combination.

"These type of things, Huddy, you're smarter. Joe don't know my mind. Only you do."

Been setting this score up the whole time. Gave Del's name to Joe, but he was giving Joe's name to Del, even if he didn't supply Joe's real name.

"The only one who knows this plan is you, because you're here and he's not."

"We're in *his* house," Huddy says.

"This ain't a house. Not yet."

"Look. Do your time, come out, come back here . . ." Huddy speaks carefully, to slow down Harlan's thinking, but all it does is lengthen the incarceration.

"I've already done that."

"Do it again," Huddy says, faster, a small sentence, but now the words feel unimportant, Harlan's life mere repetition. "You've already run away, too. To Florida." Huddy wants to speak of a beginning, not an ending, not something late.

"Go farther, then. This time."

But Huddy can't imagine Harlan in a different part of the country. "I'm supposed to tell the police about crimes. That's part of my plea."

"You ain't gonna say a thing. 'Cause I didn't say nothing about you. Don't tell Joe! That ain't fair. Don't tell no one. Something goes wrong, I don't want Joe standing over my body."

And Huddy doesn't want that either.

"I know what I'm doing," Harlan says, and he gestures at the outside corner, the tight miter joint, as if robbery were just another house project fitted exactly right. Look how skilled and responsible he is.

"It's two against one," Huddy says.

"So what?"

Which is true, every game the brothers played was uneven, even if the one wasn't always Harlan, and even if it was almost never Joe. But these other two will have guns. Both carrying, and you can bet Del's got another one stashed in his car, on a side panel or in the center console. Huddy doesn't say this, because when he told Harlan about the bodyguard, it didn't stop but only abetted. Harlan slipped a gun out of Huddy's store, so Huddy will slip one out of this story.

"Where you gonna meet him?" Huddy asks, and Harlan shrugs as if it were just some small errand.

"Where does *Joe* meet him?" Huddy asks. If Joe were here, they'd make fun of Harlan, and then they'd all go back to Joe's house and make fun of Joe, and then drive together to Huddy's for his laughing turn. He sees Harlan's hand shaking and he calls his brother's name and points a finger at the tremble to put the crime off, but Harlan screams, "Let me finish this room!"

Huddy shakes his head. He's in Joe's house, with Harlan building it, and the three of them, however close, will never get closer. But, like Harlan said, Joe isn't here, and Huddy looks at Harlan, and Harlan looks far off, as if the room were lengthening, so Huddy will leave, too, let Harlan make his room. He walks to the front door, studies it—maybe Joe hung it himself. This is Joe's house and no matter how much Harlan works with it, it will never be his. Huddy opens the door and exits and feels defeated and released. He drives out and over to Joe's, passing midway a row of pillared houses, set back in the woods, which reminds him of the deal's origins even though the widow lives on a different street, only a mile away but in the countryside.

When he reaches his destination, he doesn't know if he should go inside and warn Joe about Harlan, or go back to Harlan and warn him about Joe. He should call the police, provide information and whereabouts; he should give up Harlan. He should call Del and tell him not to answer his phone. He should do all, some, none of this. He wants Harlan to get away, to get the money, for no one to get hurt, and to get some of the money for himself without joining Harlan and for Joe to get none. He wants to prevent and benefit. Maybe Harlan will drop the robbery, or accidentally cut fingers on the chop saw, just stow away traceless with a bandaged hand. The longer he sits out here, his car idling rough and trembly, the more Huddy feels like a trespasser, and when a light switches on in Joe's expensive house, and something flickers behind the thick curtain, he drives away and turns a corner and feels like he's fleeing. Heading west, he senses that he's reached a distance equal to the north-south divide of his brothers and he slows but refuses to turn back and interfere, he keeps driving and separating, into the city, he's had enough with showing up at other houses. He has spent the last five years sitting behind a counter, waiting for people to come to him. Home isn't neutral, more like hiding, but it doesn't seem like the wrong location. Huddy enters and locks the glass outer door and shuts the inner door and locks that, too. He flicks on a light, then kills it, and he imagines watching from outside, as if it were a signal being sent to himself, or just the house short-circuiting. The house is silent except for his shoes, so he kicks them off. He sits in the dark, in the corner, and when Christie walks in, he doesn't move, and then he says, "I don't know what to do."

"About what?" she says, and he can't even answer that.

"I don't know who to tell what."

"Are you in trouble again?"

"Where's Cody?" he says, looking up.

"Where do you think?" she says.

"Sleeping?"

She smiles, but Huddy doesn't, because it's one more thing he should know. But then she laughs, and soon he joins her, and the doors are locked and windows are latched and barred and the blinds are drawn, and the room is sheltered by the wide porch. His small house is as secure as a fortress.

When he hears about it, in the middle of the next afternoon, it's from Joe. Eventually, the story will be everywhere, headlines announcing a botched robbery, and three dead bodies, two men in a car, and a third man bleeding out on the driver's side. A resident hears gunshots that he thinks is construction work in one of the many unfinished houses, until he doesn't hear more firing, and calls the police. Huddy will follow the subsequent articles and news segments and wonder if any cash or gold went missing—it seems a low number but more likely Del's own estimation of his take was inflated. Joe didn't arrive until after the police and paramedics, according to reports, and Huddy won't question the order of the gathering, the emergency vehicles and then Joe, just as he won't ask if Joe stood over Harlan, as long as Joe doesn't ask what Huddy knew and where he searched beforehand and what he might've stopped. When the police trace Del's cell-phone records and ask Huddy about a call he made the day prior to the robbery, Huddy will explain that Del was a regular customer, always on the lookout for bargains—his story reinforced by the weight bench which he points to without hesitation. The police will knock at Joe's door, too, both of the perpetrator's brothers will be questioned, because of the pawnshop meeting and the crime scene, but both will be cleared of any connection, their business transaction and their land ownership incidental and unrelated, and the case will be closed around the shooter.

And Huddy can then begin to forget Harlan's final dragging steps on his own legs, and untug the weight on his chest of the bullet in Harlan's body, and also silence Joe's voice, aching and shamed and unconcealed, screaming over the phone line, "He's dead"—especially Joe's voice, which Huddy will not hear in his head, saying, "Lying on the street. Harlan! Dead. On my damned street!"

Sixteen

A MAN STANDS AT the front door of Bluff City Pawn and Fine Junk. He's just left Lifecare Blood Services, in the next building, but the window sign here says CLOSED, even though it's near noon on a Saturday. He walks up to the bus stop, sits on the bench, maybe the store will open before the bus arrives to take him elsewhere.

The store opened at ten, after Huddy picked through yard sales for camera equipment and movies, grabbing the newer releases and staying away from the old-old duds, and then hit a couple estate sales, where he bought a silver platter and a candelabra and an antique headboard and footboard. He brought the merchandise back to his store, posted all the A/V items and furnishings and decor on eBay, and then he locked up and went out again, to a midday auction on Summer Avenue, in a store a half-mile past Liberty Pawn, which is now another Cash America, the owner selling out to the chain.

Huddy goes inside and signs in and gets his number and grabs a seat on a side bench and before long the auctioneer up in the booth starts the microphone patter, the floorman catching quick bids for dinner plates and arrowheads and rough-hewn lumber and toy planes and a box of children's books and floor lamps and memorabilia and pottery and flatware. The action of the room is both dull and hurried. Huddy sits and waits. He can't trap the cash like he can in his shop, because he can't set the price and stop the raises, but he has a feel for what everything brings, and he can still make money on the buy, get 35 percent or even double on most sells. He buys an ornate picture frame—he'll bust the picture out—buys a Limoges jewelry holder, buys a display case for twelve and a half dollars. He outbids the others for a mahogany bedroom suite, but loses out on Tiffany pieces to a bad bidder in the second row who always bids first and then stops, but for some reason, maybe he's a collector, he has no limit on good glass, and he keeps raising, going back and forth with Huddy, as the floorman catches and shouts with his arms flinging this way and that, and the auctioneer's eager voice rises, like some cheerful speech impediment, a pricing error to correct fast, until Huddy's profit margin gets squeezed enough and he drops out. Next is a cowbell, and then a spice rack, and a cast-iron doorstop, and a karaoke machine, and vintage medicine bottles, and Memphis Tigers cufflinks, and Huddy appraises the stuffed tables and shelves, and hears the prices spasm, and decides there's nothing left. He could wait around for the Hummels, but he knows the couple in the front row is only here for figurines. He takes his tickets to the payout window. Behind him, the noise is raucous, but it's just the auctioneer opening the bidding. There are a few newcomers here who build too much value in their mind—one rookie paid over retail—which is fine, as long as it's for what Huddy doesn't want. Huddy gathers the smaller items and loads them in his truck, and hauls the suite out with a man who attends the storage-unit auctions, first of the month, the man boasting about a Bose box that didn't have a Bose inside it, but old celebrity photographs that'll fetch more money than the stereo he expected to find. This new story has replaced the nightmare from last month, when the man bid three hundred dollars on a storage room filled with boxes and boxes that contained only concrete samples, thousands of pounds that the man was legally bound to remove within twenty-four hours.

Huddy returns to his store, driving across an overpass with GOD LOOK spray-painted on the cement barrier. At a stop sign near railroad tracks, he watches a man walk an empty shopping cart into the tall weeds. He wonders if the glass collector will be at the next auction. If so, maybe Huddy can get to the auction earlier, see if there are multiple lots of glass—a couple of months back, there was both Tiffany and Heisey glass—and Huddy'll negotiate, corner the man and say, How 'bout you take the first lot, I'll take the second, that way we leave each alone and keep both bids down. He passes a sedan with the trunk open, the latch bungee-corded to the bumper, the kitchen appliance tipped down inside. He sees barbershops, nail salons, all with signs saying WE BUY GOLD. Huddy wants to walk in and say, I'm gonna start cutting hair in my pawnshop if you keep buying up the gold. A tempting confrontation, but instead he imagines himself with scissors in his own shop, snipping bangs for gold. Sometimes, after he leaves the auction, he hears the auctioneer's voice, the price bumping and vibrating and bumping again in his head, and if Huddy's bothered by it, there's always the radio.

He reopens the door, brings the merchandise in, checks his online accounts. The DVDs selling like always. Buy something for a dollar, sell it for two, and do it a lot of times. Find the market value and blow them out. He is thinking about one last shopping spree, maybe late afternoon, to a salvor who called earlier about salvage goods, a furniture buyout, leather sofas with a little light smoke in them that you can't even smell. Huddy wasn't sure about nonsmelling smoke, but the man also talked about store returns, these shelf-pulls from a major electronics retailer, and Huddy said sure, he'd come look. He sees a man enter with a bandage in the crook of his arm—which means next door. "I got there too late," the man says. "They telling me my blood's worth twenty-five bucks before ten A.M., but only twenty after." The man shakes his head at the missing five, stares at the fingers of his hand.

Ever since the bank opened and the CASH PAID banner went up, Huddy's been hearing about midmorning rate switches, about donors rejected for insufficient iron. The next customer comes in, and the blood donor slips out, toward the bus stop, where no one congregates, to face the road and stick around there or inch back.

"I pawned a mower here, for a time," the customer says, and Huddy thinks he remembers, the mower and this man for six months. "I paid it out. Then I was . . . out of town a stretch. Back now."

Which might mean jail, but Huddy doesn't ask.

"Now, I'm working. Full week. Not this week. This week, I got but two days, but next week's full, and I'm hoping it stay that way."

"What can I do for you?" Huddy asks.

"Listen, man, I got this TV."

"Flat screen?"

The man shakes his head. "Big, though."

"Can't take it."

"See, here's the thing, I ain't selling it."

"I can't do nothing." Huddy stares at the man, at his front shirt pocket stretched and empty.

"I got this room, where I'm staying. And the lady, who owns the place, see, she wants to watch TV every night. She got her own TV in her own room, but she wants to watch with me, you hear? But

I don't want nothing to do with her. My situation, I need to have women out of my life, just for a while. But she runs the house. And she's in my room all day, watching the TV, and that's good, because if she weren't, somebody else'll steal it. So it's good that she's in my room, but it's bad, I can't have it no more, she's got to go. I gotta do something to correct this—"

Huddy looks outside as Joe's car pulls up to the curb. Joe parks and steps out, and then he reaches back inside—Joe who he hasn't seen in months, carrying a gun case that Huddy hasn't seen in longer.

"The TV, this lady, my room," the man says, shaking his head, as if the story were mixed up or maybe it's just Huddy half-hearing and understanding. "I'm wanting to bring my TV, duck it here for a while, and then, you know, I get my own place and come back for it. I'm getting my own place next month, but I'm already starting to argue with her."

Huddy eyes the hard case, watches it tilt and slant in his brother's hand, Joe's fingers gripped around the center handle but the case not staying level, wobbling up and down. The inside weight tells Huddy it isn't empty.

"You got family?" Huddy asks.

"Naw, man, that won't work. Family's a situation."

And Huddy looks at Joe, who places the case far down from the man—the caution is another reason the gun is contained there—and stares warily at him and then at Huddy without nodding.

"Friends, too."

"You want me to warehouse it?"

"That's it."

"I ain't a warehouser," Huddy says.

"Just for a bit. I figure, since I done business with you before, we do this thing, and then the next thing, I pay on this, what I bring you."

"You want me to store it for free?"

"Asking a month," the man says. "You can have the TV if I don't come get it thirty days."

Huddy doesn't answer, unsure why he's not going against him.

"I'll bring it tomorrow?"

Huddy nods.

"The TV ain't too big," the man says, as he leaves.

"I never done that," Huddy says to Joe, wondering if Joe thinks he's soft or crazy.

"Got it back from the bondsman," Joe says, eyeing the case, as if it were some machine or instrument that he'd never understood how to make work. "I'm coming together with a group of builders. Four-man partnership, split up the liability. Gonna build minimum-size houses, on zero lots. The market looks to be coming back that way. Reviving."

And Huddy realizes that Joe is mentioning recovery—these broke builders put together to get themselves unbroke—only to tell him why the gun can now be his.

"I already lost Heritage Cove, so now I'm getting what else went under. We're all swapping foreclosures. These other builders, the four of us—" He stops, their eyes meet, and Joe glances away as he shakes his head. He looks around the room, trying to see what's different. No guns, but overall the floor looks full, the inventory replenished. Most of the items were bought elsewhere, Huddy could add, which means higher cost but no waiting on the pawn cycle, and they're priced here for show, but also online, so Huddy's on Lamar but not *just*.

"You sold twenty, and I said you'd get one after twenty," Joe says, as if it were a promise, and not the deal, that got broken, and Huddy nods to believe it. "And, like I said, don't need a license to sell an antique. Guess that applies to both of us now." The gun, previously half-owned and then taken, is now returned as a gift, like some defaulted loan that Huddy, with Joe's forfeit, is reconfiscating from himself. Huddy feels both remorseful and excited, and he'll control both without denying either. The sale of this gun won't change Huddy's life, but it will start to. He'll go to bigger auctions, move into commercial equipment, or even pallets of new clothing stacked high, and maybe before long he's doing bulk purchases on home-theater systems, tractor-trailer loads on who-knows-what. Huddy went to one once, this all-day affair, and bought some industrial switches, but that was it, staying silent on the big-ticket machinery.

Joe turns away, for a long moment, so Huddy will remove the case without Joe watching, and Huddy touches then grips the handle and lifts the case and brings it around to his side and lowers it downward to the floor. Joe turns back, relieved but distressed to find the case out of sight. His eyes stick on the empty counter. "Blood bank's set up. That was fast."

"Tell me about it. They didn't even slow down for hunting season."

"I heard something. About that widow Yewell. About her house."

"What's that?"

"Her son's family moved in with her. In the guest house. When she dies, they'll take it over. Guess she ain't selling. Maybe she never was."

"Too bad. You might've been old money by then."

"Not in my lifetime. Those classic lines run too deep."

Huddy watches his brother laugh, Joe's adult life out in

Germantown adding up to such a minimal number. "So you build-ing small houses?" Huddy asks.

"Yeah. Still big, but smaller."

"You lose weight?" Huddy asks, because his face looks thinner.

"No," Joe says. "You're the second person that's said that."

"Who's first?"

"Lorie."

"She should know."

"Weight's the same. Weighed myself yesterday."

"Maybe the scale's wrong."

Joe rubs his belly. "I don't know what y'all ain't seeing." He looks side to side at his wide waist. "I ain't a pound less. Doctor got me eating even more pills."

Huddy looks at Joe's gut, then back to his face. Not thinner but sunken. Maybe it's just his eyes. "Don't worry," Huddy says, "you'll outlive us all."

Joe's cheeks redden, and Huddy wonders if that's what's changed, some color leaving his face that only comes back with guilt. Maybe he's not thinner but thinned-out inside. "Harlan," Joe says, star-tled—it's the first time the name's been said between them in months, and now Joe's face is raw and swollen. Huddy watches Joe glance at the counter before him, and his eyes squeeze shut and twitch open. "He said Lorie looked like mama."

"Don't look a thing like her," Huddy says.

Joe nods. "He said, 'They got the same skin.'" And what Huddy sees in Joe is what he feels stirring in himself, with thoughts of Harlan alive and in trouble and sometimes not. He nods at Joe. With eye contact, they both feel complicit, so they both look off.

Joe shifts to change subjects, but can't. "He said, 'Mama's skin was so good, she even looked good in the casket.'" He steps away from the counter, even though the case has been moved around and under. Huddy watches him dig a finger at the corner of his eye.

And then Huddy starts telling a Harlan story, too. From their days working together, when an old customer, Miss Lottie, came in about a heating problem in her house, and she got to talking about her health, about her recent stroke, her sense of direction real bad with new places, but her head's mostly clear. "My memories is strong," she said, and to prove it she said, "Genesis, Exodus, Leviticus, Numbers, Deuteronomy, Joshua, Judges, Ruth, First Samuel, Second Samuel." And when Harlan heard her, he said, "Look at that, she's a historian." Huddy tells all the way to the Bible books, but then realizes his own memory is wrong. The story didn't happen with Harlan. It happened later, after he was gone, months after Joe's phone call. Huddy had shared it with an imagined Harlan, the Harlan inside himself, who gave the punchline. Joe looks at Huddy, at the collapsed tale. Huddy could tell it anyway, replace parts of it—the woman says her line and Huddy supplies his Harlan answer—but Huddy doesn't want to lie to Joe, and he doesn't want to say Harlan was there when he wasn't. And since the whole point of telling the story was that he was, the end of the story can't be told. Still, it feels wrong to Harlan to leave him out; the punchline feels like some belated words that Harlan somehow said. Huddy waves his hand to forget.

Instead, he says to Joe, "Lucky you got me here. I'm in and out, here and there. It's best to reach me at home, these days, at night, if you're looking." He hears the information extend to invitation, and Joe tries to reply, mumbles at the phone on the counter. Next week is bad, Joe says, but after is better, a visit tentative enough for both to agree upon.

Joe shifts to leave, but then stays still. His eyes squint. "He . . . had . . . this cigar box."

"Huh?" Huddy says, at the slow talk.

"I had my rubber baseball that daddy gave me," Joe says, and it's only after hearing daddy that Huddy understands the meaning. "And you had your toy gun."

"We all had guns."

"Yeah—but you had yours *more*, you know?"

Huddy nods. "Banner-50."

"And Harlan had his cigar box. With a knife in there, right?"

"Case knife. Granddad's."

"Was it?" Joe asks.

"Yellow handle."

"You remember that?"

"He also had an arrowhead," Huddy says, and for a second he has to double-check he's not recounting the noonday auction table, but he can place the item in both spots. He sees Harlan studying it with a magnifying glass, which was there, too. Which Huddy lists to Joe. Harlan eyeing the surface, examining a color or detail. He'd use the glass against his other objects.

"Yeah. He'd be staring through that thing with full force," Joe says. "He'd wake up and he'd go to that box. He was real quiet with it. Seemed like the only time he was quiet."

"Found the arrowhead with me."

Joe's eyes level then lowered, wondering where he was, all by himself and far apart, his two brothers elsewhere together.

Huddy remembers roaming the woods, no, a field, and he looked over and Harlan was crouched to the ground, lifting the flint out of the grass. Huddy wanted to snatch it, to claim he'd seen it the same time and not second, but the feeling passed and the prize was Harlan's without struggle. Still, Harlan saw how Huddy hated not finding it, so the two of them searched the field all over for a double, their heads bent to the spaces before their feet.

"Arrowhead. Magnifying glass. Pocketknife," Joe says, his fingers diagramming a triangle, to see these objects separate and not lumped together in his mind. "What else?"

The box on a bedroom shelf. Harlan pulling it to the floor. "I think there was a magnet," Huddy says.

"Yeah. That's right," Joe smiling, the flood of memory warm and sudden. "Lot of little things in there."

"His treasure," Huddy says. "His little pile of goodies."

"Lucky Strikes," Joe says. "Half a pack. At least, that's when I remember seeing 'em. Probably other things. But that's most of it." Joe nods to himself. They've remembered enough of Harlan's collection. But then he closes his eyes to get more. "Forgetting anything?" His eyes strain half-open.

"Can't think of much else," Huddy says, but he can—there are so many trinkets to swap and mix with the contents of the box—so Huddy thinks hard and sharp on it. A key chain, a button, a whistle? Toy car, train? Huddy lifting the lid wide, his eyes searching end to end. A shell, a buckle, a lure, a pin, a medallion, a lighter to burn things with? No, he tells himself, none of those was there, and nothing else's been missed. "That's all of it."

"You sure?"

Huddy raises the top again, gazes inside over and over. "That's everything."

A sly smile from Joe, and his body trembles in a laugh. "That brain of yours, it sure done remember stuff." He shakes his head. "Even stuff that scatters to the wind."

"Scatters and comes back. I just saw your baseball, auctioned off."

"What?"

Huddy grins, and Joe sees he's taken the bait. His body sways another laugh.

"Hey, my baseball never wore out." He cups his hand like he's holding it. "Might fetch a good price, still." Thumb rubbing fingertips; Joe signals the money being made. He clenches his lips, his fist, and nods. Then he leaves once more, and Huddy watches the car back out and turn toward Lamar and accelerate up, and Huddy looks beyond him to the busy street where a truck barrels along the outside lane and Huddy winces at collision, but Joe is still gliding up to the lot's edge. He coasts and brakes and waits for the truck to pass, and then for a car speeding, and then his brake lights switch off and he surges east.

A man walks in after and asks about ladders. "Got two of 'em," he says, and Huddy says, "Let's see." The man comes back with them, splits the legs. "They got some hiccups. Some age." He steps onto the bottom rungs.

"There he goes," the blood donor says, from the other side of the room, and Huddy didn't see him re-enter, he must've lost track of the man's whereabouts when Huddy was staring down at the case. He watches the man gaze upward, and Huddy turns back to the ladder.

"See," the customer says, stepping higher, then climbing two more till he's past halfway and stops. Huddy stares at the climbing man as the ladder legs shake and steady, and the man calls from above, "Now I'm up here."

ACKNOWLEDGMENTS

This book was informed by many conversations, and I would like to thank the following individuals for sharing their time with me: To Vince Miles, for the years of friendship. To Carole Hinely, for leading me into Germantown. To Charles Salvaggio and Hank Akers and Joe Kroboth, for the lessons in home building. To Jeff Brown and Barry Brown, for welcoming me into their shop. To Mary Liz Foster and Tempe Chancellor, for showing me their horses. To Jeff Todd, for the drives. To Ken Strong, for the pond.

To Vince Higgins, John Mayr, John Bates, John Kanne, Thomas Mitchell, Don Yount, Mimi Atkinson, Warren Balman, Joel Barron, Martin Boldt, Kenny Brooks, Fred Calcagno, Amber Dermont, Michael DeSain, Ronald J. Engelberg, Hans J. Farnung, Sgt. Michael Freeman, Sr., Don Grove, Ruth Irick, Kordell Jackson, Dave Kielon, Brett Krasner, David Krasner, Blaine M. Mattison, David Merz, Vernon Paradise, Michael Picow, Holiday Reinhorn, Frances Rosenberg, Lamar Todd, Walter Wills.

To my former colleagues at Rhodes College, especially Marshall Boswell. To my colleagues at the University of Rochester, especially Joanna Scott (thank you, Joanna, for all of your wisdom and advocacy), James Longenbach, John Michael, Jennifer Grotz, and Kenneth Gross.

To my agent, Ethan Bassoff, for his belief in the book and his indefatigable work ethic; to all the folks at Lippincott Massie

McQuilkin. To my editor, Rachel Mannheimer, for her guidance and judgment; to George Gibson and everyone else at Bloomsbury.

To my parents, for everything, and to Susan, who listened and encouraged and saw what this book was long before I did.

A NOTE ON THE AUTHOR

Stephen Schottenfeld is a graduate of the Iowa Writers' Workshop. His stories have appeared in numerous literary magazines and have received special mention in both the Pushcart Prize anthology and *Best American Short Stories*. He teaches English at the University of Rochester in New York.